To the volunteer firefighters,
the *pompiers* of the Périgord

CHAPTER 1

The three skulls transfixed him. The first, the original that had been unearthed after seventy thousand years, was not quite complete. Beside it stood a reconstruction, an exact copy artificially filled in with the missing parts of the jaw and cranium. Behind them, glowing eerily in the museum's carefully crafted lighting, was a copy or perhaps a casting of the same skull made from an almost transparent blue plastic. Maybe it was a trick of the light that made it seem larger than the others. Reluctantly, Bruno Courrèges shifted his glance back to the original, whose caption said it was the closest to a perfect Neanderthal skull ever found. It came from the rock shelter of La Ferrassie, a place he passed each day as he drove from his home to his office at the *mairie* of St. Denis, where for the past decade he had carried out his duties as the local chief of police in the Périgord region of France.

The region boasted an extraordinary wealth of prehistoric remains, including painted caves and carvings from stone, deer antlers and the tusks of mammoths. Bruno had become an enthusiast who had now visited all the known caves and was a regular visitor to the museum of prehistory in Les Eyzies, close to his home. This skull, however, made him think of the curious obsession of his friend J-J, chief detective for the *département* of the Dordogne, with another and more recent skull. Bruno knew this skull well, since its enlarged photograph had for three decades accompanied J-J to every office he had occupied. These days it was fixed to the back of J-J's door, where he could see the skull from his place at the imposing desk that was standard issue for such a senior official. His visitors could not miss it as they left his room. His fellow cops often speculated why J-J submitted himself willingly to this constant reminder of his first big case, the one he had failed to solve as a young detective some three decades earlier.

J-J claimed not to remember why he had called the skull Oscar, but every policeman in southwestern France knew the story. A truffle hunter out with his dog in the woods near St. Denis had found a tree downed by a storm. The fallen trunk blocked a small stream tumbling down the slope and forced it into a new channel. The rushing water had then eroded a small bank and exposed something that had attracted the hunter's dog: a human foot, partly decomposed and partly nibbled by woodland creatures. The hunter had called Joe, Bruno's predecessor as the municipal policeman in St. Denis. Joe had visited the site and in turn had informed the Police Nationale in Périgueux, and they had sent J-J, their newest young detective, to investigate.

Determined to make his name with this unexpected case, J-J had rushed to the scene, established a security cordon, demanded spades from the *mairie* and help from the local gendarmes. With their support he had carefully unearthed the remains of a healthy young male in his twenties with long blond hair and perfect teeth, dressed in a T-shirt which still bore the faded logo of some long-forgotten rock band. The body's own bacteria and the insect life and soil microbes had done their work in the year or so since the death, as estimated by the medical examiner. Too little flesh remained for any cause of death to be evident.

The fact that the corpse had been deliberately buried persuaded J-J that he had been murdered.

To the horror of the watching gendarmes, J-J had donned medical gloves and carefully removed the remaining earth that still covered much of the body. He then commandeered a steel sheet about a meter wide and two meters long, along with a forklift truck from a nearby builders' depot, and had the body moved out of the woods. He had been careful to dig far under the body. Using staves of wood beneath the steel sheet, he ordered eight gendarmes to carry it like some heavy military stretcher, down to the flat land adjoining the campsite below. It was then taken by truck to the morgue in Périgueux for a forensic autopsy.

J-J had then spent an hour foraging in the soil beneath where the body had been for any sign of a bullet. Nothing useful had been found, even when the gendarmes with metal detectors and volunteers from the local hunting club had made a careful fingertip search of the vicinity. They had found the sites of two small fires, remnants of charred wood ringed with stones, and some disturbed soil which, on examination, turned out to be a latrine. The burial site was but a short walk from a popular commercial campsite. It seemed to have been a regular place for what the French called *le camping sauvage,* where people squatted on a temporary and unofficial campsite in the woods without paying the fees required for a formal campground that offered showers, toilets, a bar and a shop.

In those days before DNA had transformed the forensic profession, J-J challenged himself to discover how the man had been killed. In the morgue, when the remaining flesh and organs had been painstakingly removed in the hope of finding a bullet or perhaps some evidence of poisoning, J-J had peered at every rib in search of a scratch that could have been made by a knife. Finally, he persuaded the investigating magistrate assigned to the case to let him try one last, desperate measure. He used his own money to buy a large metal pot, removed the body's head and went to the kitchens in police headquarters to demand the use of a mobile cooking stove. He moved it into the courtyard and proceeded to boil the head until all the flesh had fallen away.

This took some time, and the aroma at first intrigued and then horrified the other policemen in the building, along with those members of the public with business there,

11

and the two local news reporters who had a small office near the entrance. The stench itself was unforgettable and unavoidable, and soon local shopkeepers began to complain. The mayor and the prefect arrived to demand an explanation, each of them wearing a mask that had been soaked in some mentholated liquid. By the time they arrived, the local radio reporter had already broadcast the news that the local police were cooking a corpse.

When the policemen began to grumble, J-J had been summoned to the commissioner's office, where he showed his letter of authorization to boil the skull. It had been signed by the magistrate who had by then departed on a long-planned weekend trip to visit his parents in Brittany. In those days before mobile phones, there was no immediate way to reach him. The commissioner then announced that he had some urgent business at the Bergerac police station, almost an hour away, that required his personal attention. The mayor and prefect found themselves met by the deputy commissioner, who had been told of the magistrate's authorization and pleaded to his visitors that there was nothing he could do. His youngest detective was leaving no stone unturned in his pursuit of a murder case.

"You might at least have insisted that this unpleasant procedure take place in some remote location rather than in the center of the city," the mayor said, the force of his protest somewhat diminished by the mask, which made the deputy commissioner ask for every statement to be repeated. Finally, he led the two distinguished visitors, one representing the city of Périgueux and the other the Republic of France, to the small courtyard where they found J-J, oblivious to the stench, stirring the steaming pot amid clouds of pungent steam.

The mayor strode forward and turned off the bottle of gas beneath the mobile stove. At the same moment, J-J hauled the now fleshless skull from the pot with a pair of heavy tongs and waved it at his visitors in a manner that made them back away nervously. He then announced, his face beaming with pride, "It worked. See for yourselves, messieurs. He was bludgeoned to death!"

The mayor, prefect and deputy commissioner each looked at the telltale cracks between the eye and ear sockets of the gleaming white skull as the two local news reporters entered the courtyard, notebooks at the ready.

"We are looking for a left-handed killer,

messieurs," went on J-J, who had become a policeman after a boyhood devotion to the detective skills of Sherlock Holmes. "You will see the wound is on the right side of the victim's head."

"Could this not have been established more simply, perhaps by an X-ray of the skull?" asked the prefect.

"Indeed," replied the deputy commissioner. "But you will doubtless recall that you refused to endorse our proposed budget for modernizing our police laboratory and installing an X-ray facility."

J-J, intent only on the skull and the clues it offered, did not notice the reporters scribbling in their notebooks. The mayor, who had an eye for such things, and who vaguely recalled having told the local hospital to refuse police requests to use their X-ray machine on the grounds that the public health came first, was already regretting his decision to demand an explanation from the police. He regretted even more his suggestion that the prefect should accompany him to put a stop to the foul stink that was spreading through the historic city of Périgueux. Now the mayor thought it best to retreat.

"Well, the cooking is now over, the smell will soon disperse and a vital clue has been found," the mayor said. "It only remains to congratulate the police on their ingenuity in difficult circumstances. I think we can now adjourn, my dear deputy commissioner, and leave this enterprising young detective to his duties."

It was the event that made J-J's reputation with the press, the public and above all with his colleagues in the police. Even the commissioner forgave him when the prefect reconsidered his earlier verdict and approved the budget for a state-of-the-art facility, including an X-ray machine, for the new police scientific laboratory. This was little compensation for J-J, who then embarked on a long and fruitless attempt to identify his corpse, even though the mayor had persuaded the local hospital to let him use the X-ray machine to document an unusual double break in the body's left leg, made some years before death. J-J had been confident that medical records would eventually enable him to confirm the name of the most celebrated corpus delicti in the history of the Périgord police.

There had been no local report of a missing young male person with fair hair and no such missing person reported in France in the twelve months that the medical examiner estimated had been the maximum time since death. J-J went through Interpol to ask other European countries whether they had any candidates on their lists of missing persons, and even tried the United States, Canada, Australia and New Zealand, all without success. As the Berlin Wall came down and relationships improved with the police of Russia and Eastern Europe, J-J widened his search. Through French embassies, he made contact with the medical associations and the health ministries across Europe, seeking a doctor who might recall treating the unusual leg break. He turned his attention to the T-shirt on the body and researched the rock bands of the last decade. He tracked down the members of the Austrian band featured on the T-shirt; they had enjoyed a brief success and sold several thousand T-shirts in Germany and Switzerland on the strength of it. But that was a dead end, too. Months passed and then years, but J-J's labors, to which he devoted much of his spare time, were all in vain.

He had a body, or at least a skeleton. He had a murder and had identified the murder weapon as a collapsible spade, produced in large numbers by the U.S. Army and widely available at army surplus and camping stores around the world. What he did not have was an identity, only the photograph of Oscar's skull that covered the back of his office door.

And so Bruno, shifting his gaze from the three skulls in the museum display case to the even larger case alongside, which showed an artist's reconstruction of a Neanderthal face from the original skull, had the first glimmerings of an idea. The face did not look primitive. It was almost entirely human but with elements of our primate ancestors, with the same heavy jaw and prominent bone ridges above the eyes. The reconstruction seemed more real because the artist had also produced not simply a face but the whole body from the ancient skeleton of La Ferrassie. The man was sitting, a thick and brawny arm outstretched as he made some point to a small child sitting rapt with attention before him. The child's face had also been reconstructed from a Neanderthal skull, and the scene was to Bruno's eyes wholly convincing.

He paused at the next display case, startled at the sight of an attractive young woman with a defiant or perhaps proud pose of her head. She was clad in furs with beads around her neck, her eyes looking sidelong at some scene that made her watchful, perhaps even suspicious. She had a high forehead, sensuous lips and prominent cheekbones. She had been reconstructed from a partial skeleton found at the Abri Pataud rock shelter in Les Eyzies, just along the long main street from the National Museum of Prehistory where Bruno now stood. The skeleton of the body, a young woman of sixteen or eighteen years, had been found with the skeleton of a newborn child, and her skull had been found four meters away, protected by some stones that appeared to have been deliberately placed. She was a Cro-Magnon, or early modern human, who had lived some twenty thousand years ago, nearly twenty thousand years after her people had replaced the Neanderthals.

Bruno shook his head in awe rather than in disbelief at the sight of this woman whose face moved him so deeply. There was a lively intelligence in her features and a self-reliance in her stance that made him realize with a start of surprise that this was a woman who attracted him. He could imagine seeing her in a crowd on the street outside, or gazing out from the window of a passing train, or sitting at another table in some outdoor café. He let the fantasy run on, imagining sharing glances with her across the crowded tables, perhaps arranging to meet. This was a woman who stirred thoughts of might-have-beens.

The next face surprised him again, since he recognized not the face but the headdress she wore, a skullcap of dozens of tiny shells, carefully pierced and then sewn together. He had seen it before at the famous rock shelter of Cap Blanc, just a few kilometers up the road toward Sarlat, where prehistoric people had crafted a massive bas-relief of horses, deer and bison. They were so lifelike that they might almost be emerging from the rock into which they had been carved.

In 1911, archaeologists had found an almost complete human skeleton buried beneath the hooves of the central horse of the sculpture, the bones protected by rocks at the feet and more rocks balanced above the head. It was presumed at first to be male. The local landowner sold it to the Field Museum in Chicago in 1926 for the equivalent of one thousand dollars. Henry Field, the curator, who collected the skeleton in New York and wrapped it in cotton wool to be taken back to Chicago, noted at once that the pelvic girdle was female. He arranged such a blaze of publicity in Chicago that on the first day it was shown to the public, more than twenty thousand people crowded into the museum to see the first prehistoric skeleton ever displayed in the United States.

Six years later, by which time it had been seen by more than a million visitors, the skull was withdrawn from exhibition to be fully reconstructed. A detailed examination found it to be a young woman of around twenty years, five feet one inch tall, and that she had lived between thirteen and fifteen thousand years earlier. She had been buried with an ivory point, perhaps a harpoon or spearhead, about three inches long, on or perhaps inside her abdomen. This led to speculation that this weapon might have been the cause of her death, a suggestion of long-ago murder that was astutely promoted by Henry Field to bring in more visitors. He also suggested that the location of her burial suggested that she might have been one of the sculptors of the unique great frieze.

The reconstruction of this woman's face had delighted Bruno since he had first seen it at Cap Blanc, not only because she was lovely in a strikingly modern way with huge eyes, a graceful neck and high cheekbones, but because of the skullcap of shells that she wore. It made her look like some café society young beauty of the 1920s. Bruno could almost imagine her dancing the

Charleston.

"What do you think of the exhibition, Bruno? You've been studying it long enough," asked Clothilde Daumier, a short and red-haired powerhouse of a woman who was one of the museum's curators and a leading expert on the prehistory of the region. She and her German archaeologist husband, Horst Vogelstern, were good friends and Bruno had been one of the witnesses at their recent wedding.

"It's wonderful," Bruno replied. "Thank you for inviting me to this preview. I'm overwhelmed with the skill of these reconstructions."

"In that case, you can tell the artist yourself," Clothilde said, steering him toward an attractive, gray-haired woman who moved gracefully as she advanced toward Bruno. "Elisabeth Daynès, meet Bruno Courrèges, our chief of police and a good friend who has a great interest in archaeology. He even found a modern corpse in one of our ancient graves."

"Clothilde's archaeologists found it," Bruno said, smiling. "I just helped find out who it was. I'm really moved by your work, bringing these people back to life in this way. You're a great artist, madame."

"You're very kind, Monsieur Bruno,"

Elisabeth replied. Her voice was soft and well modulated, with just a hint of an accent of the Midi. "How did you realize your body was not some prehistoric skeleton?"

"Because he was wearing a Swatch," Bruno replied. "They had only been made since 1983. Tell me, madame, have you ever worked with the police in trying to reconstruct the faces of unidentified skeletons?"

"A little, but only informally. It's a considerable investment in time and effort to do such a reconstruction, and since so much of our work is seen by the courts as inspired guesswork, the police are understandably reluctant to finance such projects."

"I find it hard to understand why the courts are so hesitant when I see your work here, madame," Bruno said.

"Please, call me Elisabeth," she said, as Clothilde steered them toward a reception area where they were handed glasses of wine and Clothilde excused herself to welcome some other guests to the preview. "I understand the courts' point of view. If you study the verbal descriptions that people give of strangers, they usually describe the hair, its style and color, the color of the eyes and whether the face is fleshy or lean. Those, however, are the three elements that we cannot discern from the skull itself. What we can do is use the contours of the individual skull, which vary much more than you might think — even among family members — to reconstruct each of the forty-three muscles in the human face. So in terms of form and structure, I think we can go a long way to reconstruct the features. But the hair, the eyes, the depth of flesh — these remain our challenges."

"So the muscular structure of a face varies with the small differences in the shape of each individual skull?"

"Exactly," she said, nodding with enthusiasm. "We use a laser measurement system to map the precise shape of each skull down to fractions of a millimeter, put them into a computer which creates a three-dimensional model, and then we use a high-precision 3D printer to give us the head. We then use the laser again to compare this printed skull with a cast we make of the original skull to check that they are absolutely identical. Developing and perfecting that system took a year of work, but now it's almost automatic."

"Why bother with the computer-printed version when you have a cast of the original skull?"

"Because we can do so much of the work on re-creating the musculature on the computer where it's easy to make adjustments," she replied. "And with the computer, we can share images of our progress with colleagues elsewhere in France or in other parts of the world. When we reconstructed the face of Tutankhamen, the computer allowed us to stay in constant touch with the National Geographic people in Washington and with the Cairo museum."

"And if you knew the hair color, and that the body was that of a young man in his twenties, athletic and probably without much body fat, could you reconstruct something in which you would have confidence?"

"I always have confidence in my work, Monsieur Bruno, but should I assume that you have some particular skeleton in mind and that you're hoping to enlist my help? I'm afraid that my schedule is already impossibly full. Perhaps Clothilde has told you of our project to re-create the entire family of hominids from the earliest times, *Australopithecus, Homo habilis, Homo ergaster,* Flores and, of course, Neanderthals and *Homo sapiens.* That takes all my time."

"I understand. But do you have some young associate or student with such skills?"

"Most of what I learned in this area came from Jean-Noël Vignal, whom I met when he was at the forensic institute in Paris. You might consult him. But tell me about this body."

Briefly, Bruno recounted the story of J-J and Oscar, and she suddenly interrupted him.

"But those dates, you say 1988 or 1989, that's when I was here in the Périgord," she said excitedly. "I was working at Le Thot, the park that's attached to the Lascaux cave. They asked me to reconstruct a mammoth and a group of human hunters. That was part of my earliest work in this field. I'd been working in the theater on costumes and then on masks for the national theater in Lille, and I really became interested in ancient humans when I was making models for the prehistory museum at Tautavel in the Pyrenees. So I have a personal connection to this region at the time this young man died. Give me your card, and I'll talk to some colleagues and see what might be possible. Now I really must circulate, but thank you for your interest and your kind words."

They exchanged business cards, and she scribbled a personal mobile phone number onto the one she gave him.

"Au revoir, madame, and thank you for your exhibition and also for your help."

CHAPTER 2

Bruno put his idea to the back of his mind until he heard from Elisabeth that she had a possible candidate, Virginie, a young student at a design school in Paris who was looking for a project she could submit to complete her diploma. Her mother was Spanish and her father French, and she had been raised in Madrid and the French naval port of Toulon. She had spent the previous summer vacation on an internship in Elisabeth's studio.

"Virginie is good, knows my techniques, and her work is meticulous," Elisabeth said. "I'll keep an eye on her progress with you, and if this works out as I hope, then I'll probably offer her a job in my studio when she graduates, since I know her professor and we agree that Virginie shows a lot of promise. She can continue to live on her student grant, but she may need help with rent and so on, unless you can find her a place in a student hostel. And she'll need a workshop."

"That sounds great, Elisabeth. Thank you so much. I'll discuss this with J-J and get back to you," Bruno replied. He immediately called J-J to invite him to dinner, but warned him they would first be visiting a new exhibition at the Les Eyzies museum. He asked J-J if he still had access to Oscar's skull.

"It occupies pride of place in our evidence room here. Why?"

"I'll tell you later. Do you still have a budget for cold cases?"

"Certainly. It's part of the training budget. We assign new candidates to unsolved old cases to see how they shape up. What are you up to, Bruno?"

"I'll let you know over dinner, J-J. But I think you'll like the idea."

Bruno planned a simple meal before he left to meet J-J at the museum. He would serve some salmon he had been curing for the past three days. The marinade was made of peppercorns, dill, salt, pepper, crushed juniper berries and lemon zest, with a shot glass of eau-de-vie drizzled over the mixture before it went into the fridge. The sauce to accompany the gravlax was made of Dijon mustard, cider vinegar, honey and sunflower oil. He had cooked a casserole of venison the previous day and had made an apple pie that he would serve cold with ice cream.

Knowing that Fabiola was on duty at the medical center that evening, he invited her partner, Gilles, as well, suspecting he would be intrigued by the prospect of reopening an investigation into Oscar's death. He also invited the mayor of St. Denis, whose political skills might be useful if J-J met some official resistance to reviving his old obsession with Oscar. They met at the museum shortly before it closed, each relieved to be in an air-conditioned space and escape from the brutal heat wave that had gripped southwestern France for the past week. Clothilde showed them around Elisabeth Daynès's exhibition while Bruno explained what he'd learned from his talk with her.

"Normally, a project like this would cost a fortune, but Elisabeth has a young student who is keen to reconstruct Oscar's face from his skull as part of her diploma," Bruno explained. "I was told she's very good — Elisabeth told me she wants to hire her for her own studio."

"You're proposing that we could get something close enough to Oscar's real face that we might use it to identify him?" J-J asked. "But how do we go about making sure enough people see it?"

"Publicity," said Gilles. "This is a great story and it's very visual, custom-made for TV and social media. You have the skull and the reconstructed face and a long-ago murder. I'm sure my former editor at *Paris Match* would want a story on that, and so would *Sud Ouest* and TV newsmagazines. It's just the kind of quirky, offbeat story they love to wrap up a news bulletin." Gilles leaned back, made a mock-solemn face and adopted the half-sonorous, half-folksy diction of a newscaster: "And now, from Périgord, how the archaeologists are helping police investigate a thirty-year-old murder that has never been solved . . ."

"I see what you're getting at, but I'm not sure I can persuade the powers that be to give me a budget for this," J-J said, but his eyes were bright as he kept looking at the reconstructed faces of the women in the display case. "Still, I'd certainly like to give it a try. Nobody could deny that these faces are amazingly lifelike."

"You don't need a budget," said the mayor. "The artist will be working for free, or for not much more than pocket money. She's doing this project to get her diploma and she has her student grant to live on. I can have an informal talk with the mayor of

29

Périgueux, and I'm sure we can get her a place in a student hostel. You have plenty of room for her to work in that police science lab of yours, J-J. And since the original murder took place in St. Denis, I imagine we can find some modest funds in our tourism-promotion budget if required, so long as we can eventually put the reconstruction of the face on display for the tourists. Gilles is right, this is something that will catch the public imagination."

They took a last look around the exhibition, pausing once more before the exhibition case that depicted the life-size reconstruction of the Neanderthal man with the child and beside it another display of a young Cro-Magnon man, spear in hand and poised to throw it.

"It's a funny thing about these men with their straggling beards," said J-J. "It makes them look less modern somehow than the women."

"Yes, I see what you mean, but imagine trying to shave with a piece of flint," Bruno replied.

"You're both missing something," said Gilles, a note of excitement in his voice. "Look at the Neanderthal man with that animal fur draped loosely around him. And then look at the Cro-Magnon guy with his

30

spear from tens of thousands of years later. His furs have been deliberately fashioned into trousers and a jacket. I'd never thought of it before, but the Cro-Magnons must have invented the needle, which gave them the technology of sewing. It meant they could wear garments that were much better suited to surviving cold spells and ice ages. Maybe that's how they flourished while the Neanderthals died out."

Later, in Bruno's living room over their aperitifs, protected from the heat outside by the thick stone walls, the mayor observed that it was a different kind of technology that now interested him. He turned to J-J and asked if he'd ever thought of using the DNA from Oscar's skull to help identify him.

J-J shook his head. "It was all too new at the time, very expensive and not too reliable."

It wasn't until 1984 that a British scientist named Alec Jeffreys first established that everyone's DNA is unique, J-J explained. The police were still studying the science behind it, but a defense lawyer was quick to take advantage, and two years later the lawyer used DNA in a British court in a case of two girls raped and murdered to show that his client was innocent, even though he'd already been convicted. DNA was then able to establish the real culprit. That made news, and the following year it was used in another rape case, in Florida. France took some time to start using the technology, first proposing to keep a national DNA database only in 1996. It began with sex offenders, but its use was not extended to those convicted of serious crimes until after the 9/11 terrorist attacks in the United States.

"Even today, we only have something like five million people in our national database," J-J said. "The British and the Americans each have over twenty million. But it was French police scientists who showed its limitations. There was a case of a woman's DNA connected to several murders in Austria, Germany and France, and French detectives established that the DNA came from a woman working in the factory that produced the cotton swabs used to collect the DNA from swabbing inside the mouths of suspects. The killer was finally caught and turned out to be a man. There's no doubt that DNA has revolutionized police work."

That seemed a natural point to pause, thought Bruno, and he invited his guests to the table, brought out the salmon and asked how Oscar's DNA might be useful today.

"I've been thinking about that," said J-J. "I'll start by running it against the national database, which is a long shot, but it's getting better. Then I'll ask for a Europe-wide search through Interpol. I can work on that tomorrow. Our own lab can take a sample of the skull and get the DNA."

"Isn't Jacqueline supposed to be back soon?" Gilles asked the mayor, referring to the half-French, half-American historian who spent one term teaching each year at the Sorbonne, another at Columbia University in New York and the rest of her year in St. Denis. She now rented out her own renovated farmhouse nearby and lived with the mayor, an arrangement so mutually agreeable that it seemed to have subtracted several years from each of them.

"She'll be back Friday," the mayor said. "She stayed on for some conference in Washington at the Cold War research center that relates to her next book, something about some hoard of Stasi documents from the former East Germany. She e-mailed me to say that Jack Crimson is also attending the conference. Apparently he's on some British committee that determines which official documents are to be declassified."

"So Jack will be back here as well?" Bruno asked. He was fond of the former British diplomat and intelligence official whose daughter, Miranda, helped Bruno's friend Pamela run a nearby horse-riding school. They had recently started offering cooking courses to fill Pamela's *gîtes* in the winter months when tourists were scarce. Bruno and other friends had been roped in to help demonstrate the local cuisine.

"No, Jacqueline told me that Jack is going back to London for a few days for some committee meeting, probably relating to the conference in Washington. He'll be back later next week."

The conversation drifted off to sports and then through politics over the venison until interrupted by Bruno's phone. He didn't recognize the number of the caller but thought he'd better answer and was surprised to hear the voice of his cousin Alain, who was in the air force and the relative to whom he was closest.

"Bad news, Bruno," he began. "It's about Mum, she's had a stroke and been taken to the hospital in Bergerac, the one on avenue Calmette. It happened sometime last night, but I just heard about it from my big sister. I'll get some compassionate leave and head there tomorrow. Apparently she can recognize people, but she can't talk."

"Sorry to hear it," said Bruno. "What time

do you expect to be there?"

"I'll have to sort out the paperwork at the base for my leave tomorrow morning, and then I'll drive up. I should be there at about four, and I'll stay with Annette for a day or two. Should I expect to see you?"

"I'll get there as soon as I can after four," Bruno said. "Maybe we can have a drink together afterward and catch up. It's been too long."

"Okay, see you then." Alain ended the call, leaving Bruno pensive about his aunt and his childhood in the overcrowded tenement in a grim public housing project where all six children shared a bedroom, even the eldest, Annette, who was fifteen.

Bruno only ever saw her and the other siblings when he paid a duty call to his aunt on her birthday and at Christmas, each time taking her a bottle of his homemade *vin de noix.* Annette and the eldest brother, Bernard, both lived in Bergerac, in public housing. The other three siblings had all moved away, and Bruno had lost touch with them, except for Alain. Annette worked in the kitchen of the Bergerac retirement home in which her mother had been living. Bernard had been unemployed for years, claiming disability allowance for a bad back which did not seem to stop him from taking part-time jobs as a painter and decorator, working off the books and only for cash.

Alain was a senior warrant officer at the air defense control training center at the Mont-de-Marsan air base south of Bordeaux, better known as the home of two fighter squadrons equipped with Rafale interceptors, France's most advanced warplane. The youngest of five children, Alain was just a year or so older than Bruno, and they had grown up together when Bruno, age six, had been taken in from the church orphanage by his aunt. It had not been a happy home, and Bruno had long suspected that the main reason for his welcome was the more generous welfare payment his aunt received as a *famille nombreuse* at a time when the French state was trying to increase the population. The food, he recalled, had been better at the orphanage.

"You look like you had some grim news," the mayor said as Bruno returned to the table with the apple pie and ice cream. His friends nodded sympathetically when he explained the news of his aunt's stroke.

"I don't recall any of your family coming to St. Denis to visit," the mayor went on, when they had all been served.

"My aunt came for a weekend in the early days, and it was plain she didn't like it, being woken by the cockerel, the silence for much of the time and the lack of town sounds and street noises," Bruno said, half smiling and feeling a mixture of affection and regret.

"She was never a reader and she couldn't get over the fact that I had no TV. She thought the Dordogne Valley was pretty and liked the castles but refused to visit any caves, thought they'd give her claustrophobia. Her youngest, Alain, is roughly my age, and we always got on. He came for a weekend when I was playing in one of those old-timers' games against the youth team, and he liked it a lot. He's thinking of settling near here when he gets out of the air force in a couple of years. He'll have a decent pension after twenty-five years."

"There's a program I worked for when I was in the Senate, to let long-serving veterans spend their last year training to be teachers," the mayor said. "That might suit him. And we're always short of teachers here in the countryside, particularly men."

"I'll mention it when I see him at the hospital tomorrow," said Bruno. "But I know he's been thinking of setting himself up in business. He learned to be a radar tech and electrician and now teaches air defense systems, so he's good with computers."

"Is he married?" asked Gilles.

"Not yet. Like me, he can't find the right woman."

"You find them all right, Bruno," said Gilles, grinning widely. "You just don't seem to be able to get them to the altar. It must run in the family."

"Maybe you're right," Bruno replied with a rueful smile. "Isn't there an old saying, Always the bridesmaid, never the bride?"

"It's a song from some Hollywood film," said Gilles. "But I think the girl who sang it eventually married the man of her dreams. So, Bruno, that means there's hope for you yet."

CHAPTER 3

Bruno anticipated a depressing visit when he arrived at the hospital the next day. His ancient Land Rover had no air-conditioning so he had driven the forty minutes from St. Denis with all the windows open, the radio giving news of forest fires in Provence and the Landes. The parking lot seemed to radiate heat from the relentless sun, and he was sweating freely by the time he reached the hospital doors.

Although looking forward to seeing Alain again, he felt oppressed by memories of his childhood, knowing that he was an afterthought. He had been the charity kid, expected to be endlessly grateful for being taken in to his aunt's poor, noisy and overcrowded family home. There had been some happy moments, but in childhood there always were impromptu games of soccer in the street outside the apartment block; birthday parties; his growing friendship with Alain. They served to remind him of the wretched times, the way Bernard the bully, seven years older, would hit him with casual regularity and say that Bruno's dead mother was a whore, a word Bruno was too young to understand.

In the hospital, he found his aunt in a small ward of eight people, all elderly. The place smelled of disinfectant and cleaning fluids with an underlying hint of urine. She was the only one with a visitor, Alain. Bruno kissed his aunt on both cheeks, gave her the flowers he'd brought and received a grunt of acknowledgment in return. He embraced Alain, found a spare chair and sat down on the other side of the bed from his cousin and announced that he was pleased to see his aunt looking better than he'd expected. She grunted again, waving the fingers of one hand in frustration at being unable to speak. Her face seemed to have been divided into two halves, one normal and the other melted like so much candle wax. The left side of her mouth and her left eye were drooping, and the skin sagged with them.

Bruno wondered how sad he truly felt, how far his somber mood was simply a product of the gloomy hospital ward. He knew he had little real affection for his aunt, a woman he usually remembered as tired or angry, always ready to swat one of her brood of kids with a soup ladle or hairbrush or whatever was in reach. He could not recall ever being hugged by her, but he knew he should feel grateful that she'd taken him in from the orphanage.

With an effort, Bruno thrust away these thoughts, and he and Alain exchanged small talk, trying at first to include her with talk of the family, her care in the hospital and the kindness of the nurses. Being unable to join in seemed to upset her, so they sat quietly, each of them holding a hand. Bruno had her cold left hand, which seemed almost lifeless. Soon she drifted off to sleep and snored.

"It's good to see you, Bruno, despite this sad occasion. It's been far too long," Alain said. "And thanks for coming."

"Good to see you, too," Bruno replied with a grin. "You're not looking bad for a man of your advanced years."

"Just eighteen months older and wiser than you, Bruno," Alain said in mock reproof.

Bruno laughed, genuinely pleased to see the only cousin with whom he stayed in regular contact, the one who'd taught him how to swim in the Bergerac municipal pool. Even though Alain liked soccer while

Bruno was a devoted rugby man, Bruno still knew they had a lot in common. He thought they looked roughly the same age. Each of them had kept his hair and looked trim and fit. Alain's hair was blond, while Bruno's was dark, and Bruno was four or five centimeters taller. Alain had a heavier, almost stocky build with wider shoulders, but Bruno thought there was a family resemblance in their features.

"When are you getting out into civilian life?" Bruno asked.

"Less than two years to go. That's still the plan, even though it will mean I have to start buying my own clothes," Alain said, with a twinkle in his eye and a smile, as if he had some good news to share. "But it looks like it will be a very different life because I might not be leaving alone."

"You've met someone?" Bruno asked eagerly.

"A tech sergeant at the base, her name's Rosalie Lamartine," Alain said, his eyes lighting up as he spoke of her. "She'll have done twenty years when my twenty-five are up, so she'll get a decent pension. It's kind of tough with the rules against fraternizing with people of different ranks, but we've spent some weekends together and had a great two-week vacation in Senegal just before Christmas. That's when we each knew this was it."

"I'm really happy for you, Alain. That's great news. I'd better start saving for a wedding present." Bruno punched his cousin lightly on the arm, and they both laughed, grinning at each other in a way that took them back to their boyhood friendship. "Are you planning to marry once you're out?"

Alain nodded. "Maybe before if Rosalie gets the promotion she expects. Then we'd be the same rank and could qualify for married quarters. She's young enough to have kids, which is something we both want. She's terrific, cheerful and funny. I think you'll like her."

He took out his mobile phone, punched at some symbols to call up his collection of photographs and proudly showed Bruno his favorite pictures of his new love. Tanned a little more pinkish red than brown, and dressed in a light blue bikini that barely covered her ample figure, she was smiling fondly at the camera while holding a fat slice of watermelon. Her lips and cheeks were still moist from its sweet red flesh, and one oval black seed was stuck to her chin. Bruno noted the dark hair and laughing brown eyes, good cheekbones and a generous mouth and nodded in approval. She was an attractive woman.

"You're a lucky man," said Bruno. "She's glorious. *Le bon Dieu* has sent you a real gift. From looking at her, you can tell she has a sweet nature."

"Yes, she does, and the troops like her." Alain's eyes were glowing as he studied the photo. "And here she is in uniform. She carries her rank easily."

He called up another photo of the same woman in standard camouflage dress, her eyes fixed on the assault rifle she was stripping. Her hair was piled up beneath her beret and showing off her neck. In another photo, still in uniform, she was chatting with some soldiers, male and female, with an expression that was firm but not unfriendly. The troops were sitting up straight and looking at her with respect.

"Bring her to St. Denis for a weekend so I can get to know her." Bruno grinned with genuine delight. "You can have the honeymoon suite, a whole top floor to yourselves, and I'll keep my basset hound from coming up to roust you out at dawn. I'm afraid I can't answer for the cockerel."

Alain laughed. "It can't be worse than a bugle calling reveille. And I'll look forward to seeing your place again and trying your cooking. You might even have to give me lessons, since the Armée de l'Air won't be taking care of my meals in the future. I've told her a lot about you, and we saw a couple of articles in *Sud Ouest* about some cases you solved. Rosalie was impressed, but she said she was happy she'd got the handsome cousin."

Bruno grinned again. "What are you going to do when you're out?"

"I'm not sure. Rosalie is interested in a new program, training to be a teacher during our last year in the military, while staying on full pay. So we could be back in civilian life in just over a year. She's thinking of going to a vocational school, which is also something I could do. That would mean two salaries plus two pensions, so we'd be pretty comfortable. Between us we've saved enough of our pay to put down a deposit on a house. We're thinking of settling somewhere near Bergerac, maybe in the wine country around Pomport or St.-Laurent-des-Vignes. That's where we spent our first weekends away together."

"It sounds like you have it all worked out," said Bruno, feeling just a hint of envy. Still, Alain's good fortune meant there was hope for Bruno yet.

"How about you?" Alain asked. "Any woman in your life, or are you still carrying a torch for the policewoman in Paris? Isabelle, is that the one?"

"I still see her from time to time, and I still feel like a lovestruck teenager whenever I'm with her, but we both know there's no hope of settling down. She's devoted to her career."

"Maybe one of the bridesmaids will catch your eye at our wedding. I'll count on you to carry the ring and to make a speech."

Bruno was trying to think of a suitable reply when a student nurse approached them and said the specialist was free to see them. She directed them to an office down the corridor and began checking the monitors of the various patients.

"Are you the next of kin?" asked the middle-aged woman behind the desk. A stethoscope hung around her neck, and there were shadows under her eyes. She looked close to exhaustion but straightened up when they entered and gave the two men a half smile before settling her features into that look of infinite patience that Bruno recognized from his friend Fabiola as the sign of a good doctor.

"I'm her son and this is my cousin, her nephew," Alain said. "She raised us both, so he's like my little brother."

Bruno felt himself almost absurdly pleased

to hear Alain's words. He'd never thought of himself in that way. He'd half assumed that he and Alain were similar types, Alain in the air force and Bruno in the army and then the police. They were both men whose messy, chaotic childhoods had steered them toward the structured camaraderie and routines of military life. He was still glancing sideways at Alain as the doctor began to speak.

"My name is Dumourriez, and I'm the specialist who's been treating your mother since she was admitted yesterday morning," the doctor said. "I'm afraid I have bad news. We gave your mother a scan this morning, and the results are not at all encouraging. She's had a heavy stroke, and there are signs of serious brain damage. I'm sorry, but don't expect her to be capable of rational speech again. Her heart is in bad shape, and she wasn't in good health to begin with. I don't think we'll be able to do much more for her than to make your mother comfortable for the time she has left."

She paused and picked up a file from her desk and opened it to a page that Bruno recognized to be a printout of a scan.

"Your mother certainly won't be able to return to the retirement home where she was living. They aren't equipped to care for her. We can't keep her here, so she'll have to go either to a geriatric ward or, if her condition continues to decline as I expect, then she should go into hospice. Perhaps you should discuss this with the rest of the family, and we can meet again tomorrow when I've had a chance to see how she's reacting to treatment."

"You think she's dying?" Alain asked.

"We're all dying," the doctor said with a shrug and a clearing of the throat that might have been a morose laugh had she not been so visibly tired. "Your mother is pretty close to the end and not really in touch with the world around her."

"But I'm sure she grunted when she recognized me, and she squeezed my hand when I sat beside her," said Bruno.

"That was probably an automatic reaction. Please don't get your hopes up. And she's almost eighty. That's a pretty good age, close to the average, and it's clear she didn't have an easy life. I don't think she's able to feel any pain. I wish I had better news for you."

The doctor rose to signal that the meeting was over. She ran a hand through her graying hair, pushing it back from her face. Bruno wondered how many such conversations with relatives she had gone through that day, that week. She handed Alain a sheet of paper.

"Here's a list of the local hospices," she said. "I've marked the two that have a vacancy. I recommend the first one if you can get her in. The atmosphere is better, but you'd better call them as soon as you can. You might want to check in with the help office on the ground floor who can give you more details and make the booking. Under the new rules we've already had to inform the retirement home that your mother won't be going back there, so you'll need to clear out her belongings."

"What new rules?" Bruno asked, keeping his voice neutral, though there was something in his tone that made the doctor look at him properly for the first time. Although Bruno was wearing the usual red jacket that he donned when he wanted to appear civilian to a casual glance, the doctor took in his uniform shirt and the usual police pouches at his belt.

"Gendarme?" the doctor asked.

"Municipal, from St. Denis," Bruno replied, lifting the left side of the jacket to show the police badge attached to the chest pocket of his shirt.

"The *conseil général* of this *département* brought in the new rule last year," the doc-

49

tor explained. "Here in the Dordogne we have one of the oldest populations in France, one in seven is aged seventy-five or older. That means an unusual degree of pressure on retirement homes, geriatric wards, hospices — and on people like me. For you, monsieur, it means significantly less crime, since most crimes are committed by younger people."

"Not white-collar crimes, madame," Bruno replied.

"Touché." The doctor gave a curt nod that she softened with a half smile. "You're right, and I think Montaigne said something about violence being the preserve of the young, but avarice the temptation of age. In my experience all ages seem to be vulnerable to greed."

"Montaigne seems to have written most of the wise things we eventually come to appreciate," said Bruno, finding himself admiring this overworked but still kindly woman. He felt guilty for taking any more of her time. "I think we understand the extraordinary pressures you are under and thank you for what you did for this woman," Bruno went on. "When do you expect to move her to a hospice."

"Tomorrow, two days at most. I'll keep her under observation, monitor her heart and reactions, see if there's any reason for hope, but I have to say that I doubt it." She glanced at the file open before her on the desk and looked up to address Alain. "We have contact details for your sister Annette, but you might give me your mobile phone and e-mail, just to keep you informed. One more thing. The file says your mother had no religion. Are you sure she wouldn't want the last rites? Most people do, just in case."

"Pascal's wager," said Bruno. "Better to believe in God, since if he exists you will be rewarded. If he doesn't exist, you won't lose anything by believing in him."

"Exactly. Is that how you believe?" the doctor asked.

"If God exists, I doubt he can be so easily fooled," Bruno replied. "If we are to be judged, it will be by our acts rather than on any number of our pious professions of faith."

The doctor nodded. "Good luck, messieurs, and I'm sorry for your loss. Short of a miracle, this old lady is passing peacefully away."

CHAPTER 4

Bruno's aunt never regained full conscious-
ness and died a few days after she was
moved to the hospice. The funeral was a
quiet affair, just Bruno, Alain, Bernard and
Annette, and half a dozen of his aunt's
friends and former neighbors. Some more
residents from the retirement home turned
up for the brief buffet lunch that was held
after the cremation. Her other children had
sent wreaths, saying they were unable to get
time off for the funeral. Nobody except
Bruno seemed much surprised by this.
Warned that the retirement home would offer only coffee and fruit juice with the
lunch, Bruno and Alain had each brought a
couple of bottles of wine. Most of it disappeared down Bernard's throat. Alain
made a brief speech about his mother,
Annette cried, and within forty minutes it
was over.

"I haven't had time yet to go through her

things," said Annette when only the family remained. "Not that there was much after she moved to the retirement home. They only let her have one of her own chairs. So there was a photo album, some clothes I'll give to Action Catholique, a couple of cushions she'd embroidered and a few photos in frames, her own wedding and mine, along with pictures of you and Alain in your uniforms. Not a lot to show for eighty years. I'll go through the papers she left when I have the time. And there was a half-empty bottle of that *vin de noix* you made for her, Bruno. I think Bernard grabbed it."

Bruno smiled ruefully at the thought. It was little enough for the woman who had taken him in and raised and fed him for eleven years before he'd gone in the youth wing of the army. He had half hoped that there might be something of his mother's in his aunt's belongings, but he doubted it. On his visits to his aunt, he had pored over the battered photo album, trying in vain to find at least a picture of the young woman who had given birth to him and almost immediately left him as a baby at a church door and then disappeared. His aunt had refused to discuss her sister, saying she was long dead and Bruno had to move on and learn to live without the woman who had abandoned him. Sometimes there was a wistful tone in his aunt's voice when she said that. Bruno thought that in her way, and when the large family gave her the occasional moment to herself, she missed her little sister.

The death of this last connection to someone who had known his mother made Bruno pensive as he drove back to St. Denis. He'd always resisted the idea of tracking her down, even if it was only to find out when and how she had died. He knew her first and maiden names and the date of her birth within a year or two, presumably in Bergerac. He should be able to find the number of her identity card and then use his police access to troll through various government data banks to learn what he could. There seemed little point in doing so. Occasionally he had fleeting thoughts about her and about his unknown father. He'd have liked to know what she looked like, and what strange fate had driven her to carry him inside her for nine months, to give birth to him and then to leave him before a week was out. But he knew he could never do more than scrape the surface of her life, and the search would probably

he collected from his gutters. He then headed for Hubert de Montignac's wine cave in St. Denis to buy a bottle for that evening's dinner party. The event had been arranged by Pamela and Miranda to welcome home Jack Crimson and also Jacqueline, who was coming with the mayor. The rest of the usual gang from the Monday evening dinners would also be there: Gilles and Fabiola along with the baron and Florence, the science teacher at the local *collège.*

As always on Monday evenings, Florence's twin toddlers would be coming and sleeping over with their playmates, Miranda's two children. Bruno smiled to himself, thinking with pleasure of the moments when all four kids thundered down the stairs, fresh and sweet smelling from their bath and racing out to the stables to find the dogs and say good night to the horses.

Which wine should he take? The local wine store was too full of choices, with giant vats at one end selling wine in bulk for less than two euros a liter from some device that always reminded Bruno of petrol pumps. At the other end were the expensive bottles of Château Petrus, Cheval Blanc, Le Pin, Lafite and Latour that cost hundreds and even thousands of euros each. In between were separate stands for Bordeaux, for Burgundy, for sparkling and dessert wines. There was another stand for the wines of Bergerac and, along one wall, an array of what Hubert boasted was the widest selection of malt scotch whiskeys outside of Scotland. There were more shelves for bottles of vintage Cognacs and Armagnac, a small library of books on wine, displays of glasses and decanters and a selection of local delicacies from foie gras to fruit cordials and rillettes.

Hubert, the owner of this and a small chain of other such wine caves in the region with two more in Paris, was more than just an old friend. He was also one of Bruno's business partners, a fellow director of the town vineyard. Hubert knew that Bruno seldom spent more than ten euros on a bottle, but Bruno said this was a special occasion and on Hubert's advice paid twenty euros for a bottle of Château Bélingard's Cuvée Ortus from 2016.

"You should decant it a good hour before serving," said Hubert over a friendly glass of white wine from the town vineyard, and Bruno swore that he'd do so.

He drove on to Pamela's riding school where his basset hound, Balzac, recognized the sound of his elderly Land Rover and turned from his play with Pamela's two sheepdogs, Beau and Bella, adopted after the death of their owner, an old sheep farmer. Balzac gave a long welcoming howl and then raced to greet his master. Bruno crouched down as his dog galloped toward him, his long ears flapping like a pair of furry wings and his tongue hanging out like some fat pink necktie. Bruno laughed aloud at the sight, spread his arms wide and braced himself to receive the thirty kilos of flying basset.

"I've only been gone since this morning," Bruno protested as Balzac lathered his neck and jaw. Then Beau and Bella came up, more sedately, and Bruno set off past the chicken coop he'd helped to build and went to the stables to visit his horse, Hector. Bruno stroked his glossy neck and gave him his carrot. All the ponies were gone, which meant Miranda must still be out with the schoolgirls. Bruno could hear the sound of Pamela's voice from the paddock, encouraging the novices to sit up straight and relax their hands as they trotted their horses around the circular fence.

He waved to Pamela and leaned on the fence to watch the riders, checking his watch. He was a little early. He, Pamela and Fabiola had arranged to give the horses their evening ride in good time before dinner. Pamela called out that Jack was in the office, so Bruno strolled across, greeted the jovial Englishman and put his bottle of Ortus on the desk before embracing him.

"Good to see you, Bruno, and you, Balzac," Crimson said, bending to fondle the dog's long ears. "I missed you both when I was away. It's such a pleasure to have dogs in my life again," he went on. "And it's wonderful for the grandchildren, not just Balzac but those two sheepdogs you brought us from that poor old farmer. You know my grandkids smuggle them up to their rooms at night, thinking we don't know." Crimson shook his head and chuckled. "Growing up with dogs and horses is a great thing for the young."

"We humans have been domesticating dogs around here for thousands of years, so we've all sort of grown up together," said Bruno. "How was your trip to Washington, and London?"

"The politicians over there are almost as weird as ours in England," Crimson replied with a bitter laugh. "I suppose every country has the right to go completely crazy once in a while, and it's now the turn of us Anglo-Saxons. It's good to be back in the Périgord, and I'll look forward to trying that bottle of Ortus — *Hortus deorum quo ortus es,* if I remember my Latin. Risen from the garden of the gods."

"How was the conference?"

"Interesting but somewhat frustrating. It's thirty years since the Berlin Wall came down, but our American friends are still sitting on a treasure trove of Stasi intelligence files that the scholars think might well be unclassified or at least more widely shared. Our friend Jacqueline was particularly outspoken, as you might imagine, but without success."

"I thought you British and the Americans had always shared intelligence under that famous special relationship you talk about," Bruno said.

"We share a great deal, along with the Canadians and Australians, but not everything. And this stuff is still quite sensitive. The Americans say, quite rightly, that they distributed a great deal of this archive — it's called the Rosenholz dossier — to the relevant NATO partners. We and the Germans, Dutch and Scandinavians have been allowed to examine anything that the CIA says concerns us."

"But not the French?" Bruno asked.

"No, not the French, nor the Italians and Spaniards. It's partly fear of leaks, but as you may know there's an old feud between the CIA and French intelligence that goes back to de Gaulle's time. Did you ever hear of a man called Philippe de Vosjoli, the only French intelligence man who ever defected to the United States?"

Startled, Bruno raised his eyebrows and shook his head at the same time. This was news to him. The very thought of a French official "defecting" to a NATO ally was extraordinary.

"It's all ancient history, back in the 1960s, long before you were born. It was all tied up with the Cuban missile crisis. De Vosjoli was the French intelligence liaison man at their Washington embassy with good contacts in Cuba, and he got some of the intelligence that alerted the Americans to the missiles the Russians were installing. The Americans trusted him, and when de Vosjoli refused to obey orders to start spying on American nuclear technology, he was recalled to Paris. Fearing arrest or worse, de Vosjoli refused to go, and the Americans gave him asylum."

"But the Americans did share their nuclear weapons technology, with you British and with us — I remember Jacqueline wrote a book about it," Bruno said, frowning. "It was comical. Congress had passed some law about not telling the French anything, so a ridiculous charade was arranged in which the French scientists would put forward an idea for warhead design, and their American colleagues would shake their heads if it was wrong but nod if it was right."

"Nuclear technology was only the half of it," Jack replied, reaching into a cupboard and bringing out a bottle of Bowmore and a couple of glasses. He poured them each two fingers, added a splash of still mineral water and handed one to Bruno, saying, "Cheers." The two men chinked glasses and sipped appreciatively.

The Americans had obtained a Soviet defector, Jack explained, a major in the KGB called Anatoliy Golitsyn, who began exposing important Soviet agents all across Europe. He'd identified John Vassall in the British defense ministry; Heinz Felfe, who was West Germany's deputy head of counterintelligence at the time; the Canadian economist Hugh Hambleton, who was working in NATO headquarters; and the Swedish air force colonel Stig Wennerström, who gave the KGB Sweden's air defense plans and the complete design dossier for their new Saab Draken jet fighter.

Above all, Golitsyn had claimed that the French government was thoroughly infiltrated, with one agent in de Gaulle's cabinet, others in the interior and defense ministries and the quai d'Orsay. It was so dramatic that JFK wrote a personal letter to de Gaulle to warn him. The French sent a team over to interrogate Golitsyn, tested him with some real and some fake NATO documents, and he was able to spot the right ones that he said he'd read when they came across his desk in Moscow.

"The French team thought he was genuine," Jack went on. "But their masters back in Paris suspected it was all a CIA plot to undermine de Gaulle. That's when de Vosjoli was recalled and refused to return. It was one of the factors that led to de Gaulle pulling France out of NATO's military wing. It's all a lifetime ago, but intelligence agencies have exceedingly long memories."

Bruno shook his head. "Amazing but all ancient history. And where does this Rosen-something dossier come in?"

"It's Rosenholz, and I don't know why it's called that. It was the master list of all Stasi intelligence agents. Truckloads of files of index cards were burned after the Berlin Wall fell, but Erich Mielke, the minister in charge of the Stasi, ordered microfilm copies made and kept them in his office. He sent one set of copies to the KGB liaison center in Karlshorst, and a year later, after the Berlin Wall came down, a defecting Soviet file clerk sold them to the CIA in Warsaw, allegedly for sixty-five thousand dollars — probably the best deal the Americans made since they bought Manhattan Island. There's a lot of disinformation about this. Another theory says some very senior Stasi officials bought themselves immunity with the files."

"And these were the lists of all the foreign spies the Stasi had recruited? All over the world?"

"That's right but even more than that. Some two hundred and eighty thousand files in all, mostly East Germans. Something like fifty thousand West Germans were in the files, but only about a thousand of them were serious agents. We investigated just over a hundred British citizens who were named in the files, and nobody was ever prosecuted. Most of them were peace and antinuclear campaigners, well-meaning idealists whom the Stasi thought might be useful. Some of the stuff was clearly invented or exaggerated, probably so that the real Stasi agents could inflate their claims for expenses. The Stasi's selection control was pitiful, always after quantity rather than quality. But some of the people recruited in Germany and Scandinavia and at NATO were very important indeed."

"And France?" Bruno inquired, finishing his glass of malt scotch and shaking his head when Jack offered a refill.

"Who knows? The CIA isn't telling. Back in 2003 they claim they gave the Germans the full archive, at least relating to Germany — nearly four hundred compact discs. But some parts of it were deliberately not given to the Germans: for example, the British material. The Germans have been nagging us for them, but we took the view that releasing all this unattributed and some-times invented stuff about idealistic — if naïve — British citizens forty years ago would do more harm than good. Most of those people in the peace movement just wanted a dialogue across the Iron Curtain and to outlaw nuclear weapons."

"But if these files contain names of signif-icant Stasi people in France, it must be in all our interests to expose them," Bruno began. Then he paused before continuing more slowly. "Is distribution not a political decision that an elected president should make rather than an intelligence agency? And what if the Americans know of these Frenchmen, some of them in important positions — they could blackmail them into spying for the Americans? What then?"

"You can't have it both ways, Bruno. You can't expect the Americans to share secret material with their allies one minute and then accuse them of blackmailing Frenchmen to spy on France the next. I see your point, but even if the Americans gave the stuff to Paris, would we ever know if they'd given everything, or held the best stuff back? We don't know that they've given us everything about Stasi operations in Britain. In fact, some of my old colleagues strongly suspect that there's some stuff about Stasi operations with the IRA and gunrunning via Libya that may be missing, probably to protect Irish Americans who were involved."

A car door slammed in the small parking lot outside, and through the window Bruno saw Fabiola and Gilles, already in their riding gear.

"Time to ride the horses," he said. "Thanks for the drink, and the very illuminating conversation. See you at dinner. And do me a favor and decant the Ortus."

"I will indeed, and I've brought a bottle of David Fourtout's red, as served at the George Cinq Hotel in Paris," said Jack. "People tell me it's the finest wine made in the Bergerac. And I've got a couple of bottles of Château Lestevenie brut chilling in the fridge, and I'm sure you'd agree that's the best of our sparkling wines."

"Aren't we lucky that we have so many great wines that can compete for that title?" Bruno said, grinning. "Yes, it may be the best of our white sparkling wines, but what about that lovely rosé brut from your friends at Château Feely?"

"We must do a comparative tasting," Jack replied. "Enjoy your ride and make sure you're back in time for the roast lamb. Jacqueline asked Miranda for it specially and I made the mint sauce — an English delicacy."

"Some French gourmets would say that's a contradiction in terms," Bruno said, laughing as he left. "But don't tell Pamela or Miranda that I said so."

CHAPTER 5

Bruno found Pamela in the stables, saddling Primrose. He changed into his riding boots and was just saddling Hector when Fabiola and Gilles joined them.

"We'll only take our four horses out this evening, the other ones have been working all day," Pamela said as she put the bridle onto Primrose's head. "I thought we should head up the ridge for a gallop, blow all the cobwebs away and work up an appetite for dinner."

Although the heat wave continued, it was almost a perfect summer's evening for a ride, a soft breeze helping the heat to fade from the day. Their shadows were beginning to lengthen as they trotted through the paddock and then walked the horses up the long slope to the ridge, the two sheepdogs loping out ahead. Balzac was trotting along beside Hector, who was pulling at the reins in his eagerness to run. Bruno saw Fabiola had the same problem, tightening the reins on the Andalusian she rode. Gilles brought up the rear. As always, he was riding the elderly mare, Victoria, although he was more and more comfortable on horseback and would soon be ready for a younger and less sedate horse.

Pamela paused when she reached the ridge, and the others gathered alongside, all looking down at the valley and across to the hill of Limeuil, where the two rivers came together on their way down to Bordeaux and the sea. It was a view of which Bruno never tired, enjoying the way that the houses and red roofs of St. Denis clambered up the hill to his right. They were matched perfectly by the way Limeuil's houses did the same to his left, with the small château of La Vitrolle with its apple orchard and vineyards between them.

"Are we all ready?" asked Pamela, and nudged Primrose with her heels and loosened the reins to let her run.

Beneath Bruno, Hector needed no urging and leaped forward after her, came alongside while still accelerating and then forged ahead, with the Andalusian at Bruno's stirrup and Balzac's sonorous bay of joy at the prospect of a run still ringing in their ears. The two sheepdogs were silent, running easily at Pamela's far side until the horses steadily drew ahead and Bruno felt his eyes narrow against the wind of their passage. He thrilled to the sound of the galloping hooves and the rhythm of Hector's muscles in delivering this apparently effortless speed. It was exhilarating to be part of this racing unit of horse and man, moving in such perfect harmony as they sped along the two kilometers of the ridge.

It seemed to end too soon as the belt of woodland approached and Hector, by now three lengths clear of the others, began to slow of his own accord. He knew this ridge and its boundaries as well as Bruno and drew to a halt, breathing easily, at the gap in the trees that led to the bridle trail that led down to the village of Bigaroque. Pamela liked to claim it had been named by the English in the Middle Ages when they had controlled southwestern France. Bigaroque, she argued, had been called Big Rock from the rocky outcrop that dominated the bend in the river that led to Le Buisson. It seemed plausible to Bruno.

They dismounted to walk their horses across the bridge and then cantered through the valley, flanked by fields of maize crowded too close together in a way that made Bruno tighten his lips at the thought of all the fertilizer and underground water this form of intensive farming required. Along with its fisheries policy, it was one of the aspects of the way Brussels ran Europe's agriculture that infuriated him. He counted himself as a good European, but he was outraged by the monstrous gap between the rhetoric of Brussels about the need to alleviate climate change and the harsh reality of its policies on the ground. Soon after they dismounted again to cross the bridge at Limeuil, they were passing on the far side of the river the vineyards that were run by the town of St. Denis, and his mood eased at the knowledge that these grapes were now being farmed organically. They took the railroad crossing that led to St. Chamassy and then the trail back to Pamela's riding school, which gave them one last brief gallop before it came into view.

At the stables, they removed the bridles and saddles and rubbed down their horses before filling their water troughs and mangers, the dogs waiting by their own food bowls until they were fed. Pamela and Fabiola went indoors to shower, and Gilles and Bruno stripped to the waist and washed themselves in the stable sink. They each kept towels and clean sweatshirts in the stables. With their hair still wet, they patted their horses good night and led the dogs to the main house. Gilles paused at Fabiola's car to take out a bottle of red wine from the vineyard of Court-les-Mûts, their special *cuvée* called Des Pieds et des Mains, whose grapes were trodden by human feet in the traditional way. Bruno nodded his approval, and then his phone vibrated. He saw it was a call from Claire at the kennel and answered at once.

"Bonjour, Bruno," she said. "Carla is getting ready to go into labor sometime tonight. I think Balzac will be a daddy by tomorrow morning."

"That's wonderful news," he said, laughing with delight as he spoke. "Is there anything I can do? Would you like me to come up to help you?"

"No, it's me she'll want alongside and it's not her first litter. I checked with the stethoscope and all the pups are doing well, nine good little heartbeats. I imagine she'll have them early in the morning, so I'll send you an e-mail rather than wake you up."

"When can we come and see them?"

"You can come anytime, but I'd rather keep Balzac away for the first couple of weeks because Carla will get nervous. Some sires can be tricky. I'm sure Balzac will be well behaved, but I want to keep Carla calm.

You'll remember I warned you about this when you were here. And don't worry, you still get first pick of the litter, and from the heartbeats she'll have enough pups for you to have two."

"Just so long as they're all right and Carla, too, although you know I still prefer to think of her as Diane de Poitiers."

"How could I forget?" She laughed. "Do you use her pedigree name because you're a bit of a snob, or do you have a thing for royal mistresses?"

Bruno laughed in return, more in delight at the coming of Balzac's pups than at Claire's teasing. "It's the royal connection, of course, nothing but the best for Balzac. And you know I'm not as much of a fan of Carla Bruni's music as you are. Thanks for the news and my best wishes to Carla-Diane. Call me anytime if you need anything."

They ended the call, and Bruno instantly called Isabelle, his old flame, whose gift to him Balzac had been, and who had accompanied him to the mating earlier in the summer.

"Bruno, good to hear from you, but I'm in a meeting . . ."

"It's just to say that Diane de Poitiers is going into labor. Balzac will be a father by the morning. I'll hang up."

He just heard a whoop of joy and the words "That's wonderful" as he closed his phone, wondering what the others at her doubtless high-level security meeting would make of that. Knowing Isabelle, she'd probably share the news with them anyway. He paused a moment before going into the house to join his friends. He'd always thought that one pup should go to Florence's children. They adored Balzac, and on her teacher's salary there was no way that Florence would be able to afford a basset hound. He couldn't think of a better home. But a second pup was more complicated.

He could probably get a thousand or fifteen hundred euros for a pedigree pup, but he had no intention of doing that. He did, however, feel an obligation to the mayor, who had given him his first basset, Gigi, from one of his own litters. The mayor had never replaced Gigi's mother when she died, and Bruno knew from his affection for Balzac that he missed having a dog in his life. It would also mean that Balzac would be in the same town as his two puppies. But since the mayor had not found a new dog, did that mean at his age he didn't really want one? His friend the baron had said as much after the death of his own dog, a gigantic *dogue de Bordeaux.* Bruno felt sure that if the offer were made, the mayor would feel bound to accept it, but he'd hate to feel that it was an imposition on the man he'd come to think of almost as a father. Perhaps he could try raising the matter in a round-about way. And Yveline of the gendarmes had said she'd be keen to have a female pup. He'd have to think about this before announcing the news to all his friends. He pocketed his phone and went into the house.

He was greeted first by the scent of roasting lamb and then by two small children arriving like little bullets to clamber at his legs. They were Dora and Daniel, Florence's children, keen to tell him of their latest exploits at Pamela's swimming pool, where Bruno had taught them how to swim earlier that summer. Then he was besieged by Miranda's two children, who were now old enough to play rugby with the *minimes* and wanted to tell him of their last practice. He would normally have been there to help with the coaching, but he'd been at his aunt's funeral.

Disentangling himself, but with Dora on one arm and Daniel on the other, Bruno greeted Florence, Jacqueline and Miranda. He was then embraced by the baron, who took one of the children so that Jack Crimson could hand Bruno a glass of white wine and lead him to the big dining room where the table, already laid and with a row of candles waiting to be lit, was set for ten. He saw four open bottles of wine, his Ortus, Jack's red from Les Verdots, Gilles's foot-trodden wine and one of the mayor's favorite Pécharmants from Château de Tiregand. Then there was one mystery bottle wrapped in a black sock. This was doubtless from the baron, one of the blind tastings he sometimes offered to test his friends. A smaller table stood at the far end with places for the four children.

"*Mon Dieu,* this is terrific," said Bruno. "A fine homecoming for our two globe-trotters. It could almost be Christmas."

"And here's a gift for you, Bruno," Jacqueline said, embracing him. She gave Bruno a wrapped parcel, about the size of a book, though it was soft and pliable when he took it. He thanked her.

"Aren't you going to open it, Bruno?" asked Dora.

Bruno unwrapped the parcel to find a chef's toque. It was white, pleated, nearly a foot tall and embroidered with the words TOP CHEF. He immediately put it on his head, his hair still wet.

"Now I have something to live up to," he said. "Thank you very much, Jacqueline, but I don't think I'll be able to match Miranda's roast lamb, and a little bird told me that Grandpa Jack has made a secret sauce, just for all of us, to go with the baron's secret bottle."

"Florence, Pamela, Miranda and I got aprons that look like the American flag," announced Fabiola. Gilles said he'd been given a T-shirt bearing the unmistakable face of the American president, which he found to be very ironic, suitable only for wearing in bed. Fabiola instantly vetoed that idea, unless Gilles was prepared to sleep alone. Crimson and the baron had each been given the same T-shirt, which made Bruno feel all the more grateful for the chef's toque.

"We're starting with a chilled soup of vegetables from the garden before we have the lamb we got from Sylvestre, that friend of Bruno's with the sheep farm on the hill overlooking St. Chamassy," Miranda announced, steering them to their seats. "I told him you'd be one of the guests, Bruno, and he said he knew what you liked."

Bruno nodded courteously, but his heart sank a little. Sylvestre knew that Bruno liked a hogget, a young sheep between one and two years old with rather more of the taste of mutton than the ones born in the spring. He was far from sure that all his friends shared his fondness for the dish, but then a newborn lamb could hardly feed ten adults and four hungry children. Bruno also knew that the English tended to prefer their meat less pink than the French. Well, the wine would make up for it, he thought, eyeing the row of bottles with pleasure. The baron's mystery bottle was in the classic shape of a Bordeaux, so he could rule out a Burgundy or some wine from the Rhône Valley.

At least they had clear glasses. Bruno had an embarrassing memory of an evening of wine tasting with Hubert, along with some other friends who thought they knew about wines. Hubert had poured the wine in another room, then served it in black glasses. Without the customary visual clue most of those present, including a sommelier from a well-regarded restaurant, had had no idea whether they were drinking white or red. It had been a lesson in humility that Bruno would not soon forget, even though he'd been sure he'd recognized a Chablis in the first glass. At least it had turned out to be a Sancerre, so he'd got the color right.

The soup was excellent, red and yellow

peppers with cucumber and peeled tomatoes, served with a generous scoop of *aillou,* a blend of crème fraîche and *fromage blanc* with garlic and parsley. Had it been his soup, Bruno might have been tempted to add a little fresh mint, but then he recalled that Jack was making a mint sauce.

"Alors, mes amis," said the baron, rising to take up the covered bottle and pour each of the adults half a glass. "In this moment between the soup and the lamb, let us seek to identify this mystery wine. And I'll give you a clue. It comes from within a hundred kilometers from here, so you can rule out the Médoc and the Loire and Languedoc-Roussillon."

They all twirled their wine, held their glasses against the light of a candle and then sniffed. Bruno, knowing that his taste buds were still sensing the garlic in the soup, drank some water first, before sipping. He wondered if the baron were testing them with one of the smaller appellations, a Buzet or even a Duras. It certainly was not a Cahors. It was a familiar taste, if not a Bergerac, then very close to it, possibly one of the new and very small classified regions, like a wine from the old *bastide* of Domme, farther up the Dordogne Valley. He didn't really know.

The baron went around the table. Jack thought it was a Montravel, at the western end of the Bergerac region. Gilles thought it came from farther south, the Saussignac. The mayor was still thinking, and Bruno admitted he was guessing, but he thought it was a *vin de pays* from the Périgord, somewhere nearby, but he was sure it wasn't from the town vineyard. He suggested it could be a wine from Domme. Finally the mayor put down his glass and said he thought it was a Buzet.

"You're all wrong, but Bruno came closest," the baron said. "It's from the Domaine de la Voie Blanche, just this side of St. Cyprien, so it is indeed a *vin de pays* of our own Périgord, stored in terra-cotta amphorae just as they did in Roman times. I bought a couple of cases and brought one along tonight, so I'll leave the other eleven bottles here for future dinners together in the hope that you all enjoy it as much as I do. Now drink up and let's attack the other bottles."

Miranda brought in the lamb on a giant platter, surrounded by roast potatoes and whole heads of garlic. The scent of the rosemary, on a bed of which the lamb had been roasted, filled the room. Jack excused himself, left the room briefly and returned with a gravy boat which he announced was his traditional English mint sauce. When the baron asked how it was made, Jack replied that he crushed finely chopped mint leaves into a spoonful of sugar and a little olive oil until it had turned into a rough paste, then thinned it out with vinegar. The baron's eyes widened. Gilles and the mayor exchanged glances. *Mon Dieu,* thought Bruno, the things I do for international understanding.

Meanwhile, Jack had wrapped a napkin around his hand, used it to seize the bone at the end of the leg and began to carve the thick end of the shoulder that was still attached. He was using one of Pamela's Japanese knives, and the slices of lamb fell away like butter. Miranda began serving these more cooked slices to her father and Pamela and to her own and her children's plates, and the pinker meat to her French guests.

Bruno's own portion was perfect, obviously very slowly cooked at a low temperature, and the roasted heads of garlic squeezed out their delicious tender flesh when he pressed them lightly with his knife. He took a sip of the Cuvée Ortus he had brought and thought it the perfect accompaniment. He then raised his glass to Miranda to tell her that her lamb was an

Anglo-French triumph. The others raised their glasses to toast her, the children following suit with their own glasses of mineral water.

"My friends at school say they are allowed a little taste of wine in their water, Mummy," said Miranda's eldest son. "May we try that?"

She glanced at her father, then at Pamela and at Bruno, who gave a very discreet nod. Bruno carefully poured a teaspoon of wine into the boy's glass, turning it a very pale pink and telling him that this was a very important moment and the other children would be allowed their own taste of wine when they were older. That seemed to satisfy them, although Bruno was sure that Mark's younger sister would manage to sneak a sip when the grown-ups weren't looking.

"I think this may be the moment to introduce you all to my secret sauce," said Jack, raising the gravy boat containing his mint concoction. Bruno gamely accepted it and used a spoon to put a small helping of a thin green sauce onto the side of his plate. He dipped a morsel of lamb into it, dreading what the mint and vinegar would do to his enjoyment of the bottle of Tiregand that Gilles had started to pour.

In fact, the mint and the sharpness of the vinegar went well with the lamb, but the sugar seemed to Bruno a bizarre and unnecessary addition. Still, in the interest of friendship he tried another portion, and this time he was accustomed to the sweetness of the sugar that had at first surprised him and began to see that this could work. Perhaps if he tried a little honey instead of the sugar . . . and then he was aware of a female voice in full and vehement flow.

"I think it's shameful, a deliberate denial of history," declared Jacqueline. "The British have long had a thirty-year rule before the release of government papers, why not the Americans? We in France are now full members of NATO, committed to the common defense, so what possible reason could they have for withholding the Rosenholz dossier? It's more than thirty years ago."

"Secret papers are not released in Britain after thirty years, only routine ones, and they have to be cleared by a weeding committee of historians and officials," Crimson replied. "And you know perfectly well, Jacqueline, that France is even more cautious about releasing state papers than the British or Americans."

"I know that, Jack, and you're right," she replied. "But I don't see why serious historians in democratic countries have to work in the dark just to protect the reputations of antiquated politicians and officials for foolish or shameful decisions they took in secret when they were in power."

"What shameful and secret decisions are you talking about, exactly?" asked Gilles, in a voice that silenced the rest of the conversation around the table and reminded them all that he still wrote for *Paris Match* when he chose. "Is this all to do with that Cold War conference in Washington you attended?"

Jack laid down his knife and fork, looked up at the ceiling and said, almost with a groan, "Now we have the media involved."

"About time, too!" said Jacqueline, tapping the table for emphasis. "In fact I think I should write an op-ed for *Le Monde* about it." She looked around the table almost fiercely before going on. "The Americans have been sitting on a vast trove of Stasi documents, listing all the East German agents around the world, and they have shared the German sections with the Germans and the British sections with the British. France by contrast is still deemed too untrustworthy for the CIA to let us know just how badly we may have been penetrated by East German intelligence."

"I see your point, but it's all a long time ago," said the mayor.

"In historical terms, and in terms of official careers, it is uncomfortably short," Jacqueline replied. "Imagine young French students, recruited when they were in their twenties at Sciences Po or some other springboard into government. They would now be in their fifties, in senior positions with another decade or so in office. Imagine the damage they could do."

"But the Stasi has been extinct for thirty years," said Fabiola. "For whom would these officials be working now?"

"The Stasi shared everything with the KGB," Jacqueline replied, more calmly this time. "Moscow would be in a position to force those people to work for them. And so would the Americans, so long as we in France don't have the documentation to expose them."

"Sounds like a hell of a good story," said Gilles. "And I see why you might want to run this in *Le Monde,* but you'd get a far bigger audience if we ran this in *Paris Match.* And we could keep your name out of it so the story doesn't start being about you again, as it did before."

Everyone around the table recalled Jacqueline's last foray into the secret history of the Cold War, which led to the resignation of a French cabinet minister with whom she had once enjoyed an indiscreet liaison.

As silence fell, Bruno filled everyone's glasses with the bottle from David Fourtout, modestly titled Le Vin. He asked the baron what he thought of it, hoping that the conversation would drift off into new directions. Florence, who was sitting like Miranda at the end of the table closest to their children, then asked a question.

"If the Americans share this material with the British and the Germans but not with us, then it comes down to a question of trust. Why don't they trust France?"

Jacqueline looked at Crimson, Bruno looked at the mayor, Pamela looked at Gilles, and finally the baron spoke.

"As a lifelong Gaullist, I always appreciated his insistence on an independent foreign policy that put French interests first," he said. "De Gaulle did so during World War Two and after it, and this sometimes rubbed our British and American friends the wrong way. Bruno, what's that story about President Lyndon Johnson's reaction when he was told that de Gaulle was pulling out of NATO and insisted that all American troops leave French soil?"

"President Johnson told his secretary of

state, Dean Rusk, You ask de Gaulle if that includes our men in the Normandy cemeteries who died to liberate France." Bruno paused a moment and looked around the table. "Much as I admire de Gaulle, I have to say I feel a little ashamed each time I think of that question."

CHAPTER 6

Bruno awoke just before six when his cockerel announced the new day, and since he'd drifted off to sleep thinking of Balzac's pups, he jumped out of bed to check his e-mails. Just before the news headlines sent automatically from *Sud Ouest* and the radio news from France Inter in his in-box, there was mail from Claire Mornier at the kennel, timed at three in the morning.

"Félicitations à Papa Balzac," it read. "Nine beautiful pups born well; five little Dianes de Poitiers and four Brunos."

Bruno laughed, jumped up, bent down to caress his dog and tell him what a wonderful father he'd be and with so many offspring to his name. He swigged some orange juice from the fridge, donned his tracksuit and running shoes and led Balzac out onto the familiar trail through the woods. The birds were far too happy with their new day to interrupt their singing for a lonely runner, and the extraordinary but somehow harmonious range of their various songs reinforced Bruno's sudden conviction that the world was full of little miracles and that he couldn't wait to see its latest gift.

Twenty minutes later, back at home, he turned on the radio, lit the gas beneath his kettle and e-mailed Claire to thank her for the news and to ask if it would be convenient for him to come and see the puppies at around eleven. He jumped into the shower, shaved, put a fresh egg on to boil and made coffee before he dressed in his summer uniform. Back in the kitchen, he refilled Balzac's water bowl, sliced the remains of yesterday's baguette and fed the pieces into the toaster before going outside to feed his chickens, collect six fresh eggs and replenish their water.

His egg and coffee were ready, so sharing the grilled baguette with Balzac he began to plan his day. He could be at his desk in St. Denis before seven-thirty, deal with the mail and paperwork, escort the mothers and toddlers across the road to the *maternelle* just before eight. He'd have plenty of time to patrol the town and show his face at the *mairie* before leaving for the kennel at around ten, first dropping off Balzac at the riding school. He found an old egg carton for the six fresh ones and grabbed a jar of his homemade pâté from the pantry and a sack of the dog biscuits he made for Balzac as gifts for Claire, and set off for town in his ancient Land Rover. Using his official police van for his personal trip to the kennel would not be right.

It was on the short drive into town that he thought about the mayor and how to offer him one of Balzac's pups without making him feel he should pay for what Bruno intended as a gift. Best to be as straightforward as possible, he thought. He parked in the main square, since it was not a market day, and went to his office to open his mail and check that there was nothing urgent on the computer. Shortly before eight, with Balzac on his leash, he set off for the *maternelle,* pausing only to greet his acquaintances as they opened their shops and hurried to work. St. Denis was a town that rose early. Balzac amiably tolerated the petting of the toddlers once they and their mothers had safely crossed the road.

He and Balzac made their usual circuit of the town, past the retirement home, the church and the cemetery, turning at the gendarmerie to head up to the old main street before turning back onto the rue de Paris and back to the main square. The

91

mayor was standing at the desk, chatting with his secretary and Roberte from the social-service team and waiting for his fancy coffee machine to finish his morning brew.

"Bonjour, Bruno, and you, Balzac," he said, and turned to tell his secretary to make another cup for Bruno. "Do you have a minute for me?" he asked, steered Bruno into his office, closed the door and said, "I'm a bit worried about this CIA dossier business. My instincts tell me this might not be the best time for Jacqueline to start making a fuss about it, least of all in *Le Monde.* What do you think?"

"It's a sensitive issue," said Bruno. "It may ruffle some feathers, both among our own security people and across the Atlantic, but that doesn't mean it should not be aired. Our secret agencies sometimes seem to forget they work for a democracy. Against that, I can't say I like the idea of some witch hunt for old Stasi spies in the current political climate with fake news and the superheated rhetoric of social media. I remember what Jack Crimson said about those well-meaning British peace activists who were listed as agents in those Stasi files. I assume the French counterespionage people have been aware of this prospect for many years and tried to deal with it."

"That's my feeling, or at least part of it. I'm also a bit worried about Jacqueline putting herself back into a very public controversy with all the social media trolling that's likely to follow."

"That has to be her decision," said Bruno. "I'm confident she'll think it through, and we both know she takes your own views seriously."

The secretary tapped at the door with the toe of her shoe and came in with a tray of coffee when Bruno let her in. A gust of her freshly applied perfume drowned out the delicious smell of coffee as she swayed past him, fluttering her enormous eyelashes. He sighed inwardly, thanked her with a cool smile and held the door open for her to leave, knowing that her flirtatious ways would never change.

"There's something I wanted to tell you," Bruno said after she left. "Balzac's puppies were born in the small hours of this morning, five females and four males. After your kindness in giving me Gigi when I first came to St. Denis, I'd like you to have one, and I'm sure Balzac would agree."

The mayor put down his coffee cup and beamed first at Bruno, then at Balzac, and said, "That's wonderful news. I'm very happy for him and for you, and I'm touched by your offer, but I don't think I want to go through all the serious business of training a puppy at my age. These days I like to sleep later than basset hounds. I remember chatting to the baron about it after he lost his dog, and he said puppies were best raised on a working farm or in a house with children. I tend to agree."

"I get some pups instead of a stud fee, and I thought I'd give one to Florence's children. I was saving the other for you."

"Thank you, but no, and I don't think Jacqueline is nearly as much of a dog lover as you and me. In fact, she's thinking of getting a cat. But I'm sure you'll find a good home for the second hound, and I think it's a good idea to offer one to Florence's kids, but I'd raise it with her first. She might well think she already has enough on her plate. And the children feel they have a share in Balzac already."

"I hadn't thought of that," Bruno admitted. "You're right. I'd better check with her first. I thought I might drive up to the kennel later today and take a first look at the new puppies."

"Give them all my warmest good wishes and make sure you don't let one of them pee on your hand. That means he or she owns you. But you might want to join me tomorrow at noon in Périgueux. The prefect has called an informal conference over this heat wave, whether we should impose controls on water, special measures for old people who are vulnerable, setting up cooling rooms in retirement homes and so on. They're worried about another disaster like the *canicule*."

A surge of unusual heat in 2003 had led to many deaths, mainly among the elderly and infirm. The rivers had been unusually low, and the water levels so sparse that fire engines had to come in relays to pump cooling water from their hoses onto the nuclear power stations. Successive governments had ever since been acutely aware of the dangers and noticeably more sensitive to warnings of climate change. A recent surge of forest fires in southern France had sharpened the swelling sense of alarm. The government had made much of the purchase of four new specialist firefighting aircraft.

Bruno agreed to accompany the mayor and suggested that, if they had time, they could visit Virginie, Elisabeth's student who had started work at the police lab in Périgueux. After checking that he had an e-mail from Claire confirming that he'd be welcome, Bruno dropped off Balzac at the riding school and set off for the kennel.

He put in his earphones and called up on his phone the app of English lessons that Pamela had given him. He was at the third level now, which meant that Jack and Jill were no longer navigating the London Underground or watching the changing of the guard at Buckingham Palace. They were now at an industrial museum in a place called Telford and admiring the first iron bridge. It was mildly interesting, and he felt slightly virtuous at improving his imperfect command of the language. Mouthing the English words, he drove out through Rouffignac and Thenon and past the magnificent Château de Hautefort and up the familiar road to the kennel. It had taken barely an hour.

He paused before pulling into the main courtyard, admiring the familiar spread, the old barns converted into a kennel and the large paddock filled with the big Malinois dogs that Claire raised for the military. They were bounding around a score or so of basset hounds who had cleverly developed their own game of running in and out between the legs of the Malinois. He smiled as he watched, thinking that he could imagine Balzac enjoying that, and pulled in to park his Land Rover as Claire came out to greet him.

"Bonjour, Bruno," Claire said. "It's good to see you, and the puppies are enchanting. How's the new father?"

"Blissfully ignorant of his new status," Bruno replied, smiling widely. He handed her the eggs, the foie gras and the small sack of homemade dog biscuits he'd brought her. "I'm sure his pups are too young for these, but Diane de Poitiers and the other dogs may enjoy them."

"They certainly scoffed down the last bunch you brought," she said. "I even tried one myself and liked it. Let's go see the new family."

She led him to the familiar converted pigsty, which he had known as the mating chamber and was now a maternity ward. Before going inside, Claire turned, a serious look suddenly appearing on her face.

"Stay back well behind me, kneel down so you don't intimidate her and don't say a word until I say it's all right," she said firmly. He nodded, understanding that Claire was in charge here.

"Even then, speak very softly," she went on. "Don't touch her and please don't move toward the puppies. In the unlikely event that one of them pulls back from the teats and crawls toward you, stay absolutely still and let them explore you a little but please don't react and don't stroke them. The mother is very protective just now, and she might reject one that has your unfamiliar smell. It was an easy birth, no complications, but still, she's exhausted and with a pup on almost every teat she has enough to deal with without you. Understand?"

"Yes, I get it," he said. "May I take some photos on my phone?"

"Not if you have automatic flash. I already took some for you on my phone when she was sleeping. I'll take some more over the next few days and forward them to you. And if I tell you to leave, please do so quietly and without abrupt movements."

She opened the door, and Bruno saw the red light from the infrared lamp and heater. He was surprised to see it being used in summer. There was a strong scent of dog and milk and something indefinable, not at all unpleasant and faintly reminiscent of truffles. He wondered if the scent might carry some universal fertility hormone. Claire slipped in, pulling the door shut behind her, and he waited for a few moments before she opened it again and gestured him in.

Bruno did as he was told, moved slowly, crouching, and staying by the door, letting his eyes grow accustomed to the red light.

The scent was even stronger now, and as he looked ahead he saw what seemed to be a crawling, heaving mass of legs and heads and squirming bodies. It reminded him of some kind of hive, a complex but single organism. The image stayed with him until he was able to pick out the individual puppies. They seemed to be mainly the usual mixture of black, brown and white in various individual patterns, and there were two who were pale brown and white. Even in the red light, the pads of their feet were as pink as their mother's teats, and he smiled at the memory of Balzac as a pup, the soft underflesh of his paws just as pink before they hardened and became dark. The fullness of Diane's teats was striking, and the pups were piled on top of one another to reach them. Each of the pups seemed to be affixed to a teat, except for one very small one who was nuzzling at its mother's lowered head. He felt a touch of awe as he watched, fascinated, aware that as a male he was privileged to be present at this most intimately female of moments.

One, a black, brown and white pup on the upper tier of teats, seemed to lose his grip and fall off, tumbling over its siblings below and then rolling a little on the bed of hay. The mother nuzzled the pup, using her nose to push the tiny creature back onto the pile to a vacant teat. But the pup seemed curious. Bruno could not even see if its eyes had opened yet, but it raised its head a little and moved it from side to side as if sniffing curiously at this new world before letting its mother ease him back to feed.

He tried to count them in the constantly shifting kaleidoscope of fur and legs and pale pink tummies, but it was impossible. He assumed Claire had counted them as each one of the litter was born, and he was impressed that she had already determined their gender. To his untrained eyes and in the dim red light, there was no visible difference between them.

The mother was now trying to push the tiny brown-and-white one toward a teat, so the rather bigger puppy, the one who had seemed curious, was now crawling over her hind legs and seemed to be heading toward Claire. Gently, its mother pushed it back and helped it clamber over a row of siblings to find an empty teat on the second level. Bruno could have stayed to watch this for hours, thinking it was far more interesting and affecting than any television.

"I'm thinking of giving one of them to two young children I know," he whispered. "They are twins, a boy and a girl, nearly four years old, and the children of a good friend back in St. Denis. They adore Balzac, and I think they'd love a basset of their own. When could I bring them to see the puppies?"

"It's very difficult to restrain children, so not before three weeks, and I'll be keeping them here for another month after that until they are weaned and able to take solid food," she replied. "Grown-ups can come and take a look at the puppies after about a week or so."

"I liked the curious one who kept moving around, and I even thought he was looking around himself," Bruno said once they were back outside in the open air. "And the little brown-and-white one who was nuzzling at its mother's nose. The others still seemed glued to their milk."

"The first one is the pick of the litter, so he's yours by right," Claire said. "The little one is the runt, and she's also yours since there are nine. If you want a third pup, you'd have to buy it and don't forget the vet fees, the vaccinations, the pedigree registrations and so on. When you add it all up that usually costs between three and four hundred euros for each puppy."

Bruno nodded, saying he understood. He'd never thought of a third puppy being part of the deal.

"I have five of the litter sold already from preorders, at fifteen hundred each, and I'll have no trouble selling the rest," Claire went on. "Bear in mind that I'd like to book Balzac in for servicings two or three times a year in the future for my other bitches. All his pups are perfect, he gets a large litter and his own pedigree is impressive, so you can expect lots more pups to give away or sell."

"*Mon Dieu,* I could almost make a living out of this," Bruno exclaimed, surprised that his dog was so commercially valuable. "I had no idea."

"I've already had two inquiries from other kennels whether Balzac would be available to service their dams," Claire went on. "You could lend him out for service every month or two, for which you can charge three hundred euros a time. Or you could take a pup or two pups from each litter to sell, so you see how the money soon mounts up, if that's what you want. Your Balzac is a little gold mine. Bassets are starting to become very fashionable these days since they are so good with children and they look so special."

"I'd have to consider that," said Bruno, surprised at the thought. "I think I'd want to know something about the homes his pups would be going to. I mean, he's my friend as well as my dog. I don't like to think of Balzac as some sort of rent-a-sperm, breeding all comers for cash."

"They wouldn't be all comers." Claire laughed. "Pedigree ladies only, preferably named after royal mistresses. I don't think you realize just how special Balzac's pedigree really is; he comes from the old royal pack at Cheverny. That means we can trace his ancestry back for more than three centuries. In human terms, he's a duke or a count or something, maybe even a pretender to the throne."

Her eyes twinkled as she said this, and they both laughed together at the absurdity of it.

"That's what breeding is all about," she said. "So it's like a fairy tale. You're the commoner, the poor but honest woodsman, secretly raising and nurturing the heir to the throne. Meanwhile wicked and jealous aristocrats seek to hunt him down. You could even write an opera about it."

"The mind boggles," said Bruno. "Maybe he has an evil stepmother with two ugly daughters, each determined to catch him."

"That's Cinderella," she replied, grinning in return. "Or maybe it's the tale of the prince who is raised among the common people and learns to love them while moving secretly among them, avoiding the greedy nobles. And then he seizes the moment to mount the throne and chooses to marry the poor but honest country girl who helped protect him through many dangers."

"And they all lived happily ever after," said Bruno, smiling a little wistfully. "Do children today still get told those old stories? Tales in which goodness and loyalty are eventually rewarded and wickedness punished? I fear they don't hear them when they're little, and I wish they still did."

"Were you told them?" she asked, quietly.

"Yes, I was, by the nuns in our orphanage," he said, enthused by the memory. "There was always a Bible story but then a fairy tale, all of us children on our little cots, our eyes wide, rapt with attention, while a nun read to us all aloud. I haven't thought of that for years."

He felt a prickling in his eyes, as though he was about to shed a tear. So he took a deep breath, blew his nose and looked away at the bassets and Malinois romping in the pasture.

"You're an unusual man, Bruno," she said. "Sometimes it's hard to think of you as a policeman. Isabelle is a lucky woman."

"You have really built a special place here, Claire," he said, not knowing how to respond to her remark. He glanced at his watch. "Sorry, but I'd better get going."

"Well, I'm glad you and Balzac have become a part of it," she said briskly, and led the way back into the house, saying, "There's time for a coffee before you have to go."

On the return journey, J-J called. Bruno pulled off the road to answer and was struck by the excitement in J-J's voice as he said, "We've had a breakthrough. That special forces guy who was killed in Mali, Louis Castignac, Oscar's posthumous son — since we know he was born in April 1990, Oscar must have been here in June or July the previous year to have fathered him. And while Max and his sister have the same mother, they have different fathers. We've traced the next of kin he listed through army records. It's his younger sister, named Sabine. And would you believe she's a cop, so her DNA was also on file. She's a gendarme based in Metz, near the German border."

"Sabine would have to be Louis's half sister?" Bruno said. "Your Oscar could hardly have fathered another child once he was murdered."

"So what? She's still the official next of kin."

"J-J, wait a second. Does this gendarme, Sabine, know that she's a half sister? I mean, she's already mourning the death of Louis in Mali. Is the fact that they have different fathers going to shock her all over again?"

"Merde," J-J replied. "You're right. And the answer is that I don't know. We'll have to cross that bridge when we come to it. I called the general of the gendarmes here, and he's arranging for her to be temporarily assigned to us. She's flying to Bordeaux in the morning and will get here early tomorrow afternoon, so I'll want you here for a conference sometime around two."

"That's fine. I have to be in town for a prefect's meeting at noon," Bruno said.

"Her name is Sabine Castignac, age twenty-eight, born in Bordeaux, just over a year younger than her brother — I mean half brother, Louis. She's been in the gendarmes for six years, just been promoted to sergeant, and she's passed the exam for officer training school. So although you're right that this will come as a shock to her, we'll have to hope she'll be able to deal with it professionally."

Mon Dieu, Bruno thought to himself. J-J

was never the sensitive type, but this was cold-blooded, even for him. He would have to find a way to steer J-J toward handling this young female colleague with considerably more care.

"Congratulations, J-J, you must be pleased. It looks like all your years of work on Oscar are finally paying off," Bruno began. "But what do we know about Sabine's family? Are her parents still alive? It's the mother we need to talk to — she's the one who knew your Oscar and got pregnant by him, so she should be able to give us his real name. And there must be family photos. We'll need all that and the date of their wedding, along with the birth certificates of Sabine and her late half brother, Louis.

"And does Sabine know what this is all about?" Bruno asked. "She may be in for quite a shock to learn that she and the man she thought was her brother had a different father. Might it make sense to bring in another woman to support her through this? I could ask Yveline, the *commandante* of gendarmes here in St. Denis. She's as wise as she's smart, and I suspect Sabine is going to need all the help she can get. And now that Sergeant Jules has bought a house, there's spare lodging at the St. Denis gendarmerie, where Sabine could stay while your investigation proceeds. She could be a real asset if we handle this right."

"Good thinking, Bruno. You ask Yveline, and I'll clear it with the gendarmes here. Sabine's train gets in around two, so let's all meet in my office at two tomorrow."

J-J ended the call and Bruno sat for a long moment, thinking of the drama of a long-ago murder investigation that was about to engulf Sabine's family when they were still mourning the death of their son in Mali. J-J would leave no stone unturned and no family privacy untouched in his determination to resolve the frustration that had nagged at him throughout his career.

Maybe the whole family was aware that Sabine and her brother had different fathers — but what if they were not? Bruno suspected that it would hardly have been a good start to the marriage if Sabine's mother had told her new husband that he was not the father of her newborn son. And how would Sabine handle the conflicting loyalties to her family and the police?

Worse still, Bruno suspected that the investigation was unlikely to come up with any clear answers about a murder that had taken place thirty years ago. Oscar had never been reported missing by family and friends, so there were no relatives still grieving and seeking closure for their loss. Witnesses were likely to be dead or forgetful, and leads would be thin. J-J's obsession was likely to tear a family apart for a very dubious outcome.

CHAPTER 7

Virginie, the young woman recommended by Elisabeth Daynès to reconstruct the face from Oscar's skull, had only been at work for a few days when Bruno and the mayor visited her at the police lab in Périgueux. At Bruno's suggestion, they had arrived in the city in the mayor's air-conditioned car with some time to spare before the prefect's meeting, thus giving them the opportunity to meet Virginie. Having left Claire at the kennel the previous day, Bruno was struck by the contrast between the two women. Claire had been solidly built, full of self-confidence in her skills and her profession, a woman of cheerful disposition with an interesting, almost playful sense of humor. Virginie was a much-younger woman, far less sure of herself, almost desperately serious in her approach to a task that could make or break her career.

"Are you settling in all right?" Bruno

asked her, after introducing himself and the mayor, and pointedly not looking at the metal ring Virginie wore in one nostril and the studs in her eyebrows and lower lip. "Is there anything that you need?"

"Everything is fine, and Madame Daynès told me to say that she sends you her special regards," she said. "I'm really grateful for this opportunity, and everybody here has been very kind and helpful. I even have my own room at the student hostel, which is more than I had in Paris."

Virginie was wearing a white lab coat that was far too large for her, hanging down to fluorescent-orange running shoes. Her sleeves were rolled up to reveal a complex geometric tattoo above one wrist. Her pink-dyed hair was pinned up into a tight bun revealing pretty ears that rose into a slight point, almost like an elf's. Her eyes were splendid, huge and dark, though she wore no makeup. Bruno knew that she was in her early twenties, but she looked no more than sixteen, and he suspected she might attract a constant parade of curious and admiring policemen inventing reasons to visit the lab. He'd better have a word with J-J about it.

"Where's Oscar?" the mayor asked. Virginie looked blank.

"The skull," Bruno explained. "That's

what J-J, I mean Chief Detective Jalipeau, has always called him."

"I see. I was told to call him Exhibit A," she said, and gestured to a corner. "He's over there on a rotating stand in that thing that looks like a microwave. It's a laser linked to a computer, making an exact image in three dimensions from which the 3D printer is building the copies I'll work on. Madame Daynès will be able to monitor what I'm doing in real time."

"Copies?" Bruno asked. "Why do you need more than one?"

"To try alternative eye colors, different noses, different hairstyles and body mass index." She sounded impatient, almost bridling at someone who seemed to question her skill. He gave a friendly nod to encourage her, and she seemed to relax a little.

"It only costs a little bit more for the extra plastic," she said. "Six or seven euros each for an identical skull. That's how I was trained to work."

"J-J told me the dead man's hair was quite long and blond, not shoulder length," said Bruno. "You should check that with him."

"What's your schedule here?" the mayor asked. "I mean, how long do you think it should take?"

Virginie lifted her chin and gave them both a determined look. "I'll work as long as I can every day, six days a week. I know it's urgent. But look at that." She gestured to a large poster on the wall, a detailed illustration of the human facial muscles. It looked fiendishly complicated.

"I'll have to re-create each muscle, precisely calibrated to the shape of the skull beneath. I was already told that this was needed as soon as possible, so I'll work as fast as I can without sacrificing accuracy."

"Good for you, and your priorities are the right ones," the mayor said, nodding his approval and trying to put her at ease. "But we can't let you come to the Périgord without enjoying the sights and the food, so you can understand why we're all so devoted to this region."

"I'll be happy to pick you up and take you down to our area on some convenient weekend," Bruno said. "You need some time off, and you could meet my dog and my friends and the horses, some good food and a swimming pool. Make a weekend of it. I could pick you up here on a Saturday and get you back here in the lab on Monday morning. We can put you up with friends. After seeing the exhibition at the museum, people will be fascinated by your work.

"That reminds me," he added, handing her a brown paper bag. "There's some of my homemade pâté de foie gras in there with a jar of my own onion confit to go with it, a homemade *saucisson* and a local cheese made by a friend of mine. Just so you know how good the local food can be. And I think you'll like our local Bergerac wines, too."

She blushed prettily and gave them a lovely smile which almost made up for the tattoo. "Thank you, that is very kind. I should say the food's not bad at the student hostel here, much better than the one in Paris. Even the police canteen here does a great salad buffet. And their coffee is free."

"I'm delighted to hear it," the mayor said. "Here's my card with my office and mobile numbers and my e-mail. Just let me know if there's anything I can do to help."

"And don't forget to tell me when you'll be free to visit us in St. Denis," Bruno chimed in. "We can arrange to take you to the museum in Les Eyzies to see Elisabeth's exhibition that puts all of her — and your — work into context."

The two men climbed the stairs from the lab, and Bruno took them on the shortcut through the busy police canteen, where dozens of cops — traffic, uniformed and plainclothes — were tucking into their *steak-frites*. One or two friends from rugby or previous cases nodded and waved in recognition as Bruno strolled through, but one very big cop in uniform, whom Bruno did not know, called out loudly and with an unpleasant sneer in his voice, "Watch it, boys, it's the country copper. How are the sheep shaggers down there in the Périgord Noir?"

This was no time to take offense, Bruno thought, and he replied amiably, "They're leaving all the ewes happy." He walked on through a ripple of laughter and then turned at the door, raised his hand in a friendly wave and declared before slipping out, "I just hope you big-city guys can say the same about your own partners."

"Do the city cops always tease you like that?" the mayor asked as they left the building.

"Yes, but it's something you get used to," Bruno said. "Male-dominated societies like the cops and the military tend to be clannish, always ready to challenge outsiders. There's usually no harm meant, and a joke can almost always take the sting out of it. But that guy was trying to be offensive. I think I'd better keep an eye on him in the future."

He and the mayor headed up the road to the *préfecture,* wishing they had taken the car as the saunalike heat rose from the paving stones. The mayor observed that it was markedly warmer than in St. Denis and began discoursing on cities as heat sinks, a lecture that took them to the *préfecture* for what turned out to be a predictably disappointing meeting. The prefect, as representative of the French government, had summoned a selection of local officials to ensure he could claim they had been consulted and that he had political support for the unpopular measure of imposing water restrictions. These would ban the watering by hose of all private and municipal gardens and also outlaw the refilling of private swimming pools and all car washes. Local fire brigades would make their own preparations to tackle forest fires.

Sitting beside Bruno, the mayor of St. Denis asked if the much greater use of water for crops would continue. Yes, of course, the prefect replied. Agriculture was a state priority. So that would naturally include orchards and market gardens, the mayor queried. Indeed, said the prefect. The mayor sat back and murmured to Bruno, "That means I've saved your tomatoes."

And probably saved your own reelection,

thought Bruno privately. But he was most struck by what the prefect had not said. This heat wave was not only a problem for swimming pools and watering lawns. Perhaps he should have a word with Albert, the chief *pompier* in St. Denis, about possible precautions against forest fires.

The gathering of mayors and local police and fire chiefs broke up, grumbling as always about officials from Paris never understanding rural concerns. The mayor stayed to mingle, and Bruno, knowing he could get a lift back to St. Denis with Yveline, excused himself and headed for J-J's office. There he was told that the meeting would be held in the much larger office of Prunier, as *contrôleur-général* the senior police officer of the whole *département.* He and Bruno had first met as opponents in the army-police rugby match, which both men saw as a firm basis for an enduring friendship, however irritating Bruno's loyalty to St. Denis could occasionally be for Prunier's much greater responsibilities.

Bruno also thought highly of Prunier's taste in coffee and smiled as he recalled introducing Prunier to Léopold, the big Senegalese in the St. Denis market who imported and sold excellent coffees from Africa. Like Bruno, Prunier had become a convert and bought kilos of the stuff for his home and persuaded the manager of the police canteen to buy it, too. As he entered the police headquarters, Bruno's nose caught the familiar and welcome aroma. No police station could run for long without vast quantities of the stuff, and Prunier had won the hearts of his force by insisting that everyone should drink the same excellent coffee that he did, rather than the usual sludge of most police canteens.

"Bonjour, Bruno," said Prunier, advancing from behind his desk to shake hands and pour Bruno's coffee. J-J waved an amiable greeting from one of the comfortable armchairs that faced Prunier's desk.

"I see you escaped from the prefect's meeting almost as fast as I did," Prunier said, smiling as he handed Bruno his drink. "My secretary has just heard from her counterpart at the general's office that this gendarme Sabine Castignac is on her way here, accompanied by Commandante Yveline, and in a state of some distress. Apparently Castignac's superiors in Metz had neglected to inform her that her only brother was in fact her half brother. She'd only been told that she'd been reassigned to us and to take all available family albums with her."

"Knowing the gendarmes, I am not at all surprised," said J-J. "They are not the most sensitive of colleagues."

Prunier nodded sadly, then added, "The general here is a decent guy, and he took it upon himself to brief her more fully before she joined us, so at least we're spared that."

"I'm glad Yveline is with her," said Bruno. "We'll try to take better care of this Sabine in St. Denis. But won't the family photo albums be back at her family house?"

"We'll find out," said J-J. "She's from Bordeaux originally, so we might take her home for a family reunion. Obviously we'll need to question her mother about the identity of the real father, and I'm not looking forward to that."

"So not only Sabine but her parents are not aware of the DNA findings from her brother?" Bruno asked.

"Apparently not," said Prunier, pausing as they all heard a quiet knock at the door. "So let's be as professional and as courteous as possible to this young woman. There's no need to make the family drama even worse." He raised his voice and called out, "Enter."

"Bonjour, Monsieur le Commissaire, Bruno, J-J," said Yveline. "Allow me to introduce Sergeant Sabine Castignac of the

Gendarmerie Nationale."

A young woman marched to Prunier's desk, came to attention with a soft thud of rubber-soled boots and gave a brisk salute. She was wearing full-dress uniform, the stripes on her epaulette gleaming so new that Bruno suspected she'd attached them while traveling from Metz. Her promotion to sergeant must have been very recent. Her blonde hair was tucked at her neck in a tight bun, and she was sturdily built with big shoulders, and her skin had that glow of health and fitness that comes from long hours in the gym. Her eyes showed no hint of tears, so whatever shock she had experienced in her general's office had been overcome. The hands, properly aligned on the seams of her trousers, were large, strong and looked well kept. To Bruno's eye, she was an impressive young woman whose face was dominated by a determined chin and a nose that had at some time been broken and clumsily reset. In a man, he'd have thought it was a rugby injury, but more and more women now played the sport. He'd ask her about that; it might establish a useful bond.

"Reporting for duty, sir," she said, still at attention, in a strong, clear voice with no apparent regional accent.

"At ease, Sergeant, and please sit. Would

you like some coffee?" Prunier asked. "I gather you now know what this is all about."

"No coffee, thank you, sir," she answered, taking a hard-backed chair and sitting at attention, her eyes on the wall above Prunier's head. "Yes, I have been briefed on the situation regarding my late brother, Louis. I now know that his DNA shows that he's my half brother, fathered by an unidentified murder victim some thirty years ago, and not by the man who brought us both up. I'm still trying to come to terms with this news and with the implications for my family."

"I realize this comes very late, but please accept my condolences on the death of Louis on active duty in Mali," Prunier said. "And my apologies for bringing you this unsettling news about his parentage. Allow me to introduce Commissaire Jean-Jacques Jalipeau, chief of detectives for the *département,* and Chief of Police Bruno Courrèges of the Vézère Valley. I'm sure we can count on your professionalism in helping us investigate this unsolved murder."

"Yes, sir. We always seek to cooperate with our colleagues of the Police Nationale." She said the words as if she had learned them by rote. She glanced at Bruno and added hastily, "And our colleagues of the Police

121

Municipale, of course." She paused again. "I mean, we're all on the same side."

Prunier said nothing. J-J raised his eyebrows, doubtless thinking of all the turf battles he and every other member of the Police Nationale had waged against the gendarmes. They liked to think they were the only police who really mattered, with a pedigree that went back far beyond their formal foundation in 1791 as the shock troops of the French Revolution. In fact, they had begun as a highly politicized paramilitary force dedicated to the suppression of the Catholic faithful, the monarchists, feudal aristos and their bourgeois allies and all the other enemies of Liberté, Égalité, Fraternité. They had found some obscure soldier who died in battle against the English at Agincourt in 1415, the Prévôt des Maréchaux Gallois de Fougières, and adopted him to give themselves an even longer and more impressive pedigree. In 1934, after considerable research, Gallois was officially declared to be the first known gendarme to have died on duty, and his remains are forever buried under the monument to the gendarmerie in Versailles.

"The general sent me a copy of your file," Prunier said, opening a manila folder and glancing through it, turning the pages quickly. "It's very impressive. I see you are a keen mountaineer and that you volunteer for the ski patrol at Gérardmer. I didn't know the Vosges hills were high enough for skiing."

"Yes, sir, Gérardmer is only about twelve hundred meters at the highest point, but I've had some good skiing there. It can be icy, which is how I broke my nose, and it's not as magnificent as the Alps. Still, it's only two hours from Metz."

"Right. I understand you were asked to bring any family photo albums you might have."

"All the family albums are back home in Bordeaux. I brought with me the photos I had in Metz, two of my parents' wedding photos and one of my brother, I mean my half brother. They're in my bag outside the door. Should I get them?"

Prunier nodded. She went to the door and brought in a large duffel bag with wheels, opened it and removed three framed photographs. Prunier stood them on his desk so all could see them.

"This first one is my parents at their wedding," Sabine said. "The second one is the group photo with my grandparents, my father's *témoin* and my mother's *demoiselle d'honneur.* This last one is my brother,

Louis, when he graduated from the special warfare training center at Perpignan."

The photo of the wedding couple was slightly faded but clear enough. The groom looked some years older than his bride, maybe in his midthirties, and each of them looked slightly stunned as they smiled, dressed in clothes that must have been fashionable at the time. The groom's wide lapels and even wider tie matched the exaggerated shoulders of the white wedding dress of a bride whose face had been heavily made up. Bruno suspected she'd have looked more attractive without makeup. The group photo, in which she was laughing with a slightly taller but equally young woman, showed her to be slim and attractive with dancing eyes, a generous mouth and a long, elegant neck. Bruno was mildly surprised that this young bride had produced a daughter like Sabine, whose physique must have been inherited from her father.

"Is that the *demoiselle d'honneur* with her?" Bruno asked.

"Yes, Dominique, my mother's best friend ever since they were kids. They met the first day of school and were almost inseparable afterward. I think of her as my aunt. She was wonderful in my mother's last illness.

124

She held us all together, even though she was grieving as much as we were."

"You mean your mother is dead?" J-J asked, in a voice that carried his disappointment at learning that his key witness was no longer available. This was news to him, to Prunier and to Bruno.

"Yes, sir. Last year. Cancer. At least she didn't get to know that Louis had been killed in Mali."

"Did you have any idea that your mother had this, well, extramarital liaison that produced your brother?" Prunier asked, trying to use a gentle voice.

"No, sir. I don't think anybody did. Except maybe Tante-Do, I mean Dominique. That's what I always called her. They lived in the next street, so we were always in and out of each other's homes. If anybody can help you, she can. She and Mum were as close as sisters, except they never seemed to have a row. They used to go on holiday together. I know they came to this area for a final girls' fling just before the wedding. I was thinking on the train and I suppose that could have been the time that Mum had her little — I don't know what to call it. Accident? Adventure?"

"I think the term 'final girls' fling' should cover it," said Bruno, and then caught himself, wishing he'd remained silent. He was relieved to see Sabine smile.

"I suppose it would," she said, glancing at him and still smiling, but more to herself than to him. "Funny how you never think of your mother that way, young and silly and having fun, getting drunk and making mistakes. I suppose we all have to be young once. Even you, messieurs."

Sabine glanced at J-J, a man approaching retirement, and then at the middle-aged Prunier and at Bruno without the least embarrassment at the clear implication that she saw them all as verging on the prehistoric. Behind her, Bruno noticed, Yveline was trying to suppress a grin. He gave her a discreet wink and then leaned forward to get Sabine's attention.

"When you said your mother and her best friend came to these parts for that last fling before the wedding itself, do you mean they came to Périgueux or somewhere near here?" he asked.

"I'm not sure where it was, but it was some kind of local folk festival called a Félibrée, where there was lots of music and dancing. It was Tante-Do's idea to go camping, but I forget where it was exactly. Tante-Do would know. It was like a private joke between her and my mother. They'd say to one another, 'Do you remember the Félibrée?' Or sometimes they'd refer to the Bois de la Vézère, which I think was the name of the campsite. And then they'd both giggle like a pair of schoolgirls and tease me about being far too young for it."

"The wedding was in July 1989, and your brother was born when — in April the following year?"

"Yes, April third, he was a real Aries, always the action man. I'm a Scorpio."

The room fell silent for a moment as everyone mentally counted the months of gestation and tried to work out when it was that the unknown Oscar had impregnated Sabine's mother and just how long that might have been before he had met his own death.

"In the first week of July 1989, the annual Félibrée to celebrate the Occitan language and culture was held in St. Denis," Bruno said, knowing that he did not have to explain the event to J-J and Prunier. The city of Périgueux had recently been the location of the hundredth anniversary of the festivity.

"It was long before my time, and we haven't had one in St. Denis since then," Bruno continued. "But that's where Oscar's body was buried. Sorry, I should explain that Oscar was the name J-J gave to the unknown murder victim. It's reasonable to suppose that the St. Denis Félibrée was where and when your brother was conceived."

"It's time we went to your home in Bordeaux to get the family photos, talk to your father and interview this Tante-Do," said J-J, lumbering to his feet. "If anyone can tell us what happened at St. Denis, it will be her."

"I'd rather go alone, at least to talk to my father," Sabine said, her chin thrusting even more forward. "It's just him and me now, and he knows nothing of all this. Coming after Louis's death, it will be a blow to him, and he's not in good health."

"No, it's not just you and him. There's also an unsolved murder, and you're a cop," J-J said bluntly. "He may be your father, but he's the only one I can see at this stage with a motive for murder. He's my lead suspect."

"You'll have trouble getting much out of him," Sabine replied coldly. "He's got early onset Alzheimer's, and he's been in a home since my mother went into the hospital for the last time. We'll be lucky if he recognizes me or understands what we're trying to ask him."

CHAPTER 8

J-J was sufficiently sensitive to wait in the car while Sabine entered the nursing home where her father lived, close to the university on the western fringes of Bordeaux and the vineyards of Haut-Brion and Pape Clément. Bruno, who had been in the rear seat between Yveline and Sabine, got out to stretch his legs. J-J, in the front passenger seat beside his aide and usual driver, Josette, clambered out to lean against the hood and instantly lit a cigarette. He must have craved one, never allowing himself to smoke when there were others in the car.

"We might get something from the photo albums even if Sabine's father can't tell us anything useful," Bruno said.

"I'm pinning my hopes on this Tante-Do, and maybe on that facial reconstruction," J-J replied. "It's hard, running into this setback after getting my hopes up with the DNA findings. I was wondering if there's anything to be learned in St. Denis — maybe you can pick something up from the campsite the two girls used."

"It's still there, still in the same family, and the parents who used to run it are still around. I'm sure they'll help if they can, but it's a long time ago."

"You think I'm on a wild-goose chase, don't you?" J-J turned to face him.

"No," Bruno replied firmly. "I got this started again with the facial reconstruction theory. I know it's a long shot, but this is a murder. We have a duty to press on. And maybe we can at least get a photo or a reconstructed face, enough to help find out who he was."

Sabine came to the door and gestured for J-J to join her. In the car, they had agreed that squeezing all of them into her father's room would not help. As J-J went inside, Yveline and Josette climbed out of the big Citroën once Josette had located Tante-Do's address at the beauty parlor she owned in the car's navigation system.

Bruno was admiring the handsome mansion that had recently been converted into a nursing home and research center for senile dementia. It looked old, perhaps eighteenth century, with tall windows and pleasant gardens where old people in wheelchairs were sitting in the shade beneath a stately avenue of lime trees that looked almost as ancient as the house. Some of the patients had small dogs on their laps. Bruno had read that such pets helped to connect the residents to the real world and improved their health as well as their moods. That made sense to him.

"Heaven spare us from ending up in a place like this," said Yveline. "It seems a sick joke on the part of the Almighty, to grant us longevity but take our brains away."

"I don't think the Almighty had anything to do with it. Modern medicine, better diets and maybe doctors are better at diagnosing it, even if they can't cure it," Bruno said. He recalled what his aunt's doctor at the hospital had said about one in seven in the region being over the age of seventy-five and repeated the statistic to Yveline.

"*Putain,* what's that going to do to our taxes?" she asked. "Maybe J-J has a point in smoking. They'll probably kill him before he goes gaga." She looked across the car at him. "Tell me, do you ever think about euthanasia?"

"Not really," he replied, surprised by her question. "There's no simple answer. I can think of circumstances where it makes sense, but I can also see it opening the way

131

to a great deal of abuse. And it would put a heavy burden on the medics we'd expect to do it."

"So we stick with the law as it stands, even though we know the law is sometimes an ass?"

"So long as the laws are made by deputies we elect, and whom we can evict in another vote, we stick with the laws that we as cops swore to uphold. It's not the laws that are an ass, it's us, the people and the deputies who make the laws. The laws change along with us. When we were born, Yveline, both abortion and homosexuality were illegal. Even slavery used to be legal. Maybe we change too slowly, but at least we change."

The main door opened, J-J holding it for Sabine, who was carrying a stack of photo albums. Once she stepped out, J-J offered her a clean handkerchief, took the books from her and went to the car, leaving Sabine standing by the door, her face turned away, her shoulders shaking. Yveline walked past J-J and stood beside Sabine, putting an arm around the young woman's shoulder. Bruno heard Sabine tell Yveline that she ought to be accustomed by now to her father's condition, but each time it depressed her anew.

"He didn't even recognize his own daugh-

132

ter," J-J said, his voice solemn. He stood by the back of the car until Bruno opened it so he could place the photo albums beside Sabine's luggage. "The poor guy is in a different world altogether. He couldn't stop reciting something like a shopping list or an inventory of groceries, over and over. Sabine said he used to be deputy manager of a supermarket. That's where he met her mother, who was a cashier. I don't think he ever knew we were there, not me, not his daughter."

J-J let out a long breath. "*Putain,* this job. Sometimes it gets to you. It's never the obvious things, the decomposed bodies. Yes, the women and kids beaten up, those little bloodied faces that break your heart. But it's also something you just don't expect, like trying to make contact with this old — this poor old man."

He lit another cigarette, breathed in deeply, coughed hard and spat. "Right, on to Tante-Do at the beauty parlor."

Her place was larger than Bruno had expected, filling both sides of a double-fronted modern building on a busy street. A beauty parlor and a hairdresser shared a single entrance door and seemed to be two parts of a single business. The hairdresser's premises went back about twenty meters and looked two-thirds full. The beauty parlor smelled of scent and pampering and was smaller than the hairdresser's place, little more than a receptionist's desk and a counter where two women were having their nails done. They turned to stare as the receptionist gave a professional smile of greeting that stayed fixed on her face even as the police uniforms piled in behind J-J. Behind her were two doors, one marked SALON and the other SPA.

"Madame Dominique?" asked Sabine. The receptionist stared briefly at the uniforms and then pointed them to the stairs between the two businesses, saying they'd find her in the office on the next floor.

"Sabine, what a pleasure!" exclaimed an elegant, carefully coiffed and extremely thin woman with a complexion that seemed as white and smooth as porcelain. She rose from behind a modern desk covered with sheaves of accounts. She was wearing a pressed and pleated white blouse with a high collar and a scarf at her neck. She must have kicked off her shoes beneath the desk because she shuffled her feet a little and suddenly seemed five or six centimeters taller. Bruno knew that she must be in her early fifties, but to his eye she looked no more than forty, until he looked at her hands. Behind her was a tall, old-fashioned wooden hatstand that carried a medical-style white coat on a hanger.

"And are these your colleagues?" she went on as she came from behind the desk. She spoke brightly, although she had to know this was no social visit. "Please, all of you, come into my room at the back. I assume you're here on business."

Sabine smiled and nodded before introducing J-J, who showed his police ID and allowed Bruno's and Yveline's uniforms to speak for themselves. They followed Dominique into a comfortable sitting room. A half-open door revealed a kitchen, and some steps led up carpeted stairs, presumably to a bedroom or two. Bruno assumed that she lived here, above the shop.

"Madame, we are investigating a murder that we believe took place during the St. Denis Félibrée that you and Sabine's mother attended some thirty years ago on the eve of her wedding," J-J began, and went on to explain Oscar's discovery at St. Denis and the new DNA evidence. "It seems very likely to us that you were with Sabine's mother when she had her liaison with the man who was then murdered. We are hoping you can help us discover who exactly he was."

Tante-Do sat back, looking stunned as she stared at J-J, then at Bruno and Yveline before her gaze came to rest on Sabine. Slowly her features relaxed into a sad smile.

"So the family secret finally comes out," she said, addressing Sabine as if the others weren't present. "I'm sorry it had to emerge like this, Sabine. Your mother never wanted you or your dad or poor little Louis to find out. Not that she ever regretted her little adventure, and, believe me, nor did I."

Tante-Do gave a grin which made her look much younger and then chuckled with what Bruno assumed was a happy nostalgia. "I only knew him as Max and he came from somewhere in Alsace, a good-looking guy, a bit of a blond beast," she said, lighting a cigarette. After her initial shock she appeared unfazed by the police visit and the questions.

"Max was a good-looking guy and I might have been interested, but I had my own *mec,* his friend Henri. In fact, it was Henri who picked me up first on Thursday evening and then your mother and Max really took to each other. He was a great dancer. We had a great weekend together, the four of us, and then on the Sunday morning the two guys vanished, just disappeared." She paused, as if suddenly recalling the social niceties.

136

"Can I offer you some coffee?"

"No, thank you," said J-J, putting his phone on the coffee table between them. "I'm recording, if you have no objection. It has no legal status, but it will help to jog my memory — and perhaps yours — when you give the formal statement that I'm afraid we are legally obliged to take."

Tante-Do shrugged, and J-J said, "The witness has signaled her agreement to the recording."

"I was against the marriage from the start," she began. Then she glanced up at Sabine and said, "Sorry, Sabine, but your dad was too old and too boring for your mother. I think he represented stability, reliability, if you like, and that was what she craved. You may not know this, but your grandfather, your mother's dad, walked out on his family when she was little. He just disappeared, and your mother never heard from him again. That would have been in 1972, maybe '73. Your grandmother had a hard time raising your mother alone."

Dominique went on to explain that she understood her best friend's need for stability but could never understand her choice of husband. She had tried talking her out of the marriage, and it was her idea to have a last fling before the wedding. Dominique

137

had originally thought of a rock festival but chose the Félibrée as a suitably wholesome event. She found and booked the campsite, bought the bus tickets and announced it as a surprise prewedding gift.

"Which days were these, exactly?" J-J asked.

Dominique looked irritated and almost snapped out the words, "It was a long time ago."

"Please, Tante-Do," said Sabine, gently.

Dominique nodded, closing her eyes in an effort to remember. "We got there on the Thursday evening and spent the Friday and Saturday and a bit of Sunday at the Félibrée, and we caught the bus back to Bordeaux after a late lunch on the Sunday."

"Thank you," said J-J. "Please proceed."

"My real motive was to give your mother some fun," she said, looking directly at Sabine. "And that maybe meant she'd meet another guy, or realize she was too young to get married. At least I could help her have a last good time. And she did. She and Max just clicked in a big way, very passionate, could hardly keep their hands off each other, kept slipping away into the woods for another quickie. Mind you, I wasn't much different with Henri. I really thought it was working. On that last night in our tent she

138

was thinking of canceling the wedding, but then the next morning the guys had gone. That was the Sunday, as I said. Just disappeared, leaving no trace. Your mum had been abandoned all over again, so I wasn't surprised when she squared her jaw and went ahead with the wedding. But she regretted it ever after."

Dominique paused, looking abashed as Sabine gave something like a sob that she tried to cover by clearing her throat.

"I'm sorry, sweetheart," Dominique said to her. "But I suppose it all has to come out now."

"What were the surnames of these two young men?" J-J asked.

"I have no idea. I've forgotten, if I ever knew them. A family name was hardly important to us." She stubbed out her cigarette fiercely, as if erasing a memory.

"Can you tell us anything else about them?"

"They were both of them big, fair haired, well muscled and very fit, bronzed from the sun. Real golden boys. They'd been working in the strawberry fields around Vergt to make some money and were planning to go down to the vineyards to pick grapes before heading back to university in Strasbourg. We were in a proper campsite, but they wanted to save their money so they were camping *sauvage* up in the woods. They had a small tent, a sleeping bag each, an army-surplus water canteen each and lots of wine they drank from the bottle. They'd sneak into our campsite for a shower."

"And that was where you, uh, connected? Up in their tent?"

"What, in their shared tent? We weren't into orgies." She laughed. "Weren't you ever twenty? We did it in the woods, up against trees, in the river, on the bank, in their tent, in ours." She glanced up at Sabine. "It might have been the happiest time of your mother's life, at least until she had you and Louis. Just a few glorious days, but some people don't even have that to remember."

"Do you think that was when she became pregnant?" Sabine asked, speaking over J-J, who had been about to ask something else.

"We both thought that, and by the time she knew, she was married. And she took that seriously. She was determined to make that marriage work, and she did — after a fashion. She was devoted to you and your brother. But he never looked a bit like your dad, and when he was growing up I kept seeing bits of Max in him, in his eyes and his build. She tried to deny it to herself, but we both knew who his father was."

"So, to sum up: all you know of him is the name Max," said J-J. "That he was from Alsace, a student at the University of Strasbourg and a good dancer. He was with another young guy, Henri, also from Alsace, and they'd been making money in the strawberry fields in Vergt. Did you ever learn what subject they were studying, or their hometowns? Did you exchange addresses or phone numbers?"

Dominique shook her head, but slowly, as if careful of her hairstyle. "Henri was studying something to do with wine. He told me he'd spent some time in the Alsace vineyards as part of his studies."

"Had they done their military service yet?" Bruno asked.

"I don't know. It never came up." She shrugged.

J-J jumped in with his own question. "How did you learn they'd gone?"

"We were going to meet at a café in the square for croissants and coffee, and they didn't show up. We waited and then went back to the campsite, thinking they'd have left a message in our tent, but there was nothing. We went up to where they'd been camping, and they were gone. There wasn't a sign that they'd even been there. Your mother was distraught, went all around the festival, sure they'd be there. I just thought it was time to move on and put it down to experience. Your mother wasn't like that, Sabine. She took it to heart."

"Do you have any photos you kept of that trip, anything that might show the faces of these two men?" J-J asked.

Dominique laughed. "There were no mobile phones back then, so we weren't taking photos of everything all the time like they do these days. Your mother had a little camera, but I don't know that she used it much."

"These two men, Max and Henri, how would you describe their relationship?" asked Bruno. "Were they close friends, real buddies, or was there any kind of tension between them?"

"They were just friends spending the summer together, making some money and chasing girls. We didn't spend a lot of time talking, but they seemed to get on just fine. Henri picked me up, and Max and your mum just seemed to hit it off from the start. It wasn't like the guys were jealous of each other. They both seemed pretty happy at what they'd found, and so were we."

"What contraception were you using?" Yveline asked, the first time she had spoken since entering the room.

"I was on the pill, but she wasn't. She wanted to start having babies as soon as she was married, the whole motherhood and nesting thing. I made sure she had some condoms."

"Do you know if she used them?"

Dominique shrugged. "She said so, but if she did, they didn't work."

"If you saw either of these guys again, would you recognize them?" Yveline asked.

Dominique gave a mocking laugh. "You mean even though they'll be bald and probably fat? Even if I did recognize them, I probably wouldn't want to. But, yes, I suppose I might know their faces if they hadn't changed too much."

"I'd like you to do a photofit, work with a police artist to re-create their faces as best you can," J-J said. "And if we can find any photos of the Félibrée, we'd want you to look through them. We might also want your help in staging a reconstruction —"

"I've got a business to run here," Dominique interrupted. "I can't just drop everything for some ancient case."

"Madame, let's understand one another," J-J said. To Bruno's ears his voice sounded dangerously calm. J-J leaned forward and turned off the recording system on his phone before he spoke again.

"You are a material witness in a murder case, probably the only one. From what you have said already, you may be the last person to have seen the dead man alive. Inevitably, that makes you a suspect, and that gives me grounds to detain you. If you want me to arrest you and make you do as I ask, that's up to you. One way or another, I will require you to cooperate with my investigation. And if I am forced to arrest you, I will have this house and this business torn apart by a bunch of cops to make sure we miss nothing. I will also be sure to alert the local newspapers and TV stations to send cameras and photographers. You will briefly be famous, or perhaps infamous. And after that, you might not have much of a business to come back to when we let you out. Your choice."

Dominique stared at him coldly before shrugging again. In a bitter voice, she said, "For this I pay my taxes."

"You know our motto, Dominique," J-J replied calmly. "Honored to Serve."

J-J and Dominique glared silently at each other for a long moment before they were interrupted.

"Please, Tante-Do, we really need your help with this," Sabine said.

Dominique shifted her gaze and changed

her expression to look fondly at her old friend's daughter before replying.

"For you, sweetheart, anything."

Mon Dieu, thought Bruno. That was astutely done, one of the best performances of good cop, bad cop that he'd ever seen. And natural rather than deliberate.

"By the way," said Bruno to J-J in a low voice as they all returned to the car for the drive back to Périgueux. "That young woman, Virginie, working on the skull — she's a pretty one and she was in the lab alone when we saw her. Can you keep a paternal eye on her? You know what cops can be like."

As he said this, Bruno suddenly recalled the big guy in uniform who'd made that nasty remark about country cops and sheep shaggers in the police canteen.

CHAPTER 9

Back at the commissariat of police in Périgueux early that evening, Bruno collected a
fat file of photocopies of J-J's original
inquiry into Oscar's death and drove back
to St. Denis with Yveline. He turned down
Yveline's offer to join her and Sabine for
dinner, thinking it would be better to let the
two women establish their own rapport. It
was too late for the evening ride of the
horses at Pamela's, but he went there to
pick up Balzac and then drove home. He
took Balzac for a long walk along the ridge
as the dusk deepened. He made himself an
omelette and a salad from the garden. After
a less-than-illuminating hour or so with J-J's
files, Bruno made a final check of the
chicken coop, drank a last glass of the red
wine from the town vineyard and went to
bed early.

He woke just before six after a solid eight
hours' sleep, took Balzac for a long run

through the woods, showered, shaved and picked up a bag of warm croissants and two baguettes from Café Fauquet as it opened at seven. Soon afterward, he was at Pamela's riding school, collected a hatful of fresh eggs, let himself into the kitchen and heard the shower running upstairs. He put the kettle on for coffee, set out cups and plates and began halving and squeezing oranges until the shower stopped. The kettle was boiling, so he made the coffee, and after a moment he heard Pamela's voice from upstairs, "Is that you, Bruno? I can see Balzac at the stables and I can smell coffee."

"It's me and breakfast is ready unless you want a boiled egg."

"I'd love one and I can see Gilles and Fabiola coming up the lane. Better put two more eggs on."

He put four eggs into a pan he filled with boiling water and set the alarm for five minutes. He took butter and a jar of Pamela's homemade apricot jam from the fridge, added two more cups, plates and eggcups and began squeezing more oranges.

"There's nothing like a breakfast someone else has made for you," she said, kissing him lightly. "It feels like being in a hotel." She sat down and began pouring out orange juice as Gilles and Fabiola arrived. Bruno began to brew more coffee.

"I have news," he announced. "Balzac's a father — nine pups; four males, five girls, all doing well. I went up to the kennel yesterday to see them. I'm going to ask Florence if she'd like one for the twins."

"Don't mention it in front of them or they'll give her no rest until she gives in," said Fabiola. "Gilles and I were saying the other day that we'd be interested, but we can't agree whether we want a boy basset or a girl."

"There's no hurry," Bruno said. "Apparently Balzac has a much grander pedigree than I ever thought, and he's been such a success that the kennel wants him back again to father another litter in a few months. So if you can't agree this time, you'll have another chance."

They ate quickly and within ten minutes they were trotting past the paddock, each with an unsaddled horse on a leading rein. Pamela took them along one of the shorter routes, since each of the horses would be working later in the day. She restricted them to a canter, a pace so measured that even Balzac could very nearly keep up. But it was also a pace too slow for Bruno to lose himself in the thrill of Hector's speed and the insistent rhythm of his hooves. He found himself thinking of the way Sabine had stood at the door of her father's nursing home, sobbing quietly with her back to them; the way J-J had told Tante-Do that she had no choice but to surrender to J-J's own determination to pursue this ancient case that had never lost its grip on him. At what point, Bruno asked himself, does justice so long delayed, inflicting so much pain as it grinds through the innocent lives of others, start to become absurd?

"What is it, Bruno?" Pamela asked when they were back at the stables, after Fabiola and Gilles had departed. "You're miles away, distracted. I thought you said all the puppies were fine."

"It's not that," he said, looking out through the stable door, barely aware of her behind him, standing still with the bridles in her hand, about to hang them on the hook by the sink. "It's this case that's been on J-J's mind for the last thirty years. There's been a small breakthrough, and he's determined to pursue it, though I fear it's not going to lead anywhere. And it's my fault, really. I had this idea when I saw the exhibition at the museum of faces rebuilt from the original skulls. I got his hopes up, and the more I think about it, the more I wonder whether we should have just left it as dormant as it's been for the last thirty years. This damn investigation has already started eating away at people."

He let out a long sigh. "Sorry, I shouldn't be bothering you with all this."

"We're not just friends, Bruno," she said. He heard a jangling as the bridles dropped to the floor, and she came up behind him, wrapped her arms around him and buried her face in his neck. He could hardly hear her, had to strain to catch the muffled words.

"We have a history, you and I, so you can share stuff with me all you want. Lord knows I dumped more than enough on you, about my mother, and about that sad mistake of a husband I had." She squeezed him hard. "Let's go and make some coffee."

She took his hand and pulled him along behind her, the pair of them clomping over the courtyard, still in their riding boots. There was the sound of a car, and then a cheerful *toot-toot* of a car horn as Miranda, waving cheerfully, drove her kids off to school.

"I ought to be there, seeing the kids across the street," he said.

"You know you're probably the last cop in France who still sees children across the road, but you don't have to do it today. Come and have some coffee, and you can just guess what Miranda's thinking we're up to, seeing me haul you across the yard like this."

In spite of himself, he laughed, caught up to her and hugged her tightly.

"You are very special, Pamela. And thank you. But no coffee. Duty calls." He turned back to the stables, pulled off his riding boots, rinsed his face with water and headed off to see Joe, his predecessor as the town policeman of St. Denis, and the man who had called in a very young J-J thirty years ago when a body had been found buried in the woods.

Joe kept goats, geese, and chickens and bred pigeons. He fed his large extended family from a vegetable garden that was fenced more securely than some prisons to stop the goats from invading. He also made the worst wine Bruno had drunk since his days in the army. But he had taught Bruno how to be a neighborhood policeman, and he still knew everybody in the town and around it. He lived in a small hamlet a couple of kilometers outside St. Denis, and Bruno found him in his garden, installing taller sticks to support his tomato plants. He greeted Bruno, came out of his garden and gave Balzac an affectionate pat.

"Remember that spot in the forest where you found the body buried near the campsite all those years ago?" Bruno asked. "Could you take me there?"

"I can probably find it if you tell me what this is about," Joe said, steering Bruno to a chair in the courtyard and then going into the kitchen to bring out two glasses and a murky bottle of his own eau-de-vie. It was better than his wine. He poured out two slugs, and Bruno explained about the DNA, the dead soldier in Mali, his half sister and their mother's best friend.

"I want to get a feel for the place where the killing happened, try and bring it into focus in my mind," Bruno said. "And then I'd be grateful if you would come with me and talk to the people who ran the campsite at the time. I know their son who runs it now, but the older ones are just acquaintances. Maybe they might recall something."

"Do you have any photos of these two girls who stayed at the campsite?" Joe asked.

"I can get them." He pulled out his mobile, called J-J and asked him to e-mail the wedding photos of Sabine's parents to his phone.

"They aren't very good, a wedding photo of one of the girls, with her *demoiselle d'honneur.*"

"Maybe you should talk to Philippe Delaron, see if his father left any copies of the photos he took of the Félibrée. It was a big event for St. Denis, and the *mairie* paid Delaron to take photos for the local press and for the town records. The *mairie* made an exhibition of the photos that was very popular, and Philippe's dad made a small fortune selling prints of people. Find those old photos, and you might find the girls and their boyfriends."

Bruno sat up excitedly. "That would be terrific, if they still exist. But when Philippe closed the camera shop, I think he cleared out a lot of old stuff so he could rent the place out. Still, it's worth a try."

His phone gave a double buzz, the sign of incoming e-mail. He opened the attachment and saw the wedding photo. He zoomed in with his fingers to get a close-up of the bride and her maid of honor and showed it to Joe, who pulled out his reading glasses.

"Pretty girls," he said, squinting. "You would think I'd remember them, but it's been thirty years and there were a lot of people at that Félibrée. I can't say they ring any bells, but let's go down to the campsite and into the woods."

They took Bruno's van, Balzac grumbling

that his usual place on the passenger seat had been usurped. They parked at the busy campsite, and Bruno went into the office to greet Hilaire, the owner, explain his mission and to ask if Hilaire's parents were around. He was told they'd be at home. Hilaire promised to call them and say Bruno would be coming to see them.

Joe led the way to the back of the campsite, which looked full at this time in the holiday season, where they were confronted by a sturdy fence and thick hedge. That was new, Joe observed. In his day it had been more of a token boundary of wooden posts with two planks nailed between each post, easy to climb in or out. They walked back to the entrance and around the side and then up the wooded hillside, Joe moving like a man thirty years younger despite the undergrowth.

"Ten euros a night per person these days, even with a tiny tent, so I imagine there'll still be people camping *sauvage* and finding a way to sneak into the dances," Joe said when he paused for breath and looked around, as if hoping to see landmarks.

"We were up here often enough at the time, you'd think I'd remember," he said. Then his eye caught an outcrop of rock, and he headed for it and paused at the small and soggy hollow below it. "The stream trickled in there, that's why the ground is damp. But I don't see where the stream goes out. It just seems to disappear into the ground."

"It's a hot summer," said Bruno, wiping his brow and the back of his neck.

"Worse than hot," Joe said. "It reminds me of the *canicule,* that heat wave in 2003 when so many old people died in the cities. But I can't think when I last saw a stream just disappear. This little bog is about the only damp spot I've seen. Look, little footprints in the mud, voles and mice looking for water. And the undergrowth is all dry as a bone."

They clambered up another slope beside the rock, hauling themselves on young trees that wouldn't even have been saplings thirty years ago, and came to an overgrown bank. A large scoop had been taken or perhaps dug out of it, a place that was now filled with dry bracken. Ferns normally didn't die off until the fall.

"That dip in the ground is where we found the body," Joe said, pointing. They walked along the face of the bank for about twenty meters and came to a sheltered, flat stretch of grass, maybe six or seven meters square. Against the bank was a small ring of stones enclosing charred earth and ashes.

"Looks like that fireplace is still being used," Bruno said. "It's a good thing they sheltered the fire. It wouldn't take much to set all this dry stuff alight." There had been no rain for weeks.

Joe nodded and pointed to a square patch where the grass was paler. "Somebody had a tent there very recently. Nice to know the old traditions don't change. I remember J-J going all over this area with metal detectors. All he found was an old can opener and a camping spoon."

Bruno went back to the spot where the body had been found, clambered up onto the top of the bank and looked around, trying to imprint the scene on his memory, to allow for the increased girth of the nearest big trees and mentally to erase the new growth around the scene. He knew it was hopeless, but he kept trying to force his imagination to see the place as it had been. It was a calm but brooding spot, only a few scattered rays of sunlight coming through the thick and multilayered canopy of the trees.

Usually in a place like this he'd expect the air to be heavy with the smell of moist earth and vegetation. Instead, the air seemed almost dusty. As Bruno moved to one side his foot caught on something. He bent down to find an old stake buried in the ground, the kind that might have been used to secure a tent rope. He pulled it out and it came with a short length of dirty plastic ribbon. He could still make out the stripes of white and red that had been used to mark off a crime scene.

"Where you're standing is where J-J set up his base," Joe said. He was casting around, poking at the low undergrowth with a stick.

"What are you looking for?" Bruno asked.

"I'm trying to find the tracks. J-J persuaded the gendarmes to let him use a forklift truck. That's how they got the body out. It's hard to find anything after all this time. Thirty years of leaf fall and rotting branches have put a whole new layer of soil over everything."

"J-J said he found a couple of fireplaces and a latrine. Do you recall where they were?"

"The latrine was off to the side of the campsite and a bit downhill. They found it with the metal detector because they'd put their empty cans of food down there before filling it in. One of the fireplaces was pretty much where you saw the current one, but I forget where the other one was."

"Anything else you recall, anything that strikes you, jogs your memory? It must have been a big moment for you, a lot of press interest, tourists coming to watch all the police activity."

"Yes, the gendarmes set up a perimeter at the bottom of the hill for crowd control. After the first day J-J sent me round to ask the local hunters and mushroom and truffle pickers if any of them knew the area, if they'd seen anything."

"I don't see any green oaks or hazelnuts so I wouldn't expect truffles around here," said Bruno.

"There's the odd hornbeam, and you can find truffles around them. I saw one or two on the way up here with the blackened ground around the trunks. I might come up here with the dog, see if there are any *estivales* here. They don't mind the earth being dry."

Estivales, or summer truffles, were not greatly prized, but they could flavor a mild olive oil or make truffle butter. Bruno sometimes used very thin slices on top of a salad or pasta, or to help give some taste to the usually flavorless white mushrooms sold by supermarkets, the *champignons de Paris.*

"Thanks for showing this to me," Bruno said. "Let's go back and visit Hilaire's parents. They may have something."

The aged couple, who greeted Joe with affection, had prepared their living room for the arrival of guests. Coffee cups, side plates and small glasses were lined up on a coffee table in the middle of a square formed by the fireplace, a sofa, two armchairs and a big TV set that was screening some daytime soap opera. Hilaire's dad, Antoine, used his remote control to lower the sound, and his wife brought in a plate of *gâteau aux noix* and coffee.

"Usually we'd go outside, but it's too hot today, even with the parasol," she said. "I suppose it's this global warming they go on about."

"You're very kind," said Bruno as Antoine filled the tiny glasses from a bottle of Vieille Prune, a plum brandy that Bruno recognized from Hubert's wine cave.

"I don't know how we can help," Antoine said. "We spent hours being questioned by a young detective at the time, but we really couldn't help him. He went through the list of our bookings for that week, but there weren't many credit cards in those days. It was a cash business, and the few people who bothered to book would call up and usually just use their first names. The police tried tracking them down but got nowhere. It

159

wasn't like these days where you have to give a credit card number when you book, and Hilaire has to take note of identity cards and passport numbers. It all has to be accounted for and documented now."

"You can't get away with anything on your taxes anymore," Joe said with a friendly chuckle. "It's the same with that cottage we rent out to tourists. It all has to be registered with the *mairie* these days."

Bruno ignored Joe's comment and spoke to Antoine. "I've read the statement you gave to the police at the time, and you said you knew that people who were camping *sauvage* would quite often come in and use your bathrooms and the bar. You said you never kept track of them. Why was that?"

"It was just me and Marie and our peak time was the school holidays, so she had her hands full with our children. I couldn't afford extra staff," Antoine said. "And the bathrooms were coin operated, a one-franc piece to use the toilets, another franc for the communal showers, so it wasn't as though it was free. It wasn't just the *sauvage* campers — other tourists nearby would come in to spend money at the bar I ran and buy snacks, and they'd use the little shop we had for bread and milk and other basics. There was no way to keep track of them all. And you didn't have to, in those days."

"Did you bring any souvenirs with you when you left?" Bruno asked. "Photo albums, that sort of thing?"

"The police looked through the ones we had, but they were mainly family snapshots, when we were building the site, family parties, the children growing up, that kind of thing," Antoine said.

"Have some cake, please," Marie said, pressing the plate on the visitors. Bruno and Joe each took a slice of the walnut cake and drank their coffee. She turned to her husband and asked, "Had we started that camper-of-the-week business back then?"

"What was that?" Bruno asked.

"It was something we put up on the bulletin board every week, a photo I took of one of the campers doing something," her husband said. "There was a guy who caught a big fish in the river, another one who was a bodybuilder and used to lift weights, kids playing with animals, or if some guy was playing a guitar, that kind of thing. It was a friendly gesture, something to give a sense of community and to get the campers to pay attention to the noticeboard."

"And you'd make a few francs selling prints to people," said Marie. "And being

161

you, you'd always take a photo of a pretty girl."

Bruno's ears perked up. "Did you keep any copies of these pictures?" he asked.

"I did," said Marie. "Nostalgia. I kept them all in a box, and then when we retired, I started sticking them into a couple of scrapbooks. Would you like to see them? They're all dated. I put the week they were taken on the back of each print."

"I'd be grateful to see the one for 1989," said Bruno. "You remember the time of the Félibrée? That was when we think the murder took place."

Marie said she'd just be a moment, rose and went into another room. She came back after a minute or two with a large scrapbook, about the size of a tabloid newspaper.

"This is the first year we started doing these photos of our camper of the week," she said, and leafed through the first few pages. "Here's the week of the Félibrée, some pictures Antoine took of the town. You know how they always cover the streets at rooftop height with paper flowers. It looked so pretty, and it gave a bit of shade — it was a hot summer. And little Hilaire was starting to use the camera, so there are some of his photos in there as well."

She handed the scrapbook to Bruno, who

162

was sitting alongside Joe on the sofa, and Joe immediately found a photo of his much younger self looking rather sour as he stood beside a stage where a woman seemed to be singing.

"I remember that," Joe said, smiling. "She was singing some old Occitan song and she had a terrible voice."

He leafed on through photos of people in traditional local dress, surprisingly puritan to Bruno's eye, mainly black and white with the odd scarf or sash to add a touch of color. There were more photos of peasant dances, and then the campers of the week, each with a tiny pinhole at each corner where it must have been tacked to the noticeboard. There was a young man playing a recorder, a toddler trying to ride on a patient-looking dog, and then a pretty girl whom Bruno recognized.

It was a close-up of the head and shoulders of a tanned and slim and very attractive young woman in a bathing suit, or perhaps the top half of a bikini. She was standing by the side of the swimming pool, some of the bathers visible as they stood in the shallow end, watching her being photographed. Her head was cocked a little to one side, and she was giving a broad smile, or perhaps she was laughing.

Bruno pulled out his phone, called up the wedding photo J-J had sent him and showed it to Marie.

"Would you say this was the same young woman?" he asked her, pointing to the image of Dominique.

"Yes, I think it is. I'm almost sure of it, and I think I remember her, always very cheerful, always on the dance floor. I think she was a hairdresser because I remember her showing some of the other girls different styles. And we nearly used another photo of her, cutting some young man's hair. I remember he was very blond and very tanned. A good-looking boy."

"Would you have any more photos of her, like the one with the young man, or did you keep just this one?"

"Just that one, I think. We didn't keep the ones we didn't use."

Bruno turned to the next few pages. There was an old man fast asleep in a deck chair, an empty bottle of wine beside him, then a toddler looking intently at a curled-up hedgehog, and a boy juggling oranges. He leafed through to the end of the book, but there was nothing else that caught his eye. He turned back to the image of Dominique.

"You say you recall her being cheerful. Do you remember anything about her friends, the people she was with?"

"She had a girlfriend she was always with. I think they shared a tent."

"Do you have a magnifying glass I could use?" he asked, turning back to Dominique's photo.

Marie left the room again and came back with her sewing basket, opened it and took out a small magnifying glass. "I need it to thread the needles these days," she said. "My eyesight isn't what it was."

Bruno studied the bathers in the pool behind Dominique. There was a young woman who looked like Sabine's mother standing in front of a young man, his muscular arms wrapped around her and his face half buried in her neck. He had blond hair and was very tanned. He examined the other bathers, but none of them looked at all relevant, mainly families with their children.

"Would you mind if I borrowed this album to make some copies and maybe blow them up? I'll make sure you get it back, but the detective needs to see this. I think you might have here the first image of the murdered man."

"Not very good of him, is it?" Marie said, taking the scrapbook and the glass. "You can't see much of his face."

"It's more than we found so far," said Bruno.

CHAPTER 10

Bruno dropped Joe off at his house and drove on to the *mairie,* scanned the photo of the much younger Tante-Do and Sabine's mother onto his desk computer and sent a copy to J-J with a note identifying the happy couple in the pool behind Dominique. Yves, the forensics chief, would have some computer wizardry to blow up the detail. He printed out two more versions, one for him and the other for Sabine. Then he called Philippe Delaron, the local newsman and photographer for *Sud Ouest,* who was on his way back after photographing a couple in Les Eyzies who were celebrating their joint hundredth birthday. They arranged to meet at Fauquet's.

"I'm going to have to install air-conditioning if these summers go on like this," said Fauquet, bringing a welcome glass of cold beer to Bruno's shaded table on the terrace. "If it wasn't for the ice cream, I'd go broke."

Bruno had only taken his first long swallow when Philippe arrived. "Unless this is urgent, Bruno, I'll have to go to the office to send these photos back to the paper. They're for one of those pages that gets printed early. I'll be there awhile, but later this afternoon I have to go and take some photos of the *pompiers* doing some new training because the prefect has put out an alert for forest fires. But I'll gladly have a beer with you."

"I wanted to join you at your office, see if you can track down those photos your dad took of the Félibrée thirty years ago. I remember you telling me he kept everything."

"That's true, he did. But I didn't. I had to clear out the shop when we started renting it out, including the storerooms and studios upstairs. I only kept the stuff I knew would make money, like those photo books of old St. Denis they sell in the tourism office. Wedding and baptism photos I kept, because a lot of people lose them and want to buy them again when they have a big anniversary. I offered all the rest to the *mairie.* You know how the mayor loves anything historical. But he didn't take much."

"What about the Félibrée photos?"

"There was a whole box of that stuff. Dad must have shot rolls of it, and that was one thing the mayor took. But Lord knows what he did with it, and if it was stored in that old basement, you remember it got flooded. They could be ruined."

"What did you give him, negatives or prints? The prints might be gone, but the negatives could be okay."

"Both, because the *mairie* had paid my dad by the day for covering the Félibrée, so they were the legal owners. Dad was pretty thorough. He put the negative rolls back into those sealed plastic canisters, and each of the prints had its own plastic cover. Maybe they survived."

"Did you hang on to any of the Félibrée photos?"

"Yes, I selected the best because next time we have a Félibrée here, I'll put out a photo book of the last one. I've saved maybe a hundred and fifty prints."

"I'd like you to take them out for me and I'll come by your office once I've checked something with the mayor."

"What's this about, Bruno?"

"Can't tell you yet, but there may be a good story in it for *Sud Ouest.* If so, you'll be the first to know. I'll give you a clue. Did you shoot that exhibition that's now on at the museum in Les Eyzies?"

"The woman who rebuilds faces from prehistoric skulls? Yes, I was there at the opening reception when you were. I even got a shot of you and the artist and Clothilde chatting together."

Bruno saw a blank look in Philippe's eyes as his mind began working overtime, searching for a connection. Maybe he'd given Philippe too strong a hint, but so far nobody but the investigating team knew of any connection between the dead man and the Félibrée.

"The beer's on me," Bruno said, rising and leaving a five-euro note on the table. "I'll see you in a while."

The mayor recalled getting the Félibrée photos from Philippe but was not quite sure where they had been stored. He asked Claire to bring him the registry book for the archives. He leafed through, ran his finger down a page and looked up. "The box went first to the basement, but when we had the flood alert I had most of that stuff shifted up to the new registry behind the Trésor Public. The treasurer there has a key. I'll give him a call to say you're coming."

"Tell him I won't be alone. There are many rolls of film, thirty-six images each, so

I'm going to need help from Sabine, the gendarme from Metz whose half brother was fathered by Oscar. She's been attached to our gendarmerie."

"Bring her to the *mairie* at some point so I can say hello and give her my condolences on her brother's death. I'll call the treasurer."

Bruno called Yveline, who answered almost crossly, "Bruno, where have you been? I've sent you a couple of texts."

Bruno felt instantly guilty. He tried to be good at answering e-mails, but he hadn't yet learned to make his phone an extension of himself and seldom bothered to check for text messages.

"Sorry, I was out in the woods at the scene of the murder, so I didn't get a signal. How's Sabine and what are you up to?"

"We're in Les Eyzies, with your colleague Juliette. I've been showing Sabine around our beat, and we ran into her and are having coffee. What's up?"

"Can you meet me at the Trésor Public in St. Denis? I'm going to need your and Sabine's help. I'll be in the archive at the back, and we have a lot of Félibrée photos to look through. I think we might have a lead. Give my regards to Juliette."

"We'll be with you in twenty minutes,"

171

Yveline said and ended the call.

Bruno went to Philippe's office, the ground floor of a small terraced house at the far end of the rue de Paris. Philippe lived upstairs and rented out the neighboring house that had been his father's and grandfather's camera shop until the coming of mobile phones had overtaken the family business. Fortunately for Philippe, he'd already started taking sports photos for *Sud Ouest* and quickly turned it into a full-time job as regional correspondent for the whole valley from Le Buisson up to Montignac. He and Bruno had a complicated relationship of mutual dependence that made them part allies and part adversaries. Bruno had the stories, and Philippe had the means of publicity, so each found the other useful. They also liked each other, which helped, and Bruno had kept the teenage Philippe out of trouble over a youthful escapade that involved a stolen car that was damaged and Philippe and his friends working for months to pay off the owner and the garage.

"Here are the prints I've saved for the Félibrée book," said Philippe, handing Bruno a cardboard box. "Did you track down the others?"

"Thanks, Philippe. The mayor saved the others in the archives. I'll tell you as much as I can as soon as I can. In the meantime, keep this to yourself. Have fun with the *pompiers* and give them my best. If I have time, I might drop by to see this new training for forest fires."

"Did you see the weather forecast?" Philippe asked. "They say this heat wave is going to last into next month."

"The tourists will love it. Thanks, Philippe."

"Here's something you might need," Philippe said, reaching into a pocket and handing Bruno a loupe. "Screw it into your eye socket, and you get good magnification while your other eye can see the wider context. Take good care of it — it was my father's, and I'll want it back."

The town treasurer, a fellow member of the hunting club, showed Bruno into the long room at the back of the treasury building that contained the archives. Bruno put down the box of prints and was shown how to use the catalog that identified where each item was to be found by row and shelf number. There were copies of registrations for births, marriages and deaths going back to the nineteenth century, property tax records and handwritten annual reports from local officials. There were even old cadastre maps, showing who had owned every plot of land in the commune, that went back to before the French Revolution. Testing the system, he looked up the reports by the town policeman that went back to Napoléon's day, when such officials were called *gardes champêtres,* rural guards. Joe's reports were also here, but not Bruno's. Since he was the current holder of the post, Bruno's reports for the past decade were kept in the mayor's office. Bruno made a mental note to come back and glance through all this stuff one day.

Bruno knew the mayor had planned the archive system not only for the convenience of the town administration but also for his own purposes. He was writing the definitive history of St. Denis from the Neanderthals who were buried at La Ferrassie seventy thousand years ago and the Cro-Magnons who engraved bears and mammoths on the walls of a local cave. His account went on through the Bronze and Iron Age peoples, the Romans, the Arab invasion, Charlemagne's visit, the three centuries of the English occupation, the Wars of Religion and up to modern times. The last Bruno had heard the mayor was about to tackle the period of the French Revolution.

"You'll find the photographs at the far end on the left," the treasurer said, handing

Bruno the key. Bruno glanced around, saw a large table with two chairs and more chairs stacked against the wall. That would do. But he'd need a table lamp.

"Commandante Yveline from the gendarmes will be joining me in a few minutes," he said. "Would you have a magnifying glass and a table lamp we could use?"

"Of course, Bruno, but what's all this about?"

The treasurer was as keen as Philippe to be the first to pick up the latest gossip, Bruno realized. He smiled and said, "It's a matter of identifying someone. I'm sure the mayor will let you know the details when he can."

Bruno first found the box with all the negatives and beside it three larger boxes for the prints of all three weekdays of the Félibrée. There were more boxes for each of the days of the weekend. He'd just finished carrying them to the desk at the front of the room when Yveline and Sabine knocked and came in, carrying a magnifying glass and a table lamp.

He greeted them both and said to Sabine, "I have a present for you." He took out the print he'd made of the photo from the campsite and said, "Look behind Tante-Do at the couple in the swimming pool."

"Oh, it's my mother," Sabine exclaimed. "And she's looking so happy and beautiful. Can I keep this when we're done?" She beamed at him. "Thank you, Bruno, that's terrific."

"I'll get you a copy, but look at the guy embracing your mum with most of his face hidden," Bruno said. "I think that's Max, your brother's biological father. But now we have nearly two thousand photos of the Félibrée to go through. We are looking for your mum and Tante-Do and hoping to find them with these two young men, Max and Henri.

"We need to organize the way we do this," Bruno went on. "I have a box that contains about one hundred fifty of the best photos, selected by the son of the photographer. I'll start with that. Why don't you start at the box with all the photos from the weekdays, and one of you skims each print to see if there is any sign of your mum and Tante-Do. The other then looks at it more closely with the magnifying glass to see if there are young men with them. That's what we're looking for, images of Max and Henri. Pay special attention to Thursday evening, when they all met at some dance. And please be sure to keep them in order for each day, or we'll be lost. When I've gone through the selection, I'll take the Friday box and you two can take the Saturday. And if you think you find something, let us all know."

"That makes sense," said Yveline. "Let's get started."

They got to work, Bruno with the loupe screwed into his eye, the two gendarmes side by side, Yveline making the first scan, and then Sabine examining each chosen print closely with the magnifying glass. Bruno was about halfway through the box of Philippe's selections, with six of the photos to one side for closer perusal, when Sabine said, "I think I've got something."

Bruno and Yveline crowded around her to examine a print of a musician in a black hat playing a very old-fashioned musical instrument. A crowd surrounded him, Tante-Do and Sabine's mum in the front row. There was a man behind Tante-Do with his arm around her shoulders, only half of his face visible. Behind Sabine's mum was a man bending down, though only his eyes and forehead could be seen.

"That's a good one," said Bruno. "Put it to one side." He handed Sabine one of his business cards. "Keep that with it and note the date it was taken. We'll need a system to identify each of these shots — let's call this one the musician."

Toward the end of his batch, Bruno found an image of people dancing, and there was a decent shot of Sabine's mother facing the camera. Her eyes were focused on a taller, fair-haired man who seemed to be dancing with her. His face was only in profile. Tante-Do and her escort were not in the picture.

"There's one," he said, and the others came to look. Philippe's selected prints were not dated, but he scribbled "Dance scene, mother and Max" on a card as Sabine and Yveline examined the print. Meanwhile Bruno went through the rest of the selection, picking out two possibles and asking the two gendarmes to examine them.

"There's my mother, moving out of the photo. Is she holding the hand of that blond guy behind her who's drinking from a bottle of beer?" asked Sabine. "I think that might be Max."

Bruno finished Philippe's selection and began to attack the box of prints for Friday. By the end of their session, they had seven photos with more or less clear images of the two young women with their young men. To Bruno's disappointment, there was no single clear image of either of the men's faces, but they had profiles and half faces, eyes and brows, ears and hands, for each one.

He suggested they examine the possibles again, one by one, which resulted in one shot of Sabine's mother kissing Max's nose and giving a clear image of his mouth and chin. If he assembled the various photos, Yves at forensics should be able to put together a complete face. Henri, however, remained elusive. They had his eyes and forehead, his profile, his hands and a shot of the back of his head. There were no scars, no tattoos nor any other distinctive markings, nor any clear image of his full appearance. Still, Bruno thought, Yves should be able to put something together.

"This is quite something," said Sabine with a catch in her voice as she scanned again through the various photos of Max. "That's my brother's chin and his eyes and they're even his hands. There's really no doubt in my mind that he's my brother's father. I'm sure of it."

"Let's go through the possibles for Henri one more time," said Yveline. "But this time we'll go through the Friday ones you looked at, Bruno, and you go through the others."

They went back to work for another hour and came up with one photo that Bruno had missed. A group of people were dancing, among them Tante-Do with her back to the camera. Henri was facing her, his nose and eyes obscured by one of her arms, but his mouth and jaw were clearly visible.

"That should be enough for the forensic experts to put together photos of each man," said Bruno, much relieved. "I'll get some more index cards and paper clips from the treasurer so we can identify each one by the day it was taken. Then we can put together two envelopes, one of Max and the other of Henri, get them up to J-J, and let the forensic guys go to work to assemble the complete faces."

"This calls for a drink," said Yveline. "The gendarmerie is a stone's throw from here and I have some wine in my apartment there."

"Good idea," said Bruno. "Just let me draft a receipt for the treasurer for each of the photos I'm taking. Do you realize we've been at this for nearly four hours? No wonder my eyes feel tired."

"It's not like we've cracked the case," said Sabine. "We can put together a couple of images of two unknown guys, one of whom was murdered by a blow to the head, probably on the Saturday night. But we don't know that. We aren't sure that it was then that he was killed, rather than later. We don't know his real name nor where he was from. And if we can't prove when exactly he was killed, we certainly don't know by whom. You seem to be assuming it was Henri, but there's no proof he was the killer."

"You're right, of course," Yveline replied. "But we're a long way farther down the trail than we were when you arrived from Metz. I thought then that this was the longest of long shots and that we were just indulging the obsession of J-J, an old detective who could never forget the big case he failed to resolve. Now we have a real suspect, a face, a name and a witness who can place him at the right place at the right time."

"We have thirty-year-old bits of a face, a probably false name and a witness who saw no crime being committed," said Sabine.

"You're both right," said Bruno, who was still sorting prints. He swiveled in his chair to face the two women. "We have more than we started with but a lot less than we need, which is not unusual for this stage of an investigation. But we know the next step, which is to wait for forensics to put the photos together and then see where we are."

"If Tante-Do says the face looks right," Yveline was saying, "then J-J can run it through the facial recognition software against known offenders, ID cards, driver's licenses, passports, all that stuff."

"We'll need a magistrate and a court order to do that," said Sabine.

"That's for J-J to handle," Yveline replied. "This is his case, and he really wants it wrapped up and done. He can fix it."

Bruno watched this exchange, struck by the thought that he'd never seen two women cops thinking a case through before, arguing in an amiable and positive way without regard to their different ranks. It was refreshing when he compared it with the close but often stormy relationship he shared with J-J. Bruno knew his friendship with J-J could never have prospered if he had been in J-J's chain of command, as Sabine was under Yveline. Knowing that Sabine had already qualified for the two-year course that would make her an officer, Yveline had treated her as such, even though Sabine had been a simple gendarme only a week or so earlier. Sabine, courteous and affable rather than deferential, seemed to Bruno to treat Yveline more as a slightly elder sister than as a superior.

Over the past year and more, Bruno had watched Yveline rebuild the small squad of gendarmes at St. Denis after her predecessor, a pompous but incompetent male officer, had almost destroyed their morale. Yveline had the good sense to make an ally of the veteran sergeant Jules, whom Bruno had long ago befriended through the hunting club. Overweight and close to retirement, he was an experienced policeman and a shrewd judge of people. Jules was loyal to those superiors he judged deserving of his support, and he gave Yveline his full backing and a great deal of discreet advice. In return, Yveline had helped Sergeant Jules maintain his long and successful rearguard action against being posted elsewhere. Bruno knew that without Sergeant Jules's friendship, his own task in St. Denis would have faced many more obstacles. And these days in St. Denis, Yveline's gendarmes, Bruno as the town policeman and his mayor, along with the Police Nationale represented by J-J at Périgueux, all worked together in unusual harmony.

"I think we have to wait and see what J-J says when Yves puts all the Max and Henri photos together and lays the results on his desk," Bruno said. "We may not have a murderer, but we've come a long way toward identifying the victim, which J-J has been trying to do for three decades. Let's see where we go from there. We've done good work today, and I think Yveline is right: we've certainly earned a drink."

They returned the key and receipts to the treasurer, and Bruno took the cardboard box of prints. The three of them walked up the slight rise to the stucco-fronted building with the flaming-grenade escutcheon of the gendarmes. Yveline told the duty officer she'd be in her apartment and then led the way through the yard to the housing block behind and punched the access code into the electronic lock on the entrance door. Gendarmes had traditionally lived in barracks, but since the 1960s they had increasingly been housed in these newly built blocks where married gendarmes could live with their families.

Yveline as *commandante* was housed in a two-bedroom apartment with a balcony on the first floor. The rooms were not large, but she had made her home cheerful with sunny yellow walls covered with batik prints and masks from a holiday in Indonesia. The wooden floors of her living room had been sanded and covered with Persian rugs, and two Vassily armchairs of leather and chrome tubing faced an antique chaise longue. The rear wall was filled with shelves containing books, framed photos of her family and sporting career and a bar. In one corner was a TV set, in the other a small desk.

"Scotch, wine or beer?" she asked, taking glasses from the bar.

"White wine for me," said Sabine. Mopping his brow from the heat, Bruno asked for his to be mixed with mineral water as a spritzer. Sabine then said she'd have the same, told Yveline she admired the way she'd done the room and asked to use the bathroom, adding that she knew the way. All gendarme housing was the same.

As Yveline poured the drinks, Bruno's phone buzzed. He opened it to find an e-mail from Claire at the kennel, with three photos attached of Diane de Poitiers and her puppies. He examined them with delight. The first one was as he had seen them on the day of their birth. But the next two were a day or so later, and he could see their new energy and curiosity from the way they sprawled over and around and crawled away from their mother. One was so near to the camera it was almost a close-up. He showed the photos to Yveline, and then to the returning Sabine, and they cooed and enthused over the playful charm of the baby bassets.

"You remember I said I wanted one from when you first took Balzac to the kennel," Yveline said. "And I looked up the kennel website, and I know they cost about fifteen hundred each, so I've been saving."

"Boy or girl?" Bruno asked.

"I want a girl."

Bruno gave her a broad smile. "Done. But I'm not looking to make money out of this. I'm really happy that the puppy will be going to a good home, and I'm sure Balzac will enjoy having his daughter around," Bruno replied. "I think I'll get a lot more pleasure from seeing more happy bassets pottering around St. Denis with equally happy owners."

"It's a deal, so let's drink to that, even if Sabine's right and we are being premature about identifying Max and Henri."

CHAPTER 11

Just after dawn the next day, Bruno reached the tree at the top of the hill near his own home. It was the point at which he usually turned on his morning run, pausing for a moment to look across the Périgord landscape and allowing Balzac to catch up. From this point there was not another house to be seen. Ridge succeeded valley and then there were more and more ridges all the way east as the land steadily rose to the extinct volcanoes of the Massif Central, the very heartland of France.

A snuffling at Bruno's feet made him bend to caress his dog and reminded him that he should consult Florence about taking one of Balzac's puppies. He set off trotting again down the long and shallow slope that led to a track that gave him an easy kilometer or so along level ground that led back to his home, to a shower and breakfast. Twenty minutes later he left for St. Denis, to be ready to patrol the crossing across the main road from the post office to the nursery school, the *maternelle*.

He was there some minutes before eight, chatting with various young mothers he'd known since they were schoolgirls and whose weddings he'd attended, before holding up the traffic to let them cross the road to the school. Florence was one of the last to arrive. Once they had crossed, he waved thanks at the cars that had stopped and then greeted the young twins, Dora and Daniel, and then Florence.

"Lovely to see you, Bruno, but I'd better take the kids inside."

"I'll wait," Bruno said. "I want to talk with you if you have time."

With the other mothers watching, he was careful to make it a polite greeting between friends. As one of the most eligible bachelors of St. Denis, he was nervous of rumors about his private life and he still rather regretted that with Pamela he had broken his usual rule of no romantic liaisons in his own commune. He liked Florence and admired her greatly, and he found it hard to forget the fetching sight of her in a green bikini when he'd been teaching her children to swim. When they had swum their first length of the pool, Florence had leapt into the water to hug him in delight and he could still recall the tantalizing feel of her breasts against his chest.

"It's about Balzac," he said when she returned, glancing at her watch, since the classes she taught at the *collège* started in a few minutes. They began walking to the bridge. "You know I took him up to a kennel for mating. Well, the puppies have been born, and I wondered if you thought it would be a good idea for Dora and Daniel to have one."

"That's very kind, but I don't think I could afford —"

"It would be a gift, Christmas and birthday combined for both of them," he said quickly. "I thought I'd better consult you first, before saying anything to the children. I don't want to get their hopes up."

"That's so thoughtful of you, Bruno, thank you. Let me think about this for a day or two, okay?"

"Of course, I know you have quite enough on your plate without having a puppy to house-train."

"It's not that, I'm wondering whether we have enough space or enough garden, or enough time to give him morning and evening walks. It's such a responsibility, and the children are still kind of young for that.

But of course they'd love to have a basset puppy and so would I. You know how they adore Balzac."

"That's why I suggested it," he said. "But it's up to you. Take your time. Balzac will have more puppies in the next few years, so there's no hurry. And it does mean walking the dog twice a day, that's for sure."

"Still, I'd hate to deprive the children of such a gift, and it might even be good for them. I'd better sleep on it," she said as they reached the *collège.* "I'm really touched that you thought of this." She stared at him for a few seconds and went inside.

Bruno's phone buzzed to say he had a message, and as he pulled it from the pouch he felt the different vibration of an incoming call, this time from J-J.

"I just sent you a copy of Yves's two composite pictures, one of Max and the other of Henri," he said. "They look very convincing to me. I'm waiting to hear back from Tante-Do to see what she thinks. If she says they're good, we can prepare to launch a media campaign. And Virginie says she should have Oscar's reconstructed face in a few days. She refused to look at Yves's picture, saying it might influence her."

"Good for her. Please send copies to Yveline and Sabine," said Bruno. "And if you're

190

going to release the photos through your press office, maybe you should send copies to Gilles. He said he'd try to do a piece for *Paris Match.*"

"Right. And let me know what you think when you see them. For the moment I won't stand down those cops in Strasbourg who have been going through old university records and class photos from the late 1980s, looking for two students called Max and Henri."

Bruno hung up and looked at the composite photos, first Max and then Henri. He recognized in each one parts of the various photos he'd sent to Yves, but the compilations looked dramatically better, like real people. And the more he looked at Henri, the more he had a sense that he'd seen this man before, but when he was much older. The shape of the face and head and something in the eyes and mouth rang a distinct bell in Bruno's memory, and it was linked to St. Denis. The man was not a resident, but he'd visited the town within the last two or three years; Bruno was sure of it.

When could it have been? At a market day? Or at some cultural event or political meeting? As he closed his eyes to try to remember, Bruno could almost imagine hearing the man's voice, as though he'd exchanged words with him rather than just seen him passing by.

"What's happening to you?" came Pamela's voice, and his eyes opened. "You looked like you'd gone into a trance."

She was carrying a shopping bag, and he saw a big baguette and caught the delicious smell of fresh croissants. She must have been to the Moulin bakery nearby.

"I was trying to remember someone I know I've seen, but I can't remember where." He showed her the photo on his phone.

"I know what you mean," she said. "I get the same sense that I've seen him before, maybe at a market stall, or a *brocante,* trying to sell antiques, or a garage sale — that sort of thing. There are so many of these events it's hard to place him. Could it have been one of the antique-book fairs?"

None of them felt quite right to Bruno. He sent the mayor a copy of Henri's photo, suggesting that he print it out and show it around the *mairie.* No sooner had he done so than his phone buzzed again. Once more it was J-J to say that Tante-Do had declared Yves's composite photo to be the very image of her lover of thirty years ago.

"See if your friend Gilles can get that photo into *Paris Match,*" J-J went on. "We've got our press office trying to get it on the TV news bulletins and promising them photos of Virginie's skull. Now is the time to use that local reporter of yours, Philippe. This is going to work, Bruno!"

Bruno thought it best to coordinate all this from his office, so he said goodbye to Pamela, went to the *mairie* and then called Gilles and Philippe before printing out a larger image of Henri than the one he had on his phone.

"Here's that story I promised you, Philippe," he told Delaron. "We've called in an expert who works with that woman you photographed at the museum who rebuilds faces from prehistoric skulls. Right now, she's rebuilding the face of a victim from the skull of a man who was murdered in St. Denis thirty years ago. I can let you have a photo of the man identified as the killer, and we want you to run it in the paper tomorrow to see if anyone recognizes him. How does that sound as a story?"

Philippe was suitably enthusiastic, and asked Bruno to make sure J-J let him into the police lab to photograph Virginie and her skull. He would leave for Périgueux right away. No sooner had Bruno put down his desk phone than his mobile buzzed again. This time it was his cousin Alain, saying that he had managed to obtain a pass for a weekend leave for him and Rosalie. Would it be convenient for the pair of them to visit Bruno, arriving late Friday afternoon? Of course, Bruno replied automatically, not letting himself worry about what threatened to be a weekend consumed by the hunt for Henri. He'd make it work somehow. They had a car, there were caves to see, and it was perfect weather for Alain and Rosalie to take a canoe trip down the Dordogne. He would prepare a welcome dinner that evening and on Saturday maybe visit the *marché nocturne* at Audrix, where they could buy their food and wine at the stalls and dine in the open air in the medieval square.

The next call that interrupted him came from Sabine on her personal mobile, not from the gendarmerie. She had just heard from Tante-Do about the photo of Henri.

"Tante-Do says it's him for sure. So what happens now?"

"J-J is organizing a media blitz, TV and newspapers, national and local, and everyone being asked the same question — do you know this man?"

"But do these things work? We'll get hundreds of false leads, all over France. The chances of this working can't be good."

"It's a standard tool of police work, and it has worked before," Bruno replied. "All those false leads will have to be checked, but we might get the one we want. It's the best chance we have, Sabine, and now that we have the photo we have to try it."

"What happens then?"

"Any good prospect will have to be seen in person by Tante-Do. If she still says this is the man, J-J will not only interrogate him around the clock, he'll go through the guy's life with a fine-tooth comb, checking and double-checking everything. J-J has been looking for this murderer for thirty years. He's got almost as much invested in this as you do."

"Could this put Tante-Do in danger?" Sabine asked. "I really wouldn't want that to happen. I couldn't live with myself . . ."

"J-J can organize a police guard for her, but we're not at that point yet, and you'll be with us every step of the way. J-J will listen to you. He's a good cop and a decent guy."

"There's something else. What should I be doing now?"

Bruno suddenly realized that Sabine felt frustrated and underused. "I'll talk to J-J," he said. "I'm sure he has you in mind for the crucial phase, checking out the leads we get from the public and being there with Tante-Do when she verifies Henri's identity."

"Right, I get it. I'm babysitting the key witness."

"We wouldn't have her if not for you, Sabine."

"Okay, Bruno, thanks. If there's anything I can do . . ."

"I'll let you know," he said and heard her sigh before she closed the call. He began to think what he might do to help her through this. With a team of gendarmes to run, Yveline had only limited time for Sabine.

Bruno sighed also, making a mental note to call J-J about it. Then he sat back, thinking what to make for dinner with Alain and Rosalie. It was Friday, and although he had no idea whether Rosalie was religious or not, French tradition still called for fish. They'd be eating outdoors, so he could barbecue some trout or red mullet, or perhaps make something more ambitious with scallops and a creamy risotto flavored with a grating of summer truffles. Bruno had all he needed for a salad in the garden, but he might crumble some Roquefort over it instead of a separate cheese course. Nobody would want a heavy meal in this weather. For dessert he had some peaches in his garden.

This should be a family dinner, just the three of them, to give Bruno and Rosalie a chance to get to know each other. Nobody had to drive, since they were staying with him, which meant they could enjoy their wines. He'd serve a kir royal for the aperitif, crème de cassis with a lovely local sparkling brut from Château Lestevenie that was in his fridge. Then a really good white wine, a Cuvée Quercus from Pierre Desmartis at La Vieille Bergerie, ending with some Monbazillac that would match the strong cheese in the salad and would also go splendidly with the dessert.

If the baron had been out fishing that morning, he'd have told Bruno if the catch had been good. And on Friday mornings he usually played golf. Today's market was in Le Buisson, just down the road, so Bruno drove there, exchanged his uniform jacket for his red *blouson* and removed his képi. He went directly to the fishmonger he knew, who had bought his stock that dawn at the Arcachon quayside and driven directly from the coast to the market. Standing in line, Bruno studied the fish spread out on the long ice-packed counter with the centerpiece of a big fresh tuna, about twice the size of Balzac. He considered the cod and

197

the plaice, the red mullet and the mackerel, thought briefly about the still squirming crabs and scallops, before finally deciding on the *écrevisses*.

They were the red American crayfish, originally from Louisiana, and they had almost completely replaced the traditional white-foot crayfish that were native to the Périgord. He selected two-thirds of a kilo and also a half liter of the fishmonger's own fish stock and bought some Roquefort and fresh cream from Stéphane. On the way back, he stopped at the Moulin bakery for a fat, round *tourte* of bread. Everything else he already had. He was just parking outside the *mairie* when his phone buzzed. It was Isabelle, calling from Paris.

"Thank you for the photos of the puppies," she said. "I think we can be very proud of our handsome Balzac. There's one that looks just like Balzac when I first saw him at the kennel, and I don't know if I can resist getting him."

"Not while you have the job you do," he said. "You'd spend half your time trying to find a puppy sitter while you're off in Brussels or Berlin, and the rest of your time worrying about whether he was eating right or getting enough walks. Still, it's good to hear your voice."

"The same goes for me. That's not why I'm calling. A little bird in the media here tells us that *Le Monde* is running what could be a rather embarrassing op-ed on Sunday written by your friend Jacqueline. Do you know anything about it?"

"What's embarrassing about it?" he asked. "It's no secret that the Americans don't share with us like they do with the British. And the Stasi business was a long time ago."

"We have very long institutional memories," she replied. "So you know exactly what I'm talking about. Is there anything you can tell me?"

"Only that she and Jack Crimson were at a Cold War historians' conference in Washington on some East German intelligence files, and Jacqueline is upset that those files were shared with the Germans and Scandinavians but not with us. She thinks some French agents might have been recruited when they were young enough to still be in place today, there's a risk that they could have been blackmailed to work for the Russians, or even for the Americans."

"*Merde,* she must mean the Rosenholz dossier. That's a problem."

"Jack Crimson didn't seem too concerned about it."

"Jack doesn't have a prima donna president who likes to think that he can have a special relationship with Washington, just like the Brits. Ever since Brexit, the Élysée has been dreaming of France becoming the Americans' key security partner in Europe, a geostrategic coup that puts Paris back in the top rank."

"With him as the essential go-between," said Bruno. "It's a fantasy. The British haven't been in the top rank since the end of World War Two."

"Ah, but the British never claimed that they could speak for Europe. The Élysée thinks that we can."

"And you?"

"I'm still a cop at heart, Bruno. I've learned to deal with things as they are, not as I'd like them to be. Putting all that aside, Jacqueline's op-ed means that I have a problem. We've been talking discreetly with the Americans about sharing the Rosenholz dossier with us, and discussions are at a critical stage. If a political row blows up in Paris over this, we'll be back where we started."

Bruno sighed. "Knowing Jacqueline, I really don't think there's anything I can do here that would not make matters worse. In fact, I'm going to add to your troubles. Gilles was there when Jacqueline spoke about it, and he's doing a piece for *Paris Match*."

"Merde," she said. "I guess we have to live with it." Then her voice changed. "It's good talking to you. Why not come up to Paris to see me this weekend with Balzac and forget all that? We can all curl up together and look at pictures of his puppies."

"There's nothing I'd like more," he said. "But my cousin Alain, the only member of the family I'm close to, is arriving this evening with the woman he plans to marry."

"Is that the one in the air force?"

"That's right, but he's getting out in a year or so, getting married and moving somewhere near here to start a new life as a teacher."

He kept his voice cheerful, not mentioning that the key to the new life that Alain was hoping for was settling down with Rosalie to raise a family, something that Bruno increasingly feared would never happen to him. Listening to Isabelle's voice made it all the more poignant.

"You'll like that," she said. "I remember thinking that day that we met him for lunch how close the two of you are, how much of a childhood you'd shared. So if we can't enjoy Paris together this weekend, let's plan one when this business with Rosenholz and with Oscar is all over. Promise?"

"Promise," he said, thinking of her apartment just off the boulevard Voltaire and recalling breakfasts in bed and later a light lunch by the Pont Marie and taking the Métro to her favorite museum. She had shared it only with him, she had said: the Marmottan by the Bois de Boulogne, home to the paintings owned by Monet's family. "I'll count the days."

"Me, too, and please send me lots more photos of the puppies."

With the sound of a kiss, she ended the call and Bruno sat immobile for a long moment, hoping again that there might be a crack in the wall that kept them apart: her craving for Paris and the promise of a glittering career, and his for the peace of the Périgord, his horse and dog, his home and his garden, the lazy, embracing sweep of the Vézère as the river wound its way through the gentle hills and ancient caves around St. Denis. But she would no longer be the vibrant, ambitious Isabelle if she came back here, and he would no longer be Bruno if he left.

He took a deep breath, climbed out of the van and strolled halfway across the bridge to look down at the river. He could never remember having seen it so low, its flow so feeble, its sandbanks filling more than half its width. He went back to the van, took out the crayfish and cheese and the stock, thinking they'd be spoiled if he didn't put them into the fridge at the *mairie* until he could go through his paperwork and then return home to cook.

He turned, looking across the square at the Hôtel de Ville, standing on its thick stone pillars, and known to all as the *mairie* rather than by its formal name. The familiar noticeboard carried its usual announcements of forthcoming events: the anglers' competition, the antiques sale, the annual Noir Vézère book fair of *polars,* as the French called crime novels. It was when he saw the reference to the Foire des Vins that suddenly the gods of memory smiled upon him.

With a start he remembered that it was under those same arches that he had seen the older version of the young Henri in the photographs he had spent so many hours examining. It had been at a Foire des Vins, two or three or perhaps four years ago, and the man had been standing behind a stall, selling his own wine. Had Bruno tasted a glass or two? He could not remember, but he distinctly recalled the face, the light cotton jacket the man was wearing over a black T-shirt, his height and his heavy build.

Bruno raced up the *mairie* stairs to his office, took the enlarged photo of Henri from the printer, put the food into the fridge, got back into his van and drove the short distance to Hubert's wine cave, thinking he had not a moment to lose. He burst into the store, ignoring the cheerful greetings of "Bonjour, Bruno" from his friends among the staff, went behind the sales counter and into the offices, barely knocked and thrust his way into Hubert's private lair.

"Bruno, it's always great to see you. But you look a little harried," Hubert said.

Bruno thrust the photo at Hubert. "This man, a winemaker, he was at one of our Foire des Vins. The photo was taken thirty years ago, but do you know him?"

Hubert put the photo under his desk lamp and put on the glasses he was too vain to wear in public. "I'm pretty sure it's Henri Bazaine, mostly he makes a run-of-the-mill Bergerac from an old family property near St.-Laurent-des-Vignes. He married into it, as I recall, and almost all the wine he makes goes to the cooperative. Frankly it's all that most of his wine is fit for. But you know winemakers and their little vanities. He makes a small amount of a reserve red wine which is pretty good, not as good as he likes to think, but certainly very drinkable. I'd like to sell some here, but Henri likes to sell his special wine privately. He's kind of a recluse, lets his wife and young son and daughter do most of the marketing and go to the wine fairs. He likes to stay in the *chai* and the vineyards. Why do you ask?"

"Are you sure?" Bruno asked, the urgency almost painfully evident in his voice. "Would you swear to it?"

"I don't know about swearing, but it's him, all right. I think he was from Alsace originally and came down here for the *vendange* as a student, picking the grapes all over the Bergerac to earn a bit of money. He caught the eye of Mathieu's daughter, Mathilde, and pretty soon a baby was on the way, so Mathieu grumpily consented to the marriage and took him into the vineyard. Of course, if Mathieu had any sons, it would have been a different story. But the marriage worked out well, it must be thirty years now."

"What's the name of the vineyard?"

"Le Clos de Bazaine, the old family name. I think Henri adopted the name when he married to please old Mathieu. And now can you tell me why you're so interested in Henri Bazaine? It certainly can't be because of his wines."

"I can't tell you right now, sorry. But when I can, and we sit in this room, enjoying a glass together, I'll give you the full story from its beginning right here in St. Denis. In the meantime, I'm afraid I have to ask you not to say a word."

"My lips are sealed," said Hubert, smiling. "Let's have a glass together of this wonderfully refreshing white from Château Jaubertie as the world outside bakes in the heat. And you can tell me how seriously we should take this sudden alarm over forest fires."

CHAPTER 12

Bruno could not explain the instinct that told him not to alert J-J to his discovery of the identity of Henri, or at least not yet. It was partly because he was far from sure that he had the right man. But also he wanted to get his own sense of this possible murderer, to look into his eyes and see how much of Hubert's story he could discreetly verify. The last and most cogent reason was that Bruno felt above all that he should not alert Henri that the police were on his track at least until an independent witness had identified him. Someone with the nerve to commit murder and to keep it to himself for three decades, to create a new life for himself with a wife and family and build for himself a new and apparently successful business, was not a man to be trifled with.

In the meantime, he could do his own research. Back in his office, where a bottle of the Jaubertie he'd tasted now lay in the *mairie*'s fridge alongside the crayfish, Bruno fired up his computer, rubbed his hands together and began by searching for the website of Henri's vineyard. It was disappointingly thin. Unusually, it did not seem to welcome visitors for tastings, and there were none of the usual vineyard photos, family histories, copies of press reviews and price lists that he'd expected. The place seemed deliberately to be running under the radar. The police data bank showed no criminal record for Henri Bazaine, just some minor speeding offenses.

The website of the Inter-Professional, the overall administrative body for the Bergerac appellation, was more helpful, showing that the vineyard was now a relatively large property for the region with forty hectares of vines, more than double the size it had been twenty years earlier. For somebody making wines mainly for the co-op, where prices were low, that was unusual. Most successful vineyards in the region depended on the higher prices they could command for premium wines like Monbazillac or Pécharmant, or by gaining a reputation for their better wines through winning medals and prizes.

By contrast, there was more to be found on Henri's father-in-law, the late Mathieu

Bazaine, in a newspaper obituary. He had been a local councillor and served one term as mayor of his commune. His family vineyard had been devastated, like so many others, by the great frost of 1956. Mathieu had returned from serving in the Algerian War to rebuild the vineyard, becoming active in the cooperative and producing cheap wines for the new supermarkets. He had also been on the board of the local Anciens Combattants, the veterans' association.

He called the baron, another Algerian War veteran, who laughed at the mention of Mathieu's name.

"He was a *fainéant,* a real poser, always turning up at Remembrance Day parades with his medals, and he spent his entire time in Algeria working in the motor pool at the big base in Oran, never on what I'd call real active service," the baron said.

"Certainly he never saw combat. He spent most of his time wooing the very plain eldest daughter of a rich *pied-noir,* married her and then used her dowry to rebuild his vineyard here. She must have been at least ten years older than him and so obviously on the shelf that her family was more than grateful to get her married off. He inherited a small place from his dad, just seven or eight hectares. But when Algeria became independent in '62, all his wife's family came to France and put more money into the business, doubling the size of the place."

"How well did you know him?"

"Well enough to have lunched with him a couple of times at Anciens Combattants events. I think I even dandled his little girl, Mathilde, on my knee when she was a kid, and I recall one ceremony when she came along with him dressed like she was going to her First Communion. She was no beauty, just like her mum. Maybe that was why her wedding was such a low-key affair, but she got herself a good man who did wonders for that vineyard."

"Did you meet him?"

"Only at the wedding. I think I was only invited because Mathieu wanted to get close to my dad, who was president of the Société des Gastronomes de France. We were both invited, and my dad said I should go, just to show the flag."

"Are you at home?" Bruno asked. When the baron said he was, Bruno asked him to stay there and drove directly to the old *chartreuse* that he knew so well. He found his friend mowing his extensive lawn and showed him the composite photo of Henri that Yves had prepared.

"That's him, all right, good-looking guy,"

the baron said. "I think his name was Henri. I could never work out what it was he saw in little Mathilde, except maybe for the family vineyard. Still, I gather the marriage has lasted, which is more than you can say for a lot of marriages these days."

Bruno thanked him and then apologized, saying he had to go, explaining that he would tell the baron about Henri when he could, but now should cook for the visit of his cousin Alain.

"Was that the one I met, the one in the air force?" the baron asked. "I remember him, a decent guy. Bring him around for a drink if you have time."

Bruno nodded and said he'd try to drop by, but maybe the baron would like to join them at the Audrix night market on the following evening. He made a mental note to call some other chums about Audrix.

"Good idea, I haven't been there yet this year," the baron said. "Let's invite the whole gang. We can all meet for a drink here at six, and then get there by seven. I know the village mayor. I'll ask him to hold a table for us."

Once back home, after greeting and feeding Balzac and the chickens, he called Pamela, Jack, Gilles, Florence and the mayor to suggest they all gather at the baron's house tomorrow to meet his cousin and his bride-to-be and then go up to Audrix. Then he called Sabine on her personal mobile to invite her to join them, to meet his friends and experience the local tradition of the night markets. Suddenly with a touch of guilt he recalled Virginie, the young woman working on Oscar's skull at the police lab in Périgueux. He called her mobile and invited her to come down for the weekend, but she had already bought a ticket for an open-air concert in the Jardin des Arènes, the old Roman amphitheater. Could she come the following weekend instead? Of course, he replied.

It was time to start preparing the meal, the cold soup first — vichyssoise. In the garden, he dug up a single potato plant, which gave him four fat ones, nearly half a kilo. He pulled out two medium-sized leeks and two small onions and snipped off a bunch of chives. Back in the kitchen he peeled the potatoes and onions and stripped off the outer leaves and tops of the leeks, keeping only the whites. He sliced and chopped them into small dice, then began to fry them in duck fat over a very gentle heat. Ten minutes would let them cook without browning as long as he kept turning them.

He returned quickly to the garden with a wicker basket, loaded it with three fat carrots, a head of celery, eight shallots, a fat lettuce, a cucumber and some cherry tomatoes and darted back to turn the cooking vegetables of the vichyssoise. When the onions and leeks were soft, he slowly added a half liter of his own chicken stock and a wineglass full of water, bringing the vegetables to a simmer until he was sure the potatoes were cooked through. For the moment he thought there would be enough salt in the chicken stock, but he'd test it later, once the dish had cooled.

Suddenly his ears pricked up as the radio, tuned to France Bleu Périgord, began reporting "sensational developments in a murder inquiry that has been unsolved for three decades. The victim of the murder, which took place in the woods near St. Denis, has never been identified — until now. The crucial breakthrough in the case came thanks to the museum of prehistory at Les Eyzies, where an exhibition of prehistoric faces that had been reconstructed from their skulls inspired local police to bring in an expert to reconstruct the face of the murder victim. Here's the chief of detectives in Périgueux, Jean-Jacques Jalipeau."

"For the Police Nationale, a murder

inquiry is never closed," J-J said. "We have new information and new tools, so we are working hard now to push this to a conclusion."

That was it. Bruno looked up at the radio in surprise as it moved on to the next item. There must have been a leak, he thought. That was a nonanswer from J-J, framed with unusual caution for a man so normally outspoken. Could the leak have come from Philippe, who regularly worked with the radio station? Bruno thought not; Philippe knew a lot more about the case than just Virginie's work on the skull. The leak could have come from a cop who knew of Virginie's work. But did this mean that Bruno should contact J-J right now with the news of Henri Bazaine?

Bruno paused to think, wooden spoon still in his hand. If Henri had heard that news bulletin, might he try to flee, to disappear again as he had thirty years earlier? That was not a risk Bruno had any right to take. He put down the spoon, picked up his phone and called J-J only to reach his message service. Bruno reported that the man in the photo had been identified as Henri Bazaine, winemaker of Le Clos de Bazaine near Bergerac, by Hubert and by the baron, both of whom J-J knew. He recommended that J-J arrange for Tante-Do, suitably escorted, to be brought from Bordeaux to verify the identification.

He washed and chopped the lettuce, peeled and sliced a cucumber and put them into a salad bowl with the cherry tomatoes, crumbled and added the Roquefort cheese. He cut two slices of bread from the *tourte* and toasted them, ready to be cut into cubes to go into the salad once he'd added the vinaigrette. The bowl for the walnut oil and the white-wine vinegar stood ready by the chopping board.

He peeled and chopped the shallots, then cut a head of garlic from the braided rope that hung from a kitchen beam. He peeled and sliced two cloves and began peeling the carrots and celery before slicing them into a julienne of fine strips with his mandoline. He was planning *écrevisses à la nage,* crayfish that would seem to float atop a bed of the julienne.

He put a hundred grams of butter into a pan over the lowest possible heat and went to the garden for a sprig of thyme, three sprigs of tarragon and a bay leaf, and tied them together as a bouquet garni. He put the shallots and garlic into the pan with the now melted butter and softened them slowly for about ten minutes. He added the crayfish and sautéed them until they were bright red. Then he poured a glass of Cognac, struck a match and flambéed the crayfish. Once the flames died down, he removed the crayfish and began slowly adding a bottle of Bergerac Sec white wine to the sauté pan. He added the bouquet garni, sea salt and *piment* d'Espelette, the red pepper from the Basque country, and raised the heat for five minutes to reduce the liquid.

The vichyssoise was now cool enough to go into the blender to become a smooth puree. He stirred in the two hundred grams of Stéphane's cream and put the bowl into the freezer to chill. He went out to the rear garden, picked three plump fresh peaches from his tree, washed them, peeled and halved them, removed the pits and put them into the fridge on a plate, cut side down. He would leave the last stage of cooking for the arrival of his guests.

He'd already prepared the bedroom for Alain and Rosalie, putting fresh sheets on the double bed and fresh towels in the bathroom when he'd cleaned it that morning. On impulse he went to the garden, plucked two red roses with long stems and put them into a long-necked wine decanter that he took upstairs and placed on the bedside table. He checked his watch and saw that he was in good shape, so he took a quick shower and changed into khaki slacks and a polo shirt.

Bruno was just putting new candles into his two terrace lanterns when his phone buzzed. It was J-J, who said he'd got Bruno's message, and Tante-Do and Sabine would be going to Henri's vineyard in the morning. Sabine had been given an unmarked police car and, with Yves going along for security, would be picking up Tante-Do in Bordeaux at nine. They should be at the vineyard soon after ten. Tante-Do had been instructed to wear dark glasses and leave the talking to Yves and Sabine, who would say they had heard from Hubert's wineshop that they should try to buy a bottle of Henri's reserve red. J-J himself would first be going to the Bergerac wine cooperative to get more confirmations on the photograph. Did Bruno want to be there?

He explained about his cousin's visit. He'd arranged tickets for Alain and Rosalie to visit the Lascaux cave at ten the next morning, which meant they would be leaving about nine. They could have lunch in Montignac, then he'd urge them to take a canoe trip in the afternoon from the fortress of Castelnaud down the Dordogne River to the next fortress, Beynac, that loomed above the river from its clifftop. Bruno said he could be at the Bergerac vineyard by ten to meet Tante-Do and Sabine. Being in the military, Alain and Rosalie would understand if he pleaded urgent and unexpected police duty.

"Then I'll tell Yves to expect to see you at the vineyard. You'll be in civilian clothes, of course, but carrying your police badge, just in case. It's up to you, but I don't think you need to go armed. Yves will be wearing a concealed weapon in a holster, and I'll be nearby. I don't expect to be long at the co-op, and I'll have a couple of my men with me. I'm not planning an arrest at this stage, just starting with a few questions. I've checked his ID card, which has him born in '68 in Belleville, in the old Red Belt of Paris. By the way, he lied to Tante-Do about being a student — Strasbourg University never heard of him. Still, let's not forget this could be a case of mistaken identity. He might not be our guy."

"This is how we find out. By the way, I heard you just now on the radio. Was there a leak?"

"We're looking into that. Thanks for getting Hubert and the baron to confirm the photo. See you tomorrow."

Bruno sat in his garden, thinking about

the confrontation that would be coming at the vineyard in the morning and whether Tante-Do, Hubert and the baron could all be wrong about Henri. It was just possible. He got up, remembering to pick some parsley, and was heading back to the kitchen when Balzac gave his customary bark of warning a moment before Bruno heard the sound of Alain's car coming up the hill.

Rosalie was even more attractive in person than in the photo on Alain's phone. She greeted Bruno with a broad smile that came from her eyes as well as her lips, and he felt the immediate impression that she was one of those fortunate people who had been born cheerful and stayed that way. Almost as tall as Bruno, she was wearing flat ballet shoes and a short-sleeved summer dress in thick stripes of white and light blue. She greeted Bruno and then bent down to pat an enthusiastic Balzac, finding just the right spot to make him kick a rear leg in delight. Alain stood by, beaming proudly.

Bruno took Rosalie's overnight case and led the way upstairs to show them their room, suggested they might want to wash their hands after the journey, adding that drinks would be served outside when they were ready. He took three champagne flutes to the small table on the terrace and went back for the brut and the cassis.

When they came downstairs, Alain presented him with a bottle of champagne and Rosalie gave Bruno a small, wrapped parcel, saying, "Alain tells me you were always a great reader and that as a boy you loved Sherlock Holmes, as did I. So here's a modern writer's attempt to do a Sherlock, but it's about his brother, Mycroft. I read it when it was first translated, and I thought you might enjoy it as much as I did, unless you get enough detection in your day job."

"That's very kind of you," he said, hugging her in thanks and catching a hint of roses from her newly applied scent. "Thank you for the champagne and for the book. I'll look forward to both. Meanwhile, here's some Bergerac champagne, although we're not allowed to call it that, even though it's made in the way invented by Dom Pérignon long before he went north to teach the people in the Champagne how to do it. Would you like it with cassis or without?"

Alain chose it with, and Rosalie asked to try it without and stood a moment to sweep her eyes across the vegetable garden, the avenue of truffle trees, the chicken run and the roses that climbed up the front of the house.

"It's lovely here, a charming spot," she

said. "Did those roses you put by our bed come from the climbers by the door?"

Bruno shook his head and pointed to the cluster of rosebushes at the corner of his driveway, pleased that she noticed his gesture. He told them of their booking for Lascaux in the morning and of his own police business.

"I have to leave here just after nine," he said. "And I need to make my usual patrol of the Saturday market tomorrow morning at about eight, so I think we should go down to St. Denis for coffee and croissants in my favorite café, and then you can go to Lascaux and I'll head for Bergerac. And I really recommend you take a canoe ride on the way back from Lascaux. Tomorrow evening we're having drinks at a lovely small château that belongs to a good friend, and then we'll head to a tiny village with some more friends to have dinner at a night market."

He explained that they could park at Beynac, and the canoe rental people would drive them upstream to Castelnaud, from where they could launch their canoe into the river and paddle gently downstream with the current back to Beynac. Two formidable medieval castles, Castelnaud and Beynac had changed hands several times, but usually one was held by the English and the other by the French.

"If you have time, it's worth visiting Castelnaud and the Museum of Medieval Warfare inside it," Bruno said. "At this time of year they have fencing exhibitions, and you might see them fire one of the *trébuchets,* the heavy artillery of the Middle Ages. Amazing machines, they can toss an eighty-kilo rock as far as two or even three hundred meters. The Crusaders learned to use them from the Saracens and brought them back to Europe."

Aware that he was prattling, Bruno gave Rosalie a rueful grin and said, "Sorry, but this kind of thing captivates boys of all ages, and I think Alain might like it."

"Not just boys," she said, smiling back at him. "Why do you think I joined the military? That sounds great and thank you for arranging all this."

As Bruno refilled their glasses, she asked, "How far does your land go?" He pointed to the top of the hill behind the house and said it ran from there down to the hedge in the lower field, where some cows were quietly grazing.

"Do those Blondes d'Aquitaine belong to you?" she asked.

"You know your cows, Rosalie. No, they belong to a neighboring farmer. He uses my pasture and gets a dozen of my eggs each week, and I get a lot of free veal in return."

"Are we eating veal tonight? Alain tells me you're a good cook."

"No, I thought in this heat we should have something light, but a lot of it will have come from this garden."

"I can't wait until Alain and I have a garden of our own, but I think we'll be turning to you for advice. And what are we eating?"

"It's a surprise," Bruno replied, and suggested they move to the larger table he had laid for dinner and brought out on a tray the bowls of chilled vichyssoise to which he'd added some fresh parsley. He poured out glasses of the Cuvée Quercus, cut some bread from the *tourte* and said, *"Bon appétit."*

"Delicious, and I suspect these are your vegetables," she said. Bruno smiled inwardly as he thanked her for the compliment, aware that she was working hard to make friends with the cousin of her future husband. This was an interesting aspect of etiquette. Here were two people of a similar age and background who might in other circumstances have been attracted to each other, and each of them was trying hard to please the other out of their affection for Alain. Bruno could foresee many Christmases, birthdays and

New Year's Eves being spent together. The thought of such shared family events pleased him.

"Would you like to come into the kitchen while I finish the next course?" he asked, and they joined him with refilled glasses once the bowls had been cleared.

He boiled water, put the julienne of carrots and celery into it and reheated the white-wine sauce, adding the crayfish once it began to simmer.

He drained the julienne, thoroughly mixing the carrots and celery together to make the *nage* and spooned a generous portion into each of three warm bowls, added the crayfish and then offered Rosalie a teaspoon of the sauce to taste. She nodded her approval, and he poured the sauce into the bowls.

It was still light enough to eat without candles and, with the odd word and murmur of appreciation, they devoted their attention to the food and wine. When the *écrevisses à la nage* had gone, Bruno brought out the chilled Monbazillac to go with the Roquefort salad. Finally, Rosalie pushed back her plate, wiped a last chunk of bread around the bottom of her salad bowl, popped it into her mouth and closed her eyes.

"That was great," she said when the morsel was finished. "I'd never have thought of a dessert wine with the salad, but the Roquefort made it just right. Brilliant, Bruno, altogether a terrific meal."

"There's a small dessert to come," Bruno said, smiling as Rosalie gave a mock groan of pleasure. "I'm delighted that you enjoyed it."

He lit the candles as they began to eat their peaches, topped with the remainder of Stéphane's cream. Alain and Rosalie declined coffee, and they sat with the Monbazillac until the last glow had faded from the distant ridge. Bruno blew out the candles in the lanterns, and the stars all seemed to explode into view overhead, so they watched them, trying to trace the more familiar galaxies, until the moon rose and it was time for bed.

CHAPTER 13

Before seven the next morning, Bruno stepped out of his front door in his running gear and was surprised to see Alain and Rosalie similarly dressed and limbering up in the garden.

"I told Rosalie you were a jogger," said Alain. "So are we, along with most of the air base." Rosalie gave him a wide smile and said that after the dinner of the previous evening she felt she really needed to run. Air bases were flat places, thought Bruno. Maybe he should spare them the path up the hill through the woods. He led the way at a moderate pace down the driveway and up the grassy lane that led to a gentle slope, lengthening his stride on the long ridge that stretched for three usually windswept kilometers until the land dropped to the Vézère Valley below.

The earth was so dry that Bruno saw small puffs of dust rising at each step, but on this already warm day there was no wind to blow it away. They ran side by side, Rosalie between him and Alain, each of them moving easily and running well within themselves but still outpacing Balzac. It was, thought Bruno, even more companionable than the dinner they had shared the previous evening. The only animals up here were sheep with their lambs. Balzac had been taught not to bother them, and the sheep in turn ignored the visitors but still edged away from the ridge itself, seeking the little shade on the western side of the hill while the sun was still low in the sky.

Bruno increased the pace on the way back, and the two others stayed with him. Balzac, who was by now way behind, stopped in his tracks as they approached and gave a happy bark of greeting until they raced past him and he had to start chasing them all over again. Bruno glanced at the others when he trotted the last fifty meters up his driveway to the terrace. Like him, they were sweating very slightly, their chests not heaving. He approved. They obviously ran as much as he did.

"I'll put some coffee on and then take a shower before we head down for the best croissants around," he said as Balzac finally trotted up the driveway to rejoin them. "By the way, do either of you like riding horses?"

"I do," said Rosalie. "But then I grew up on a farm near Lisieux, which is why I recognized those cattle last night. We didn't have horses, but some of my friends did. Alain told me you have a horse of your own, but I don't see him."

"Hector stays at a nearby stable, a riding school run by friends of mine," Bruno said. "We usually go out to exercise them in the mornings and evenings. I only started riding recently and I love it."

Alain was making friends with Balzac, who was lying on his back, the flesh of his lower jaw hanging down from his teeth in what looked like an extremely happy grin. Alain was running both hands over his chest and flanks. He looked up. "Didn't you tell me you were breeding him?"

Bruno nodded. "The first litter of his pups was born just over a week ago. I went to see them and they're wonderful."

Alain looked at Rosalie, who was smiling broadly. "We've been thinking about getting a dog when we're married," he said.

"That solves the problem of your wedding present," said Bruno. "Tell me the date, and I'll not only be there, I'll time Balzac's future matings so you get a puppy once you're hitched."

"That's much too generous," said Rosalie. "I know how much a basset like this one costs."

"Alain is the only real family I've got. And I think the two of you would count as a great home for one of Balzac's pups. Now that that's settled, I'll put on some coffee."

Twenty minutes later, fresh from their showers and coffee mugs in hand, Bruno was introducing Alain and Rosalie to his chickens and his cockerel, Blanco, named after a legendary French rugby star. They were suitably impressed by the two geese, Napoléon and Joséphine, and their latest brood of half-grown goslings. He explained the three kinds of truffle trees and the different varieties of mushrooms he found in the woods that rose up the slope behind the cottage.

"I see you have apple trees, pears, plums and cherries," Rosalie said, looking at his small orchard behind the chicken run. "Where did you get the peaches we had last night?"

"Come see." He led them to the back of the house where he had a peach and an apricot tree espaliered against the rear wall and a fig tree at each end. Rosalie nodded approvingly and then looked into the barn where he kept his tools, a big freezer and shelves filled with glass jars of his various preserves of different jams and pâtés, confits of duck and *enchauds* of pork.

"The only thing you're missing is beehives and goats," she said jokingly. "Then you could be entirely self-sufficient."

"I'm not sure I'd want that," Bruno replied. "Not having them means I can swap my jams and confits for someone else's honey, or for their fresh trout from the river. And I prefer cheese made by people who really know what they're doing, like my friend Stéphane, whom you're about to meet in the market."

Shortly thereafter, having enjoyed Fauquet's croissants and some of his gossip about the strange business of J-J and the reconstructed skull, Alain and Rosalie accompanied Bruno on his tour of the market. They bought some cheese from Stéphane, Mara des Bois strawberries from Marcel and fresh foie gras from the stall of the Lac Noir farm. After briefly showing them his office, he waved them off on the road to Lascaux and then set off in the other direction for Bergerac in his Land Rover.

Henri's vineyard, Le Clos de Bazaine, was south of the city, mostly on the plain but part of it on the ground that rose on the far side of the road to run along the flank of the long, north-facing slope that was dominated by the high stone towers of the castle of Monbazillac. Despite the conical roofs that topped the towers, the place looked like a medieval fortress until one was close enough to see the Renaissance windows. Bruno drove slowly past the entrance to Henri's traditional farmhouse with outbuildings and barns, one that must now be the *chai* where he made his wines and another where he stored them.

Henri's vineyard looked old-fashioned to Bruno's eye. Well-drilled rows of vines, separated by strips of mown grass and gravel, were all the same height and bulk, which meant the vineyard was not organic. Bruno wondered just how many chemicals Henri used to get that disciplined but unnatural effect. Fewer and fewer of the Bergerac vineyards looked that way anymore, as more and more winemakers joined the organic revolution. He glanced up the slope, where most of the vines straggled and looked wilder, as nature intended. He wondered whether Henri's better wines came from the slopes, although they would have little protection from the chemicals that were pumped over the vines on the flat side of the road.

Outside Henri's farmhouse were a dusty

Toyota Land Cruiser, a Mercedes sedan that looked new and an older Renault Twingo. With no other car to be seen, he drove on to park in the entrance to a farm lane and kept an eye out for the gray Renault he knew Sabine would be driving. His phone buzzed.

"Is that you, Bruno?" came her voice. He explained where she'd find him. She had just turned off at Gardonne, on the main road from Bordeaux to Bergerac. He had arrived a little early, and she'd be with him in five minutes. While waiting, he tried to work out how best to handle the coming confrontation. It would have to be fast, just a simple and friendly question about his wine to ensure the real prize, a chance for Tante-Do to get her eyeballs on him. She should stay by the car while Yves and Sabine knocked on the front door and Bruno tried to get into the barn to see if Henri might be there. He'd better stay in the background, since Henri might just remember him wearing a police uniform at the wine fair in St. Denis.

When Sabine's car arrived, Bruno waved her down, climbed into the backseat and explained his plan. They drove into the courtyard, climbed out and Sabine and Yves walked slowly to the main door while

Tante-Do leaned against the car. Bruno tried the building on the left, which had double sliding doors, slightly open. He squeezed through, calling out Bazaine's name, and saw that this must be the *chai.* Six tall stainless-steel vats stood on one side, four on the other, everything spotlessly clean. There was no reply to his calls. A locked door on one side of the barn had a glass panel and seemed to lead into an empty office, from the little of the room that Bruno could see. He went back to the courtyard and across to the other barn, which was locked. He walked back to the car. Yves and Sabine were still waiting at the front door until it was opened by an overweight young woman with short blonde hair, who said, politely and loud enough for Bruno to hear, "We don't take visitors here at the vineyard."

"We heard from Hubert de Montignac in St. Denis that you make a very good reserve wine, and we'd like to buy some," Sabine said. "He told us you only sell it here."

"Bonjour, Mademoiselle Bazaine?" Yves asked, smiling and with a hand outstretched. "We've come here specially because Hubert told us your wine was worth the trip. Is Monsieur Bazaine here?"

"Sorry, but we don't —," she began and

then a tall, well-built young man with fair hair appeared behind her.

"I'm Monsieur Bazaine the younger, and my sister is right," he said. "We don't sell from here, only from the cooperative, and you can find our wines in most supermarkets." He began to close the door.

"Excuse us for interrupting your day," Sabine said in friendly tones. "But it's not the co-op wine we want, rather the special reserve you make. Perhaps your father could help us. Is he here? Monsieur de Montignac told us your father was very proud of it."

"We're all proud of it," said the young man. "Dad's not here right now." He paused, looking uncertainly from Yves and Sabine to Tante-Do and Bruno waiting by the car. Then he seemed to make a decision. "I'm sorry you had a wasted journey. Just wait here a moment."

He ducked back inside, leaving his sister on the doorstep, and Sabine asked her brightly, "Are you a winemaker, too?"

"I'm learning," she answered grumpily and then her brother reappeared, a bottle of red wine in his hand. He thrust it at Sabine and said, "Here, sorry we're busy, but this is the wine."

"How much do we owe you?" Yves asked, pulling out his wallet.

"Ten euros will do it," said the young man, and almost snatched the note from his hand, pulled his sister back and began to close the door.

"If it's as good as I hope, how do we buy more?" Sabine asked.

"Write to us. We sell mainly by mail. Thanks for coming." The door closed.

Yves and Sabine stared at each other, shrugged and returned to the car, displaying the bottle. It was labeled as a special reserve from four years earlier. Bruno knew it had been a decent year.

"That's a very strange way to treat customers," Bruno said loudly, but there was no reaction from the house. Tante-Do was already inside on the front passenger seat, and as Sabine drove off, Tante-Do turned to Bruno, removed her dark glasses and said, "That young man is the spitting image of his father thirty years ago. I'm sure of it."

"Look at this," Sabine said, handing Bruno a photocopy of a newspaper article with the headline "Love Blooms among the Vines," and a photo of a bride and her new husband, who was very clearly Henri — but it could have been the son they had just met.

"I spent hours at a microfilm reader yesterday going through old newspapers for the relevant time period," Sabine said. "I reckoned I'd have to start searching three months after the murder and the first six months of the following year. That's what I eventually came up with."

"Well done," said Bruno, impressed, and realizing that he should have thought of that. The caption to the photo gave Henri's original name, before he changed it: Henri Zeller. The name reminded Bruno of one of the Alsatian brasseries in Paris where he'd eaten a fine *choucroute royale.*

"What do we do now?" asked Tante-Do.

"We find J-J and check with him. It's his investigation," Bruno said, wondering if the radio news story the previous day had alerted Henri and induced him to disappear again. Yves called J-J, who answered that he was waiting in the car park at Monbazillac. Yves explained what had happened, and J-J suggested they join him. Bruno gave Sabine directions.

"Do you think he's fled?" J-J asked once they had joined him.

"I don't know. He could have been inside the house or just out shopping. I didn't see anyone working in the vines," Bruno said. "What did you learn at the co-op?"

"They confirmed that it was him in the photo, but that was all. He's a member of the co-op in good standing but seldom appears at meetings and refused all requests to go on the board or take any part in management. They called him a bit of a loner and said they used to deal with his wife. Now they deal mainly with his son, who's well liked and respected and knows the business — he took the wine course at the University of Bordeaux. Apparently Henri travels a bit as a wine consultant; they call it an oenologist. Maybe that's how he earned the money to expand the vineyard."

"Unusual for people to pay for a wine consultant who mostly makes wine for a co-op," Bruno said. "Customers usually want much better credentials than that. Did they say where he consults?"

"Canada was the only place they mentioned," J-J replied. "We've started checking on his passport and movements. I have his bank account details from the co-op, so we'll soon have his credit cards, cell phones, all the usual data. And one more thing, now that we have a photo for Max, the murder victim, I'll ask Interpol to try again on medical records for that unusual break in his leg. I'm told those data banks are a lot more complete than they used to be. Maybe we'll get lucky."

"Let's hope so," said Bruno. "What about Henri's income? Did you get to see the co-op accounts?"

"Yes, he seems quite wealthy. The co-op said he was the first of them to push for the bag-in-the-box and almost all his wine is now sold that way. You know the things, fifteen euros for a five-liter box. He gets just over a third of that, one euro ten per liter, and he usually produces about a quarter million liters a year. The co-op pays for the boxes, delivery and marketing, and he gets a share of the profits the co-op makes, which netted him another nine thousand euros last year."

"He has to pay for labor, the picking, his winemaking equipment, insurance, social costs, fertilizer and taxes," Bruno said. "But don't forget that every few years there's a hailstorm or some expensive blight or a drought, and if we don't get some rain soon he won't have much of a harvest this year. Still, he should usually be clearing close to a hundred thousand a year."

"Certainly more than you and I make combined," said J-J, shrugging. "He has no labor costs. His family helps him work the vines, and the grape picking is all done by the co-op machines. And you and I probably work longer hours. What's more, he drinks for free."

"We're in the wrong business," said

Bruno, laughing. "If it wasn't for the company, J-J . . ."

"Very funny," J-J replied. "Sabine can take Tante-Do back to Bordeaux. I'll get the Paris police looking into Henri's background, now that we have his real name. He was born there so they'll check his school records, get the address where he grew up and the names of any relatives, all the usual. They should have something for me on Monday."

"You still running a media blitz with the photos on Monday?" Bruno asked.

"We might as well. It can't hurt and it puts a spotlight onto him. And if it panics him into taking off, all the better. We'll have his credit card numbers, his passport and the details of his cars. He won't get far."

"What if he just uses cash to buy a train ticket to Italy or Spain?"

"And then where does Henri go?" J-J replied, staring out over the slope that led down to the wide plain of the Dordogne Valley, the slender spire of the great church of Bergerac on the far bank. "Henri's found a safe haven here that has sheltered him for the last thirty years. Do you think he's the type of professional criminal to have fabricated a second identity with a false passport, secret bank accounts, all that?"

"I don't know. It's unlikely but possible."
As Bruno spoke he knew that J-J was thinking aloud, but he felt he was at least a step behind the way J-J's mind was working. Bruno knew better than most that J-J's bullish manner and appearance concealed a profound and subtle intelligence. He'd been a successful detective for thirty years and had navigated the complexities of police politics to reach his current job. Bruno would never underestimate him.

"Do you think Henri's going to stay here and brazen it out, just plead that all your witnesses are mistaking him for someone else?" Bruno asked.

"Guilty or innocent, it could be his best bet, if he can bring forward someone who says they've known him since way back when they were kids together in Paris, and if he can come up with an alibi for the time of the murder." J-J's voice was thoughtful, almost detached, as though he were thinking of something else entirely. "Even if he admits to being Tante-Do's Henri, we still need evidence that he killed Max."

Bruno nodded. Identifying Henri was one thing. Proving that he was the one who had killed Max was something quite different.

"But if we can't prove that he was Max's killer, maybe if we look hard enough we can find something else." J-J turned to look at Bruno directly. "Any ideas?"

"None at all."

"You're the hunting-club man, Bruno. I'm surprised you didn't know that Henri is a member of the Pomport Club, just a few kilometers south of here. And he's a crack shot, they tell me."

"You've lost me, J-J. Where are you going with this?"

"Where did he learn to shoot? What was his military service? You still have that friendly contact in army records?" When Bruno nodded, J-J said, "Give him a call on Monday and see what you can find out."

"Will do. What do you do now?"

"I'll do the obvious. I go to Henri's house, show my police ID and ask for him. If he's not there, I ask where he is and when he'll be back. I leave my card and ask him to call me. If they ask why, I'll say I have some questions for him."

"You're a *commissaire,* the top detective in the *département,*" Bruno said. "That would scare anybody."

"You could be right, but it makes no difference if I send a junior. Henri will still end up talking to me. That will be just as scary if he only learns it's me when I walk into the interview room next week. He'll see my rank when he gets to see my card, presumably sometime later today. The sooner he learns that I'm interested in him, the more time he has to worry, perhaps even to panic. Never underestimate the panic factor in police work, Bruno. Over the years it's probably caught as many criminals as fingerprints."

CHAPTER 14

Alain and Rosalie had got a lot of sun on their canoe trip, their faces glowing red but nonetheless beaming with delight as they came hand in hand from the car to join Bruno on his terrace. Balzac darted from his spot by Bruno's feet to welcome them, circling around them twice and then standing before them appealingly, one paw raised, until Rosalie bent down to stroke him.

Bruno had spent two pleasant and calming hours weeding his garden, scything some long grass behind the house and cutting off the faded roses. He feared for his flowers if some rain did not come soon. For the past few days he had watered only the vegetables and had followed a tip from Marcel in the market. Bruno had planted discarded plastic bottles upside down at strategic points. He'd punched a very small hole in the various bottle caps, screwed them back on, cut off the bottoms of the bottles and then half filled each one. From the healthy look of his tomatoes, peas and lettuces this primitive drip irrigation seemed to work.

"Lemonade, coffee, tea?" he asked his guests. "We should leave for the baron's place in about half an hour. Do you want to shower first?"

"That's okay," said Rosalie. "We took a dip in the river before we returned the canoe. It was spectacular, those amazing castles, one after another, and that little village that clambered up the cliff was too pretty for words. And we saw them fire the smallest of the *trébuchets*. Very impressive. They said some of the damage to the castle was done by catapults like that."

"And how was Lascaux this morning?"

"Amazing," she said. "I had no idea that it was so beautiful and that those prehistoric people were so smart. The only way they could see to paint without covering all their chalk walls with soot was to invent a special kind of lamp that used a juniper twig as a wick in rendered reindeer fat. How long did it take to develop that? I'll never think of those people as primitive again."

Bruno smiled, accustomed to the enthusiasm of visitors, but still pleased. "There are many more caves worth a visit, twenty-four painted caves and over a hundred with various engravings. One is so big you take a train to get deep inside, and the walls are covered with mammoths."

"I told you we'd need more time here," Alain said, putting his arm around Rosalie's waist.

"On the way to the baron's place we'll stop to pick up a friend called Sabine, a young gendarme who's on temporary assignment here."

"I'm getting out of these bathing trunks I'm wearing under these slacks," said Alain. "We'll go up and change, but we won't be long."

The eyes of Sabine and Rosalie widened when they drove along the baron's driveway and saw his four-hundred-year-old home. It was a *chartreuse,* the local name for a building that was smaller than a château but larger than a manor house. The rear looked like a fortress, a fifty-meter stretch of stone wall with a tower at each end, a bleak façade broken only by a few windows, recently added. It formed one side of a square in the small hamlet that had grown up around the building, mainly cottages for families who had worked the land of the baron's ancestors.

By contrast, the front of the *chartreuse,*

framed by a long avenue of apple and walnut trees that led up to a thickly wooded slope, was open and welcoming. Tall windows suggested the height of the rooms within, and stone steps, wide at ground level but narrowing as they rose, led up to a venerable set of double doors studded with iron. The bottom half of the doors was much darker, and the baron claimed they were scorch marks from an attempt to burn out his ancestor in the turbulent years after the Revolution. Since that same ancestor had survived to become one of Napoléon's generals, the attack had been briskly defeated.

At some point large French windows had been installed on either side of these steps, and from one of them the baron emerged, carrying a tray of drinks and glasses, to welcome his guests. He put the tray down on a round metal table, painted white, which stood on a stone terrace that stretched along the whole front of the building. Big terra-cotta urns that reached above Bruno's waist were filled with bright red geraniums.

"Welcome," he said, advancing to greet the four of them with the stride of a much younger man. "Alain, it's good to see you again, and Bruno, please introduce me to this lovely young woman. If you are marrying Alain, my dear, then he's a lucky man. And Sabine, you must be the young gendarme of whom Bruno has spoken."

Then he sat on one of the garden chairs to greet Balzac, who seemed to assume that the baron was a member of the family, along with all the other friends of Bruno that Balzac saw almost every day and with whom he invariably spent his Monday evenings.

"Your welcome is as courtly as your home, monsieur," Rosalie said as a car horn tooted and Fabiola's Twingo swung into the driveway. Fabiola parked and her partner, Gilles, and Florence walked to the terrace as Pamela's elderly *deux-chevaux* then came into view, followed by the mayor's car. Balzac at once raced off to greet each of them, and not for the first time Bruno wondered if his dog's hearing was so acute that he could recognize people by the sound of their car engines.

"Looks like we're all here," the baron said, making introductions. "Bruno, would you take care of the drinks while I greet the others."

Three bottles, white, red and rosé from the town vineyard, stood on the tray with bowls of nuts and olives and a smaller bottle of cassis. Bruno began to serve, thinking it

247

might be time for Hubert and Julien to add a sparkling wine to the town's production. There were chairs enough for all on the terrace, but they gathered instead under the shade of a cypress tree. Balzac snuffled around the feet of each one of them, waiting for the inevitable snack that would come his way. Bruno served drinks while Rosalie and Alain met his friends and Sabine went around with the snacks.

"Make a note in your diary for Monday afternoon, Bruno," said the mayor. "We're having that forest fire rehearsal that was postponed last week, but it's going to be much bigger with some *pompier* experts, people from the other communes and the *préfecture.* Your colleagues from Les Eyzies and Montignac will also be there. It starts at two."

"I'll be there," said Bruno, handing the mayor a glass of kir. "Let's just hope the rehearsal never turns into a reality." He went back to the table to fill and serve more glasses and then managed to have a quiet word with Gilles.

"Have you and Jacqueline conferred on these articles you're writing on that spy business?" Bruno asked him. "It's tomorrow they come out, isn't it?"

"Yes, Jacqueline is in Monday's *Le Monde,*

which will be available in Paris late tomorrow afternoon. My piece goes up on the website at five tomorrow, with a longer piece with photos in next week's print edition."

"What photos have you found?" Bruno asked.

"Gisela, of course, sometimes called the spy of the century. Her real name was Gabriele Gast, who went from think tanks into West German intelligence, the BND." Gilles went on to explain that Gisela was an attractive woman, and there was a romantic angle with her Stasi handler. That made her story perfect for *Paris Match.*

"Then there was the biggest spy of all, Rainer Rupp, code name Topaz," Gilles went on. Rupp had worked at NATO headquarters in Brussels and photographed secret documents in his wine cellar at home. He had a British wife who tried to persuade him to stop but stayed loyal to him. He handed over the crown jewels, the locations of cruise and Pershing missiles, NATO's strategic plans and its assessment of what the Warsaw Pact could do. A lot of that material was given the Cosmic Top Secret classification, NATO's highest, and was sent to Moscow right away.

"Then I list some of the spies exposed in the Rosenholz dossier in various countries,"

Gilles went on. "This raises the obvious question: Why would there not be Stasi spies in France? Rupp was recruited when he was a young student leftist in 1968, when our own student revolt would have been a happy hunting ground for the Stasi and the KGB. Most of this stuff is available if you know where to look for it."

"What about Jacqueline's article?" Bruno asked.

"As you might expect, hers is much more policy based, on the implications of the continued lack of trust between Paris and Washington, with the Rosenholz dossier as Exhibit A. Predictably for *Le Monde,* her piece is aimed at the policy makers, whereas mine is aimed at ordinary people, the office worker on the Métro. It's the same story but with different targets, and you know how people always love to read spy stories. I threw in some stuff about how we expelled Dick Holm, the CIA station chief in Paris during the Clinton years, for running an operation against France."

He gave Bruno a shrewd glance. "Is this just gossiping for your own interest, or are you asking this on behalf of somebody?"

"A bit of both," Bruno acknowledged.

"I can guess who is interested," Gilles said, grinning. "It's not a problem for me if

I e-mail you my article tonight. It's already ancient history, anyway. I filed my final version just before I came here." He took out his phone, tapped a few buttons and said, "There you are. On its way to your private in-box. Say hello to Isabelle for me."

Bruno strolled discreetly into the baron's kitchen, read what Gilles had sent and forwarded it to Isabelle, with a note saying Gilles sent his regards. That was how it worked. Gilles had done Isabelle a favor and would doubtless expect one in return. Jacqueline would probably not be so helpful.

Back in the garden, Bruno went up to where she was chatting with Rosalie, Sabine and Pamela and asked if he might refresh their drinks. They handed him their glasses, he refilled them and, when handing them back, he managed to steer Jacqueline aside and ask if her *Le Monde* piece was running the next day.

"So they tell me. I hope it makes a stir," she said amiably.

"If it's anything like your remarks over dinner the other day, I'm sure it will," he said. "I never cease to be surprised at the way history thrusts its claws from the past into our present. It must be even stranger for you, a historian of the Cold War, to find it here again thirty years after it ended."

"If it has ended — that's the question," she said. "Every one of us here is a child of the Cold War, Bruno. It shaped us, defined our politics and reshaped our economies and our systems of government. Not just the Russians and Americans, but we in Europe in our own way also became national security states, each of us shaped by our own military-industrial complex. The past always lives on in very profound ways, particularly in our security agencies and defense bureaucracies."

"I remember once in Sarajevo, taking shelter in a bunker at the airport when the Serbs were shelling it, and I was reading a piece in *Le Monde* about the Cold War being over. It certainly didn't feel like it."

"I remember reading articles like that in those days," Jacqueline said with a chuckle. "I may even have written one or two suggesting that the Balkan wars were the sign of a return to the traditional wars of national interests."

"National interests never go away," said Bruno. "Just look at this Franco-American suspicion you're writing about."

"I think you might enjoy my *Le Monde* piece," she said. "I make the point that the Americans still assume that their interests are equally the interests of the other members of the NATO alliance, particularly with Russia making trouble again and China playing its own superpower games. In reality, most of us NATO allies have moved on, not just to our traditional national interests but to the new interest of our Europe."

"You may be a little premature in that judgment, even though they'll love to hear that in Brussels," he said.

"We'll see. But wouldn't you agree that it's better to be early in thinking publicly about these things rather than too late?"

"You're probably right. But there is such a thing as being right too soon. Didn't you write a book about those people who went to fight in Spain against Franco in the 1930s? Premature antifascists, you called them."

"I did, and if you recall my conclusion, I noted that some of those Spanish war veterans who came to France as refugees became a hard core of our own Resistance here in France in the big war."

Suddenly the baron was clapping his hands and calling, "Drink up, it's time to go to Audrix for dinner. I'll go with the mayor and Jacqueline. Bruno, you take Sabine, Alain and Rosalie and Balzac. You can show them where to park and save a place for Pamela when she finally limps in after her *deux-chevaux* makes its slow and painful way up the hill."

The tiny hilltop village of Audrix clustered around a small square that was dominated by the simple twelfth-century stone church on one side, facing the very small *mairie* on the other. To one side stood the local inn, the precisely named Auberge Médiévale, with a good restaurant where Bruno liked to eat on the terrace. To the other side was a road that was wide enough for a row of a score or so of stalls, selling the usual range of wines, cheeses, strawberries, grilled meats, ducks and chickens, salads and pastries that were common to all the night markets of the region.

Some night markets liked to offer different foods, like St. Denis's stalls of Vietnamese, Caribbean, Moroccan, West African and Indian-style food from Mauritius, gifts of the old French colonial empire for which Bruno felt grateful. Audrix remained proudly traditional; the specialties were dishes based around roasting chickens and barbecued steaks along with snails from a local snail farm and raw foie gras sautéed with a sauce of honey and balsamic vinegar. And then there was the village bread oven, a beehive-shaped structure of stone which baked fresh bread and pizza, all surrounded by a paved space without walls but covered by a much wider roof supported by wooden beams. This was where the musicians played and the visitors danced. Thanks to the passionate Greens on the local council, the village had banned the use of plastic plates and utensils, so beneath the *mairie* was a stall where crockery, glasses and cutlery could be hired for a modest deposit.

When Pamela arrived, Bruno and his group strolled up from the parking area in the fields, pausing to admire the gigantic straw sculptures of a mammoth and a warrior of ancient Gaul, at which Balzac always paused to lift his leg. Bruno assumed it was his dog's way of paying respect to such magnificent structures. The baron and his friends had secured a large table on a patch of higher ground beside the *mairie* and had spread out their own plates, glasses and cutlery from their various picnic hampers. Bottles of wine had already been bought and opened. Florence was standing in line for salads, Fabiola for cheese, Gilles for roast chicken and lamb chops, Jack Crimson for bread and pizza and Jacqueline for the foie gras. Everybody had put twenty euros into the communal pot and planned to spend any remainder on dishes of strawberries and cream.

The musicians were local favorites, a band composed of an accordion, a guitar, drums, a saxophone and a woman in a blonde wig who dressed and performed like a prewar torch singer. They made a living summers by playing each night at a different market in the region, offering popular French classics of cabaret numbers mixed in with bal musette dance music and romantic ballads. Bruno enjoyed it hugely, making a point of dancing with each of the women in their group, and with several more, friends whom he came across while strolling past the food stalls.

After his first stroll, trying to decide what he would eat, Bruno went around the rear of the church. Balzac followed him and at once joined some children playing on the grass. Bruno waved at two of them whom he recognized from his tennis classes. And then he used his burner phone to call Isabelle on the private number.

"Thanks for the *Paris Match* piece," she said. "And give my thanks to Gilles. There's nothing much that's new in it, but he certainly makes it all sound sensational. Maybe he should try a new career as a spy novelist. It's Jacqueline's piece I'm more worried about."

"It's all policy based, Franco-American relations," Bruno replied. "But it all hinges on Gilles's point that the Stasi were recruiting among the student left in Germany in '68 and they'd almost certainly be trying the same in France. It seemed a bit odd to me since any of that generation would be in their seventies by now and long since retired. Other than some cerebral stuff about the new Cold War and national versus European interests, that seems to be it. I shouldn't imagine that will cause you any real problems."

"That's not what they're saying in the Élysée," she said. "Anyone recruited back in the sixties could have recruited promising candidates from the next generation of bright youngsters they were supposed to be training and supervising. There are already people warning that this could lead to a witch hunt in the bureaucracy, sniffing out suspected spies and sleeper agents among the *énarques,*" she added, referring to the graduates from the elite ENA, the École Nationale d'Administration, who filled the higher ranks of the state bureaucracy and the boards of directors of France's top corporations.

"But all these people are routinely vetted by our own security people, just in case,"

Bruno replied.

"Yes, but the point Gilles missed in what he wrote about Rainer Rupp was that the guy was an idealist. He wasn't a passionate supporter of East Germany, far from it. He just thought that the Cold War arms race could be made less dangerous if each side knew what the other was doing and thinking and convinced himself that he was in the right place to do that. He even claimed he helped prevent World War Three by reassuring the Warsaw Pact that NATO was not planning a surprise attack back in '83, when Ronald Reagan was talking about the Evil Empire and Star Wars and scaring the pants off the Kremlin."

"These are very different times," Bruno said.

"Up to a point, Bruno, but the current American administration is not exactly reassuring. It's no secret that most European capitals worry that we're all skating on very thin ice, whether we look at trade, at security policy, arms control, relations with Russia, the Middle East, China, I could go on. Some of the advisers around our president are almost panicking about it."

"This is all way above my head," Bruno said.

"Yes, but you understand why the Rosenholz dossier has suddenly become a very hot topic here in Paris. I have to go but thanks, and kisses to you and Balzac."

Bruno stood a moment looking out over the valley, the sounds of some old dance music drifting to him from the far side of the church, accompanied by the scents of different foods from the night-market stalls. The contrast between the innocent pleasures of this peaceful village deep in the rural heart of France and the mood and politics in Paris that Isabelle had described disturbed him deeply. It suggested a vast and dismaying gap in perceptions and concerns between the Parisian elites and the people who voted them into office and entrusted them with power.

As a very minor and tiny cog in the vast machinery of the French administration, Bruno was scared by the scale of this gap. Nor was Bruno at all comfortable at having shared his friends' articles and views with Isabelle. He told himself that he'd only passed on Gilles's piece with his tacit permission; Gilles was familiar with this game of complicity between media and officialdom. And while he had shared nothing of what Jacqueline had written, he'd passed on her views, not that they were secret. Everything would soon be available to anyone who bought *Le Monde* or *Paris Match.*

That did not stop Bruno from feeling he had participated in something underhand. It was not so much guilt as feeling bad about making use of people he considered his friends, and thus people who had reason to trust him and the right to assume that they could converse with him in confidence. And he could not fool himself by claiming to have acted from patriotism nor from some sense of duty to the French state. Not at all. He had acted simply to render a small service to Isabelle, a woman he would rather not disappoint.

Putain, it was a lot more than that. He still loved her, still thrilled like a schoolboy at the sound of her voice, still dreamed of somehow squaring the impossible circle of contrasting ambitions that kept them apart. Even in those blissful moments when they shared the same bed, they had different dreams. Perhaps he should force himself to end it. It would hurt, he knew, but pain eases with time. He would someday emerge from such a grim ordeal of self-denial and heartbreak. He'd be bruised but free to look elsewhere and perhaps to give his heart fully and honestly to another.

He breathed out a long sigh. As he'd told

Isabelle, this was all far above his own head, and Bruno knew he was hungry. He went back to buy another bottle of wine from the woman from Domaine de la Voie Blanche, who made the wine the baron had offered for his blind tasting. And that, Bruno recalled as he tried to decide between the foie gras and the lamb chops, had been the dinner when Jacqueline had first talked of the Rosenholz dossier.

Enough of that, he told himself. This was a Saturday night. He went back to the table to invite Sabine to dance. Food could wait.

CHAPTER 15

The next morning there was no sound from the guest bedroom upstairs when Bruno rose and took Balzac out for their morning run. He'd bought a couple of extra loaves in Audrix the previous evening so he could make breakfast at home. Looking in at the chicken coop on his return he saw that his hens had been particularly generous that morning, with ten eggs to cradle in his arms as he went into the kitchen. He left six out and put four into the large crockery bowl he kept in his pantry. He then went out with Balzac to his row of truffle trees and began tapping the ground with the long twig he called his wand as he watched for the shimmering dance of a rising fly.

"*Cherche,* Balzac, *cherche,*" he said, and the hound padded forward to sniff at the point where Bruno had placed his wand and then began to paw gently at the ground. Bruno moved him to one side and scraped with his trowel until a summer truffle, perhaps the size of a golf ball, emerged. That would do. Usually he'd have put it with the eggs for a couple of days so the scent could seep through the porous eggshells, but he'd grate this one onto the omelette he planned.

He showered and dressed, set the table on the terrace, brought out butter and his homemade apricot jam, squeezed orange juice and, as he went back inside to make the coffee, he heard the shower running upstairs. His guests were awake. He went to the garden to pick and wash a small bunch of fresh parsley. He peeled and chopped two cloves of garlic, brushed the truffle clean, shaved off half-a-dozen slices and waited until his guests descended before cracking the eggs and announcing that their breakfast would be an *omelette aux truffes*. He whisked the eggs, added salt, pepper and the remainder of Stéphane's cream before pouring a little olive oil and dropping a large pat of truffled butter into his frying pan. He tossed in the garlic and as it sizzled he added the egg mix and began to make his omelette, lifting and then lowering the pan to spread the liquid and running a wooden spatula around the sides to stop it from sticking.

When he judged it to be almost done,

Bruno grated the remainder of the truffle onto a surface that was still slightly liquid, folded the omelette over, adding the slices of truffle, and took it out to the terrace. He tore apart the parsley leaves and sprinkled them on top and served while Alain broke off chunks of bread for each of them and Rosalie poured out the coffee.

"A perfect country breakfast," said Rosalie, tapping her stomach when the omelette had gone along with all the bread and a third of the jar of Bruno's apricot jam. "I'll go on a diet when we get back."

"And we missed our morning run," said Alain.

Rosalie smiled and put her hand on his and gave him a dreamy, loving look that suggested to Bruno that they had enjoyed a very different form of exercise this morning already. He smiled at the thought, happy that Alain had found such a suitable partner.

"I think you're well suited, you two," he said. "I look forward to seeing more of you when you're out of the air force and married and settled somewhere nearer."

"We've been talking about that. There's a vocational school in Sarlat we might consider, as well as the one in Bergerac. We heard about it over dinner last night from Florence. And she said we might be able to do as she did, earning the teaching diploma while actually working."

"But Florence already had a university diploma," Rosalie added. "Still, she said vocational schools were more interested in craft skills, and she asked me to send her the qualifications we got from the air force. She's on the executive committee of the teachers' union and says she'll try to make it work. The mayor said he'd help if he could."

"It makes sense to have a good look around," Bruno said. "You know what they say in the army — time spent in reconnaissance is rarely wasted. Sarlat will be full of tourists, but if we leave now we'll beat the rush. It's a handsome old town and worth seeing for its own sake."

Soon after, they set off in Bruno's Land Rover, Rosalie with Balzac in the back. She and Alain began looking up to admire the great overhang of the towering cliffs that sheltered the town of Les Eyzies. They were in Sarlat not long before nine, and the town was starting to stir, with stalls of cheese, *saucissons* and souvenirs being set out in front of shops. The streets were not yet crowded, so they could admire the town's old center.

Other than the shopwindows, it was a

place that seemed barely changed over the past four hundred years. Renaissance town houses led to a grand square and cathedral and narrow alleys that were full of restaurants and shops selling local delicacies. Bruno took them around the back of the cathedral to see the Merovingian royal tombs from the centuries after the Roman Empire fell, and to the Lanterne des Morts, a tall, conical tower built eight centuries earlier from whose top a lantern glowed each night to mark the place of the dead.

"St. Bernard came here to preach the Second Crusade," Bruno said, warming to his role as guide. "And there are Knight Templar signs engraved inside the tower. This was where the rebellion against English rule began in the Hundred Years' War. The town was a Catholic stronghold in the Wars of Religion and went through a bitter siege but held out. There's a lot of history here."

Alain stopped to look at a real-estate agent's window, and Rosalie picked up a photocopied leaflet that listed local houses for sale. They stopped for coffee at a place Bruno saw had a bowl of water outside for customers' dogs, so Balzac could drink, too. Bruno glanced at the copy of that morning's *Sud Ouest* that lay on the counter. A third of the front page was covered with the composite photo of Henri with the headline "Unsolved Murder — Do You Know This Man?"

Inside was Philippe's photo of Elisabeth Daynès at the Les Eyzies museum standing beside the Neanderthal skull she had reconstructed. Alongside it was a photo of the skull Virginie was working on. Although it was unfinished, to Bruno's eyes it was already uncannily like the composite photo of Max that he had helped put together. The caption read, "At last, after thirty years, we reveal the process of rebuilding the face of the unknown victim."

Bruno nodded approval, thinking that J-J's media blitz seemed to be going well. He wondered if he'd had similar success with the national press and TV. He called Virginie to tell her how impressed he was but had to make do with leaving a message on her answering service. Immediately afterward his phone rang again. It was J-J.

"I was just thinking about you," he said. "I'm in Sarlat, admiring your coverage in *Sud Ouest.* Did you have any luck with Henri?"

"Yes, he's coming to the Bergerac police station for an interview tomorrow at ten," J-J replied, sounding very cheerful. "Do you want to be there? Sabine is bringing

Tante-Do for the confrontation. And our hotline has already had two calls saying it's Henri Bazaine. I think we'll get a few more after the responses come in from the TV news programs."

"Great. I'll see you before ten tomorrow in Bergerac." He ended the call, picked up his coffee and joined his friends outside.

"I mean it about wanting one of Balzac's pups when we get out of the air force and find a place of our own," Alain said. He gently scratched the area where Balzac's silky ears joined his pointed skull, and the dog groaned softly with pleasure as they sat on some spindly chairs outside the coffee shop.

"That's agreed," Bruno said. "I thought I'd show you one or two more sights and then take you to the town vineyard just outside St. Denis. We're proud of it. We can have a light lunch there and taste our wines before you have to get back to the base. Have you some kind of curfew?"

"No, but it's at least a three-hour drive and we want to be back in time for the evening meal at the base, which means putting on our uniforms. The town vineyard sounds like a good plan."

"I really like it around here," said Rosalie. "We haven't quite ruled out moving to

Bordeaux, where we'd have a lot more options with technical schools. The house prices look steep, though. And with you nearby, we'd have a ready-made social life if we moved here."

"You don't want to go back to Normandy?" Bruno asked.

"No, the weather's better down here. Our farm was sold when my parents split up, and the family is spread out all over the place. I've got a sister who's a surgical nurse in the South Pacific, in Nouvelle Calédonie, where we're planning our honeymoon, and a brother who works in insurance in Paris."

"Well, you'll both be more than welcome if you want to move to this area," Bruno said as he looked around at the thickening flocks of tourists assembling in groups behind guides lifting colored ribbons on poles. "The crowds are starting to move in, so let's head back and I'll show you one of my favorite old castles on the way."

He took them to Commarque, a medieval fortress founded by Charlemagne and built up over the centuries to become one of the largest castles in Europe. They walked down the path through the woods until they reached the valley floor, and suddenly there it stood, the great walls and tower standing proudly against the sky. Children were trying their hand at archery farther down the valley. Beyond them the special breed of cattle that thrived on marshland was grazing among the several tiny rivulets to which the River Beune had shrunk. Bruno told the story of the dead woman he'd found at the bottom of the cliff on which the tower stood, and the Templar remains that had been unearthed in one of the caves beneath the castle.

"I think that was in the paper, something to do with Arab terrorists. I remember reading about it, just about the time Alain and I were getting together," said Rosalie. "They had your photo in the paper, and that was when Alain told me you were his cousin."

"It's quite a place," said Alain, looking up. "I'd like to come back here and take a good look, climb up to the top of that tower. There must be a terrific view."

"There certainly is," said Bruno. "It was built to be high enough so that signals could be sent by beacon across to Sarlat. The hills were bare of trees in those days. They were all cut down for charcoal to feed the forges around here that were busy making swords and armor for the knights. Much of the land around is full of iron ore. Those cave paintings you saw used the iron-bearing clay to get the red pigments, and around St. Denis they were still making cannons for warships in Napoléon's time. They used to ship them down the river to Bordeaux."

They drove back to Les Eyzies, crossed one of the great bends of the River Vézère and then a second at Campagne — "Another château," Rosalie announced — and through St. Denis to the town vineyard.

The vines spread out along the hillside, hectare after hectare, and Bruno pointed out first the small château that was at the heart of the terrain where Julien had lived when trying to make a success of it as both vineyard and hotel. Overstretched and in debt, and distracted by his wife's terminal illness, Julien had been rescued by the mayor, Hubert and other local businessmen who had bought out his debt and knuckled down to make the new town vineyard a going concern. Bruno had played a minor role in the saga, sufficient to get him awarded some shares and an appointment to the board of directors. He had used his savings to buy more shares and took great pride in the vineyard's progress.

They found Julien and Hubert in the big barn that was now the *chai,* where the wine was made and bottled. They were looking worried but cheered up at the sight of Bruno and warmly greeted Alain and Ro-

271

salie and led them across to a modest table that was the best St. Denis could offer as a tasting counter. Despite the mayor's best efforts, the plan for a vineyard visitors' center was still on the drawing board.

After greeting them all, with a special pat and a bowl of water for Balzac, Hubert poured out small glasses of the previous year's dry white for each of them, explaining that it was a classic blend of sauvignon blanc and semillon grapes.

"It's three euros twenty a bottle, but you can have Bruno's discount, three euros even," said Julien. "Or we offer a five-liter box at fifteen euros, with Bruno's discount. That's a good buy."

"I could drink a lot of this," said Rosalie. "It's refreshing and has a lot of fruit without being sweet. And I like the name, Demoiselle de la Vézère. Tell me, what's this dry weather doing to the vines this summer?"

"It varies," Julien replied. "The old vines have sunk deep roots and can take water from far below the surface. You know, a bit of stress makes for better wine. But a lot of the young vines we've planted over the past few years are really suffering. Hubert and I have just been talking about it. We certainly need rain, the sooner the better."

"What kind of wine do you usually prefer?" asked Hubert.

"I'm no expert," Alain replied with a smile. "Red with meat, white with fish and after the first couple of sips of the stuff they serve us in the air force, I'm damned if I can tell the difference."

"*Mon Dieu,* Bruno, your cousin's an honest man," said Hubert. "Not many of our customers would admit that. See what you think of this one, Alain. We call it Seigneur de la Vézère, and it's our standard red. It's two years old, half Cabernet Sauvignon with a quarter each of Merlot and Malbec. The same price as the white."

"It's a lot smoother than what they serve at our canteen," Alain replied after taking a sip. "I like that."

"Now try this one, the same blend of grapes but from our older vines, and it has spent six months in oak barrels. See if you can taste the difference."

Rosalie and Alain sipped and nodded. "It leaves a lovely taste in my mouth," she said.

Alain agreed adding, "I agree, and it has more flavor. How much is that?"

"Four euros fifty a bottle but you can buy five liters in a box for twenty-five euros, and it stays in top form for six weeks, two months if you keep it somewhere cool."

"Why is it more expensive?" Rosalie

asked, reading out the name on the bottle, Chevalier de la Vézère.

"Oak barrels are expensive," said Julien. "Even the cheapest ones are more than six hundred euros each, and the really good ones from old wood with a tight grain are a thousand or more. What's more, you don't want to use them for more than three years, four at most. Then we sell them secondhand to Scotland for their whiskey."

"Really?" Rosalie asked. "But whiskey's a spirit. Does it change in the barrel?"

"The color changes most. Like most spirits, whiskey is colorless at first. The color comes from the wood, but you get a slightly different flavor from a sherry barrel from Spain than you do from one of our barrels. And that's not just the wine, it's the toasting. Look," he said, pointing to a row of barrels. "These are marked NOISETTE, but they're made of oak, not hazelwood. The term comes from the color of the toasting. All barrels are toasted on the inside. It used to be done over an open flame, but these days they use a blowtorch. *Noisette* is a very light toasting, but some heavy wines like a Syrah or a Malbec from Cahors benefit from a much darker toasting."

"Well, we've learned something today, and I think we've found the wines we'll serve at our wedding," said Alain. "I'm driving, so no more tasting for me, but we'll buy a box of the white and another of the good red."

"When's the happy day?" Julien asked.

"As soon as I get my promotion. It should come through within the next month or two," Rosalie said. "Then I'll be the same rank as Alain, and we can marry and move into married quarters. These wines are for our engagement party. You'll come, won't you, Bruno?"

"Of course, and we look forward to your being regular customers in the future," he said.

"And I'll send along a bottle of champagne with him to help you celebrate, with my compliments," Hubert added.

"Good luck with the rain," Rosalie said as Alain paid for his boxes and Bruno told Hubert they were heading for lunch at the Domaine.

"We only want something light," she added. "Bruno made us one of his truffle omelettes for breakfast."

They ate on the paved terrace behind the Domaine with a view over the swimming pool and tennis courts to beyond the gardens and parkland: *salade chaude aux gésiers* for her, a *confit de canard* with salad for Alain, and Bruno chose a *salade chèvre.*

He and Rosalie shared a small carafe of the town white, and Alain drank mineral water.

"What does it mean, your being a director of the vineyard?" she asked.

"Lots of meetings, at least once a month," he replied. "Keeping an eye on the finances, and last month we agreed to postpone building the new visitors' center until we see how this year's *récolte* comes out. If we get no rain, we'll need to economize. The best meeting was when we chose the names for the wines. Then there is the marketing strategy to discuss, which I don't know much about. But I did push hard for our wines to be on sale at all the *marchés nocturnes* in the region because they're less expensive than most. We only charge six euros a bottle when most vineyards want eight or ten. And we now provide the house wines for several of our local restaurants."

"It's a real surprise, Bruno. I never thought of you as a businessman."

"I'm not," he replied, laughing. "I'm a country policeman trying to do what's best for our town. Hubert and Julien really run the show."

Back at Bruno's home, their bags packed and loaded in the car with the wine, Bruno embraced them both, saying that they would always be welcome in St. Denis and promised he'd keep an eye out for a possible home for them. Rosalie crouched down, followed by Alain, to say their own farewells to Balzac. To Bruno's approval, they seemed to enjoy the generous lick of affection the hound bestowed on each of them. Being Balzac, he gave Rosalie a second and even more enthusiastic slathering and watched with Bruno as they drove off.

CHAPTER 16

The next morning at the Bergerac police station, Bruno was drinking coffee with J-J, Sabine and Tante-Do and leafing through the national newspapers. There were only some small stories with photos of Henri on the inside pages. Save for the local and regional press and TV, J-J's vaunted media blitz had been something of a disappointment. Most of the papers focused instead on the new scandal of possible German spies in France, following up on Jacqueline's op-ed article. The reports usually began by citing *Le Monde* but then went on to cannibalize Gilles's post on the *Paris Match* website, repeating the names of spies and even printing the photo portraits he had used.

"Do we need a new witch hunt against the left?" demanded *Libération,* the daily that seemed to Bruno to have one foot anchored in the socialist center-left and the other one waving out around the various anticapitalist sects, militant feminists and even more militant vegetarians and environmentalists. "Better late than never for a housecleaning of security risks," suggested the center-right *Le Figaro*. "Reds under our beds?" asked the populist *Aujourd'hui*.

"Those damn friends of yours have stolen my media campaign, Bruno," J-J grumbled, but his heart wasn't in it. He kept glancing at the clock in the borrowed office, and his eyes were bright at the promised confrontation of Tante-Do with Henri. He was also pleased when Bruno informed him that his predecessor, Joe, had also recognized Henri's photo and was prepared to testify that he recalled seeing Henri, Max and Tante-Do together at the Félibrée.

J-J had already made them rehearse their opening gambit twice. The moment the desk sergeant downstairs announced Henri's arrival, Sabine and Tante-Do were to stroll slowly and casually along the long corridor. That would give Tante-Do a good twenty seconds to take a careful look at Henri to confirm his identity and then to greet him by name as an old friend. J-J would take it from there.

That was the plan, but it did not work out that way. Henri was not alone. He came with a lawyer. And not just any lawyer, but one of a new breed, Pierre Perle, who liked to be known as the People's Pierre. A bouncy and aggressive advocate who seemed to have learned his trade from American TV courtroom dramas, he had a genius for publicity. He also had formidable legal credentials from the University of Bordeaux as one of the top law graduates of his year and as the author of a best-selling book, *It's Your Law — and How to Make It Work for You.*

"This is outrageous," Perle almost shouted after the brief moment of stunned silence in the corridor after Tante-Do marched up to Henri and embraced him, saying, "*Salut,* Henri. It may have been a long time, but you haven't changed a bit. You're still a handsome devil."

"This is a trap, a shameful ambush of an honest citizen who has come here to perform his civic duty," Pierre shouted as Henri looked stunned, trapped in Tante-Do's embrace. "I'll complain to the courts. Commissaire Jalipeau, you should be ashamed of yourself."

Bruno saw with a start that Philippe Delaron, obviously tipped off to witness this moment, was standing on the stairs, putting aside his camera to start scribbling in his notebook. J-J merely smiled, then brought his hands together three times, very slowly, in a mockery of applause.

"There you go again, Pierre," J-J said, "making it all about you instead of about your client and whether he can help our own humble attempt to find out how a young man was murdered thirty years ago." He turned to Henri. "Monsieur Bazaine, thank you for coming to see us. I hate to interrupt that touching reunion with an old flame of yours, but perhaps you would be happier discussing this in the privacy of an office." J-J paused and then threw the People's Pierre a contemptuous glance, adding, "Although I'm sure your lawyer would prefer to have it in the middle of the market."

J-J opened the office door and gestured to the others to precede him. When Henri and his lawyer were seated before the desk, he stood facing them. "Again, thank you for being here. Allow me to introduce the chief of police of the Vézère Valley, Bruno Courrèges, on whose turf the murder took place, and Sergeant Castignac, our liaison with the gendarmes."

"And what have the gendarmes got to do with this?" the lawyer asked.

"They helped disinter the body and examine the scene of the murder, and Sergeant Castignac has unearthed their contemporary reports. She has also assisted in our research into the St. Denis Félibrée, during which we believe the murder occurred. You recall the Félibrée, Monsieur Bazaine?"

"My client has no recollection of the event," said Pierre.

"Despite the photographic evidence that he was present and in the company of the murdered man, and all this confirmed by contemporary witnesses?" J-J asked calmly, taking his seat and opening a fat file that Henri was eyeing with some concern. Bruno suspected J-J had padded it with several pages of less-than-relevant material.

"Photographs that were obviously concocted long after the event," Pierre shot back. "I'll ask the court to rule against their being admissible as evidence."

"How fortunate then that we have some living witnesses, one of them a successful businesswoman of unquestioned probity who has identified him," J-J said.

"You mean that harpy you launched at us in the corridor?"

"Harpy?" J-J raised his eyebrows. "Tut-tut, Pierre, such outrageously sexist terms don't do you credit. I'm appalled to hear you speak that way about a woman who obviously cherishes some tender memories of your client in his younger days. I think you should apologize to Sergeant Castignac here. Heaven knows what your female clients would think."

"I fear the woman must have mistaken me for someone else," said Henri, the first time he'd spoken. He had a harsh, almost hoarse voice, but his face was expressionless. "I have no recollection of her."

To Bruno, who had trawled through so many photos, this was evidently the same man. His hair color and eyes, the set of his mouth and jaw, his height and build, all matched those of his younger self. And as Bruno studied him, he noticed that his ears were unusually wide and set very close to his head, something that also matched the photos he had picked out.

"May I see your identity card, monsieur?" J-J asked, raising a hand when the lawyer started to object. "We can hardly eliminate your client from our inquiries if we can't verify who he is."

" 'Henri Thorez Bazaine, born October fifteenth, 1968, Belleville, Paris,' " J-J read aloud as he copied the details onto a sheet of paper in the file before him. He looked up and said casually, "Thorez is an unusual name. Would it have any connection to

Maurice Thorez, the old Communist Party leader? Ah well, Belleville was the heart of the old Red Belt even though these days it's become very trendy and gentrified, I'm told. What was your address there?"

"I was raised in a municipal orphanage named for Paul Lafargue, on the avenue Jean Jaurès," Henri said.

J-J asked for the name of each school Henri had attended, primary, *collège* and then vocational school. Henri had not gone to a lycée, which would have put him on a university track. Instead he'd attended a vocational school, learning general construction and electronics, and had been an apprentice with the works department of his local *mairie* in Paris. J-J asked for more details: how long he'd been an apprentice; who his teachers were and who supervised his work; how much he was paid by the *mairie;* when and why he'd stopped working for the *mairie.*

"Are you sure all this is necessary?" the lawyer asked.

"One never knows what is and isn't relevant until we check," J-J replied blandly. "And now, Monsieur Bazaine, can you tell us where you were in the first days of July of 1989?"

Henri looked at his lawyer, who shrugged.

"I don't recall exactly. It was too long ago. Probably hitchhiking somewhere in central France, heading for the vineyards to get some work picking grapes. I was aiming for the Bordeaux region but got a lift to Bergerac, so that's where I stayed."

"The first few days of July would have been a couple of months too early for picking grapes."

"I earned some money washing cars for tourists on the quayside until it was time for the harvest. I worked with a guy called Gérard Follet and we're still friends. These days he runs half a dozen automatic car washes in Bergerac and Ste. Foy and he remembers working with me."

"One of our witnesses, a farmer near Vergt, distinctly recalls you and your friend Max picking strawberries with him on his father's farm in the last week of June. Is he making it up, is that your story?"

"Must be mistaken identity," said Henri. "I never knew a guy called Max. But I can understand people making mistakes if this Max was around the area with a guy who looked like me. And I accept that there's a resemblance from the photos in the newspapers. But that's all it is, a resemblance, from three decades ago."

"I think we're finished here, Monsieur le

Commissaire," said the lawyer. "My client came here voluntarily, answered your questions and accepted that he bears a resemblance to your suspect. We conclude that you and your witnesses have all made an honest mistake and that should be the end of the matter."

"No so fast, Pierre. Naturally, we'll have to check out some parts of your client's story, and I find it hard to believe that so many witnesses have all made the same mistake. Bruno, do you have any questions for Monsieur Bazaine?"

"Yes, one or two. The first one was where you performed your military service."

"I was excused for medical reasons as asthmatic. The illness still troubles me. What else?"

"Your work as a wine consultant surprises me," Bruno added. "It's very unusual to be a professional *oenologue* whose own vineyard mainly makes cheap wines for a co-op. How do you explain that?"

"That's not the only wine I make," Henri replied, clearly stung by Bruno's mocking tone. "And it's not as easy as you might think to make a consistent and decent wine year after year for the mass market. That's a skill people want to learn, and they're prepared to pay me for it."

"And where are these clients of yours who are willing to pay you to teach them how to succeed with mass-market wines?"

"I protest," interrupted the lawyer. "These questions are entirely irrelevant to the matter before us."

"I have an important client in Canada," Henri said, raising his hand to silence his lawyer. "I'm advising him on which wines he should plant on the northern shore of Lake Ontario, which is becoming interesting wine country because of climate change. More and more of us here in the area have been experimenting with different varieties of grapes, so we've built up a lot of expertise that clients are prepared to pay for."

"I think that's enough of these irrelevant questions," said the lawyer.

"Who is your doctor?" Bruno went on, ignoring the lawyer's objection. "We should check on this asthma condition. I'd have thought the chemicals you spray on your grapes could be a problem for you."

"That's more than enough," said the lawyer, rising. "Since you have evidently exhausted your relevant questions I see no reason to waste my client's time further with these irrelevant ones. And in the future any questions for my client should come first to me. Come along, Monsieur Bazaine, we're leaving."

"I'll be in touch," J-J said cheerfully as they left. Once the door closed behind them, he looked at Bruno and Sabine. "That went pretty well, I think. Did you note that he swallowed my suggestion that he was here in the first few days of July. I'd expected him to say he wasn't even near here at that time. He slipped up there, but maybe he knew we had enough witnesses who recall seeing him. And he's clearly nervous about this — otherwise he wouldn't have hired the People's Pierre."

"I'm sorry, sir, but I can't understand why you're so confident," said Sabine, a little hesitantly. "He just stonewalled you."

"But he gave us enough to start checking and verifying. We'll find people he was at school with and at the orphanage. We could well find that was where he met Max, even though he denied knowing him. Detective work is mainly about this sort of detail, and it usually pays off. Sabine, once you've taken Tante-Do back, perhaps you could start with those schools he attended, see if there are any class photos and if any teachers are still alive. Then track down his old classmates. Bruno, have a word with that Belleville *mairie,* if you would, for the orphanage records. I'll have my team check his car-wash story and the local doctors for his claim to have asthma, although I don't believe a word of it. I'll see how many more identifications we have from the media."

"I can't stay long, J-J," Bruno said. "I have to attend a forest fire rehearsal in St. Denis this afternoon."

Bruno found a spare desk with a phone, found a number for the Paris *mairie* and asked for the mayor's secretary, explaining his task.

"I don't think we can be much help," she said. "Ever since the old Communist Neanderthals lost control of this arrondissement, we've had dreadful trouble trying to make sense of the old files. They destroyed a lot, deliberately burning whole sections of the archive trying to cover their tracks or making it difficult for their successors. That included a lot of budget accounts, school records, all sorts of special funds for labor relations, international links, so-called summer schools that seem to have been Communist holiday camps. Even the births, deaths and marriage registrations had huge gaps."

"What about the Paul Lafargue orphanage?" he asked. "We're trying to check the background of a suspect in a murder inquiry who claims he lived there."

"I've never heard of it, which doesn't mean it didn't exist. Hang on a minute, I'm just calling up on my computer the index we made of the archives and I've found a reference to it — but the note says all the files are missing. Shall I pass you on to our archives department? They may be able to tell you more."

The archives people were friendly but unable to be of much help. They did check on the apprenticeships record and found the name of Henri Thorez Zeller. He was listed as attending the local vocational school for four years beginning in 1985 when he'd have been aged sixteen. He'd started doing three days a week of studies and two days working as an apprentice. In his fourth year he was doing one day a week at the school and the rest of his apprenticeship at the public works department. The file said his marks had varied between good and very good and that he'd graduated as a qualified construction electrician in June of 1989.

"Do you have an address for him?" Bruno asked.

"The Lafargue orphanage," said the archivist. "We think it closed a couple of years after Zeller left, when Jacques Chirac was mayor of Paris and began cleaning up some of the old Communist strongholds. We have no files at all on the orphanage."

"Any health records for this guy? He's supposed to have been spared military service because of asthma."

"I doubt if these guys would have put an asthmatic into public works, even as an apprentice, but we don't have those records. Maybe the army can help you."

"Why would all these archives have been destroyed? Any idea?"

"Some of it was inefficiency. But a lot of it was covering up corruption, jobs for the boys that didn't involve any actual work except what they called political organization. There were solidarity funds which filed no accounts, public housing for *mairie* workers who never seem to have paid rent, that kind of thing. And a lot of incompetence was involved as well. Still, your man Zeller was at the vocational school, so at least you have that."

"What about his classmates? Do you have registers for them? I'm particularly interested in the murder victim, first name Max. We know the two of them were traveling together around here in June or July of 1989."

"I can have a look and get back to you."

"Many thanks, and good luck with cleaning up those archives," Bruno said, giving his phone number and e-mail address and ending the call. He quickly wrote a note for J-J on his findings and set off on the return to St. Denis. He went home first to check on Balzac, then to his office to check his e-mails, and shortly before two he joined the large group of people already gathered in the cavernous hall of the fire station. The fire trucks had all been moved outside to make room. Half the *mairie* staff was there along with Yveline and Sergeant Jules for the gendarmes, Fabiola and Dr. Gelletreau, the *collège* director and officials from the communes up and down the entire valley. He found his own colleagues, Louis from Montignac and Juliette from Les Eyzies.

"This would be a good time to pull off a bank robbery," he said. "Half the cops are tied up here."

"Not to mention the TV news cameras," said Louis, nodding at a separate stand filled with cameras and reporters, Philippe Delaron included.

"And the military," said Juliette pointing to a tall officer in an air force uniform who was chatting with Albert, the chief *pompier* of St. Denis, along with his boss, the woman who had recently taken over as head of the fire service for the *département*. She mounted a small dais, tapped the microphone to check it was working and began.

"We are now at a very high risk of forest fires, and in a highly wooded region like this with lots of scattered housing we could lose dozens of lives, not to mention many millions in property, unless we take some very serious precautions. Each of your *mairies* has been sent checklists of things they have to do, from preparing evacuation centers and emergency food and water supplies to mounting round-the-clock fire-watch stations on all the water towers. Doctors, pharmacies, medical centers and social-work teams are being sent their own checklists on supplies that could be required and plans for preventive evacuation of at-risk individuals."

She stepped down and handed the microphone to the prefect, who began by saying he supported everything the chief *pompier* had said. "If we get a major fire, I will at once declare a state of emergency under which supplies and key personnel can be requisitioned to deal with the challenge. Any disobedience of evacuation orders will result in an arrest. I should stress now that if such a fire occurs, human life will be our priority, so we may suffer heavy losses in livestock. Paris has agreed that special compensation funds will be available and that *pompiers* from other regions which are not at risk can be drafted here. *Mairies* will have to make arrangements for their housing and upkeep. From midnight tonight, a special operations center will be manned at the Périgueux *préfecture* around the clock. And just so you know how seriously we are taking this, I will be on the first night shift. Now let me introduce Commander Yvelot of the Armée de l'Air, who will be in charge of water-bombing operations."

"My team will be based at the Bergerac airport, and we will have access to a flight of water-carrier aircraft on permanent standby at the Bordeaux airport," announced the tall air force officer. "We will also be flying in chemical fire suppressants. My colleagues are currently building a master map of the region, giving each one-kilometer square its own identifying code so we can steer the dumpers to threatened points with minimal delay. We plan to issue stacks of these maps for each commune for your fire watchers, *mairies,* police and *pompiers.* We'll also have meteorologists on-site to warn us of prevailing winds, which are the real danger to the fires spreading. The bad news is they are predicting warm, dry winds from the south for the coming week, which is why this emergency has been called.

"Now, I have to speak in the name of my colleague from the army, Colonel Rostin, a signals specialist who is currently meeting in Périgueux with the local directors of all the telecommunications companies about their roles in maintaining phone links even if we lose some cell-phone towers. They are setting up a dedicated communications center at the *préfecture,* with direct radio as well as phone links to every *mairie,* gendarmerie and *pompier* station. Expect one of those teams to be setting up links in your own communes over the next two to three days."

"One more thing," said the prefect, climbing up onto the platform once more. "In terms of handling any fires, local chiefs of *pompiers* will have absolute authority. If they demand public works staff and equipment to build fire breaks, they must be obeyed. If they have to drain swimming pools to get water or requisition civilian vehicles for evacuation purposes, so be it. All fires in the open air are now banned, which includes domestic barbecues. I hope you now realize how seriously we have to take this threat. Thank you."

He stepped down to a long moment of

stunned silence.

"Well, at least the schools are on vacation so we have some evacuation centers available," said Bruno to his two colleagues.

"We don't even have our own *pompiers* in Les Eyzies," said Juliette.

"Christ, what about Lascaux?" said Louis, in whose district the prehistoric cave stood, surrounded by woodland. "I'd better find our mayor and see if we should close it."

"All St. Denis *pompiers* to me," called out Albert. "And you, Bruno, and Yveline and Jules and Monsieur le Maire.

"I've spent the weekend with some of the guys from the hunting clubs trying to identify the highest-risk zones in our area, those woodland areas that appear to be most dry and flammable," Albert began. "There are three that really worry me. The first is the wooded area along the ridge above the town vineyard and all the way past Limeuil to Terrasson. The second is on the road up to Audrix and all the way along to the road that leads down to the forest of Campagne itself. The third is the woodland north of St. Denis up to the Miremont crossroads and east to Les Eyzies. We'll need fire-watch volunteers, at least two people at each post, with binoculars and fully charged cell phones, and running shift systems night and day. Bruno, can you round up some volunteers from the tennis and rugby clubs? And anybody who has a drone — they could be useful."

"I'll do that as soon as we're finished here," Bruno replied.

"If you could do the same for Les Eyzies, Juliette, I'd be grateful," Albert went on. "Fire-watch volunteers can use cell-phone and church and water towers, whatever gives us good views. We'll have helicopters available to check out each warning. And one last thing — beware of broken bottles. A lot of fires are started by broken glass. At the right angle, it can become a lens that concentrates the sun's rays."

As he turned to go, Albert paused. "One more thing, everybody. Double-check your fire insurance."

CHAPTER 17

Bruno had to excuse himself from the usual Monday evening dinner with his friends at the riding school. He worked late into the night collecting keys to church and water towers, rounding up volunteers to watch for fires, his only meal half a cold pizza from a stack of boxes delivered to the *pompiers.* His own home was in one of the high-risk zones, so when he got home after midnight he collected a box full of essential documents. He filled another box with his most cherished books and bottles of wine. He would leave them and Balzac at the mayor's house in town. Then he fell into a deep sleep as soon as his head touched the pillow.

He woke with the cockerel's crow, skipped his usual run and packed a suitcase of clean clothes. He went out to load up his Land Rover and felt the heat of the day building unusually early. The wind was from the south, warm but now menacing, and there was not a cloud in the sky. He sent a blanket e-mail to all members of the rugby and tennis clubs calling for fire-watch volunteers, adding that they could sign up at the fire station. Then he cooked himself a hearty breakfast, a fat cheese omelette with cherry tomatoes on the side, and toasted two big slices of bread from the *tourte.* It might be his only meal for some time. He squeezed his remaining oranges and made a big pot of coffee, sufficient for a mug with his breakfast and to fill his vacuum flask for the day to come.

On the radio, France Bleu Périgord was reporting the emergency, the prefect's speech and the new fire regulations. The final item on the morning news made him sit up when he heard J-J's name and the familiar voice of the People's Pierre claiming that the veteran detective had developed "a pathological obsession" with a case he failed to solve at the start of his career.

"Now as this elderly policeman's career approaches its end, Jalipeau is riding roughshod over human rights in a desperate bid to find a plausible victim for his personal vendetta," Pierre said, sounding as though he were addressing a public meeting. "He is even using doctored photographs and dubious evidence of witnesses claiming to recall events that happened thirty years ago."

"You are representing one of the suspects in the case, and I understand you took him to meet Commissaire Jalipeau," said the interviewer.

"That's right. My client went to the police station voluntarily only to be ambushed by some heavily painted woman he'd never met who was claiming some kind of relationship with him around the time and place of the murder. This farce was staged by Commissaire Jalipeau for reasons best known to himself."

"These are serious allegations against a well-known and much admired senior police —"

"I quite agree," Pierre interrupted. "I have had great respect for him in the past, but these antics are beyond belief. Do you know he's using some unqualified young archaeologist to try and rebuild the face of the victim from a thirty-year-old skull? This is crazy, it's close to witchcraft. No serious lawyer could stand for it."

"So what are you going to do?"

"I'm filing a formal complaint with the commissioner of police requesting that Jalipeau be suspended or at least removed from this case. Moreover, I will today petition the court on my client's behalf for relief from vexatious abuse. In a free country, the police cannot be allowed to get away with this kind of behavior."

"Thank you very much. And now, it's going to be a hot day, so watch out for those forest fires. If there's a pool or river near you, this might be a great day for it. But remember, no barbecues, by order of the prefect. Turning to sports news . . ."

Bruno turned it off, finished his breakfast and washed up. He loaded Balzac into the Land Rover and drove into town and left Balzac in his office. It was too early to deliver him to the mayor. Passing the Maison de la Presse he saw Gilles emerge with the day's newspapers.

"Can you spare me ten minutes?" Bruno asked him. "My house is in the danger zone, so I'd like you to drive up there with me, and you bring back the Land Rover to park it by the *mairie* and I'll bring the police van back."

"No problem," said Gilles. On the drive there, he said that Fabiola was already at the medical center, and he thought their house should be safe.

"I'm worried about Pamela's place," Gilles went on, and Bruno realized with a sudden sense of guilt that he hadn't thought of that, not only of the danger to Pamela,

Miranda and her children but that Hector and the other horses might also be at risk.

"Have you spoken to her about it?" Bruno asked.

"Not yet. I was going to call her when I got home. Maybe she can at least move the horses to another stable."

"The stables aren't that close to the woods, but Pamela's house could be in danger."

"Don't forget about her *gîtes*. Right now they're full of tourists."

"I'll go up and see her after we get back to town," Bruno said.

Twenty minutes later, he parked the police van at the riding school, went to visit Hector and give him his usual carrot and greeted Beau and Bella, the two sheepdogs. He walked up to the house to find her in the kitchen. She was on the phone, saying "I don't think anybody really knows how high the risk is. Ah, here's Bruno. I'll ask him and call you back."

"Your stables should be okay, but this house could be in trouble if there's a fire in those woods behind. This south wind could sweep the flames right down. Let's take a look."

There were twenty meters of garden behind the house, mainly her croquet lawn and flower beds, then a low hedge and another thirty or forty meters of grassland that linked to two big paddocks to left and right. So the woods were probably fifty or more meters from the house, a distance wider than the usual firebreak. The outbuildings that had been converted into four *gîtes* were even farther from risk. The house and *gîtes* were all stone with tiled roofs, so there was little danger of sparks.

"You should be fine," he said. "But in case you have to get out, make sure you and Miranda prepare boxes now with all your essential documents and things you don't want to lose, and tell your tourists to do the same." Bruno checked his watch and asked, "May I take Hector out, go up to the ridge and see just how dry those woods are?"

"I'll come, too, on Primrose, we both need some exercise."

Ten minutes later, Bruno dismounted, handed his reins to Pamela and plunged into the woods, the vegetation dry and crunchy beneath his feet at first, but as he went deeper the trees were older and the canopy more dense. The grass beneath his feet gave way to the mulch of a forest floor, and he saw new shoots and some ferns, all still green. He bent down and brushed away the top layer of mulch, feeling a slight but reassuring dampness below.

"It's not too dry, so it won't catch fire easily," he said. "Have you looked at your spring lately?"

Pamela shook her head, and so Bruno rode farther along the ridge and then diagonally down to the rocky outcrop from which water bubbled throughout the year. It fed a small stream that ran down through the riding school to a pond that housed colonies of toads whose croakings always fascinated Balzac. The water was invariably cool and clear, and Bruno found it delicious to drink, usually filling a twenty-liter *bidon* before the regular Monday night suppers. He dismounted again and clambered through the rocks to find that the spring was still giving water, not much, but the flow in summer was always more feeble. Still, if the water table on the ridge and plateau were still feeding the spring, there would be water underground for the tree roots.

"It's still flowing, so the woodland above should be moist enough to resist anything but a massive fire," he told Pamela.

The farther they rode along the ridge, the drier the woodland below appeared to be, and when they came to the bridle trail they so often took, some of the trees were so dry that they had lost many of their leaves. Land that he knew to be usually boggy was now dry cracked mud. When they reached the hunters' cabin and took the path back to the valley, the stream that usually fed into the Vézère was barely a trickle. The horses cantered easily, but even Hector seemed reluctant to increase his pace, as if drained by the heat. How, Bruno wondered, had Arabian horses won their historic reputation for speed when they must have suffered from heat like this? Perhaps their breed had grown used to it. He didn't see himself adapting to this kind of heat.

Back at the stables, they unsaddled and rubbed down the horses, and Bruno rinsed himself at the sink and drove back to town to entrust Balzac and his boxes to the mayor, and to make his usual patrol of the Tuesday morning market. Everyone he knew asked him about the fire emergency, and he told them all of the need for fire-watch volunteers. One of the stallholders Bruno knew slightly — sold novelty T-shirts and only came in the tourist season — brandished a cell phone at him and said, "You know this cop they're talking about?"

Bruno peered at the Twitter feed on the small screen. It read: "*Flic* should be locked up," followed by "#CrazedCopPerigord."

He took the phone and scrolled up, seeing insult after insult against J-J, all with the same hashtag. Calling for him to be locked up was mild. Others claimed it should be "#CorruptCopPerigord," and that led to a second stream of different insults. There was one, referring to a long-ago gunfight when J-J had been hit by a bullet, that said, "Shooter should have aimed higher #CrazedCopPerigord."

Angered by this vicious and anonymous attack on his friend, Bruno handed back the phone and said curtly, "He's a brave, honest guy and a friend of mine. If you get robbed or your kids get snatched, you'll want him on your side."

"Aw, come on, don't take it so seriously," the stallholder called after him. "It's just a joke."

Bruno turned on his heel, controlling his anger, but his eyes were blazing. "How would you like it if somebody burned out your stall and I said that was just a joke? Or if somebody held you up at gunpoint and I just shrugged and said you shouldn't take it seriously? We're cops. We're not supposed to back away and say it's all a joke. It's not a joke to me when some cop hater trashes the reputation of a good man."

He stared around at the people who had

gathered to watch this confrontation and, one by one, they dropped their eyes. As they began to move away, Bruno felt a big hand land on his shoulder and heard Léopold's deep voice.

"I was right here in this market just before Christmas when some young thugs trashed the Vietnamese stall that sells those *nem* we all like," the big Senegalese said quietly, looming over the T-shirt seller. "This cop here, Bruno, was dressed like Santa Claus, raising money for kids. And he went for those thugs, knocked them down and took them out. Alone."

"I didn't mean anything," mumbled the T-shirt man, backing away to the shelter of his stall. "Sorry."

Bruno nodded at him coldly, turned and shook Léopold's hand. "My boys and I will be going to the *pompiers* to sign up for the fire watch after the market closes," he said.

"Thanks, Léopold, see you there," Bruno said, and walked on to the fire station. Ahmed, Albert's deputy and the only other professional firefighter on the St. Denis team, was holding the fort. The rest were all volunteers.

"Albert is getting some sleep," Ahmed said. "He'll be on watch all night. We've got some more professionals coming up from

307

Bordeaux later today and bringing some more water tenders. You ought to go home and get some sleep. We might need you tonight."

Instead, Bruno went back to his office and called an old contact in army records to see if there was any record of Henri being excused from military service because of asthma. He gave Henri's details and was promised a call back. Then he called the Belleville archives again, to see if they had any medical records of children at the orphanage suffering from asthma. They would check. No sooner had he put down the phone on his desk than the mobile phone at his waist buzzed.

"What's this crap on Twitter about J-J?" came Isabelle's familiar voice.

"And bonjour to you, too. It's good to hear your voice," he replied. "There's a publicity-hungry lawyer playing games over the Oscar case."

"That's clear from the Twitter feed, but is this guy J-J interrogated really a suspect?"

"His name is Henri Bazaine and his identity was visually confirmed by an old girlfriend who knew both him and Max — that's Oscar's real name. The guy says she's mistaken, so we're double-checking his background at an orphanage in Belleville that was long since closed and the local records were left in a mess, lots of files missing or destroyed."

"Belleville? In the old Red Belt?"

"Yes, an orphanage named after someone called Paul Lafargue."

"That doesn't surprise me. Lafargue was Karl Marx's French son-in-law. He founded the Workers' Party in France and wrote a book with the brilliant title *The Right to Be Lazy.* No wonder they liked him in Belleville. Still, it's convenient that this Henri claims to be from somewhere where the archives are a mess."

"I'm checking his military service records. He claims he was excused because of asthma."

"Would you like me to have someone take a look at the old RG files?" she asked. The Renseignements Généraux was the old police and security intelligence network which devoted much of its time to watching French political activists of both the left and right. Some of its employees were once famously discovered planting microphones in the offices of the investigative weekly *Le Canard Enchaîné.* The RG had long since been merged into a new directorate of internal security, but its files and its work continued.

Hoping the RG might turn up something useful, Bruno gave Isabelle Henri's details and then ended the call as his desk phone rang. It was J-J, announcing himself by saying, "Your mobile line was busy."

"It was Isabelle, worried about your Twitter attack."

"A man is judged by the enemies he makes," J-J replied, his voice calm. "Enough of that. I seem to recall that you had a contact with the cops in Quebec. Are you still in touch?"

"I can be. Why?"

"I'm interested in Henri's wine-consulting business. Don't ask how I know, but there are hefty annual payments to Henri from a Montreal-based corporation that owns vineyards and distilleries in Quebec and on the West Coast. It all looks legal — a friend in the *fisc* tells me the money was declared and tax paid. It's a lot, ten grand a year going back as far as we can track — over ten years — and rising to fifteen the last two years. We looked at the firm's website and it seems real, but maybe the local cops know something different."

"I can try. What have you got?"

"It's called Vins de la Nouvelle France, and it's run by a guy named Laurent Loriot, and guess what? He was born in Belleville, just two days before our Henri. It seems a hell of a coincidence. He immigrated to Quebec from France in 1991 and made good."

"You have to be joking." Bruno scratched his head, thinking hard, and said, "I just talked to Isabelle. She's looking into old RG files about Belleville. You could ask her to try Loriot's name along with Henri's, and I'll do the same with army records and a helpful guy at the Belleville archives. And she's the one with the Quebec police contacts."

Bruno tried his army records contact first, a retired *sous-officier* who had helped him in the past, who began by saying he was about to call Bruno.

"There's nothing here in the Henri Zeller file about asthma or any medical condition. He got a deferment to finish vocational school, and then we were informed that Henri Zeller had died in a road accident. We received a death certificate from the Belleville *mairie* along with someone else who died at the same time, Max Morilland. He was also on a vocational school deferment. They each had the same address, the Lafargue orphanage in Belleville."

Bruno suppressed his excitement. "What was the date on the death certificate?"

"December tenth,1989. Both men were supposed to turn up for military service the following month."

"Thank you, my friend. This is very important. Could you e-mail me a scan of those death certificates, please. We're into a murder inquiry involving a man who's been using the identity of Henri Zeller, changing his name to Bazaine."

"I'll do it now. Let me know how this turns out. You've got me interested."

Forgetting his promise to check army records for Loriot in Quebec, Bruno immediately called J-J to convey the news that Henri Bazaine had officially been dead for three decades, supposedly in a car crash with a man from the same orphanage named Max Morilland. As they spoke, his desktop computer pinged to signal an incoming e-mail. It was the scans of the two death certificates, which he at once forwarded to J-J and to Isabelle. The printed form itself looked straightforward, with the official stamp of the *mairie,* the date and the name of the doctor who certified the cause of death as a traffic accident.

"I suppose this means I can arrest him for identity theft, or for forgery to evade military service," J-J said, sounding hesitant. "I've never come across anything like this before. I'd better have a word with one of our lawyers. And this other guy, Max Morilland, do you suppose that's the murder victim?"

"I presume so," said Bruno. "It could be a coincidence. I'm as confused as you by this. Either Henri forged the death certificate or more likely got somebody in the *mairie* to do it for him and sent it to the army. But the record of Henri's death should have gone automatically to other official databases like the electoral roll and the social security register. You'd better check whether this supposed death was recorded elsewhere. And before you arrest him, do you have any evidence that he was involved in this fake certificate? He could claim he was the innocent victim of some bureaucratic mix-up, and given what I've been told about the state of the local archives in Belleville, that's entirely possible."

As Bruno spoke, his computer pinged again. The new e-mail was from the archives in Belleville, informing him that Henri had a classmate in vocational school called Max Morilland. He immediately passed on the news to J-J.

"It all seems too convenient," J-J replied.

"It reminds me of something I read about the Resistance during the war," Bruno said.

"They always wanted to have somebody inside a *mairie* who could arrange to concoct apparently genuine identity documents, working papers, coupons for food rations, justifications for travel. Maybe there was somebody doing that in Belleville and making money out of it. This was back in the eighties, when it must have been easier to get away with it. Registers were filled in by hand and kept in filing cabinets, before everything became computerized."

Bruno's computer pinged yet again. This time it was an e-mail from Isabelle, with a copy to J-J. It read, "Have passed this to Paris police and to RG. This smells fishy. We'll also take a look at Malakoff, which has had a Communist mayor since the 1920s and a sports stadium named after Lenin. RG suggests no arrests yet. We'll talk."

CHAPTER 18

Bruno had planned to sleep from mid-afternoon into the late evening before heading out at around ten to his fire-watching post on the church tower of Audrix. Already, however, he felt almost overwhelmed with all the balls he was juggling at once — the fire precautions, worrying about Pamela's house and the horses and trying to keep straight all the aspects of the murder case. He began by calling his friend at army records and asked him to find what he could of the military service of Laurent Loriot, the Quebec winemaker who was born in Belleville and had become the main customer of Henri's wine-consulting business.

Then Florence called to say that she had thought about his offer of one of Balzac's puppies and she was very grateful, but her children were still too small to take proper responsibility. Bruno said he understood, promised to save one from a future litter and then called Rod Macrae, an old rock musician who lived nearby. He'd told Bruno months earlier that he wanted one of Balzac's pups and now he could have one. Macrae was delighted, and they agreed to visit the kennel at some future weekend, but Bruno should drop by sooner to seal the deal over a drink.

The next call came from Sabine, saying that Tante-Do was becoming increasingly nervous for her own safety as a woman living alone and had asked if Sabine might come and stay with her. Bruno, feeling instantly guilty at not thinking of this, said he saw no objection, but she'd better check with J-J. Moments later, Isabelle was calling, this time to say that the latest edition of *Le Monde* had just arrived on her laptop, and she felt the expected counterattack of the French establishment had begun. As she spoke, a copy of the article appeared in Bruno's in-box.

"The New 'Finlandization' and the Danger to France," ran the headline. "As France considers how to deal with the latest eruption of the great East German spy scandal of the Rosenholz dossier, a timely warning comes from Finland. During the Cold War, the term 'Finlandization,' deployed in the American capital as a term of contemptuous abuse, described the way that the small Nordic country felt the need to remain neutral and to appease its giant Soviet neighbor. Now France is threatened with a new kind of Finlandization, following in Finland's footsteps into a dangerous witch hunt that can target many innocent officials."

The article went on to explain that on the basis of the Rosenholz files, Finland's Supo (security police) had begun to investigate as a possible Stasi agent one of the country's ambassadors, Alpo Rusi, a former adviser to the Finnish president Martti Ahtisaari. Supo had judged Rusi to be the Stasi agent called Pekka in the Rosenholz dossier, though Rusi strenuously denied the charges brought against him. He won his case, and then sued the Finnish state for slandering his good name and won again, securing a compensation payment of twenty thousand euros. As a result, the Finnish high court decided that the Rosenholz files were inadequate as proof and that they should remain classified in future.

"So why is France now trying once again to obtain these dubious records, whose validity has been publicly questioned, and to what end?" the *Le Monde* editorial went on. "Do we seriously wish to inflict on our own public servants the ordeal inflicted on Ambassador Rusi? Do we want to stage our own McCarthy-style witch hunt when such an act of anti-Communist hysteria is now widely and rightly condemned in the country that suffered it?" the article concluded.

"The key point, Bruno," Isabelle said, "is that this article is signed by a member of the Constitutional Council, which sounds to me like a shot across the bow from the legal establishment. I've already had a couple of worried calls from the Élysée, and the president himself is concerned. On top of that we have French diplomats saying that this is damaging our relations with Germany; I'm getting some snide remarks from my own German counterparts. This is becoming a very unpleasant political mess."

"I sympathize, but I don't see what I can do about it," Bruno said.

"You could try and persuade Jacqueline and Gilles to shut up."

"You and I know them both well enough to be sure that would be just the way to get them to redouble their efforts," he replied. "And it's too late."

"You may be right, but please let me know of anything else they are planning. And ask yourself why a Communist-run *mairie* might be interested in creating false identities during the Cold War. Could they have been building legends that would have allowed Soviet agents to work undercover in France? That's what worries me."

"*Mon Dieu,*" he said. "I never thought of that."

"That might even be a motive for the murder of Max," she said. "That's why I've got the RG trawling through what's left of the old Belleville files."

"You can do something for me that might shed some light on all this," he said. "Another of the Belleville orphans, Laurent Loriot, born in the same week as our Henri Bazaine, went to Canada thirty years ago and made good in the wine business. He's been paying Henri large sums for alleged wine consulting — ten or fifteen grand a year for many years. Could you check with your contacts over there and see what you can find about him and his group, Les Vins de la Nouvelle France?"

"I'll make some calls," she said. "And please keep me informed of what you learn and I'll do the same for you."

Bruno sighed and went back to his task of listing all the elderly and handicapped people living in remote locations in the commune who might be at risk. He had still to check it against separate lists for emergency evacuations drawn up by the medical center, the pharmacists and social services. Then there was the list of volunteers who offered to use their cars to pick up people who would not need a special vehicle. His phone rang again.

"Where are you?" came the voice of Albert, the chief *pompier.*

"In my office, at the *mairie.* Why?"

"You ought to be getting some rest," Albert said. "You're on watch tonight at Audrix starting at ten o'clock, according to the list you drew up. So where are you going to sleep?"

"Back at my place."

"Forget it, Bruno. Your house is too much at risk, and I'm not in a position to drop everything and come and rescue you. You'll sleep at the mayor's house. He's expecting you, and I mean now. Sweet dreams."

Albert ended the call. Bruno shrugged and decided he could make one more call, and phoned the Belleville archives — people there had been helpful before — to inform them that the Henri Zeller he had asked about was supposed to have been dead for three decades.

"I'll send you a copy of the death certificate," Bruno told the archivist. "It was one of two sent from the Belleville Hôtel de Ville to the army to explain why Bazaine and another local young man called Max Morilland would not turn up for military service."

"That's interesting," the archivist replied. "But this Zeller is the guy who's supposed to still be alive and the subject of your investigation, is that right?"

"Correct," said Bruno. "Zeller was his original name. He changed it to Bazaine when he married a woman with that name who was going to inherit a vineyard. I thought you'd like to know. And we think the man he could have murdered was Max Morilland, Henri's classmate at vocational school. You sent me that e-mail about him."

"Wow, I've never been involved in anything like this." The archivist's voice was excited. "I'd better check this with the last survivor."

"Who's the last survivor?"

"Sorry, I was thinking aloud," the archivist replied. "There's an elderly woman, the last living member of the *mairie* staff under the old regime. She's sometimes helpful. A veteran Communist, of course, but she's seen the light. She's retired, almost eighty and living with her son somewhere near you, a place called Carlux. Do you want her number? She goes by the name of Rosa Luxemburg Delpèche, which is a giveaway to her parents' politics."

Bruno took her address and phone number, toyed with the idea of driving there at once, less than an hour away, but then thought of Albert's call. The old fire chief was right. Bruno needed some sleep. And he'd see Balzac. He picked up his cap, strolled down to the mayor's house and greeted Balzac, who raced from the far end of the garden where Jacqueline was weeding.

"Bonjour, Bruno, you're in the spare room," Jacqueline said, presenting her cheeks to be kissed after waiting for the first flood of Balzac's enthusiastic welcome to recede. "I'll wake you before ten — I have my orders from Albert along with a set of very impressive binoculars for you and a map that's far too complex for me to read. Balzac stays with me, otherwise you'll get no sleep. Your case is already in the room along with towels and some mineral water. Sleep well. Oh, and the last news bulletin reported two new forest fires, one in the Lot, east of Cahors, and the other southwest of us at Casteljaloux. The Armée de l'Air sent planes dropping water."

In his days in the army, Bruno had been able to fall asleep almost at will, happily seizing any opportunity to doze off. Perhaps because he was older, it was no longer so easy, or perhaps his life was now more complicated. Thoughts of Henri Bazaine, the dead Max and the frightened Tante-Do danced in his head along with his surprise that Isabelle now took so seriously the little flutters of panic in that bizarre, self-absorbed world of French presidential politics. None of that was as important as protecting his valley from the threat of forest fire.

With that he must have drifted off, for when he heard a knock on the door and Jacqueline's voice, his watch showed twenty minutes to ten. He called out that he was up, took a quick shower and went out to the smell of fresh coffee. Places were set for three at the kitchen table and Jacqueline was mixing a salad while the mayor tipped and twirled an omelette in the frying pan.

"I'm not sure if this is breakfast or dinner, but either way I'm looking forward to it, so *bonjour et bonsoir* and thank you," Bruno said. At the sound of his voice came a scratching on the kitchen door, and the mayor used the hand bearing the spatula to open it as Balzac rushed in to greet his master as if they had been separated for weeks.

"If you could grate some of that Gruyère

on the table I'm almost ready to add it," the mayor said. Bruno complied and then began squeezing oranges from the bowl for juice as the mayor added the cheese and began to fold the omelette. Ten minutes later, refreshed and fortified, with a fresh thermos of coffee and a bag of fruit, cheese, water and a baguette, he and the mayor were in Bruno's van and heading for Audrix. There were still some customers dining on the terrace of the Auberge when they arrived, and the village's own mayor, Jolibert, was standing on the steps of his own tiny *mairie* to greet them.

"My turn tomorrow night," he said by way of greeting as they shook hands. "We had three or four small outbreaks today, nothing the *pompiers* couldn't handle. But this is the first evening when that damned southerly wind hasn't died down. It could be a bad night. Be sure to call me if things start looking rough."

"I heard the planes were busy dropping fire retardant down south in the Lot," said Bruno. "But that was hours ago."

"Rocamadour and Biron were the nearest the fires came to us today," said Jolibert. "I'm off to bed but wake me if you see a big one."

Bruno and the mayor walked slowly

around the hilltop village, able to see for at least ten kilometers in all directions except east, where the nearest skyline was dominated by a tall aerial mast. It was owned by the defense ministry and said to be a key link of French military communications.

"Has anybody suggested we should have a watching post on top of that?" Bruno asked.

The mayor shrugged and said, "Ask Albert."

Bruno did so, and Albert replied that the request had been dismissed on grounds of security.

"Understood, but have we suggested the military should do their bit and put their own fire watchers up there where they'd have a much better view than we do? It's crazy if we work with the air force to drop water but can't use their facilities to check for fires."

"You're with the mayor," Albert replied. "Ask him. He's the politician."

Bruno did so. The mayor nodded. "That makes sense. I'll call the minister tomorrow. Now you can tell me what's going on with this thirty-year-old murder inquiry that has made J-J so unpopular on social media. You and J-J seem very focused on collecting evidence to charge this Henri Bazaine with murder."

"Because the evidence is mounting up that he killed a young man called Max, but we don't know why," Bruno replied, and recounted what he had learned from the Belleville *mairie* and army records and from Isabelle.

"I see, but I'm even more worried that we've had a Communist *mairie* in Paris that has been forging documents, creating fake identities and killing them off and has since managed to destroy most of the evidence," the mayor said. "What on earth were they up to?"

"That's why Isabelle has brought in the internal security people. They're trawling the old RG files to see if they might have been building cover stories for KGB agents to operate in France."

"Renseignements Généraux? I never liked the idea of that kind of political police, neither the files they kept, the methods they deployed nor the use that could be made of them. But in this case I might make an exception. The idea that a French mayor could preside over a system in which KGB agents could be provided with apparently genuine French identities so they could conspire against the interests of an elected French government is sickening."

"They were hardly discreet about it," said

Bruno. "You remember the old Communist Party slogan, that my true homeland is the international working class?"

The mayor made a sound that was halfway between a grunt and a sigh and handed Bruno the binoculars.

"Very distant red glow to the northwest," said Bruno. "Better call it in."

The mayor called the control room in Périgueux, reported the glow and then ended the call. "A fire in the woods north of Cendrieux. The *pompiers* are there."

"You know, we're going to need a better system of forest management to deal with this climate change," the mayor said. "We can't afford this simple clear-cutting of timber and leaving loose brush and branches all over the ground. It's an invitation to fire."

"Yes, but it also provides a habitat for the insects and wildlife that regenerate the ground," said Bruno. "It's complex. Maybe you should get our local agricultural research station to make some recommendations."

"I did a little research into this recent surge in forest fires," the mayor went on. "A hundred dead in Greece three years ago and eighty dead in California, parts of Los Angeles evacuated and insurers lost more than twenty billion euros. And then there's

Australia with eleven million hectares burned, that's about the size of England. What we're doing here with fire watches, we're just reacting. We need to think ahead about what kind of forests we need, what kinds of trees in a changing climate."

"How far ahead do we think?" Bruno asked. "When trees can live for hundreds of years we need a special kind of long view."

And so the night went on, the two men chatting while eating their bread and cheese and sipping their coffee from the thermos, breaking off to report a red glow suddenly in the sky to the southeast, toward Cahors. Near dawn they reported another, due south near the old Abbey of Cadouin. Each time the control room had already been alerted.

"How does a fire suddenly break out at three in the morning, when there's no lightning, no tourists dropping cigarette butts, no sun to start a flame through a piece of broken glass?" the mayor asked.

"Albert says fire can lie dormant, just glowing for hours if there's the right amount of fuel, until a sudden gust of warm wind licks it into life." Bruno upended the thermos. "There's no more coffee and dawn is coming. What's your schedule today?"

"I shall write a letter to the minister of

defense and call him, the same for the environment minister. Since French law allows me the privilege of immediate audience with all ministers, I'd be failing in my constitutional duty as a former senator if I neglected to take advantage of such access. I'll also talk to the head of the research station. And you?"

"I have a meeting with J-J and Prunier late this morning with a police lawyer in Périgueux to see if we have enough of a case for the *procureur* to bring charges against Henri. There's a text on my phone saying I should be there. I'll also want to arrange a police guard for our main witness, the one we call Tante-Do. Then I ought to call in on Virginie, the young woman who's making a face out of J-J's skull. I feel a bit guilty about not doing more to make her welcome, so I might invite her down to St. Denis for the weekend. Fabiola is interested in the project and said she'd gladly let Virginie have her spare room, and you ought to meet her. Then at some point I'll go to visit an old lady who used to work at the Belleville *mairie* who may be able to tell me more about these fake death certificates."

"I hope you'll get some time to sleep."

"I slept well at your place and I might take a nap for an hour or so when we leave here.

After the military I'm accustomed to some broken nights. These night duties are probably worse for all the volunteer *pompiers,* and we wouldn't have a fire or rescue service without them. And it's the same for you, taking your turn on fire watch."

"If I didn't, not a single volunteer *pompier* would ever vote for me again," the mayor replied. "And they'd be right. When I think of the hours they put in . . ."

"It's not just the *pompiers,*" said Bruno. "We have more than two hundred people from St. Denis who've volunteered themselves and their cars to go pick up any old folk at risk. These are decent people that we work for."

CHAPTER 19

By nine in the morning, after a nap, a brisk ride of Hector with Balzac trotting behind, a shower and some breakfast, Bruno arrived at the address of the woman with the unforgettable given names of Rosa Luxemburg. He had to think a moment to recall her surname, Delpèche. She lived in a small cottage outside of the hilltop village of Carlux, down toward the bridge over the Dordogne. The far side of the river was heavily cultivated, but this side was so thickly wooded that the whole area looked to Bruno like a fire risk, threatening even the lavishly restored Château de Rouffillac on the slope dominating the river crossing.

He parked his police van, put Balzac on a leash and approached the wooden gate that led to a well-tended garden. He stood for a moment admiring the neat rows of lettuces, peas, eggplants and tomatoes before asking himself how on earth she watered them.

Then he saw the large cistern, rather like his own, into which the house's gutters fed. Interspersed between the rows he saw the telltale glint of plastic bottles. She was using a drip system of irrigation, not unlike his own.

"Bonjour, Madame Delpèche. Congratulations on your watering system and the fine *potager* you've made," he said, touching a finger to the brim of his cap as a tall, thin and elderly woman came briskly around the corner of the cottage. She was wearing baggy khaki pants, a blue denim shirt and an enormous straw hat. She carried a plastic bowl that looked half full of water, and she poured it into the cistern before turning to reply politely to his greeting and to stare at him with a confused half smile as if trying to remember when and where she might have met him.

"I see you save the water from rinsing your vegetables," he said. "I do the same, but I don't think you learned your gardening skills in Belleville. I'm Bruno Courrèges, municipal policeman from St. Denis, and I'd be grateful for a few minutes of your time. The people at today's Belleville *mairie* tell me you're the only person who can help make sense of what's left of the old archives."

"I'm starting to make preserves out of my vegetables because my cistern is nearly empty, and I don't see this heat wave ending soon," she said, coming forward to shake his outstretched hand and then to open the gate and invite him in. As Bruno expected, her face widened into a broad smile when she saw Balzac.

"What a wonderful dog," she exclaimed. "Do you work with him?"

"I'm training him to find truffles, but he's a fine guard for my geese and chickens."

"I had a little terrier who passed away last year and haven't had the heart to replace him," she said, going down on one knee to fondle Balzac's ears. She was spry for her age. The archivist had told him she was nearly eighty, but she looked to be in her sixties. As she rose again to her full height and took off her straw hat, he saw she had iron-gray hair, cut short, and watchful brown eyes.

"Would he like some water?" she asked, looking down again at Balzac. "I was about to make myself some coffee. You're welcome to join me. It's cooler on the terrace at the back, and you can tell me why you're here."

"It's about a man, born in Belleville, named Henri Zeller," Bruno began as they sat in the shade of an awning behind the house. Chickens pecked in the small fenced area of land that gave way to a steep and wooded cliff that rose to Carlux on the hilltop. The slope was too steep to see the ruins of the old castle at the heart of the village.

"Henri failed to appear for his military service because the *mairie* sent the army his death certificate in December of '89. The first problem is that he's not dead. He's alive and well and running a vineyard in Bergerac under the name of Bazaine. The second problem is that we're investigating the murder of a friend of his that same summer while the two men were camping near St. Denis. The dead man, also from Belleville, was called Max Morilland. The Belleville *mairie* sent the army a death certificate for him at the same time. And they had both grown up in the Lafargue orphanage in Belleville."

"Have you been to Belleville?" she asked.

"I walked through it once, from the cemetery of Père Lachaise to the park of the Buttes-Chaumont. I was in love at the time, and only had eyes for the girl. We failed to find the lamppost on the rue de Belleville that marks the spot where Edith Piaf was supposed to have been born."

She smiled and said, "I know you look the

part, but it's hard to believe you're really a municipal policeman."

"You could call my friend Montsouris in St. Denis, a train driver and a party member. We play tennis together."

"I don't think I've believed a word any party member said to me for thirty years. But don't worry. I read *Sud Ouest* and I remember seeing a photo of you and your dog when you arrested those IRA people."

"So you know I'm genuine. What can you tell me?"

"The Lafargue orphanage was very small for the number of children it was supposed to house, because most of those registered were never there. I knew it, even though I wasn't in the registrations department which managed such matters. We all knew it."

"How do you mean, they were never there?"

"They were invented, just names on lists. I assumed it was a way of getting more money from the central government, welfare payments for nonexistent orphans."

"In which department did you work?"

"I was in a section known as Fraternity, which dealt with relations with comrades elsewhere, from Italy and Britain to Poland, Cuba and above all the DDR, the Democratic Republic of Germany. East Germany."

"Why 'above all'?" Bruno asked.

"Many of our senior party cadres had been conscripted to Germany as forced labor during the war and had learned the language. Not many spoke any other language at all, and the German comrades were keen to maintain the connection, inviting us to their holiday camps and so on. I went twice, although I was most useful for my English and my Spanish. I first visited Schwerin, a beautiful place with a lovely castle on a lake. That was in the late seventies. And the second time, in '87, I was invited to Radebeul, near Dresden in the Elbe Valley, an area of vineyards. It was sad. They had no corks, so used bottle caps instead. Their old barrels were rotting and they couldn't afford stainless-steel vats, so they used enamel ones, designed for making beer. Still, the people were very welcoming."

She smiled. "The wine wasn't bad. And we had to sit through a lot less folk dancing than we did in Cuba and Bulgaria."

"Did you make friends?" Bruno asked, genuinely curious.

"Yes, there was a French couple from Belleville, Jacques and Sylvie Lefort, who had immigrated there in the fifties. They taught French and helped run a local orphanage, named for Clara Zetkin, a famous German Communist. She's buried in the Kremlin Wall. We met some of the German youngsters and were amazed at how good their French was and how much they knew about France. They would listen to French radio, watch French films, listen to French pop records, and there were up-to-date French papers and magazines in the library."

"Did you conclude that these youngsters were being trained to merge into French life?" Bruno asked.

"Yes, but I didn't think that was sinister at the time. I just thought it was a marvelous way to educate these youngsters."

"How much of their education did you see?"

"How do you mean?"

"Did you see anything special that might have been espionage training, in codes, communications, that kind of thing?"

"There was a lot of gymnastics, judo, cross-country running and hikes. At the time I just thought it was very healthy. But we didn't sit in on the classes. They could have had espionage training and I wouldn't have known."

"Did you talk politics with the kids?"

Bruno asked.

"Not really, except bland clichés about the struggle for peace, racism in America, the Vietnam War, that kind of thing. Our meetings with the youngsters were mostly organized and scripted, except when we went off for picnics in the vineyards. That was when we realized they were very well informed about France and French politics. They were bright kids. They clearly saw the difference between what they read in the French media and the spoon-fed propaganda in their own East German press. Looking back, there were some clues that their thinking was a bit dissident."

"Did Jacques and Sylvie encourage this kind of free thinking?"

"Yes, I think they did but not in any subversive way. They had no children of their own, but they were really proud of the kids they taught and loved to see the way they interacted with us. They kept a scrapbook with sections on each of the youngsters, growing up, playing sports, their school reports, their work in the vineyards. I was leafing through it one day with Sylvie and I saw photos of a couple of boys, almost young men, whom I recognized. I'd seen them in the *mairie* back in Belleville where they were working in registrations. I'd thought they were French. Even when I knew they were from East Germany, I assumed it was some sort of exchange scheme. It took some time for me to realize what their presence really meant."

"Which was?" asked Bruno.

"To insert them into French life as French citizens, presumably while still taking their orders from East Berlin."

"What year was that?" Bruno asked.

"Nineteen eighty-seven, a time of great controversy in the Belleville *mairie,* with most of the younger people thinking Gorbachev was wonderful, and most of the old guard fearing that he was betraying the revolution."

"What did you think?"

"I was confused. Gorbachev was such a breath of fresh air, an idealist, a believer in peace after all those dreadful old men in the Kremlin. But I was worried that he was naïve and that he could end up losing all the good things about socialism."

She sat forward and tapped Bruno on the knee. "You have to understand that I was born during the war, and it was clear that the Nazis had been defeated in the field by the Red Army and in France by the Resistance, which was mainly Communist. You're too young to remember, but the party used to call itself the party of *les quarante mille fusillés,* the party of forty thousand martyrs, executed by the Nazis for their courage. That was how I was brought up — that it was communism that beat Hitler, not American capitalism and British imperialism. And without the Soviet Union, what would save us from the new fascism that we all could see at work in the Vietnam War?"

"So you were torn," Bruno suggested. "You were trying to believe two contradictory things at the same time, that Gorbachev was great but that he could imperil everything the Soviet Union stood for."

She nodded. "Yes, that's right. And everything in my life, all my friends, my colleagues, even friends who were not in the party, we were all instinctively on the left. We'd all been thrilled by '68 in Paris, the general strike, the state giving in to the workers' demands, the Americans getting a bloody nose in Vietnam. I got married then to a comrade who worked on *L'Humanité,* the party newspaper. We had our son. It seemed we were on the right side of history. And yet at the same time, Belleville was changing — new housing estates, new people, a lot of hostility to the Algerians. You could feel the party's grip on the working class start to weaken. You could see the old working class starting to dissolve, just like my marriage. We divorced in 1984."

"How long did you stay at the *mairie*?"

"My department was closed at the end of '89 after the Berlin Wall came down. I got a job in a travel agency and then an old comrade helped me into a better job on the railroad, the international office where my languages were useful. When I retired, I came down here where my son works in the tourism office. He married a woman from Sarlat, so I have my son, my grandchildren, my garden."

"Did you ever hear again from Jacques and Sylvie Lefort at the orphanage?" he asked.

"No, although I wrote to them a couple of times. I tried to telephone the orphanage, but it had been closed."

"How many French-speaking kids did you see at the East German orphanage?"

"At least twenty, but there may have been more, and the Leforts told me they had been running the orphanage for more than twenty years, the total could have been many more."

"Were they all boys?"

"No, there was a separate small house for girls and young women, but I only recall seeing four girls and about twenty boys."

"And those faces at the *mairie* that you recognized from the Leforts' scrapbook, did you ever see them again?"

"No. The party was dying along with the old guard. *Mairie* after *mairie* was being lost as the party shrank. Mitterrand killed it. He brought the party into his government in 1981, which we thought was the start of great things, but he slowly embraced us to death. No, I never saw the Leforts again, but I often wondered what had happened to those young German boys with the perfect French and their French identity cards. What must they have thought as their own country dissolved and they were stuck in France."

"Did you recognize those names, Henri Zeller and Max Morilland?"

She shook her head. Bruno pulled from his small briefcase a file with the reconstituted photos of the two men. "Do you recognize either of them?"

She took the photos and examined them closely, looking from one to the other. She extracted a pair of spectacles from her shirt pocket and examined them again. "I remember this one," she said, pointing at Max. "He was a favorite of Jacques and Sylvie. I met him with them because they threw him a birthday party. He was seventeen, I remember. Neither of the two names you mentioned rings a bell. And I don't recall ever seeing the other one. Which was the one you think was murdered?"

"Max, the one you recognized. Like Henri, he had a fake French identity, birth certificate, school records and reports — all simply made up at the *mairie.* When Max had that seventeenth birthday party he was supposed to be attending some vocational school in Belleville, according to the records in the *mairie.* His entire biography was invented."

"Do you know what happened, how Max was killed?" she asked.

"He and Henri had been making money in the strawberry fields and planned to move on to work in the vineyards, and in the first week of July they were camping *sauvage* near St. Denis. They picked up a couple of girls and then disappeared. Max's body was found the next year after a storm uncovered his grave in the woods. He'd been hit over the head with a camping shovel."

"This murder was in the summer of '89?" she asked. Bruno nodded. "That was the summer before the Wall came down, when thousands of young Germans were getting out to the West through Hungary and

Austria. Maybe Max and Henri realized the Democratic Republic was collapsing and fled to a new life in France."

"Those faces in the Belleville *mairie* you recognized from the East German orphanage, do you recall their names, anything else about them?" Bruno asked.

"No, we were not encouraged to make inquiries. If any of the employment records or paychecks from the registrations department still exist, I might be able to identify them by means of elimination, but I'm pretty sure those files were destroyed."

"Looking back, what do you think they were doing in Paris?"

"I assume they were planning to start new lives in France while continuing to serve the socialist revolution." There was just a trace of irony in her voice. "Presumably they were deployed here in France as underground organizers or as spies or recruiters or as mailboxes, through whom other spies could communicate. I can't imagine what other purpose they might serve."

"Are you in touch with any other former employees of the *mairie* who might be able to help us?"

"Not still in touch, but I know one or two who moved on to other party strongholds in the Red Belt after they lost Belleville, one to Malakoff and the other one to Kremlin-Bicêtre." She gave a half smile and shook her head regretfully, as if recalling memories of happier or perhaps simpler times. She seemed suddenly aware of Balzac at her feet, gazing up at her sympathetically. She bent down to stroke him before saying, "They'll both have retired since, but I think I'd have heard if they'd died. I won't give you their names, but anyway I doubt they would talk to you under any circumstances. I think they'll probably retain more of the old political loyalties than I do."

"Do you recall anything else that might be relevant?" Bruno asked, handing her his card when she shook her head. "Well, if anything comes to mind, please let me know."

"Is that it?" she asked. "You aren't going to arrest me?"

"Why would I want to do that?" he asked, genuinely surprised by her question. "You haven't committed any crime. You were a member of a legal party, working in a *mairie* controlled by that party after it won elections. You might have had suspicions that some of your comrades were conspiring to commit or assist espionage, but you only began to suspect when it was much too late to matter. You've been very helpful. What's more, you like my dog, and he seems to like you, so he'd probably object if I tried to arrest you."

She laughed aloud. "That's a relief. I'd hate to go to jail for views I no longer hold."

"One last thing. If I take down a brief statement confirming that you believe you saw the murdered man living as a pupil at the Clara Zetkin orphanage in East Germany, where he was a pupil of Jacques and Sylvie Lefort, would you date and sign it before I go? That means he cannot have been at the Paris orphanage as the Belleville *mairie* records claim."

She nodded. "Of course. It's no more than the truth. Tell me, do you think you'll be able to bring his killer to justice?"

"I hope so, but proving murder thirty years after the event is going to be tough." He took a pad and pen from his briefcase and began drafting the statement.

CHAPTER 20

Bruno put in his earphones, put his mobile phone into the cradle on the dashboard and called Isabelle on the encrypted line. He waited until he had the double green light that said their call was secure before setting off to drive from Carlux to Périgueux. He spent the first few minutes briefing Isabelle on the Clara Zetkin orphanage, on Jacques and Sylvie Lefort, and on the eyewitness placing the murdered Max in the former East Germany as a youth.

"The witness is — don't laugh — Rosa Luxemburg Delpèche, a disaffected old Communist who worked for the *mairie* in Belleville," he added. "These East German orphans were being raised as native French speakers, equipped with French identities and then inserted into French life and jobs and education while their loyalties were to East Berlin."

"So we have the Stasi connection, but one

with nothing to do with the Rosenholz dossier," Isabelle replied. "That's very interesting because I also have news for you. Our old friend General Lannes was called into the Élysée yesterday evening to be told that they had just received a visit from the trendy and very political lawyer Maître Vautan. He arrived with a startling offer. He had a client who was prepared to give the Élysée a special version of the Rosenholz dossier relating to Stasi operations in France in return for immunity for any crimes committed on French soil."

"What did Lannes say?"

"He said he would have to consult the interior minister and colleagues in the DGSI, the Directorate-General of Internal Security. The Élysée didn't like that. They want to keep this in-house for security reasons, even though we all know the Élysée staff are the most notorious leakers in Paris."

"Obviously they agreed and he then briefed you."

"Yes, along with the minister and two people we think we can trust at internal security. And now I'm briefing you. Do you think these Clara Zetkin orphans are part of the Rosenholz dossier, or were they off the books, some special Stasi project that didn't get into the main files?"

"I don't know, but you said something about Maître Vautan suggesting his client had a special version of the Rosenholz dossier."

"That's how Vautan described it. The problem is we've been given no indication of the crimes for which Vautan's client seeks immunity. It's a blank check. They could be signing up to forgive a pedophile serial killer and heaven help anyone in the loop if this ever were to go public. Understandably, the Élysée wants some cover, which is why they want to be able to say they consulted the security services."

"I know this is quite a leap, but something described as a special version of the Rosenholz dossier in return for immunity makes me wonder if Henri might be behind this, hoping to get away with murder. He must have some credible evidence from the orphanage. What about your German colleagues? Can you get them to launch their own probe into the Clara Zetkin orphanage and Jacques and Sylvie Lefort? There must be some records of the place and of them, when they arrived in East Germany, who paid the bills. We need to know under what conditions they were given asylum or residence permits and what their status was."

"I'll do that as soon as we end this call

and I've had a chance to brief Lannes. He needs to know about this orphanage. Then I'll ask DGSI to look in their old files for this Lefort couple. When did you say they moved to East Germany?"

"Sometime in the fifties, according to Rosa Luxemburg."

"Okay, leave that with me. And what are you doing now?"

"I'm driving back from seeing this witness, with a signed statement, and heading for Périgueux where there's to be a meeting with Prunier about whether it makes sense to arrest Henri Bazaine on the false identity charge and faking his own death to avoid military service."

"The Élysée won't like that. If Henri has documentary evidence, he might not be able to deliver it if he's sitting in a cell in Périgueux. But what is it?" Isabelle demanded. "How might he have got hold of the Rosenholz dossier? The whole thing was too bulky to smuggle out before the Wall came down. Maybe he got just the French section, but how would he have obtained it from some country orphanage far from Stasi headquarters in East Berlin?"

"Maybe what Henri has is nothing to do with Rosenholz," Bruno mused, thinking aloud. "Maybe it's something different, like a register of the kids at the Clara Zetkin orphanage with their French names. Rosa, this woman from the Belleville *mairie* who visited the orphanage, said the French couple was so devoted to the kids that they kept a scrapbook of them all growing up, photos, names, school reports."

"*Putain,*" Isabelle said, almost spitting out the word. "How is that possible? Keeping something like that must have broken every security rule in Stasi's book."

"Rosa said she saw it at the orphanage in 1987. The collapse of East Germany in 1989 started when people began to flood out in the summer."

"May second, 1989, Hungary starts to dismantle the border fence with Austria," said Isabelle. "I've just called up the time line on my computer. Some ten thousand fled from East Germany in May, and another twelve thousand in June — that's the number of those who got out and applied to West Germany for citizenship."

"So, let's imagine it's May or June of '89. Max and Henri are smart boys. They see the place is collapsing and there's a way out," Bruno said. "They get to Hungary and then to Austria, and unlike the other East Germans they already have their French ID cards, their French names and they're bilingual. They decide to come to France rather than West Germany, where they'd probably be tainted as Stasi kids. As insurance, they steal the scrapbook and bring it with them. After a few days or weeks Henri realizes that there's only one scrapbook, and he kills Max to get it. Does that make sense?"

"It's plausible as a working hypothesis," Isabelle replied, cautiously. "But if the Stasi knew Max and Henri had the scrapbook, they would have moved heaven and earth to track them down and get it back."

"Only if the Stasi knew it was missing. What if Jacques and Sylvie never reported that it was gone? After all, they'd have been in trouble if they admitted to having kept a scrapbook that could identify each of these kids who were being groomed to be sleeper agents in France."

"I suppose you're right. Let me take this to Lannes. It's certainly possible that this offer comes from Henri. You'll be with J-J after this?"

"Yes, but wait: How much of all this can I share with J-J?"

"All of it," she replied firmly. "He's a professional. We can trust him."

"Even if he's robbed of a murder conviction because the Élysée agrees to the deal and hushes up the murder?"

"Yes, even then," she said. "But knowing that J-J knows might help persuade the Élysée that this might not be a sensible deal. The more people who know about it, the greater the chance of a leak. Any government found hushing up a murder would face a political storm. I should go. By the way, I e-mailed my Canadian contact at Sercars, their Service Canadien du Renseignement de Sécurité, about Loriot. We'll talk later. *Je t'embrasse.*"

The phone conversation had taken Bruno halfway to Périgueux, and he saw he'd missed an incoming call from his contact at army records. He was making good time, so he pulled off the road to return the call. Loriot, he learned, had served his twelve months in the army in 1987, mostly in a signals regiment based in Agen, because he'd listed his civilian job as an apprentice electrician.

Once in central Périgueux, Bruno realized he'd have a few minutes to visit Virginie in the police lab before his meeting with J-J, Prunier and the lawyers. He was looking forward to seeing her work on the skull, which J-J had said was close to being finished, partly out of curiosity but also as a way to check the quality of the composite photo of Max that he'd helped to assemble. However reassuring Rosa's swift and decisive recognition of Max had been from the photo he'd shown her, Bruno suspected any capable defense lawyer would be able to challenge its authenticity.

From the underground garage at the police building, where he left Balzac in his van, he came up to ground level, out into the courtyard and across to the separate adjunct building where the lab had been installed. The entrance, office and storeroom were on the ground floor, and in the basement were the lab, a small morgue and pathology room along with the shielded X-ray section.

As he trotted down the stairs, he heard what sounded like a scream, and then a woman's voice shrieking at someone to stop, followed instantly by a grunted male curse, the sound of a slap and another cry for help. Bruno found the door locked. He stood back and slammed the sole of his boot as hard as he could against the door just beside the lock. It burst open and he saw the back of a gigantic man in a police uniform, his hand up the white skirt of a woman. The male figure began to turn at Bruno's dramatic, charging entry, but too late. Bruno roared out a war cry as he slammed his boot hard up between the man's legs, then pivoted to kick the side of his knee and jerked him to one side so that he fell as his shattered knee collapsed.

As the man began to fall, the young woman shrieked again and slashed at the falling policeman's arm with what looked like a scalpel. She then raised it to threaten Bruno, blood dripping from her nose, her eyes wide in rage and shock.

Bruno backed away keeping his arms high and outstretched, open palms toward her, saying, "It's over, Virginie. It's okay. It's me, Bruno."

The white lab coat she was wearing had been ripped apart from top to bottom revealing a torn bra and a small breast that was red from some rough grasp. She was trembling with shock, but her eyes seemed to jolt and blink as she recognized him, although she kept her scalpel at the ready.

"I have to look at your attacker, he's bleeding," Bruno said, and bent down to the cop who was curled up in the fetal position on the floor, blood soaking into his uniform and onto the floor from the arm Virginie had slashed. Bruno put one knee on the guy's back to keep him in place, used one plastic cuff as a tourniquet to stop the bleeding from the man's arm and used another to bind his ankles together.

"You bastard, I'll kill you for this." The cop grunted, squinting at Bruno through narrowed eyes.

It was the cop's left arm that was bleeding. But there was blood on the fingers of his right hand. Bruno glanced at Virginie and saw a smeared trail of bloodstains on her thigh. *Putain,* what had the bastard done to her?

Bruno pulled a plastic evidence bag from his hip pocket, put it over the man's right hand and bound it into place with another plastic cuff, then used his mobile phone to call J-J.

"It's Bruno, in the police lab downstairs, where one of your cops has just tried to rape Virginie. We need medical attention for him, since she slashed him in self-defense, and I'll be filing charges of sexual assault against him. And we'll need a female cop and a doctor for Virginie."

He ended the call and turned to look at Virginie. The scalpel lay at her feet. She had her hands to her face and was trembling, her shoulders heaving as she sobbed and hiccuped.

"Virginie," he said. "Are you okay? What did he do? Speak to me."

She nodded, hands still clutched to her

face. He heard a muffled sob. Then she dropped her hands, took a deep breath, looked at him and nodded.

"Can you tell me what happened?" he asked.

She answered with the words and phrases running together. "He keeps coming in to ask me out, day after day, and I keep saying no, I'm working, I'm busy. He won't stop. And today he just grabbed me, grabbed my breast really, really hard, thrust his hand up . . ."

"It's okay, Virginie, it's over. I'm here." He was trying to make sense of the blood on the cop's hand and the smears on Virginie's thighs. He'd leave that to the policewoman J-J would be bringing.

"I need an ambulance," said the cop, lying under Bruno's knee.

"You're under arrest," Bruno said, and checked the man's arm. The bleeding had stopped, and Bruno recognized the man's face, the one in the police canteen who had made that offensive joke about sheep shaggers.

"Virginie, please, pass me your scalpel," Bruno said. She simply stared at him until he added, "I need to look at his wound, where you slashed him."

She nodded, bent down to pick it up and

357

handed it to him. Bruno cut away the sleeve of the cop's uniform and the shirt beneath to reveal a long, seeping cut running from the man's biceps down to his elbow. It did not look too deep, and the tourniquet was holding. He tightened the plastic cuff another notch and looked up to see Virginie staggering to the sink.

"Stop, Virginie. Please, don't wash anything away," he said. "We need the evidence to nail this bastard."

"I'm going to be sick," she said, and vomited into the sink.

As she spoke, Bruno heard a clattering of feet coming down the stairs, and J-J was the first in, a policewoman behind him and then a uniformed cop carrying a first-aid kit. Finally Commissioner Prunier himself came to stand, silent and glowering, at the door. J-J must have called him, Bruno thought.

"We need medical attention first for Virginie who has been assaulted, then for this cop whom I saw assault her," Bruno said. "Then I'm ready to give a statement. I should stress that I saw the cop with his hand very far up this woman's skirt and there's blood on her thighs and on his right hand. That's why I covered it with an evidence bag. I believe the blood on his hand will be that of the young woman, and

I insist that this be checked at once. The cut on the cop's left arm was made by the young woman with a scalpel in self-defense."

"Right," said Prunier, staring grimly at the scene. "Commissaire Jalipeau, you're in charge. I want a female medical examiner at once to check on this young woman and I want blood tests on the right hand of Gardien Baldin and the young woman's thighs, as Chief of Police Courrèges suggests. Nobody leaves this room until that is done. Gardien Baldin is under arrest but also requires medical attention, as does the young woman. I want statements to be taken from the three people who were in this room when we arrived."

He turned to the policewoman. "You will accompany this young woman at all times until further notice." He turned again. "Bruno, I'll take your statement myself. Come with me." He led the way up the stairs and across the courtyard to the main building and then to the elevator that led to his office on the top floor.

"That bastard Baldin is a menace, but his dad was a *commandant* here so he gets away with a lot. He's also active in the union," Prunier said once he and Bruno were in the privacy of his office. "Now we might finally be able to get rid of him."

"Let's do this right," said Bruno. "He has to be dismissed, never to wear the uniform again. And he has to go on the sex offenders list." He pulled out his phone, pressed the recording function and began to speak.

"I am recording this statement of my own free will. I arrived at the police lab at eleven-thirty a.m. on this day, July tenth, to see the progress of the work of the young volunteer, Virginie, whose facial reconstruction skills I recommended to Commissaire Jalipeau," Bruno began.

He went on to give a detailed account of what he had seen and done. He forwarded the sound file of his statement to Prunier's phone, who in turn forwarded it to his secretary sitting outside to be typed up.

"A couple of questions," Prunier said and turned on his own phone's record function. "First, have you met Gardien Baldin before?"

"I know his face by sight from passing him in corridors and the canteen, but did not learn his name until this incident."

"What made you call at the lab at that moment?"

"I had an appointment with you and J-J and arrived early, so I decided to use the time to see the progress Virginie had made on the facial reconstruction. I was the one who first proposed to J-J that we bring her here to work on Oscar's skull."

"Last question, how much force did you use to restrain Gardien Baldin?"

"I used reasonable force, since Baldin is a big man, nearly two meters tall and powerfully built. When I kicked down the door and saw him assaulting Virginie, I shouted at him to stop, kicked his groin to stop the sexual assault and then his knee to limit his movements. I then pulled him backward, which probably prevented him from being more badly slashed by Virginie's scalpel. He fell to the floor and I restrained him. I also put a tourniquet on his bleeding left arm and then called for help."

"Right, that's it, thanks. We'll get all that typed up for you to sign, and you will have to appear at the disciplinary hearing against Baldin and then at the trial. I'm suspending him from duty as of now."

"Good," said Bruno. "And there have been some developments on the Henri Bazaine case. It's a lot more complicated." He went on to explain the offer made by the lawyer to the Élysée, his own meeting with Rosa Luxemburg Delpèche and his discussion that morning with Isabelle. "I suggest that before taking a decision on arresting Henri Bazaine, you wait to hear from General Lannes, who now seems to have taken over this inquiry at the request of the Élysée."

"*Putain,* just how many French-speaking sleeper agents did the Stasi churn out from this orphanage?" Prunier asked.

"I don't know, but Rosa Luxemburg said she saw at least twenty kids, and we have no idea how many were produced in previous years. Isabelle is contacting the German security people to see what they can find out. The Leforts had immigrated to East Germany in the fifties, so they had thirty years to manufacture their fake French citizens."

"And we never found any of them, never knew anything about this? It makes my head spin. I suppose I'd better wait to hear from General Lannes before arresting Bazaine. What would you do?"

Bruno shook his head. "I don't like the idea of granting immunity to a murderer, if indeed that's what happened. But we may have no choice. If Henri really can give us information that identifies all the undercover agents the Stasi trained and sent us, it's probably worth doing the deal. Even though the Stasi is long dead, who knows if the Russians are still able to make use of these people?"

"You really think Henri Bazaine is behind this lawyer's offer to the Élysée?"

"I can't be sure, but it looks likely," Bruno said. "That gives me an idea. We can check Henri's credit cards for train bookings and flight lists to see if he went up to Paris to see his fancy lawyer, Maître Vautan. If he drove, there should be a record on the autoroute tolls. Maybe he arranged it all through the People's Pierre. Either way, I think Maître Vautan would have wanted to see something that looked like proof before he went to the Élysée. I can't see Henri giving any lawyer the original scrapbook, so he may have made a photocopy."

Prunier scribbled a note. "I'll get someone onto the travel records. What are the operative dates?"

"Henri could not have known we were looking for him until last Friday at the earliest, and the publicity about the Rosenholz dossier did not start until Sunday."

"So if we can show he went to Paris since then, it looks pretty certain. We can arrest him and then search his place for the scrapbook."

"It could be in a safe-deposit box, or hidden on his property. I don't think you have the manpower to dig up all those hectares of vines. And it might all be on microfilm, anyway. He was trained to be a spy, don't forget, so he'll know all these tricks. If I were him, I'd have buried the original somewhere very deep but kept a microfilm hidden close to hand. He could even have e-mailed some selected pages of microfilm to the lawyer in Paris while keeping the original in a safe place."

"He'd have wanted to brief the lawyer in person, so let's see if he went to Paris."

"It's worth trying," Bruno said. "But let's not expect to get a murder conviction. I doubt we'll ever be able to prove that Henri killed Max, unless he confesses."

"Well, from what you say about these East Germans with fake identities, at least it wasn't a French citizen that he bumped off," Prunier replied. "That would really stick in my throat."

CHAPTER 21

From Prunier's office Bruno went first to find J-J, without success, and then down to the basement garage to get Balzac. He went to the lab to see if Virginie was still there. Although the place was empty he was delighted to find the skull on which she had worked. It had been partly hidden by the screen of her laptop in the few dramatic moments he'd been in the lab. Now her laptop lid was closed, and the eerily disembodied head of Max — for there was no doubt that it was he — stared out across the lab.

He was bald. But strewn beside him were three cheap wigs of fair hair, each of a different length and shade of blondness. Bruno tried each one on the skull. None seemed quite to capture the curl and thickness Bruno recalled from the photo. But the shape of the face, the cast of the eyes, the prominence of the nose, the thinness of the lips and the thrust of the jaw all seemed right.

Bruno let out a soft whistle of admiration. Even without those hours of scanning through the photographs in the St. Denis archive, Max might have been identified from this reconstruction alone. Virginie had done an admirable job, and it was outrageous that one of the Périgueux cops should have treated her so shamefully. He sent a text to her phone to say, "This is brilliant. I'm full of admiration, Bruno." He added a postscript inviting her to the comfortable and welcoming company of his friends in St. Denis. He added his mobile number and then he sent a text to Elisabeth Daynès in Paris, saying that Virginie's work on the skull had exceeded his highest hopes, and when the case was complete, he'd give her a full report.

Balzac at his heels, he climbed up the stairs to the courtyard and headed for the main reception area, where he asked the cop on duty if he knew where he could find J-J and what had happened to the young woman in the lab. J-J was at the hospital with Gardien Baldin, he was told, and the young woman was with Commissaire Gouppilleau, the senior female officer at the station. He asked to be put through to her office on the deskman's phone and, when Gouppilleau answered, identified himself and asked if Virginie would consent to see him. He was told to come right up.

"Along with every other female cop in Périgueux I'd like to buy you a large drink. And that's a very handsome dog," announced a cheerful woman in a police uniform that had been extremely well cut. She was striding along the corridor toward him as he reached the top of the stairs. "It looks like you might have lifted the curse of the big, bad Baldin, the most loathed man in the station. Come in, come in. Virginie has been telling me all about it."

"I like the shoes," Bruno said, smiling as he gestured down to the defiantly nonuniform red high heels the *commissaire* was wearing.

"Good," she said. "So do I, even if I have to change into clodhoppers when I go outdoors. They help keep up my morale."

"Hi, Bruno," said Virginie from her place in a deep armchair, looking very pale and wearing a policewoman's raincoat that was about four sizes too large for her. The blood on her face had been cleaned and a bandage had been taped over her nose. Her voice sounded as if she had a heavy cold. "Thanks for turning up when you did."

"I'm so sorry about this, Virginie, and just wish I'd arrived a minute or two sooner," he said as Balzac trotted up to Virginie and put out a paw.

"Don't worry. Balzac is just trying to say hello."

"No, you stopped matters going further," said Gouppilleau. "Arriving when you did will allow us to nail a cop who has been a menace to every woman in this building, and heaven knows how many civilian women outside. How the hell did you get the better of that guy?"

"I attacked him from the rear while he was trying to stop Virginie from grabbing the scalpel," Bruno said. "She was doing a very impressive job of defending herself. I could have come up behind him in a tank and he might not have noticed. J-J is with him at the hospital. I gave Prunier a statement, and we'll need one from Virginie."

"I already took her statement. It sounds like it accords with yours," Gouppilleau said. "Gardien Baldin has been officially suspended, and he'll be charged when he gets back from the hospital. I'll do that myself and I'll personally monitor the case from now on. I already know the female magistrate I want to work on this case, Annette, in the *procureur*'s office in Sarlat. I gather she knows you."

"She's a demon rally driver," he said. "She once scared the hell out of me when I had to act as her navigator." He turned to Virginie, who was sitting forward and caressing Balzac's ears.

"Shouldn't you be at the hospital? I was worried about that blood I saw on your thighs, and it looked like he really hurt you," said Bruno.

"My breast is sore, but the blood on my thighs was where he scratched me, trying to grope me and pull . . ." She paused, her eyes fixed on Balzac. "That was when I grabbed the scalpel."

"We had Virginie checked over by a doctor," said Gouppilleau. "She has a broken nose from where he slapped her, but it's been reset. It's great, Bruno, that you bagged his right hand. The scratch wasn't deep, but that's the evidence of assault that will send him to jail."

"It certainly should," said Bruno, thinking it was never easy to win a case for sexual assault, and even less easy to convict a cop. Bruno turned to Virginie. "I came to ask you if you'd like to come back to St. Denis with me and stay with some friends of mine. She's our local doctor and he's a writer and journalist, and I'll be telling everybody what a brilliant job you've done on the skull. Our mayor wants to take you to lunch, and you ought to meet my horse, who is just as handsome as my dog. You deserve a break after all the work you put in, and I hate the thought of you going back to a lonely room in an empty student hostel."

"Bruno is known to be a gifted chef," Gouppilleau said, smiling as Bruno looked at her in surprise. "Your colleague Juliette in Les Eyzies told me about your cooking," she went on. "You'd be surprised at the breadth of our intelligence network. In this job, we women have to stick together."

"Bruno," said Virginie. "Did you mean that, the message you left on my phone, about my skull?"

"It's even better than I hoped," he said. "We put together a composite photo from various partial snapshots and you've got Max to perfection."

"But I don't think I've got the hair right."

"There's no reason why you should. Elisabeth warned us about that. Anyway, it looks like you're part of what's turned out to be a much bigger case. I can't go into details now because national security is involved, but I think someday they could be making TV shows about this case. I'm just so sorry that it involved this dreadful assault on you."

"It was all over very fast once you turned up. And yes, I'd love to come down to St. Denis and have a bit of a break. I've been working almost nonstop."

"Your work has paid off, Virginie, believe me. Now, would you like me to take you back to the hostel and get a change of clothes?" he asked.

"I wish I got invitations like that," said Gouppilleau. "We have another mutual friend in Yveline, the gendarme *commandante,* and she says St. Denis is the best posting she's ever had. She, too, says you're a good cook."

"We like Yveline, too," said Bruno, wondering why he'd been so stupid. He'd never before realized that the women, whether gendarmes, Police Nationale or municipal, would naturally have their own networks and friendships. He had his own wide range of connections, male and female, from sports and hunting clubs to the regional archaeological society. He saw them as a real asset, not only in human, friendly terms but in the way people could share skills, tips and local knowledge. It was natural and useful that the policewomen would do the same.

"Bruno, I don't want to be in your way," Virginie said. "I know you have work to do."

"Don't worry about that. I thought you might like to see Elisabeth's exhibition at the museum in Les Eyzies, which led to your coming down here," he said. "Then you might like to meet a colleague of mine, the town policewoman, and some other friends. I was on fire watch last night so I'll be spared that tonight and I'll have time to cook. But mainly I think you deserve some time off."

"I'm a vegan," Virginie said. "I hope that won't be a problem."

Bruno recalled her polite thanks for the foie gras he'd given her as a welcome gift, and struggled to keep his expression unchanged and friendly. "That means no butter, eggs or cheese, is that right?" he asked, trying to keep his voice neutral. "And no cooking with duck fat."

Virginie nodded cheerfully and said, "I don't mind watching other people eat meat and stuff. I used to eat it myself. And I don't do without butter. You can buy it made from soy milk, sunflower oil, salt and lemon juice. I even make my own vegan pastry. I could show you how to prepare it, if you like."

Twenty minutes later, after a brief call to J-J, who was still at the hospital with the suspended Gardien Baldin, Bruno and Virginie were at the student hostel where she packed a small bag, and they set off for St. Denis. Balzac was in the back of the van, and the reconstituted skull of Max had been carefully packed in a hatbox that was at Virginie's feet. Gilles and Fabiola now occupied a house that Bruno knew well. It had been Pamela's home when he'd first known her, before she and Miranda had taken over the riding school. Gilles came out from his study when he heard Bruno's van. He shook hands with Virginie, whom he'd been expecting after Bruno had called him, and showed her to the spare room to leave her bag.

"What about dinner?" Gilles asked.

"I thought I'd cook, using your kitchen if that's all right. Virginie's a vegan."

"No problem for me, but Pamela's coming with the baron, since you missed the Monday dinner." Gilles's eyes twinkled. "Let's try an experiment. You prepare a vegan meal and see if the baron notices. I doubt whether he's ever had one in his life."

"Of course he'll notice. He loves his meat."

"I bet you he doesn't — a bottle of wine on it."

"Done," said Bruno.

Gilles tactfully made no remark about the bandage over Virginie's nose, and Bruno felt it was her business if she wanted to explain it. They had time for a cup of coffee with Gilles before Bruno drove her to the museum in Les Eyzies, where Clothilde had promised to show her the exhibition of Elisabeth Daynès's skulls. Bruno put the hatbox on Clothilde's desk and invited Virginie to open it.

"This is what I was hoping for when I first saw the exhibition," he said as Virginie displayed the extraordinarily lifelike head she had made of Oscar's original skull.

"And this is why I think your work is so good," he added, pulling from his briefcase one of the photos of Max that Yves had put together from the various snapshots taken at the Félibrée three decades earlier.

"Virginie refused ever to look at this photo, saying it would influence her work, but you can see the likeness is uncanny," he told Clothilde. "It's clearly the same man."

He used his phone to take a photo of Clothilde, Virginie and the skull and sent it off to Elisabeth in Paris, as Clothilde asked Virginie what had happened to her nose.

"Just an accident," Virginie replied. "It got broken, but it's not serious and it doesn't hurt. The doctor at the police station gave me a painkiller."

Clothilde glanced at Bruno with a raised

eyebrow but tactfully left it at that. She praised Virginie's work and suggested she might like to look around the rest of the museum and visit the workrooms, usually off-limits to the public. Clothilde's colleagues were hoping to hear Virginie describe the reconstruction procedure over lunch and then take her to some other of the local sites. Bruno was wondering whether he should explain to Clothilde what Virginie had been through, when she said eagerly, "Yes, please. I want to learn more about these prehistoric people."

"We thought you might like to start with the original Cro-Magnon site where the first skeletons were found a hundred and fifty years ago."

"That sounds great," Virginie said, making Bruno marvel at the resilience of youth.

"I'll be back to pick you up around five," Bruno said. He left Virginie at the museum and drove back to St. Denis to tackle his e-mails and paperwork. He settled Balzac in his office, briefed the mayor and told him of Virginie's arrival, then he checked on Albert's fire report. There had been a serious blaze that morning in the woods east of St. Cyprien, starting in a section that had been clear-cut a few months earlier, leaving a tangle of dry branches and twigs on the ground. It was the first time Albert had called in the water-dropping aircraft, and it was now under control, but quenching the flames had required the fire engines of St. Cyprien, St. Denis and Sarlat, plus a hundred volunteers. Bruno went to open his window and leaned out over the balcony and looked out to the east, wondering if he might see the smoke, but the warm winds from the south were taking it north toward Montignac.

Why did everything have to happen at once? he wondered. The fires, J-J's obsession with Oscar, the attack on Virginie, Balzac's puppies, the Belleville *mairie,* the Dresden orphanage and the mysterious offer of the Rosenholz material to the Élysée; events seemed to be rolling in on him like so many storm clouds. And what on earth did one cook for a vegan? He smiled at himself, at the way he could always relax by thinking of menus. He would make a cold summer soup to begin and *beignets de courgettes* which he could serve with *tapenade de tomates* instead of the usual *aillou.* For the main course he could make the kabocha pumpkin dish that Ivan's new Japanese girlfriend had offered in Ivan's bistro. He'd seen the blue-green pumpkins on sale in the *bio* store. And *citrouilles rôties à la sauge et aux noix.* Roasted pumpkin with sage and walnuts was a classic French dish, with shallots, parsnips and potatoes in the roasting pan alongside. He'd remove a portion for Virginie so that for the others he could add slices of *cabécou* goat cheese, which would slump in the heat of the vegetables. He'd serve it with a salad of thinly sliced heirloom tomatoes of different colors from his garden, drizzled with oil, followed by peaches sliced into a glass of red wine.

He had everything he needed in his garden except for the pumpkins and parsnips, and he was about to make a quick trip to the local *bio* shop when the phone rang. It was Isabelle.

"Two bits of news. Despite General Lannes's objections, the Élysée wants to go ahead with the lawyer's deal; his client gets immunity in return for the Rosenholz material. And my colleagues in Canada have come up with some dynamite."

Isabelle explained that her contact in Canadian security had sent a colleague based in Quebec City, accompanied by a uniformed policeman, to visit Loriot. They told him they were investigating a Canadian connection to Henri Bazaine at the request of the French police and asked him about the payments to Bazaine. Loriot became obviously uncomfortable and said it was for consulting on different grape varieties and on techniques for mass marketing and box wines. Then they asked why he had paid Bazaine so often when immigration records show that he'd only visited Canada once. What kind of consultancy was this? Loriot became even more uncomfortable and said he wanted a lawyer. I'd told them about the faked ID papers at the Belleville orphanage, which means he would have entered Canada on a false passport, and they used that — telling him that it could invalidate the Canadian citizenship he'd later acquired. When he remained silent, they played the trump card, asking if he'd ever heard from Jacques and Sylvie Lefort of the Dresden orphanage.

"At that point Loriot collapsed," Isabelle said. "When he pulled himself together he demanded a doctor as well as a lawyer. They arrested him for making false statements on his citizenship application, suggested several more charges that could be brought, and now Loriot's lawyer is trying to reach a deal."

"What kind of deal?" Bruno asked.

"He'll tell everything he knows if he can stay out of prison and be allowed to remain in Canada."

"Does the Élysée know about this?"

"Not yet. I just briefed Lannes and he's gone back there to let them know. He's hoping that they'll now reconsider the deal with Maître Vautan."

"And in the meantime Henri Bazaine is allowed to remain free?" Bruno asked. "Has J-J been informed of that?"

"I don't know, but Lannes talked to Prunier. Isn't that the chain of command you old military guys like to work with?"

Bruno smiled because he could hear the teasing in her voice and could imagine the mischievous grin on her face as she said it.

"In principle, maybe," he said, chuckling. "But in practice, we old military guys usually find it easier to work somewhat less formally, rather like the way you and I try to keep each other informed."

He ended the call, went down to the *bio* shop and bought the pumpkins and parsnips. On the way back he saw an unusual vehicle that looked like a furniture van that had been painted red heading down the rue de la République toward the fire station. He followed on foot, to see another strange car drawn up on the forecourt. It looked like a giant off-road four-by-four with huge wheels, but it was obviously some kind of fire engine, with pump settings and coiled hoses stashed along the side. Ahmed, Albert's deputy, was standing talking to the driver of the huge van, and Bruno asked him what it was.

"A water tender, carries about eight thousand liters," Ahmed replied, before introducing Bruno to the driver who had come from Bordeaux and telling the driver he'd find refreshments inside.

"We really should have more tenders like this because there's never enough water when you're facing forest fires," Ahmed went on. "It's not like in town where you can connect your hose to a water main. And our power hoses pump out nearly a thousand liters a minute. With four hoses, we can empty a tender in two minutes."

"Can't you stick your hoses in a river and draw it up that way?"

"If the river is close enough, we do. Anything over four hundred meters away and we'll need extra pumps and we might run out of hoses, and rivers have silt and debris that can clog them. Quite a few houses around here have their own swimming pool, which is great because even a small pool can hold a hundred thousand liters. We've got drones that can tell where the pools are, and if they are near enough to the blaze to help. But if there are no pools, we're dependent on the aircraft dumping water."

"But you just pump water onto the flames, like you would with a burning house, don't you?" Bruno asked. He'd never thought much about the way firefighters had to work.

"We usually save our hoses for the really hot spots, they're the main danger. A really bad one we have to try doing a knockdown to suppress it because they can suck in enough air to create their own small firestorm. Then they can move very fast, faster than a man can run."

"What if you can't knock a hotspot down?"

"You get out fast and try to set a control line some distance ahead to stop it. That's what we mainly do on the ground, which is why bulldozers can be as useful as water when you're fighting wildfires. We try to set control lines to steer the fire into directions we want it to go, like toward a river that's wide enough to block the fire. We usually try back-burning, deliberately setting small fires ahead of the fire so it runs out of fuel. If we have enough manpower, we do cold trailing, following the fire and trying to be sure there are no hot coals or embers left that could be picked up by the wind and moved on to start a new blaze. We can use volunteers for that, but trying to set up and hold a control line is for us professionals."

"Is there anything else people like me can do?"

"The main thing is to evacuate people in danger. And we always need bulldozer drivers to help set control lines. These days people who are good with drones are really useful."

"Do you have enough skilled people?"

Ahmed shrugged. "You never have enough. But we have crews who've come in from as far north as Normandy. They're now fighting the fires in the Landes. Even with them and the aircraft, we're going to lose a lot of forest, that's for sure, and maybe some of the walnut plantations."

"Are you on duty tonight?"

"Yes, while Albert tries to get some sleep. He's running ragged already. How about you? You're on again tomorrow night?"

Bruno nodded. "What's the forecast on how long that south wind keeps up?"

"All week, at least. What are those blue things you're carrying?"

"Japanese pumpkins, an experiment — I thought I'd roast them with shallots and potatoes with a few parsnips and get some slices of goat cheese melting over the top . . ."

"Sounds interesting, let me know how it works out."

"Will do. I hope it's a quiet night for you," said Bruno.

Sunda: internativag, let and how away

"Max, I hope he's still safe," Bruno said? Creens

CHAPTER 22

Bruno picked up Virginie at Les Eyzies, brought her back to introduce her to the mayor and show him her re-creation of Max's head. The mayor was in an excellent mood, which usually meant that some event, political or otherwise, had gone entirely to his satisfaction.

"Just had the defense ministry on the line, one of the minister's staff," the mayor said. "As of tonight, the military will be taking part in fire-watch duties from their big transmission towers, not just ours but wherever there's a fire alert. A rare victory for common sense."

Virginie thanked him for his support of the project that had brought her down to the region and opened the hatbox to display the head she had crafted of Max. Bruno handed him a copy of the composite photo, and the mayor nodded appreciatively as he compared the two.

"I don't think I'd have believed it if I hadn't seen the result of your work with my own eyes. It's a remarkable achievement, and you have my thanks and my congratulations. Presumably you will have to show this to your teacher in Paris, but after that and when the court case is complete, we'd be honored to display your work here in St. Denis."

"Commissaire Jalipeau says he would like to have it for the police museum," Virginie replied. "But now that I've done the first one I'm sure I can make a replica for him very easily, and I don't think he'd know the difference."

Nor would we, thought Bruno to himself as he led her downstairs to his van for the drive back to his home to feed the chickens and pick the vegetables, salad and fruit for dinner.

"This is a lovely place and a terrific view," she said as Bruno parked in his driveway. She stepped out to admire his garden and watch Balzac trot off to see the geese and chickens. "And you have so many vegetables growing here I'd have sworn you were another vegan."

"No, I'm a happy omnivore, but I love growing and eating my own fruit and vegetables. We'll dine tonight with Gilles and

Fabiola at the house where you left your bag."

He went to the kitchen and brought out a wicker basket and let Virginie pick the *courgettes,* herbs and tomatoes he'd be preparing. He cut down onions, garlic and shallots from the braided strings that hung from beams in his kitchen. He added a carrot to the basket for his horse. Then he led her to the rear of his cottage and let her choose between the peaches, apricots and figs on his trees for their dessert. She took a selection of all three.

"Don't you entertain here?" she asked.

"Yes, often, but with a fire warning in place, the local fire chief has forbidden me from staying here overnight, since it's so close to the woodland. As the local policeman I'm on his list of essential personnel, like the mayor, doctors and pharmacists. I'm staying at the mayor's house until we get the all clear. So I'm very pleased that these fruits and vegetables we're taking away won't be going up in smoke."

"What about your chickens?"

"If a fire looks like it's getting close, my job is to organize an evacuation for some neighbors who live out of sight but quite nearby, which means I should have time to rescue the geese and chickens. I've already stored my essential documents and personal treasures in town. That reminds me, I need to bring up some wine from the cellar for our dinner tonight."

"Is that why I'm staying at your friends' house, because of the danger of fire?"

"Partly, but I also thought it inappropriate to invite you to stay with me, a single man, and it means you'll make new friends. We're also eating there because Gilles wants to talk to you about your work on the skull. He mainly writes books these days, but he was on *Libération* and then *Paris Match* for many years and still freelances, and I think he feels there might be a story in your work. Now we'll call in at the stables so you can say hello to Hector, my horse. You may also meet another friend who's coming to dinner, Pamela. She runs the riding school, a cookery school and some *gîtes* for tourists."

"I was raised in cities, so I don't ride, and I don't know much about horses."

"Nor did I before coming here. I grew up in Bergerac and only learned about the country once I arrived in St. Denis, not much more than ten years ago," he said. "I didn't ride, didn't know much about dogs or chickens or even about gardening. You can learn all these things, and every single one of them has enriched my life. I didn't know much about wine, either, but I've really enjoyed getting to know winemakers and beginning to understand a little of what they do."

"My mum always used to say you should never stop learning because life never stops offering you lessons."

"She sounds like a wise woman," he said. "Let's go and meet Hector and Pamela and two of Balzac's friends, sheepdogs called Beau and Bella."

When they arrived at Pamela's place, she was in the courtyard of the stables with her horse, Primrose, already saddled. She greeted Virginie, saying, "You must be the young artist Bruno has been telling us about, or are you a sculptor?"

"I think I'm more a technician."

"That's not what I hear about your work, and it's not what I saw at the museum of the creations your teacher made from skulls. I think what you do is extraordinary." Pamela turned to Bruno. "Do you want to take Hector out?"

"Virginie doesn't ride. And she just had a bit of an accident, broke her nose."

"Poor thing. Miranda is about to start with the beginners, putting young girls onto a pony and walking them round the ring. Would you like to try that, Virginie?"

"Not today, but I'd like to watch while Bruno goes for his ride. May I meet Hector, please?"

Bruno led the way to Hector's stall, took the carrot from his pocket, broke it in half and gave half to Virginie and showed her how to hold out her hand and let Hector find his own way to the treat. He assured her the horse wouldn't bite. He held out his own half carrot first and told Virginie to watch from the side and see how delicately the horse took it.

"You'll feel his breath on your hand, very warm, and then his amazingly soft lips and then, without you noticing, it's gone and he's chewing away."

Bruno put on his riding boots and cap as Virginie rather nervously held out her hand but then kept it immobile as Hector took his treat. He brought the saddle across, kneed Hector gently in the tummy as he tightened the girth, and Bruno then fit the bridle and gave the rein to Virginie, suggesting she lead him out to the yard to join Pamela and Primrose. They showed Virginie the way to the rail from where she could watch the ponies walking sedately around the ring as Miranda stood in the center, encouraging the little girls, some as young as six or seven.

Pamela let Primrose ease into a canter as they left the paddock by the lower path that led up a gentle slope to the church at St. Chamassy. She was deliberately avoiding the woodland, thought Bruno, perhaps nervous at the thought of fire. There was not much chance of a decent gallop on this route. It was the long, straight firebreaks between patches of forest that gave the best chance of the kind of run that Hector and his rider most appreciated. Still, with Virginie in tow he should not indulge himself; there were limits to how long one could watch little girls parading past, each on her placid pony. Within twenty minutes, they were back at the riding school, and as they rubbed down the horses, Bruno explained his bet with Gilles.

"You!" she exclaimed, laughing. "You are cooking vegan? Wonders will never cease. If this works, I might have a whole new task for you at the cookery school — we can call you the vegan master chef of Périgord, if that's not a contradiction in terms. How on earth can you cook, my dear Bruno, you of all people, without your beloved duck fat, without your cherished bouillon from wild boar, your cheese and your cream?"

"In the face of such a challenge, Pamela, I shall be inspired," he replied, grandly. He made a flourish with his hand and bowed low in the manner of some Renaissance courtier, at which point Pamela playfully threw her brush at him and Virginie appeared simultaneously at the stable door.

"Am I interrupting something," she asked, her voice hesitant, but her face was grinning widely.

"Not at all," said Pamela. "It is an old Périgord custom to throw a brush at your cavalier after an enjoyable ride." She paused as Virginie raised her eyebrows and then chuckled.

"Oh, dear," Pamela said quickly. "Please don't misunderstand me, I didn't mean to phrase it like that." She then giggled. Bruno laughed in turn and Balzac at once jumped up playfully. Virginie looked back and forth at them and inevitably joined in and began to laugh, too.

"I'm not sure what's so funny," Virginie said once their laughter had died down. "But it's lovely to laugh like that even though it makes my nose hurt." And she burst into giggles again.

"And I now have to cook," said Bruno.

"I haven't laughed like that in ages," said Pamela. "It's wonderful, except that now I've got the hiccups. I'd better head for the shower and, Virginie, feel free to use the spare bathroom. Bruno, you should leave now, and I'll bring Virginie along in my car."

With Balzac back in his favorite place on the passenger seat, Bruno drove the route he knew so well to Pamela's old house, now owned by Gilles and Fabiola. After greeting his friends, he installed himself in the familiar kitchen with his basket of fruits and vegetables and the wines he'd brought. There was a bottle of Château Lestevenie white, certified to be suitable for vegans, one of Château de Tiregand red and a bottle of rosette from Château de Rooy, a slightly sweet white wine that was unique to the Bergerac and a perfect *apéro* for a summer evening. The white wines went in the fridge, and the red wine he opened so it could breathe for a while before dinner.

First, he turned the oven on, set to one hundred seventy degrees centigrade. He chopped the pumpkins into slices about an inch thick and put them into the biggest roasting pan he could find with a small head of celery, equally sliced. He then mixed a quarter pint of maple syrup into the same amount of olive oil, poured the mixture into the roasting pan and tossed the pumpkin and celery slices until they were all coated. He added salt and pepper and put the pan into the oven for twenty-five minutes. In that time, he made the soup, chopping four fat green peppers, peeling and then chopping two cucumbers, and tossing them all into a blender with two chopped onions. He added several cloves of garlic purée squeezed through a press, salt, pepper, olive oil, tarragon vinegar and two glasses of Bergerac Sec white wine. Once the mixture was blended he put the soup into the freezer to chill.

Then Bruno washed the peaches, figs and apricots and put them into a bowl. Now he had just enough time to make the sauce for the pumpkins. He chopped a generous handful of fresh sage, put it into a bowl with a pound of walnut halves, added a pinch of sea salt and then poured in another quarter pint of maple syrup and a tablespoon of olive oil and stirred them all together. He checked his timing. The twenty-five minutes were up. He took the roasting dish from the oven, poured the sage, walnut and maple syrup mixture over the pumpkin slices, tossed them again and put the dish to one side. When he served the chilled soup, he'd put the pumpkins back into the oven. He then sliced the tomatoes he brought, making a dressing with a little walnut oil and tarragon vinegar, tossing them with a couple of handfuls of shredded basil. He was washing his hands when Gilles appeared, handing him a glass of white wine and then loading a tray with plates and glasses to set the table in the courtyard.

"Everything okay?" Gilles asked. "Will your vegan feast meet our mutual expectations? This is a bet I hope to lose."

"Who knows?" Bruno replied as they heard the unmistakable sound of Pamela's ancient Citroën *deux-chevaux.* "I've never done this before."

They went out to welcome the guests, and Fabiola appeared, looking enchanting in a sleeveless dress of light blue silk belted with a white sash. Pamela was wearing a caftan of red and gold that set off the colors in her hair, and Virginie had changed into something that Bruno recognized from Pamela's wardrobe, an Indian-style garment of jodhpurs, tight on the calf, generously cut on the thighs, topped with an embroidered silk jacket that hung to her knees. The bandage still covered her nose, and tendrils of her pink hair splayed out from a white headband.

Bruno and Gilles raised their glasses in admiration, and then the baron's venerable Citroën DS, a car that dated from the fifties but still looked like something from the future, made its own grand entrance. The pneumatic suspension made the vehicle rock gently, like some prehistoric beast coming to rest, as the baron braked it to a halt.

"This is a charming idea," the baron said, emerging to brandish a bottle of Veuve Clicquot champagne, which he proceeded to open. "I'm honored to be welcomed by three such glorious women."

He was introduced to Virginie and greeted Gilles and Bruno. They were holding empty champagne flutes, ready to hand them to Fabiola, Virginie and Pamela once the baron had filled the glasses.

"There was news on the radio, a fire in the woods east of Belvès and another north of St. Pompont, and the *pompiers* are trying to prevent them from joining up and becoming more serious," the baron said, drawing Bruno and Gilles aside and speaking in a low voice. "With this wind we could be smelling the smoke before dinner is over. We might even have to move indoors from the terrace."

Bruno knew the area, a thinly populated region with a lot of old woodland, stretching about twenty kilometers northward to one of the most celebrated stretches of the Dordogne River, where it was flanked by the three castles of Milandes, Beynac and Castelnaud. Quietly he explained to the baron and Gilles what he'd learned from Ahmed about the shortage of water tenders.

"We'd better eat soon, in case I'm called away," he said, and asked Gilles to bring out the gazpacho and start serving while Bruno went into the kitchen to put the pumpkins back into the oven. He sliced the fat *tourte* of bread and took it out to his friends on the terrace and sat down to enjoy the chilled soup.

To his surprise, Fabiola was holding Virginie's face. She had unpeeled the bandage and was looking carefully at her broken nose, still swollen and now marked by a wide, almost purple bruise.

"How on earth did this accident happen?" she asked, glancing quickly at Bruno. "I don't think you walked into a door. It looks to me as though somebody slapped you very hard. It wasn't a punch that did this."

"It's all right," said Virginie. "Just a stupid cop. Bruno came along in time to stop anything worse from happening."

Merde, Bruno thought to himself. The story would doubtless emerge when Baldin was formally charged, but he didn't want rumors to start spreading before that.

"You were doing very well on your own, Virginie," he said. "I think we'd better leave it there for now. The cop has been suspended, there's the usual internal police investigation underway and I'm told he'll be formally charged with assault. Now, we'd better eat before the next course is ruined. Red wine or white?" he asked, rising with a bottle in each hand, poised to pour.

Fabiola was not going to let it rest, ignoring Bruno to ask Virginie where she had been treated. "A police doctor. They didn't want me going to the emergency room at the hospital since the cop had been taken there after I slashed his arm with a scalpel and Bruno smashed his knee."

"This sounds rather serious," said Pamela. "Are we to presume this was a sexual assault by a policeman?"

"I'm afraid it was," said Bruno. "But please do eat up. We have what could be a serious fire south of the Dordogne and I may get called away."

He began to eat and the others followed suit, except for Fabiola.

"I'm very sorry that your visit here has been marred by this, Virginie," said Fabiola. "I thought you were working in the police lab in Périgueux. How come you were alone?"

"One of the staff was on maternity leave, and the chief technician had been taken to the hospital last week for an unexpected appendectomy," Virginie replied. "The third one was in court, testifying on forensic evidence. It was just bad luck that all three were gone."

"Virginie's work has been a great success," Bruno said, in an attempt to change the subject. "She's helping us resolve a really fascinating thirty-year-old murder case."

"A sexual assault in a police station, and the assaulting cop taken to the hospital after being stabbed by a young woman with a scalpel," said Gilles. "You won't be able to keep that out of the press."

"Nor should it be kept out of the press," said Pamela. "I've half a mind to call Philippe Delaron. What about you, Gilles? What do you think?"

"I think we listen to Virginie and Bruno and let the law take its course," Gilles replied. "This sounds to me as though it could be a messy case, a cop taken to the hospital after being stabbed and whatever you did to his knee, Bruno. The police union will get the cop a good lawyer. He might even try to get Virginie charged for assault with a scalpel, and maybe you, too, Bruno."

"Please, just stop," said Bruno, rising to take his empty soup bowl to the kitchen. "There is irrefutable evidence that this cop was engaged in a sexual assault on Virginie. I won't go into details, but this case is solid, and the two top cops in Périgueux, male and female, are determined to throw the book at the bastard."

He collected the rest of the soup bowls, except for Fabiola's, since she was still eating, and went into the kitchen to take the roast pumpkin dish from the oven, put the serving dish on a tray and take it out to his friends. To his relief, they were talking about the fire to the south and sniffing at the wind to see if there was any trace of smoke on the steady breeze. Bruno put the dish onto the table, and at once their noses caught the heady scent of sage, maple syrup and roast pumpkins. The conversation shifted at once to the food and to the red wine Bruno was serving, just as he had hoped.

CHAPTER 23

The call came for Bruno as they were finishing their dessert of fresh fruit, asking him to report to the crossroads at the Siorac golf course, where the fire engines of St. Denis, St. Cyprien, Belvès and Le Buisson were assembling. Another team was gathering at Sarlat, he was told, and a third at Gourdon. Reinforcements were on the way from Cahors and Périgueux. *Mon Dieu,* he thought, this is a maximum effort. As he rose from the table, about to apologize and go, Fabiola's phone trilled out the opening chords of Noir Désir's *Le Vent Nous Portera.* She was being summoned as well.

Bruno had a sudden image of the powerful video that had accompanied the song, a mother and her child on a beach, the wind blowing away a sandcastle as the sky darkened and the mother searched in vain for her son as the wind drove her back. He shivered, hoping it was not an omen.

Dinner was over. Gilles decided to drive Fabiola to the clinic and then report with his car to the St. Denis fire station. He and the baron were both on the list of volunteers to help drive people being evacuated to the shelter at the St. Denis *collège*. Pamela said she'd drive Virginie back to her place where she could stay the night, since Gilles and Fabiola would both be away from their home, and she would look after Balzac.

"Before we all go," said Gilles. "Just one question, to the baron. How did you enjoy the meal?"

"Very good, reminded me of a very good meal I had in the Algerian War," he said, and then paused and his face widened into a smile. "I'd almost forgotten how good a meal of simple vegetables could be."

"I win," said Bruno. "Gilles bet me a bottle that you wouldn't notice."

"But I didn't notice all through the meal," the baron said. "It didn't cross my mind until Gilles asked the question in that rather pointed way which suggested that a private wager was at stake. And since I was given that clue, I'd call it a draw, except that we all won. It was a fine meal, Bruno, thank you and good luck tonight."

Bruno called the mayor, who was already at the St. Denis fire station and who immediately asked, "What do you want me to do with your Land Rover? It will be far more useful off-road than your police van, and I've made sure the gas tank is full. Philippe Delaron is here, about to go to Siorac, where I gather the control point will be."

"Good idea, I'll come now for the Land Rover, but I'd better change into uniform at the *mairie.* Tell Philippe I'll see him at Siorac."

The parking area at the Siorac golf course was filled with police and fire vehicles, a command truck flying a tricolor beside a military signals van. A row of arc lights had already been lit against the gathering dusk. Philippe was waiting outside the command truck as Bruno arrived and was talking urgently into his phone in that disciplined way that told Bruno he was live on air to the local radio station. By now Bruno could smell the smoke. He reported to the command truck, saying he had a Land Rover available. He was given a large-scale map and a list of three remote dwellings near St. Laurent-la-Vallée inhabited by two old couples and a disabled woman. They were to be taken to the *mairie* at Coux, and then he should report back. He checked the map he'd been given against his phone, identified the three remote cottages and set off.

It took him twenty minutes to get there, an endless line of cars coming the other way, the headlights dimmed by the smoke that was starting to thicken as the evacuation gathered pace. In St. Laurent, he saw a gendarme truck with Yveline and Sergeant Jules directing traffic. He slowed, beeped his horn and waved. Yveline flagged him down and came across to his vehicle with a list. She put a tick beside the three addresses assigned to Bruno and told him to report back to her before heading for Coux.

"You won't have much time," she said. "The fire's getting close."

He found the first house easily enough, installed the two old people into the front seat alongside him and checked that they had their key documents with them and a change of clothes in a small suitcase. In the second house he found the disabled woman in a wheelchair with her young daughter, no more than eleven or twelve, Bruno thought when he arrived at their house with the Land Rover. Bruno lifted the woman from her wheelchair and laid her on one of the rear benches while the daughter folded the wheelchair, went back for a suitcase and then sat on it beside her mother while Bruno heaved the wheelchair onto his roof rack and secured it with bungee cords. The third house was harder to find, deep in the woods. By now the smell of smoke was strong, and there was an ominous glow in the darkening sky to the south.

"There," called the girl from the back. "Off to the right behind us, I saw a light."

Bruno reversed along the dirt road, saw a small unmarked turning to the right and a single light some fifty meters away in the trees. He drove down, thinking his police van could not have made it along this overgrown path. He turned the Land Rover for an easier departure, went to the front door of the house and knocked, aware of the stench of a septic tank that had not been emptied for far too long. There was no answer. The door was unlocked and he went in, almost gagging from the smell of rotting food and something else, something ominous. The main room was empty, and so was the kitchen, the sink overflowing with dirty plates. He called out the name of the couple who lived there, but there was no reply.

He checked the bathroom, at the back of the house by the kitchen, and the stench of the septic tank was even worse. He went upstairs and found an old man asleep in a chair by the bed on which an old woman lay. He was holding her hand. Bruno at first thought she was dead, but he checked her pulse. It was faint, but she was alive. He woke the man and led him, barely awake and unprotesting, down the stairs. He checked that the man had his wallet, found the woman's handbag, checked for her ID card and *carte vitale* and led the husband to his Land Rover. He had to lift the disoriented and almost helpless old man into the back, where he asked the young girl to keep an eye on him.

"Just shout if you need me," he said, and went back upstairs, about to scoop up in his arms the woman and her bedclothes until he realized they were sodden with urine. He found blankets in a wardrobe, wrapped her in those instead and carried her downstairs and put her onto the other bench in the back of his vehicle. He used more bungee cords to hold her in place.

Back in St. Laurent, he told Yveline of the condition of his last two passengers, adding that he didn't want to inflict this on the young girl for long. She had enough on her plate looking after her mother, let alone the two old people. Yveline nodded, saying the fire had started moving much faster than had been expected, and despite all the warnings on radio and TV too many people had left their departure until the last minute.

The roads were getting jammed. She sent him on his way to join a slow-moving line of cars. When he finally reached the *mairie* in Coux, there was a line of waiting cars as volunteers tried to sort out who needed medical attention and who would go to the St. Denis reception center. Bruno was surprised at the number of elderly people there, some of them sitting on a stone wall, others leaning on walking sticks, several in wheelchairs. He was impressed by their patience and stoicism, taken from their homes to an unknown place for the night.

He went in and saw the local mayor's wife, whom he knew slightly, and explained about the old man and his probably dying wife. She checked the evacuation list and told him to take his passengers to the St. Denis medical center, where they had doctors and the facilities to deal with them. Bruno obeyed, although he thought there might be better uses for his Land Rover. He took the back way to St. Denis, the hill road through Audrix, thinking the main road through Le Buisson might be blocked with traffic. It had taken him an hour to get from the last of the three houses he'd evacuated to St. Denis, a trip that would usually have taken twenty minutes. And it took him almost as long again to unload his passengers, ensure they were taken in and then drive back to Siorac.

There were lessons to be learned from this emergency, Bruno thought. He'd have to file an after-action report suggesting that dedicated evacuation routes should be made for the public in the future, with traffic allowed to use both lanes. Other roads should be kept clear for police, fire and medical personnel. The planning should have been done already, except that nobody official had anticipated a fire such as this in the Dordogne. They should have, Bruno thought, after the nine southern French *départements* had been hit by fires in the same September week three years earlier, with thousands of people evacuated and the main north-south autoroute closed.

When he got back to the assembly point in the Siorac parking area, he saw Jules beside Yveline's van, but there was no sign of her. St. Laurent had been abandoned and the *pompiers* were trying to establish a new control line to stop the fire along the D53 and D50 local roads at Veyrines. Bruno drew on his mental map of the region, thinking that the only line of resistance after Veyrines would be the Dordogne River itself.

"When we pulled out from St. Laurent,

there were fires on the hills to each side of us, moving as fast we were. It was scary," said Jules. "Looks like you got your people out just in time."

"Where's Yveline?"

"Down at the riverbank. They've requisitioned garbage trucks and milk tankers and she's trying to get them filled with water and take them up to the fire engines for the hoses. They haven't got enough tenders, since most of them were assigned to the fires in the Landes. The St. Cyprien gendarmes are collecting those aboveground swimming pools, you know the ones, thick plastic sheeting in a cradle. There's a plan to move them to Veyrines and use the available tenders to fill them so the fire engines can recharge faster."

"Sounds like a decent idea," said Bruno. "I'd better report in."

Despite his uniform, Bruno waited in line for nearly twenty minutes outside the command center before he could report. He was told to take back roads to Allas-les-Mines and evacuate some more families between there and Milandes, but to use only the small road through the woods to Envaux. On no account was he to use the Allas bridge. The main road and bridge at Allas were reserved for the fire engines. It was at that moment that Bruno fully understood the problem of the bottlenecks at the few available river crossings. Along the twenty-kilometer stretch from St. Cyprien to Castelnaud there was only that one narrow bridge at Allas.

A police vehicle drew up, blue light flashing, and Commissaire Prunier climbed out, pausing to greet Bruno as he entered the control center.

"I have an idea, let's use the *gabarres*," said Bruno, referring to the flat-bottomed boats that in the past had taken barrels of good Bergerac wine downriver to the port at Libourne. These days, they were pleasure boats that could take forty or fifty tourists on a river cruise.

"I'm on evacuation duty but can't use the Allas bridge because the fire engines need it," Bruno went on. "Given the traffic jams on other roads that means dumping carloads of old and disabled people at Allas without being able to get them across the bridge. Why don't we call out the *gabarres* from Beynac and use them to evacuate people from the dock at Envaux and take them back across the river to Beynac where they'll be safe. *Mon Dieu,* they'd be out of danger just staying on the river."

"That makes sense," said Prunier, nodding. "I'll call the mayor of Beynac and get him to organize the *gabarres* and send them to Envaux. You start evacuating people to the dockside there."

"Please make sure the control center here knows that Envaux is to be the evacuation point," said Bruno at the door. "And make sure that the mayor of Envaux knows to keep that dock open. And if there are volunteers who can help elderly and disabled people get aboard the boats, even better."

"Consider it done," said Prunier. "Now, get going."

Bruno delivered his final load of evacuees to the dockside at Envaux just after two in the morning. Several lights were on, and a group of people stood on the quay, but there was no boat in sight. The local mayor, whom Bruno had met when dropping off the first group, came to the Land Rover waving a mobile phone. As Bruno opened the door, she said, "I just spoke to them at Beynac. The *gabarre* is finally on the way. The skipper was nervous about running aground if he sailed at night but finally agreed."

"How many evacuees do you have now?"

"With the people in your vehicle, about thirty, all either old or disabled. And after that we'll have to get our own people out. We've been told the bridge at Allas is off-limits, and the radio said the fire is moving fast toward Milandes. So we're going to need a second boatload."

"Do they have a reception team organized at Beynac?"

"Yes, I've been told they have doctors and social workers standing by, and they've set up a basic medical facility in the castle." She paused, then gave him a tired smile. "It's really impressive how people are working together on this."

"A pity we can't do it all the time."

She nodded, still smiling, and he liked her at once. He could imagine the pressure she would be under, organizing the evacuation of her own village while trying to cope with the carloads of the elderly and disabled being brought to her dockside by Bruno and other volunteers. An attractive woman in her fifties with fine eyes, her hair was tied up loosely in a bun that somehow looked as if it had been done with care. This was a woman proud of herself, he realized, elected by her neighbors and evidently efficient. She smiled at him again, and to Bruno's pleasure the tiredness left her face. He had a sense of how she must have been two, three decades earlier. He thought she looked even better now. There was character in her face and pride in what she had become.

"We can offer you coffee, mineral water, wine, a cold beer or a Cognac along with a *jambon-fromage,*" she said. "I thought you might need food."

He wasn't hungry, but the idea of a baguette stuffed with ham and cheese was tempting, since Bruno assumed he'd be working all night. "Thank you, Madame la Maire. I'd love a baguette and a *petit rouge.* Have you heard from the command post?"

"Yes, I was on the phone to them just before you came. They said you were bringing the last of the evacuees, but they stressed that the wind is veering, now coming from the southwest, so to tell you that they are gathering the *pompiers* and volunteers at Castelnaud-la-Chapelle. They want to save the castle." She paused and looked at him. "Your face is filthy from smoke. You need a wash, and I imagine you could use a bathroom. Come with me."

She led him into a house whose door was open, with all the lights on. Inside was a simple office, two desks and bookcases filled with files. She showed him to an anonymous bathroom, bare but sufficient. He assumed it was part of the *mairie.* He washed his face and neck and hands, ran water over his head and ran his fingers through his hair. When he emerged she was waiting with a baguette in a paper bag and a full bottle of red wine, already opened with the cork stuffed halfway in. He looked at the label and his eyes widened when he saw it was a Margaux from 2015.

"I've got the files and papers ready to put on board," she said. "I can't take the wine, but I wouldn't want a bottle like that to go to waste. You should have it. Thank you for what you've done tonight. I heard it was you who had the idea to use the *gabarres*."

"Somebody else would have thought of it. By the way, I'm Bruno," he said. "From St. Denis."

"I know," she replied. "I'm Marguerite."

A boat horn sounded from the river. They went to the door and saw the *gabarre* approaching.

"Good luck at Castelnaud." She turned and went to the dockside, giving quiet, brisk orders to arrange for the stretcher cases and wheelchairs to board first. Bruno took a long, appreciative drink of the wine, straight from the bottle, followed by a large bite from the baguette. He chewed and swallowed and washed it down with another sip of wine. He replaced the cork, went back to the Land Rover to stash the food and bottle and then began helping the evacuees to board.

"What did you see of the fire on the way here?" he asked the skipper after introducing himself. It had almost reached the southern bank of the river just before Milandes, he was told.

"What about the château?" he asked. Milandes was a place he liked and knew well, and he felt a twinge of concern for the fate of its collection of hunting hawks.

"The village and château looked okay, protected by its big parking lot. But from that stretch from the island down to Milandes, it's woodland all the way back for twenty kilometers. The fire just raced through."

"So I wouldn't be able to drive to Castelnaud on this side of the river?"

"Not a chance, we saw the fire jumping the road. You'll have to cross the river and take the north bank."

That left Bruno no choice but to talk his way across the bridge at Allas. He waited on the dockside until told to untie the mooring rope, threw it back on board the *gabarre,* waved and then returned to the Land Rover and attached the magnetic flashing blue light to his roof before driving off. To his surprise, the bridge was clear and

nobody was guarding it. The people of Envaux could have used it after all. That would
be another item for his report.

Once over the river he turned east onto
the narrow two-lane road. It was usually
packed with tourists throughout the summer, but now it was deserted except for the
occasional ambulance, police car and fire
truck. The glow of fire loomed terrifyingly
bright across the river. The lovely castle of
Milandes was a silhouette against the fire
that had spread through the woods behind,
and the reflections of the flames flickered in
the river. Bruno was stopped by a gendarme
at the entrance to the village of Beynac,
identified himself, showed his police ID and
said he was under Prunier's orders to get to
Castelnaud.

From this point, looking across one of the
great bends in the river, he could see the
farmland in the low-lying ground illumi-
nated by the fires that covered the entire
hill behind the crops. Those woods, he
knew, ran all the way down to the great
medieval fortress of Castelnaud. There was
something almost biblical about the scene,
the red glow of the sky seeping into the
darkness of the smoke that extinguished the
stars. The bright, shooting yellow bursts of
flame seemed ready to set alight the dappled

water of the river and dance in the ripples, just as each new flare signaled the incineration of yet another tree.

The gendarme handed Bruno back his ID card and waved him on. He drove beneath the great cliff, now glowing red, on which perched the fortress of Beynac. It seemed to stand in defiance of the fires across the river, just as it had stood in defiance of enemies in siege after siege in medieval times. The road here hugged the river until it escaped the town and continued north toward Sarlat. Bruno turned south, following the riverbank to the bridge at Tournepique, and here it was the massive stone towers and walls of Castelnaud that were silhouetted against the flickering redness that loomed over the hill behind the fortress. Bruno felt a sudden lurch in his sense of time. It could be the Middle Ages once again, the embattled castle under siege.

CHAPTER 24

Bruno was waved down just before the bridge and told to turn off the road and into a field, where scores of other civilian vehicles were already parked. He did so and walked across the bridge, checking his watch. It was twenty minutes before three. Dawn would break in less than three hours. He wondered if Castelnaud would still exist by then.

Police and fire trucks filled the town parking lot and overflowed into the field where in normal times the sightseers waited for their enormous balloons to be inflated, which would take them soaring over the valley. A huge water tender was poised as close to the bank as it could get, giant hoses sucking up the river water. As soon as one left, heading for the far side of the hill where the *pompiers* were still trying to hold back the flames, a second took its place, thrusting its proboscis into the river like some prehensile beast at a waterhole. There was no sign of a third.

Dozens of men, presumably the volunteers, were stretched out on the bank, resting or trying to sleep; others were trying to help direct the fire trucks to the narrow road that led up the hill. Still more gathered around crates of bottled water that were disappearing as fast as they could be unloaded from a supermarket truck. Amid the bustle and shouting and sense of emergency, Bruno saw in the gloomy faces and lowered heads of many of the volunteers a mood of dejection, even of hopelessness. They had done their best, but it had not been enough; the fire had won. He saw something of the same faltering morale in the men standing glumly in line at a mobile pizza truck that was providing free food.

Another fluttering tricolor marked the local command center, this time with an Armée de l'Air communications truck parked alongside. Bruno wondered if the water-dropping aircraft operated at night. Presumably the pilots needed to sleep. Inside the command post he found Commissaire Prunier, one phone to his ear, staring at the screen of another phone in his hand and telling someone the evacuations were complete.

"No lives have been lost so far. We managed to get the people out on *gabarres,* those flat-bottomed boats, but the fire is still not under control," he was saying into his phone. "What we'll need in the future is a *gabarre* refitted to hold a fire engine that can suck up water and pump it out in fire hoses. Maybe a flat-bottomed barge would do. Perhaps you could put a team together when this emergency is over, Monsieur le Préfet, and run a cost-and-feasibility study. We'll speak tomorrow."

Prunier closed that phone, nodded at Bruno and showed him the screen of the other one. It was obviously linked to a drone that was tracking the front line of the fire, heading for the fortress on the hill above them that dominated the village and the river crossing.

"Hi, Bruno. It looks like we're going to lose the Eco-museum, the walnut plantations and maybe everything this side of the bridge," he said. "The *pompiers* and volunteers are all exhausted, and there are no more reinforcements. We've had to send a lot of men and equipment to Domme to protect the Frenchelon base. We're down to two water tenders, and our one remaining mobile pumping truck was caught in the fire. It got out, but its tires were burned

419

through to the rims, so it's immobilized. I protested against losing the trucks and men to Domme, but we had orders from the Élysée."

As well as the famous walled bastide fortress on the hilltop of Domme, the ridge also housed the main base of Frenchelon, the French intelligence electronic listening system that monitored the airwaves and the worldwide net, its name copied from the similar Anglo-American Echelon program. Run by the Direction Technique of the DGSE, the French equivalent of the Central Intelligence Agency, the presence of the base was an open secret in the region.

"The wind is blowing sparks and cinders right across the containment line that was made a couple of hours ago. The volunteers spent half the night making it, and then they had to run for their lives when the sparks blew right among them," Prunier added, with a shrug of resignation. "We've been promised a dawn flight of aircraft dumping water and flame retardant, but that may be just too little, too late. The fire is moving too fast. The *pompiers* can't get any closer than the fortress parking lot, and we haven't enough pumps, so their hoses haven't got the range to send water over the top of that hill."

"Have you visited the fortress?" Bruno asked. "That war museum has three *trébuchets,* medieval catapults that were used to batter down castle walls. I saw them in action here, sending fifty- and sixty-kilo rocks soaring for more than two hundred meters. They might be able to pitch water over the top of that hill and at least buy us some time before the aircraft arrive."

Prunier raised his eyebrows. "Could you make one work?"

Bruno shook his head. "I saw it done, but you'd need local experts, the guys who built these modern copies. The mayor would know who they are, or Monsieur Rossillon, the owner of the Castelnaud castle. It was his idea to have those *trébuchets* built and put into operation."

"We can't simply shoot rocks at a fire. How would we get them to deliver water?"

"We'd need sacks, maybe those hundred-liter, heavy-duty plastic sacks used for trash collection. We can use plastic ties to close the tops, put them in the sling on the end of the *trébuchet*'s throwing arm and send in barrages of water that way. The bags would burst when they hit the ground."

"Be realistic, Bruno. It may be an emergency, but we still have to live with politics. The prefect would have a fit, and the Greens would go crazy if we used plastic bags. Plastic burns, and then there's the ground pollution problem."

"Let's not tell him. It's usually better to apologize later rather than ask permission," Bruno said. But he saw Prunier frown. He tried another tack. "Maybe we can find some alternatives. Farmers use jute sacks and fishermen use waterproof ones to ship oysters and mussels in bulk. Get onto the main warehouses for the big supermarkets. They'll have some. You just spoke to the prefect. Get him to wake up the supermarket managers and get their oyster bags shipped here — by helicopter, if necessary. If that doesn't work, tell them to ship every bag of ice in their freezers. We can pour the ice cubes into ordinary sacks and fire them."

"Okay, let's try it," said Prunier. "I'd rather do something than just abandon this village and the castle."

"I'll call the supermarket manager in St. Denis. I know him well. Then I'll head up there to the bastion where the *trébuchets* are based with as many volunteers as I can round up, and you get Rossillon and his team to join me. Tell him this could be the only chance we have to save his château."

"He's here somewhere. He was one of the volunteers," Prunier said as Bruno called the home number for Simon, who managed the biggest supermarket in St. Denis. A sleepy voice answered.

"Simon, it's Bruno. Wake up. We have an emergency. Those sacks at the supermarket in which the oysters are delivered. How many do you have in the warehouse? I remember once seeing a stack of dozens of them."

"Bruno, offhand I just don't know. We send them all back at the end of every week, so we might have twenty or thirty, I guess. Why do you ask?"

Bruno explained why he wanted Simon to drive to the supermarket, get all the sacks and bring them as quickly as he could to Castelnaud. He should quote Prunier's authority, and the police on the roads would be notified. He ended the call and saw Prunier already speaking on his own phone.

"Monsieur Rossillon?" A pause. "This is Prunier, can you come to the control truck here at once, please."

"You deal with him," Prunier said. "I'll call the prefect."

"Wait," said Bruno, explaining that the police on the roads should be notified that Simon from the St. Denis supermarket was bringing a carload of sacks and should be allowed to cross the bridge with his car. Prunier told an aide to take care of it and began calling the prefect.

Usually a cheerful, energetic man, in his fifties, Rossillon was more than tired and almost swaying as he joined Bruno at the door of the control truck. Bruno introduced himself, explained his idea and saw the man's eyes brighten and his back straighten. But then his shoulders sagged.

"It's no good," he said. "They're pointing across the river, the wrong way."

"There's a bulldozer here, the one they used to make the containment line," Bruno said. "Could that turn the *trébuchets*?"

"Maybe, yes, I think they could. And I've got some of those jute sacks. We use them for the armor."

Bruno looked blank.

"When the medieval armor rusts, we put the pieces into the sacks with a lot of sand and roll them around to clean the metal. And there are more at the walnut orchard. We'll need string to close the bags up, but this might just work."

Rossillon turned and shouted some names, and a group of men came up. As he explained the plan to them, Bruno found the bulldozer driver eating a slice of free pizza at the wheel of his enormous machine. Bruno described the task, and the driver set off up the steep and curving road to the upper parking lot and the stretch of flat land where the *trébuchets* stood. By now Rossillon had gathered a score of men he seemed to know and sent most of them up the hill after the bulldozer in a couple of trucks. He sent another group to the walnut orchard and then followed his friends in a car, telling Bruno they all worked at the bars and restaurants that nestled around the castle entrance and had commercial freezers with plenty of ice.

Bruno found the Sarlat fire chief, explained this last, desperate bid to save the castle and village and said they would need a water tender. The fire chief shook his head in disbelief and said it was ridiculous. Then he said it was impossible; he was about to evacuate the remaining trucks and firemen.

"We've got to be seen to try everything, and it's the only chance we've got," said Bruno. "Our last throw."

"*Putain,* you're right. We'll give it a shot." The fire chief grinned. "They'll never believe this when they see it on TV. It's worth a try — if only to keep the TV crews out of my hair."

Ten minutes later, the two big *trébuchets* had been turned and now pointed to the top of the hill, the red glow of fire fiercely outlining the skyline. Each of the two *trébuchets* stood ten meters high, and the long throwing arm looked to Bruno even longer. Rossillon's team was hauling on the ratcheted wheels and pulleys that raised the huge counterweight and lowered the throwing arm.

"Sixteen hundred kilos of sand in that wood box," said Rossillon. "That's the counterweight. Now's the hard part. The throwing arm itself would only send it sixty, eighty meters. With the sling on the end we get the extra force, like the tail of a whip. But if we don't place the sling exactly right, it won't work."

He helped his team fix the ropes with the big leather sling to the tail of the throwing arm. A small truck raced up to him, braked, and two men got out and began hauling out sacks filled with ice cubes and loosely closing the necks of the sacks with string. It took two men to carry each sack to the sling of the *trébuchet*.

"Stand back," called Rossillon. He took a sledgehammer, approached the big machine and made sure everyone was standing well back.

"Wait, wait," came a cry as a TV truck pulled up nearby and a cameraman jumped out, as a colleague flipped a switch and the scene was bathed in arc light. A director shouted, "Okay, we're filming, let her loose."

Rossillon mouthed a curse at them and then with a powerful swing he knocked away the heavy bolt of wood that held the ratchet in place. The great weight plunged down, and the long throwing arm swung over the massive oak pivot. The sling at the end of two meters of rope whipped over and the ice-filled sack soared into the air. Bruno saw it briefly silhouetted against the glow of the fire before it dropped down.

"Mon Dieu," he said aloud in tones of disbelief. "It worked."

A cheer came up from the guys who had already started hauling again on the ratchet and pulleys of the *trébuchet* that had just fired, even as Rossillon was supervising the loading of another sack into the second, slightly smaller *trébuchet*.

"I'm putting less ice in this one because I'm not sure of the range," he said. Again the throwing arm came down, and again the bag of ice was placed into the leather sling and Rossillon and his carpenter carefully straightened the ropes attaching it to the throwing arm. Rossillon handed the sledgehammer to Bruno, saying, "This was your idea."

Bruno knocked away the block of wood

427

that had secured the ratchet and again the almost balletic swing of the throwing arm and the extra whiplash effect of the sling sent another sackload of ice over the brow of the hill and into the fire.

By this time, Prunier and the Sarlat fire chief and half the volunteers had joined them on the level ground that Rossillon called his *place d'armes* to watch the modern use of the medieval catapults, cheering as each one fired. By now they had the waterproof jute sacks filled with water from the tender. It took three men to wrestle each sack onto the sling, and then Simon arrived in his car with his oyster sacks.

"I've got thirty-six sacks here," Simon announced, throwing open the back of his car. "And on the way I called my colleague at St. Cyprien, and he's bringing another load from his warehouse. And he's calling the manager of the hypermarket at Sarlat. They should have more."

"That's great. We can forget the ice and just fire water," said Rossillon, and by this time the men had fallen into a routine. The sacks were placed empty in the sling of the big *trébuchet* before they held each one upright to be filled by a hose from the tender. Then they loosely sealed the top with string, backed away and fired it off.

Bruno began checking his watch as Rossillon and his men settled into a rhythm. It was a quarter to four. Every three minutes, one sack of fifty liters and another of around seventy liters of water, which meant seventy kilos of weight, was fired over the hill. If they could keep up the pace, that was twenty-four hundred liters each hour. Bruno told himself that maybe the glow of the fire was slackening just a little. But then he realized it was not the fire that was slackening but the lightening of the sky behind him to the east as the dawn began to break.

"I don't know if it's your mad idea or if we just got lucky," said the fire chief. He had suddenly appeared at Bruno's side with a walkie-talkie. "The fire engine in the parking lot has put down enough water to open a path halfway up the hill, so any minute now we'll use its pumps so that the hoses can start putting down water onto the crest. We'll save this castle yet."

The sacks that Simon had brought from the St. Denis supermarket had all gone, along with most of those brought from St. Cyprien. The sacks from the Sarlat *hypermarché* had not yet arrived.

"The aircraft have taken off from Bordeaux and are on their way," came a tinny but familiar voice from Prunier's mobile phone. "Estimated time of arrival is twenty-seven minutes."

"Alain, is that you?" Bruno said loudly, startling Prunier as he leaned his mouth close to the phone.

"Bruno, yes, it's me. Where are you?"

"Up at the castle with the catapults. I'll doubtless see you later." He backed off, apologizing to Prunier and explaining that the air force communications man down below in the parking lot was his cousin.

There was time for six more shots from each of the two *trébuchets* before they ran out of sacks. And then they heard the first, faint growl of the aircraft coming up over the river from the west.

"They'll pass us, turn over Domme and come in from the east, with the sun behind them," said the fire chief, facing the TV camera and speaking into a microphone. "They'll drop just a little ahead of the leading edge of the fire, so the wind will help spread the water over the unburned wood and deny the fire the fresh fuel it needs to advance. Each of the aircraft will be dumping six thousand liters of water with fire retardant. After the big fires in Provence, we bought four more of these special fire-fighting planes.

"The aircraft are purpose-built Bombardier Four-Fifteen models, originally designed in Canada as an amphibious aircraft that can operate from land or from water and can scoop up water from lakes or reservoirs," he added, as the camera swiveled upward to get a shot of the three aircraft passing overhead.

Every eye followed them as they turned and came back, dropping lower and lower until they roared almost overhead, no more than a hundred meters above the brow of the hill. They banked to follow the line of flames and then one by one dumped a great red trail of water mixed with retardant. Was it the first rays of the rising sun that made them that color, Bruno wondered, or was it the fire retardant? At that point the car from Sarlat arrived with its trunk full of sacks.

Three aircraft, each with six thousand liters, thought Bruno. And the *trébuchets* had thrown maybe five thousand liters in all, certainly less than a third of what the aircraft had delivered. But they had done wonders for the morale of the exhausted *pompiers* and volunteers, and Bruno had little doubt which of the firefighting methods would dominate the TV news reports later in the day. In the past week, the viewers had grown accustomed to film of the firefighting aircraft.

Prunier and the fire chief were looking at the mobile phone that was connected to the small drone that now lifted from the parking area below and soared up and over the brow of the hill to film the effect of the water dumpers.

"Very impressive," said Prunier as Bruno sidled up alongside to look down at the image of the fire tamed. The creeping red edge he had seen before on the images from the drone had gone, replaced by long dark stretches of doused trees with steam rising rather than smoke.

"We'll need another dump, just one more," said the fire chief. "In the meantime, the men from the Middle Ages may resume their bombardment."

"I'm not sure we can do much more with this smaller one," said Rossillon, from where he was scrambling with his carpenter over the structure that may have been smaller but still dwarfed them. "The throwing arm seems to have sprung."

"In a noble cause," said Bruno solemnly. "Fallen on the field of battle."

They loaded the larger of the *trébuchets* with another sack of water, but somehow Bruno could tell that Rossillon's heart was not in it. The sense of urgency, of their use as the last chance to save the castle, had gripped and enthused them and given exhausted men new strength. But now that the aircraft had arrived, that mood had dissipated. Every man could do the math as well as Bruno. They might as well have pissed on the flames for all the good they had done. All that work, all that enthusiasm, for delivering just a few thousand liters seemed pointless in retrospect.

"You men may be feeling that your work was in vain, but believe me, it wasn't," came the voice of the fire chief. He was addressing the volunteers and the *trébuchet* crews rather than the cameras, but Bruno guessed the man knew he was being filmed.

"I know fire, and your medieval catapults made the crucial difference in that hour before dawn when the aircraft finally arrived. I was about to order an evacuation of this side of the river, abandoning this magnificent fortress and museum to the flames. But I saw the flames die a little with each sack you hurled at them. Well done, all of you. Monsieur Rossillon, you and your team have defended your castle in the great tradition of this mighty stronghold of Castelnaud. *Pompiers, policiers, militaires,* men and women and all the volunteers, my congratulations. This was the last battle of

Castelnaud, and you have won."

He raised his hand to the peak of his helmet and saluted them all as a great cheer roared up from two, perhaps three hundred throats.

"I always suspected he had political ambitions," murmured Prunier in Bruno's ear. "Now I'm sure of it."

"Still, it was a pretty good speech," Bruno said.

The fire chief strolled across to Rossillon, who was checking the sling ropes of the *tré-buchet.*

"With your permission, monsieur," said the fire chief, taking the sledgehammer from Rossillon, who stepped back and gestured the fireman to go ahead. The sledgehammer swung back once and then again, the fire chief making sure the camera was on him. Then he knocked away the beam holding the ratchet. The great arm swung over once more, the sling whipping its final thrust, and one more oyster sack of water sailed off over the hill, spurred on by a new burst of cheers from the volunteers.

"And if this doesn't double the number of visitors to Castelnaud this year, I'll eat my képi," said Prunier.

But that didn't stop Prunier from taking his turn with the sledgehammer when

Rossillon invited him to launch the next sack. Then each member of Rossillon's team, men and women alike, was granted a turn at firing the *trébuchet* before the aircraft returned for another dowsing. This time it was judged complete. The great fire of Périgord was out.

CHAPTER 25

Bruno was about to leave the *place d'armes* for the steep curving path that led downhill when he saw a face he knew. The man was in the uniform of a *pompier,* which is why it took him a moment to realize it was Henri Bazaine.

"I thought you were a winemaker. I didn't know you were also a *pompier,*" he said. He didn't offer to shake hands and nor did Henri.

"I thought you were a cop. I didn't know you were also a firefighter," Henri replied deadpan. "I've been a volunteer in the Bergerac brigade for twenty years, and I've never known a night like this."

"Not even back at the Clara Zetkin orphanage?" Bruno asked. "I presume that's where you first learned about wine, making Riesling in the Elbe Valley. And by the way, that asthma that kept you out of military service seems to have cleared up."

Henri did not react. He just continued to look at Bruno with the same, studiedly neutral stare. Bruno wondered if General Lannes had been successful in dissuading the Élysée from accepting the lawyer's offer of a deal. After the drama of the night, all that seemed like ancient history.

"Well, thanks for your work last night, you and all the other volunteers," Bruno said.

"Thanks to you as well. Those catapults put new heart into everyone. Let's hope the politicians learn the lesson of climate change from this fire, before we have more nights like this," Henri replied.

"I agree with you on that," Bruno said. "But don't get your hopes up. Democracy is a wonderful thing, but politicians don't tend to win elections by telling people to stop using fossil fuels."

"Or to stop flying and eating fast food," Henri replied, with the glimmer of a smile on his lips. It did not reach his eyes.

"What happened between you and Max?" Bruno asked. "Was it a fight over the Lefort scrapbook?"

"I don't know what you're talking about." Henri's face was impassive once more.

"Auf Wiedersehen," said Bruno as he turned aside and walked down the hill, wondering whether it was worth telling Pru-

nier of Henri's presence among the volunteers. Until he heard from Isabelle about the Élysée's decision, it would make little difference. It was now six in the morning, a new day. Perhaps he'd be able to have breakfast with Alain before getting some sleep.

At the bottom of the hill, where a long line of vehicles was waiting to cross the bridge, the parking area was in chaos as vehicles vied to leave. They needed a traffic cop, Bruno thought, wondering whether he should start sorting out the jam. As he pondered, a gendarme emerged from the crush, blew his whistle and began restoring a modicum of order. Then Bruno saw the fluttering tricolor that indicated the command truck and beyond it the blue of the air force truck. It had not moved. There was nobody in the driver's compartment, so he hammered on the rear door. After a moment, it was opened by a sleepy-eyed stranger in air force blue.

"I'm looking for Alain," he said. "He's my cousin."

"You're Bruno? He went looking for you. He said you were the guy who got those catapults going. So *chapeau,* I doff my hat to you, but I'm exhausted and I'm going back to sleep." The door closed.

Bruno sat on the small step outside the truck door and closed his eyes, thinking how good a coffee would taste just now. And then he realized he was smelling the stuff. A cheerful young woman with a tray filled with coffee cups was heading for the command truck.

"May I buy one?" he asked, reaching for some change.

"On the house. Our café would have burned down without you guys," she said. "Take two, you look like you need them. And we'll have some croissants in a few minutes."

As she went into the command truck, Alain emerged from between two other trucks, saw the coffee and said, "Is one of those for me?" Bruno handed over a cup and they hugged each other clumsily, with one arm.

"So was it really your idea, to use the catapults?"

"Not really, I just remembered they were up there and thought it would be worth a try. But you were here at Castelnaud the other day. You would have thought of it. That reminds me, how's the lovely Rosalie?"

"Fine when I saw her yesterday morning, before I got called up here."

"You've chosen well there. All my friends

loved both of you, so you'll have a social life ready and waiting if you settle around here. But tell me, is working with the water-dropping aircraft a regular part of what you do?"

"Not at all," Alain replied. "There was an emergency call for the aircraft yesterday, and even though the aircraft are nominally part of the Service Civique, the flight crew is all ex–air force. They insisted on having our communications systems. They had some problems in Provence a couple of years ago when the cops and *pompiers* were trying to direct them. That's why we have a pilot in our truck as ground controller. I'm just running the electronics. But we haven't stopped. We were dropping water in the Landes yesterday and near Nérac before that."

"Well, thanks for helping put our fire out. You should have called to say you'd arrived."

"I had no idea where we were last night when we got here. We were just told to load up and get going so the aircraft could start dropping as soon as it was light."

Bruno grinned. "That sounds like the military I remember. But can't the planes operate in the dark?"

"They could, but they have to fly quite

low to get a concentrated drop, and in hilly country like this in the dark, it's just too risky."

Alain turned as his name was shouted from the truck, and someone in an air force uniform beckoned him. "Here we go again, off somewhere new." He handed the coffee cup to Bruno.

"Give Rosalie my best regards." They shook hands, and as soon as Alain climbed into the back of the truck its engine started, and with a beep of the horn it headed for the bridge. Bruno watched it go and then went to the command truck to say he was signing off and going home for some sleep. He found Prunier there, being interviewed by Philippe Delaron for *Sud Ouest*.

"This is the guy you should be talking to," Prunier said to Philippe. "It was Bruno's idea to use the *gabarres* to evacuate people and he was also the one who told me we should try the catapults."

"Is that right?" Philippe asked, turning to Bruno.

"A lot of people were coming up with different ideas," Bruno replied. "In the military you learn to combine your arms, air power, infantry, armor and artillery. We had the fire trucks, the *pompiers* and volunteers as our infantry and we knew the air power would

441

be coming once it was light. What we didn't have was artillery — and that was the gap the catapults could fill. When we realized just how fast the fire was moving, we were desperate enough to try anything. The important thing now is to make sure we learn from this, to make proper plans and run exercises to get everybody accustomed to working together."

"That's exactly what I told the fire chief," Prunier said. "We're forming a working group to draw up recommendations, and Bruno will be part of it."

After taking some more photos, Philippe went to interview Rossillon, and Bruno asked Prunier, "Any news from J-J about Henri Bazaine? I just ran into him; he's one of the volunteer *pompiers* from Bergerac."

"Really? So he can't be all bad. No, I haven't heard from J-J since yesterday. And now I'm going home to get some sleep and drop off this filthy uniform at the dry cleaner. You should do the same. Do you know you smell of pee?"

"It's from one of the evacuees, a little old lady with soiled bedclothes. I've been smelling it all night."

Bruno went home, fed his chickens, stripped, climbed into the shower and then turned off his phone and went to bed. He woke in the early afternoon, made coffee and had another shower before turning his phone back on. He had a dozen messages, two from the mayor, three from the local radio station, two from J-J, one from Sabine, another from Rossillon and two from Isabelle. He called her first.

"I saw you on the news with those medieval war machines," she said. "I don't think I ever saw you looking quite so filthy."

"I stank even worse," he said. "Any news from the Élysée about Bazaine?"

"Yes, against our advice, they're going ahead with the deal. Bazaine gets immunity and the Élysée gets the Rosenholz stuff." She then paused and the silence lengthened.

"Ah," said Bruno, starting to understand. "Once they have it, has the Élysée promised to pass it on to you and our counterespionage people?"

"Not that I know of."

"You mean they're going to keep it?" Bruno said, in disbelief.

"Knowledge is power," she replied. "To be fair, they don't want a witch hunt. I understand that and to an extent I sympathize with that point of view. But . . ." She paused again.

"But you're still a cop at heart," said Bruno. "And you don't want Bazaine getting away with murder."

"Exactly," she said. "But I have an idea. What are you up to this weekend?"

"If you're thinking of coming here, we can take Balzac to visit his puppies."

"I can't think of anything I'd rather do," she said. "Well, almost anything. But part of this trip might be official, depending on some meetings I have to arrange. I should be able to confirm sometime tomorrow."

"Wonderful," he said. He ignored the calls from the radio station and rang the mayor.

"I just called to congratulate you," the mayor said. "I think half the town saw the morning news on TV with you and the *tré-buchet.*"

"Good for you. Everybody else is calling it a catapult."

"And you seem to have a new fan in my esteemed colleague, the Madame la Maire of Envaux. She said on TV that you were the one who arranged the *gabarres* to evacuate people."

"Everybody is being very kind, but the truth is we mishandled the situation," Bruno said. "We misjudged the speed of the fire. The evacuation routes were not arranged in advance. Bridges that were supposed to be closed were left open, and there was too little advance planning between the police, the *pompiers* and the air force. We need to do better next time because I think there will be more wildfires like this."

"I agree with you," said the mayor. "And not just here or in Australia or California where we see them on TV, but in more and more places as climate change speeds up. Did you see they even had them in Sweden a couple of years ago?"

"Exactly," said Bruno. "Prunier is planning to set up a working group in this *département,* but you could use your Paris connections to make this a nationwide process. We need to do it."

"We'll discuss this tomorrow when you come back in. I want you to take the rest of the day off. Get some sleep."

Bruno ignored the remaining calls, and since the Land Rover still smelled of urine, he washed down the rear benches and floor and drove with all the windows open to the riding school. Balzac, recognizing the sound of the engine, was running into the stable yard to greet him. His barking alerted Hector, who gave a welcoming neigh, and then Pamela appeared at her kitchen door.

"Well done," she said, coming to give him a warm hug, with Virginie following along behind. "We saw you on TV, and Virginie found a way to download it onto her laptop and e-mailed it to me, so I sent it to all our friends. Have you seen it yet?"

"No," he said. "And I don't think I need to. I was there. I'm told I looked filthy."

"Everybody did, from the smoke."

"Bonjour, Virginie," he said.

"I'm so glad you're safe and I'm in love with Balzac, he's wonderful," she said. "I learned how to saddle a pony, and Pamela wants me to help with the little ones later today."

"Good for you. Listen, I feel the need for a ride on Hector," said Bruno and looked at Pamela. "Want to come?"

"I can't," she replied, shaking her head. "I have the big girls coming for riding lessons at four, but you take Hector out. You deserve it. Do you want to stay for dinner? Virginie is cooking us a vegetable feast."

"Thanks, I'd love to, but I have to see J-J about this case we've been working on," he said. "And I should go to the clinic and find out how some of the evacuees are doing. But first, I need a run with Hector."

Virginie came into the stables as he was saddling his horse and said, "I want to thank you for that kind message you sent to Madame Daynès about the head I made. She called me this morning to offer me a job at her studio, starting in September."

"Congratulations, that's great news," he said. "You earned it. What will you do until then? Go back to Paris?"

"I have a week more work at least in Périgueux, making the extra heads. After that, Pamela says I can stay here through the summer, learn to ride and help with the kids. She can't pay me, but I'll be able to live here for free."

"Sounds great, she'll make a fine horse-woman of you. I'm glad you've enjoyed meeting my friends. I know they enjoyed meeting you."

He walked Hector out, mounted and with a wave at Virginie, set off up the trail to the ridge, Balzac trotting at his heels. Hector seemed as eager for a good run as Bruno was. He cantered off the last shallow slope, then began to gallop almost as soon as they were on level ground. They paused at the woods for Balzac to catch up, and Bruno stared across at the familiar landscape that was still untouched by fire. He fervently hoped it stayed that way, and once Balzac joined them, Hector trotted through the trees to the long firebreak.

Balzac knew the place well and knew how fast the horse would run, so he stayed where he was, letting Hector canter at first and then move easily into a fast run, not quite a gallop. At the far end, Bruno slowed, turned and this time Hector went all out, as fast as Bruno could remember riding, an exhilaration so intense he heard himself whooping for joy until Hector slowed for the woods and Balzac barked in welcome at their return. Minutes later, the riding school came into view, and Bruno could see Pamela's swimming pool was full of water, unsullied by ashes and empty of people. It looked very inviting.

Bruno's phone vibrated. It was J-J, and he thought he'd better take it.

"How's the TV star? And have you heard the news from Paris?"

"What news?" Bruno asked, thinking it better to be discreet about how far Isabelle had confided in him, with all that it implied for the closeness of their relations.

"The Élysée is letting Henri off the hook in return for those Stasi documents he's been sitting on. Prunier heard it from General Lannes, who didn't sound at all happy about it. I'd have thought you'd have heard."

"I was up all night, firefighting. I've been catching up on sleep. So what do you do now?"

"I have a call in to Isabelle. She might have some ideas."

"I wouldn't go up against the Élysée if I were you."

"That's what Prunier said. I need to think more about all this. By the way, well done last night. We'll talk after I hear from Isabelle."

Bruno unsaddled Hector in the stables, gave him a wizened apple from the barrel and rubbed him down while Balzac snuffled around their feet. Then he strolled up to the pool, stripped off to his undershorts and dived in, his momentum taking him underwater most of the length of the pool. He rose, swam three fast laps and then floated, arms outstretched, his fingers fluttering, eyes closed, enjoying the heat of the sun on his face. He stayed like that until his head bumped gently against what he thought was the side of the pool at the shallow end, and he opened his eyes to see Balzac nudging him. He climbed out, patted Balzac and stood for a while looking up at the ridge, almost able to feel the water on his skin evaporate in the warmth. The breeze was still from the south, and he sighed at the thought that there could be another heavy night.

"There you are," came a voice. "The medieval catapult man himself."

It was Jack Crimson, grinning broadly,

dressed in swimming shorts with a big towel around his neck. He dived in, making a massive splash that showered Bruno with water all over again, then surfaced. "I heard on the grapevine that this Rosenholz dossier business is nearly settled," he said. "About time, too."

Bruno knew that Jack and General Lannes were old colleagues and that, although he was officially retired, Jack still worked as a consultant on strategic risks for some private clients. His access to old friends in British, French and American intelligence made him a usefully deniable go-between for them all. Isabelle had once described him to Bruno as a wise and trusted old owl.

"Glad to hear it," said Bruno. "I hope you'll say that to Jacqueline before she drops any more bombs on *Le Monde*'s op-ed pages."

"On reflection, I'm rather glad she aired the issue the way she did," Jack replied. "It focused a few minds, reminded people that one should not believe everything you may read in an enemy spy agency's files. Just think what damage could be done by leaking fake KGB files saying that this British statesman or that American politician had all along been in the pay of the Russians. Lies can get halfway around the world before truth gets its boots on."

He ducked beneath the water and then began breaststroking his way around a stately circuit of the pool. Bruno's mobile vibrated, and once again it was Isabelle.

"Can you meet me with J-J at Bergerac airport tomorrow?" she asked. "I'm on the morning flight from Paris, getting in just after nine."

"Of course," he replied. "It will be good to see you. Can you stay long?"

"That rather depends on how things develop overnight," she said. "I can't explain now. Maybe tomorrow."

"Can you say what brings you down here, business or pleasure?"

"Somebody has to deliver to Henri Bazaine the presidential pardon he demanded, and I volunteered. But it may become more complicated. We'll know tomorrow. And make sure you come armed."

CHAPTER 26

It was a surprise the next morning to see Isabelle emerge first from the aircraft, wearing her uniform as a *commissaire* of police and carrying a briefcase emblazoned with the RF of La République Française. He had never seen her in official dress before. When they first met, she had been a detective in plainclothes, working for J-J. Then she had been promoted to the staff of the interior minister, then to Eurojust in The Hague, the European Union's judicial coordination unit. In all of those roles she wore civilian clothes, as she did with her most recent promotion to run France's coordination team with allies and EU partners on counterterrorism. Bruno knew this had brought her a new rank, but to see her in uniform made it clear that she was on a seriously official mission. He was glad that he'd decided to leave Balzac back at Pamela's riding school.

She was followed by a man in plainclothes carrying two overnight cases, whom Bruno did not recognize. She introduced him as a diplomatic colleague without any further explanation, and then J-J embraced her in a bear hug, saying, "The uniform becomes you, Isabelle. Still, however high your reach in rank, to me you'll always be my favorite young detective."

She extricated herself from J-J's embrace, gave him a smacking kiss on the cheek and did the same for Bruno before leading the way to the waiting vehicles, saying to her companion, "This old rascal is like a papa to me — he taught me everything I know about police work when I was based down here. And this is my old friend Bruno, chief of police of the Vézère Valley, with whom I share a very special dog."

"The catapult man," said Isabelle's companion, in a French Canadian accent. "I recognize him from the news."

"You see, Bruno? You're famous," she said as J-J's driver opened the door for her.

"We'll talk later," Isabelle said quietly to Bruno. "If you could go in the second car with the *mobiles*. We're heading to Henri's vineyard."

The second car was a van almost filled with heavily armed Gendarmes Mobiles, the elite paramilitary unit, who must have come in from Bordeaux. The *chef d'escadron* greeted Bruno with a salute and a handshake, then grinned and asked if he'd brought his catapult with him. The troops laughed, amiably enough, and made space for him in one of the three rows inside.

The commander climbed into the front passenger seat, turned to face his troops and said, "This is Chef de Police Bruno Courrèges, and if you haven't noticed it, you men, he wasn't always a cop. He's wearing the ribbon of a Croix de Guerre, and they don't hand those out with the rations. I checked him out and he won it in Sarajevo for pulling wounded troops out of a burning armored car when the Serbs were shelling the airport. You may also have seen him on TV yesterday, using a medieval war machine to put out a forest fire. We're glad to have you with us, sir."

"Have you been briefed on the mission?" Bruno asked to cover his embarrassment at the praise, as they followed J-J's car down the N21 and then turned off to the right on the road to the main Bergerac vineyards.

"Standing by and providing a security escort, as required by the *commissaire.* That's all. Anything more you can tell me?"

Bruno shook his head. "I know no more

than you do. I'm not sure what I'm doing here."

He wondered why Isabelle had called in the *mobiles,* usually only employed in hostage rescue or situations requiring a heavily armed response. If she was simply delivering to Henri his presidential pardon, Bruno saw no reason for their presence. He felt as frustrated as she evidently was that the Élysée was letting Henri off the hook in return for the scrapbook or dossier or whatever it was that he was using to buy his pardon. Bruno had wondered whether Henri might not simply be handed over to the German authorities to let them prosecute him for the murder of Max, a German citizen. But the proof of that was purely circumstantial, that Henri was there at the right time and place and with a motive. Certainty of conviction required more than that.

J-J's car stopped before the Bazaine vineyard came in sight, and J-J stepped out and beckoned to Bruno to join him. He was shown into the backseat, squeezing in beside Isabelle and the diplomat.

"The *mobiles* have been briefed to come into the vineyard exactly five minutes after we go inside," she said. "It's just insurance, in case. But we don't want Henri seeing them before that, and I think you deserve to be in on the kill, as it were."

"The kill?" Bruno asked.

They pulled into the vineyard and the door of the house opened as they climbed out of the car, and Henri appeared on the threshold. He appeared to be alone. Nobody else was in sight.

"Bonjour, Monsieur Bazaine," Isabelle began. "We spoke yesterday evening, and I have here the official document from the Élysée."

"Please come inside," he said, looking curiously at Bruno and J-J and the diplomat, as if uncertain what they were doing at this presentation. "Why are these policemen here?"

"It's a courtesy, since they have been involved in the case for which you are being granted immunity."

Henri shrugged, gesturing them to enter but made no move to shake their hands as they passed him at the door. They were all steered into a large, rather old-fashioned and dark sitting room, in which the paintings on the wall were stained a motley brown, with occasional lighter patches, as if generations of wood fires had darkened them and they had never been cleaned. Some seemed to be gloomy landscapes, but

Bruno thought he could make out a cow and a stream on the one closest to him. The windows were few and low and the furniture heavy, leather and deliberately formal. There were no flowers, no books or magazines on view, no television and no sign of anything electronic except for two lonely wall lamps. Above all, to Bruno's surprise, there were no other people present. Henri's wife and children were not to be part of this encounter.

"Thank you for receiving us, Monsieur Bazaine," Isabelle said. "As I told you by phone late yesterday, I have the honor to present to you the formal document of presidential pardon for any crimes or misdemeanors you may have committed on French soil."

She placed her briefcase on a small side table, opened it and removed a scroll from which hung a ribbon of red, white and blue, which had been affixed with a seal of red wax. She handed the scroll to Henri, and he unrolled it and read carefully through the text.

"That appears to be satisfactory," he said. He pulled out a smartphone and punched in a number that had already been programmed into the device. "Maître Vautan? This is Henri Bazaine. I have the document from the Élysée. Would you care to read out the version you drafted so we can be sure the texts are the same?"

Henri listened on the phone and Bruno could make out the tinny sound of a voice reading aloud.

"That is identical to the phrasing on the document that has just been delivered to me," said Henri. "Please go ahead and surrender to the Élysée the item I entrusted to you."

He closed the phone and turned to Isabelle with a triumphant smile, as if savoring this moment. "That appears to conclude our business, madame."

She nodded at him coldly, and said, "It appears, monsieur, that your presidential pardon is allowing you to get away with the murder of Max Morilland."

"Murder?" Henri shrugged. "It was a fair fight. Max was trying to make off with the scrapbook that my lawyer is now handing over to the authorities. I tried to stop him. He picked up the spade we'd used to dig the latrine. We fought over it and I won."

"So, finally you admit that you killed him," said J-J.

Henri shrugged again. "It was him or me."

The room fell silent. Then Isabelle said curtly, "Commissaire Jalipeau, this was your case. Over to you."

J-J moved forward with great speed for such a large man and swiftly put a pair of old-fashioned metal handcuffs onto Henri's wrists. Then he plucked the phone from the hand of an astonished Henri and tossed it onto the couch.

"Monsieur Bazaine, I am placing you under arrest as the object of an extradition request received from the Dominion of Canada and formally authorized last night by the French minister of justice," said Isabelle, taking another document from her briefcase. "You are charged with blackmail, demanding money from a Canadian citizen with threats, Monsieur Loriot, and his company, Les Vins de la Nouvelle France, to the total of two hundred sixty thousand euros, together with another four hundred thousand French francs when that was the prevailing currency. You will now be surrendered to the custody of the Canadian legal attaché pending your transfer to the jurisdiction of the Canadian courts."

"This is monstrous," Henri said. "Even without my presidential pardon, I'm a French citizen and cannot legally be extradited without a legal hearing. I demand to see my lawyer."

"That is where you are mistaken," Isabelle

said, her voice flat and cold. "You are not a French citizen. You arrived in this country on false papers and have sought to disguise your true identity ever since. You are not a French citizen and never have been. Your claim to French nationality is void, and you are thus not entitled to the legal rights that pertain to that status."

With a roar of outrage Henri seemed to explode into action, raising his cuffed hands above his head and advancing as if he wanted to slam them down onto Isabelle's head. Bruno was faster. He caught Henri's wrists as he advanced, swiveled to use the leverage to force him backward, where Henri tripped headlong over Bruno's outstretched leg. He landed with a massive thud as his back and shoulders hit the floor, but Bruno kept a tight grip on his wrists to prevent Henri's head from slamming into the ground.

J-J put more cuffs, plastic this time, around Henri's ankles, and with the sound of a roaring engine and the squeal of brakes, the *mobiles* van arrived in the courtyard outside. Isabelle was already at the door to let them in. Four stayed outside by their van, each facing a different direction, their weapons at the ready. Through the window Bruno saw one of them gesturing to Henri's son, who had appeared in the door of the *chai,* to go back inside. Two more gendarmes came into the living room and pointed their automatic rifles at the figure on the floor.

Isabelle turned to the Canadian legal attaché. "Monsieur Delaurier, the prisoner is now yours. The military aircraft is now waiting for you and the prisoner in the military zone of Mérignac airport, ready for the flight to Montreal. I am instructed to offer you all facilities for the transfer of your prisoner to the aircraft. And since the presidential pardon was obtained under false pretenses, I hereby confiscate it."

"What about his family?" Bruno asked. "They should be informed. At least one of them is here. The son is in the *chai.*"

"J-J, perhaps you would inform young Monsieur Bazaine that his father is being legally extradited to Canada to face serious charges," Isabelle said. She bent down to the floor and picked up the parchment scroll, replaced it in her briefcase, closed the locks and turned to the *mobiles.*

"Messieurs, please secure the prisoner inside your van for the ride to Mérignac. And Chef de Police Courrèges, please accompany the *mobiles* and ensure the security of the prisoner on the way to the airport. We will see you at the entrance to the military zone."

"And Bruno," she said quietly once Henri had been placed inside the van and cuffed to the rings set into the floor of all such vehicles, "you know we like justice to be seen being done. J-J has made sure that you'll see some old friends at Mérignac."

The trip took ninety minutes and was uneventful, the heavy-duty air-conditioning inside the van compensating for the heat of the day outside. Bruno assumed the heavily armored *mobiles* would be in danger of heat exhaustion without it. Henri lay on the floor, glaring at Bruno throughout the trip, even though Bruno, recalling that he'd been a volunteer *pompier,* had placed a cushion under his head to spare him the bumps.

Although now best known as a civilian airport serving some five million passengers a year, Mérignac had been a military air base since 1917. Bruno was interested to see the military section, since he knew that in 1940 it was from this airfield that Charles de Gaulle flew to Britain to continue the fight for France against the Nazi occupation. As Base Aérienne 106, it was today home to Air Force Support Command, housing some three thousand civilian and military personnel, a parachute commando group and an air transport squadron. Bruno could see a French military Airbus A330 waiting on the apron as they were stopped at the entrance gate to be checked by a guard and waved inside. Troops in camouflage gear and with kit bags beside them waited in rows to board.

"We're able to use a routine flight taking French troops to northern Quebec for exercises with our Canadian allies," said Isabelle, coming to the door of the van once the *mobiles* had descended and formed a loose cordon. Bruno undid the cuffs that attached Henri to the floor and helped him out. Isabelle saluted a waiting air force officer who escorted them all into the administration building and then into a waiting room where Sabine, in gendarme uniform, was waiting, arm in arm with Tante-Do. The older woman looked as if she had arrived directly from a long session at her own beauty parlor, her makeup immaculate and her hair perfectly coiffed.

"*Merde,* not you again," snapped Henri, with a sneering glance at Tante-Do and then rolling his eyes.

"Yes, me again, Henri," she replied, her voice brittle and the knuckles of her hand tightened as she gripped Sabine's hand as she spoke. "So perhaps you can admit you recognize me this time? Well, I may not be pleased to see you, but I am delighted to see justice done, however long after the event."

Tante-Do raised her head defiantly and stared coldly at Henri and then repeated, "Justice."

The air force officer coughed, then signed a formal receipt for Henri and gave it to Isabelle. Two military policemen at once applied a separate set of handcuffs to Henri's wrists and a much looser set to his ankles. Each took one of his arms and frog-marched him outside to the waiting plane. All the soldiers on the apron turned to stare as Henri was bundled up the aircraft steps, followed by the Canadian diplomat.

Tante-Do burst into tears and tucked herself into Sabine's embrace, her shoulders heaving. Her voice was muffled, but Bruno heard something that sounded as if she was telling Sabine that the young gendarme was the only family she had left. Sabine patted her on the back and murmured some words of comfort. Bruno watched them, affected by the words, thinking that Sabine had lost her mother and brother within the last year and her father was drifting out of reality. Perhaps it was true, and Tante-Do was Sabine's family now. The thought struck

Bruno that, thanks to Alain, he'd been reminded that he also had a family, and the events of the last few days had brought them much closer than they had been before.

"That's that, J-J," said Isabelle, putting her hand on the shoulder of the old detective who had trained her in his craft and who was now staring almost sadly at the aircraft door through which Henri Bazaine had disappeared. "My congratulations," Isabelle went on. "You never gave up, and now your cold case is finally closed. After thirty years you can at last take down that ghoulish photograph from your office door."

"I suppose so, but I think I'd miss not seeing it every day," said J-J. "Somehow it doesn't yet feel that it's really over." He stomped off to the cars outside without a backward glance, leaving Bruno and Isabelle alone. Some shouted orders from an officer at the plane steps got the troops lining up, ready to board.

"And what now?" Bruno asked her. "You fly back to Paris?"

"No," she said, with a glance that was anything but official. "I go to the ladies' room, change out of this uniform into something more comfortable and then I was hoping you and I might get Balzac and take him to meet his puppies. I really want to

465

see them. After that, I have a few days off and you know how much I miss the Périgord."

ACKNOWLEDGMENTS

The idea for this novel began with a reminiscence from my good friend and neighbor, Raymond Bounichou, a retired officer of gendarmes, about a case he was never able to solve. He still has the photograph of the skull of the unknown murder victim whom he dubbed "Oscar." Raymond tried for years to identify the body of the man who had been buried in a remote woods until unearthed by a dog. It remains a mystery that haunts Raymond to this day. As a last resort, he secured a magistrate's authorization to boil the head of the corpse, which at least allowed him to examine the skull and establish that the cause of death had been a blow from a camping tool.

The mystery of Oscar came to mind when I first saw an exhibition of the work of Élisabeth Daynès. She may now be best known for her reconstruction of the face of Tutankhamen from the skull of the ancient

Egyptian ruler, which achieved worldwide renown when it appeared on the cover of *National Geographic* magazine. I was even more impressed by the way her reconstruction of the faces of prehistoric men, women and children from their skulls allows us to see not just the bones but uncannily real people. She has brought a new and highly personal dimension to the study of the long-distant past, and her work has given me and many modern visitors to the Les Eyzies museum of prehistory a striking sense of personal connection to our remote forebears.

The Rosenholz dossier is real, and its contents and its fate are much as described in this book. Its listing of the thousands of agents of the Stasi (the term comes from Staatssicherheit, or State Security) is a unique document of espionage and intelligence in the Cold War. Despite the efforts of the East German regime to destroy it and cover their tracks, the CIA obtained a copy and shared its contents with chosen allies, not including the French; the history of tension between U.S. and French intelligence services is a matter of historical record. The *Le Monde* editorial cited in the text is an invention, but its warning against taking as fact something found in the intelligence archives of a rival power is worth noting, as the Finnish security police learned the hard way.

The annual celebration of Occitan language and culture, the Félibrée, or Felibrejada, to give it the Occitan name, is a remarkable feature of Périgord life. These festivals emerged as a kind of resistance to the efforts of the Third Republic to eradicate Occitan and other local languages in schools and to make everyone speak French. As late as the 1860s, local authorities estimated that ninety percent of the Périgord spoke the *langue d'oc* as their first tongue. Then it became state policy to ban the various patois, Breton and Provençal as well as Occitan. That period is known locally as the *vergonha,* the shaming, in which local tongues were banned in class and offenders punished, often with clogs being hung all day around their necks. Since 1903 the festivals have been held in a different town or village in the Périgord each year. The songs, poetry and dances, and accompanying banquet (*taulada*) are intriguing and often magnificent in themselves; they also serve to remind us that the Périgord is not entirely France. It is older, with its roots stretching back far into prehistory, and with its own distinct mythology, language and culture.

To those of us who live in rural France, the volunteer firemen and women, the *pompiers,* are an essential and splendid part of life. They are the first responders not only for fires but for medical and other emergencies. It is hard to conceive of life in the Périgord without the skills, courage and public service of our neighbors who volunteer. I am grateful to the *pompiers* in my own village for their technical advice, and to Monsieur Kléber Rossillon and his team at the castle of Castelnaud while writing this book. Any mistakes are my own fault. I don't know if the *pompiers* have ever tried to fight fires with *trébuchets,* but those at Castelnaud are very much worth seeing in action, and I warmly recommend a visit to the whole fortress and its museum of the arts of war.

While researching this book, I was delighted to learn that the *trébuchet* team at Castelnaud had already experimented with tossing bags of water. They also alerted me to a remarkable article on this medieval technology in *Scientific American,* the issue of July 1995, which notes that some of the biggest *trébuchets* of the Middle Ages could fire weights of a ton and more (one thousand kilograms). A modern *trébuchet* built in England in the 1990s was able to fire a small car weighing four hundred seventy-six kilos (without its engine) a distance of eighty meters. The research of the thirteenth-century mathematician Jordanus de Nemore on the use of pivoting counterweights to increase the range of these missiles had an important impact on the later work of Leonardo da Vinci and Galileo and the makers of mechanical clocks.

As always, much of what I write depends on my friends and neighbors in the Périgord, on their splendid cuisine and wines, on the stories and legends they love to recount and on the landscape they and their ancestors have tended for millennia. My debt to them is very deep indeed, matched only by my gratitude to my family, always the first to read, edit and advise on my manuscripts.

Without the help of my wife, Julia, Bruno's cooking would too often end in disaster. All the recipes in this book come from the cookbooks we wrote together: *Brunos Kochbuch* and *Brunos Garten Kochbuch,* both published by Diogenes Verlag, my splendid German publishers. Julia and I are extremely proud that *Brunos Kochbuch* was named the World's Best French Cookbook of the past twenty years at the Frankfurt

Book Fair in 2015, a prize awarded by Gourmand International. The second volume, *Brunos Garten Kochbuch,* won the prize in 2020. Without the work of our daughters, Kate and Fanny, Bruno's investigations would lead up blind alleys, be stuck up trees or sink without trace. Kate runs the brunochiefofpolice.com website, and Fanny keeps track of all the characters, the books and incidents in which they appear and the meals they enjoyed. She also organized and ran the video readings and interviews that we made to stay in touch with readers and to entertain them when we and much of the world were all locked down under the threat of the coronavirus. Thanks to Julia, Kate and Fanny, the world of Bruno is a family affair.

I owe more than I can say to the help and support of my literary agent, Caroline Wood, and to the skills of my editors, Jane Wood in London, Jonathan Segal in New York and Anna von Planta in Zurich, and to the printers, copy editors, salespeople, librarians and booksellers who bring these stories to the final, crucial link in the chain — you, the reader.

ABOUT THE AUTHOR

Martin Walker served as a foreign correspondent for *The Guardian* in Africa, the Soviet Union, the United States and Europe and was also the editor of United Press International. He was also a senior scholar of the Woodrow Wilson Center and senior director of the Global Policy Business Council, both in Washington, D.C. He now shares his time between the United States, Britain, and the Périgord region of France, where he writes, chairs the jury of the Prix Ragueneau cookery prize, and is proud to be a Grand Consul of the wines of Bergerac. He enjoys writing a monthly column on wine for the local English-language paper, *The Bugle,* and with wine-making friends produces an agreeable and unpretentious red wine, Cuvée Bruno.